35-303

9.99

Honor's Price

Rocky Mountain Legacy

◆◆◆◆◆◆◆◆◆◆◆◆◆◆◆

Honor's Pledge
Honor's Price
Honor's Quest

KRISTEN HEITZMANN

Honor's Price

BETHANY HOUSE PUBLISHERS
MINNEAPOLIS, MINNESOTA 55438

Published by Bethany House Publishers
A Ministry of Bethany Fellowship International
11400 Hampshire Avenue South
Minneapolis, Minnesota 55438
www.bethanyhouse.com

Printed in the United States of America by
Bethany Press International, Minneapolis, Minnesota 55438

Library of Congress Cataloging-in-Publication Data

CIP data applied for

ISBN 0-7642-2032-2   CIP

To Jim

through it all
you're always there...
one flesh

KRISTEN HEITZMANN was raised on five acres of ponderosa pine at the base of the Rocky Mountains in Colorado, where she still lives with her husband and four children. A music minister and artist, Kristen delights in sharing the traditions of our heritage, both through one-on-one interaction and now through her bestselling series, ROCKY MOUNTAIN LEGACY.

One

Abbie Martin pressed her face to the rough ponderosa pine bark and clung to the branch with all her strength. Thundering hooves shook the trunk as the rushing force of the herd, crazed and murderous, parted in a wave around the tree. Transfixed, she stared down at the rush of bony spines, heaving sides, wide eyes, and flared nostrils.

Suddenly one longhorn hooked the buggy below and smashed it against the tree. The buggy crumpled as the cow went down, bawling when those behind trampled over it. Abbie pressed into the trunk, trying to shut out the noise. Thank goodness Monte had unharnessed the horse to run free.

She tried to see him below her in the tree, but tears stung her eyes. The dust choked the air from her lungs. She had to get higher. She reached for the sticky branch above. But the tree was slammed and she slipped, caught onto the trunk, and clung.

Abbie scrambled for a foothold, but again the tree was struck, and again. She pressed her fingers into the bark, willing her muscles to stay tight even as they cried out for release. Slowly the ground stopped pounding, though her head and heart continued. She choked, gasped, then breathed. The dust was settling.

She felt Monte grip her ankle and secure her foot on a branch. Then he climbed up behind her, warm and solid. She slackened against him, her back to his chest, her muscles spent. His breath on her neck was strained as they perched like a pair of bedraggled crows in the only tree in sight. But it was over.

"Are you all right?" He spoke into her hair.

Abbie nodded, then turned to see him. His shirt was torn and he had cut his cheek, but it was nothing to his grim face. She had never seen him look so angry; not when Blake tried to call him out nor when she shouted vile insults Monte hardly deserved. His dark eyes were ablaze with unquenched fire.

She cleared the dust from her throat. "Was it the shots that spooked them?"

"I can't think otherwise."

Abbie followed his gaze. The prairie was empty, utterly still. A brown haze of dust lingered—she could feel it on her teeth. She felt the tree sap on the side of her face where she had pressed it to the trunk. Funny how the bark smelled sweet, not pine.

She was suddenly assaulted with poignant memories of real and imagined adventures shared with Blake during her girlhood. Tree climbing for no other reason than to leave the earth behind. As she looked out across the land, she could hear his voice and unconsciously imitated it. "Ain't this a view?"

Monte raised an eyebrow.

She smiled dimly. "I can't climb a tree without finding a part of Blake up here with me."

He drew a long breath. "Here I was fearing for your life, and you're reminiscing over past loves."

"He was not my love, Monte. Even had he returned alive, I could not have cared for him as other than a friend." She knew that to be true. His death had sealed him in her heart as his return could not have.

Monte rubbed his forehead with the back of his sleeve. His hat was gone, and his dark hair tousled into unruly waves. "Can you make it down?"

"Yes." Abbie watched him lower himself to the ground. Even angry and disheveled he was dignified. How was it he always looked so . . . well-bred? He was well-bred, like the horses he kept, like the house he kept, ordered and run by former slaves who chose to come west and serve him still, though now they were recompensed.

She understood their loyalty. Montgomery Farrel commanded devotion, though you could not put your finger on what exactly he did that made it so. He didn't flaunt himself, yet you noticed him all the more. His handsome features, easy, confident bearing, and soft southern drawl were potent, yet it was something more, something deeper that drew one to him irresistibly.

Even in the depths of her bitterness, he was in her thoughts. And now ... She felt an awkwardness that had never been there, not even when she had first ridden to his ranch to accost him on Blake's behalf after the fool boy had called Monte out for flirting with her.

If she had known what would come of that day, would she have gone? Had she anticipated the heartache, would she have run doggedly to the home of the man who would claim her heart, then reject it? He landed on his feet and looked up at her. Her heart turned over. Yes. She would have gone. She would have done it all to be received into his arms now as he eased her down beside him.

For all his claims of devotion, this was their first outing together since his return from South Carolina. He had three times supped with them, but Pa had commanded his attention, as starved for Monte's conversation as Abbie herself. She was willing to sit back and listen, to watch his expressions, to hear the laughter in his voice, to quicken when the glance of his eyes met hers and lingered. Yet she had felt more uncertain of her feelings than his ... until he had kept away for three full weeks.

When today's invitation had arrived via Will, his stableboy, she had half a mind to refuse. The old feelings of betrayal and distrust raised their ugly heads and made her cross. More than cross. The thought of turning him down felt almost as good as receiving his note. But she had accepted, and here she was, shaking as much from his touch as from the stampede.

He let her go. The ground was trampled and cluttered with the wreckage of the buggy and three cows, one of which lay with eyes rolling and its massive tongue working the ground. Streams of blood ran from its mouth and nostrils. The wheezing gurgle became a bawling moan.

Without a word, Monte slipped the Colt revolver from its holster and fired. Abbie jumped. The bullet hole was squarely centered in the cow's forehead. Its eyes glazed, the tongue sagged to the earth. Abbie stared from the animal to Monte.

He held the gun silently, the pearl handle gripped in his palm. She had never before seen him use it. His face was hard, his jaw tensed. He suddenly seemed a stranger, a man she didn't know, had never known. *He had to do it. The cow was suffering, yet...*

A rider galloped toward them. The shot must have brought him. The cowboy dismounted almost before the dust settled. "Mr. Farrel! How'd you ... we didn't know ..." He swallowed hard, no doubt at the look on Monte's face. "Someone got at the herd, sir. We circled round to head off the stampede from the house, but no one knew you were ..."

Abbie stepped away from the tree.

The cowboy's mouth fell open as he took in her bedraggled state and the crushed buggy.

Monte's voice was terribly controlled. "Did you see who spooked the herd?"

The cowboy kicked the toe of his boot into the dirt. "I didn't, sir. I don't know 'bout the others. It was unexpected."

Monte drew himself up. "Take a look at these cattle, John Mason." He swung his arm over the fallen animals. "Take a good look. I trust this sort of trouble will not again be unexpected."

"No, sir." John replaced his hat. "I'll ride to the ranch fer a wagon."

"Just bring Sirocco and another. Miss Martin can ride."

"Yes, sir."

As John rode off, Abbie held back. This was a Monte she had not seen. He had always been the gentleman, even as a businessman, though in truth she had never seen him conduct business. But certainly she had never heard him speak in such a strained, heavy-handed manner. There was more here than a chance stampede.

Monte holstered the gun and looked at the fallen cows. "What a waste." He lifted the edge of the buggy top with his boot, then kicked it away.

"I'm sorry, Monte."

"So am I. This isn't exactly what I'd planned for today."

"Our best-laid plans." She spread her hands. "God has His way of—"

He turned with controlled fierceness. "I don't consider this His way."

"Of course not. But do you think I planned to be abducted by outlaws, then rescued and set free by Comanche braves? His hand was in that even if I didn't see it. It's just ... life isn't easy to figure."

Monte showed a ghost of a smile. "No, I guess not. Why is it that in your company life seems wilder than anywhere else?"

Abbie cocked her head. "Does it?"

He reached for her arm and drew her close. "You know it does, and I think you like it that way. I could even suspect at my expense."

"Monte."

"I believe you'd see the end of whatever southern ease remains my own." He wrapped his arm around her back.

"What an absurd notion."

"If you were a belle, yes. But we both know . . ."

"Don't you say it. If you bring up tracking and spearing fish . . ."

"And tree climbing."

She frowned. "As though that isn't what saved our necks just now. How would you like to have dragged me up there, swooning and blushing?"

He threw back his head and laughed, suddenly the Monte she knew.

She laughed with him, though once again it was directed at her. "You were going to tell me why you brought me out here instead of into the hills."

His eyes deepened, and the laughter calmed. "Yes. Well, it'll have to wait. I'm not of a mind to pursue it now."

"Pursue it?"

"You'll not wheedle it out." He pulled a sticky twig from her hair and released her. He turned and searched through the rubble. She could smell the new leather, paint, and varnish. The flawless seat fabric was now shredded, the stuffing in filthy clumps on the ground. His new factory-made buggy had withstood the stampede no better than his hand-built one could have.

Abbie's throat felt like both drought and grasshoppers had descended upon it. She wished they'd brought a picnic, but then it would now be demolished with the rest unless they'd hauled the basket into the tree.

The sound of hooves preluded John Mason's return with Monte's black-legged sorrel Arabian and a bay mare. "Here y'are, sir. I alerted them at the house that you'd be comin'."

"Any sign of Cole?"

"No, sir. I reckon he's still roundin' up the herd."

"Chance?"

"Back at the stable. Will's rubbin' him down."

Monte nodded. "Then you'd best see where you can be of help."

"Yes, sir." The cowboy tipped his hat to Abbie and kicked in his heels.

Monte gave her a hand to mount, then swung into Sirocco's saddle.

"My, Mr. Farrel. What a genteel outing. Race you back." Abbie dug in her heels and the mare sprang forward. She had no illusions of winning, not after witnessing Sirocco's raw speed, but she wanted to feel the rush of wind in her face and know that she had survived.

♦♦♦♦♦♦♦

Monte waited on the porch as Cole Jasper approached. Dust billowed from every step and clung to the kerchief at his neck. He looked as ragged as Monte felt, and well he might. The sun had set some half hour before, and he was only now coming to report.

Cole slapped his hat on his thigh and perched one foot on the second step. "I figured there'd be trouble." That was as near "I told you so" as Cole would dare.

"Did you get a look at anyone?"

"Not so's to recognize 'em. Three men, maybe more. Nothin' to mark the horses by, just normal stock. Far as I can tell they came up the gulch. Abbie all right?"

Monte's jaw hardened. Word traveled fast. It chafed more than it should that Cole felt justified in questioning him about her. But then it hadn't been long since Cole Jasper had been inclined to marry Abbie himself.

"Abbie's fine."

Cole replaced his hat. "Reckon I'll get some supper."

"How many men are on the herd?"

"Six."

Monte nodded. Inside, he made his way to the study and paced. If this were the first time the stock had been threatened, he could excuse his being caught unawares. Cole had suspected. He had said they were losing more animals than he could attribute to nature.

But Monte had spoken with his neighbors carefully and shrewdly, lest he say more than he intended. None had expressed any concerns, and surely no losses. In a land where men depended on honesty and cooperation, he would expect someone else to indicate trouble if there were any.

So he had considered Cole's remarks premature. But if Cole suspected, he should have been alert, watchful. How did men get close enough to spook the herd—in open country with tumbleweeds for cover, gulch or no gulch?

Monte shook his head. He couldn't blame Cole. He lifted the glass globe paperweight from the desk and cradled it in his palm. He simply wasn't convinced that rustlers were to blame. Rustlers didn't spook a herd in daylight unless they were strong enough to ignore the herders or just plain inept.

Who then? He pictured in his mind the other ranchers: Dunbar, the nearest to the east, Hodge, and Ephart. They were small, running less than one hundred head and half that in sheep. Gifford stocked three hundred head and made use of government land. He'd made one short appearance at the roundup, but they hadn't spoken.

The others didn't seem too thick with Gifford, either, but that meant nothing as he was the newest comer, setting up headquarters only that spring. Faringer and Bates got along well with Cole. Hadn't Faringer worked with him in Texas?

Monte replaced the globe. No one could have known he'd be in the draw with Abbie. It was happenstance that sent the herd their way. He rubbed the back of his neck. Maybe he was wrong to suspect his neighbors. Likely Cole did know a sight more than he, as Cole never hesitated to remind him.

He wished he had an answer that sat well. Other than Gifford, the other ranchers had been running cattle longer than he had, though his father's land claim was one of the first filed. And one of the best.

Despite its appearance, the grass—Sand Drop Seed, Buffalo, and Gramma—was as excellent as the lush green pastures of the East. The ground could be trenched to irrigate, and under Cole's management they'd fenced a choice pasture and made use of natural boundaries to provide shelter and windbreaks on the open range.

Monte had virtual control of the water source on this stretch of prairie, but he allowed sufficient runoff to satisfy ranchers downstream, such as Dunbar. He'd seen that no complaint could be made against him. Too many cattle barons took advantage of people until they had more enemies than friends and lived with their backs to the walls. Not he.

The roundup had proven a good companionship between the camps, who went as far as to share each other's chuck wagons. He had learned over the past year that the best way to keep his help was to hire a good cook. His cowboys had no complaints, and to make sure he never wanted for extra help, he gave word for the cook to feed any herder too far from his own camp during the roundup.

Though Monte had not taken part in the roping and branding

of the new calves, he had rubbed shoulders with the men and shown his interest. Despite Cole Jasper's doubts as to his abilities, Monte intended to run his cattle business from the ground up. He'd make the Lucky Star the best cattle ranch in the territory.

He flipped open the ledger book. Eight hundred head, one-fourth ready to be driven to the railhead in Denver, then freighted east to the beef markets in Chicago or Kansas City, whichever offered the better price. Freight was higher to Chicago but the market larger.

Monte figured he was a choice mark for rustlers or jealous neighbors alike. Perhaps even range pirates—men running cattle without owning land—though their biggest concern was to use the land without getting kicked off someone's plot. The two men they'd come upon during roundup had claimed to be doing just that, and no brands were recognized in the small herd, so they warned them off filed lands and sent them on their way.

Well, he would not again be caught unawares. The risk had been too great to himself and to Abbie. He closed his eyes and heard her again. *"Ain't this a view?"* The slang word had stood out like a taunt. Moments after a brush with death, clinging to the paltry protection of the single tree, she had sized up the situation and come out with that remark. No tears or clinging to him, no shivering need.

Monte sighed. The stampede had certainly distracted him from his intentions. Maybe it was for the best. Perhaps it was too soon to think Abbie had put past wounds behind her. And why not?

Had he not awakened a first love in her, then been forced by God and circumstance to honor his pledge to marry another? Would Abbie ever respond to him again with an unveiled heart? Hearing her name on Cole's lips made him want to rush over there even now and speak for her.

But with Abbie, Monte never knew what to expect. One wrong word, one push too soon and he'd rather wrestle a mountain lion.

His heartbeat increased. It was that same element that got into his blood and made him want her so dangerously much. He closed the ledger. He would bide his time. When the opportunity was right...

Two

Abbie pressed her back to the wooden pew. The cadence of the Latin sung by Father Dominic and the voices of the brothers chanting in response stirred her. It had an unearthly beauty that belonged to the cool serenity of the small adobe chapel at the mission. She breathed the incense, imagining the smoke rising to the throne of God. She raised her eyes to the carved figure of the crucified Christ.

His agony reminded her of the first priest who built the mission to bring truth to the Indians. He had been lashed to a tree and burned. But Father Dominic had followed and remained, serving now the orphans and Catholic settlers rather than the Indians, though some still came for food. They were never refused.

Abbie looked over the heads of the orphan children. They were fed in more than body. Here at the mission their minds were formed, their spirits nurtured. She loved working with them. She understood the privilege it was to teach the little ones their letters, the older ones literature and recitation while Father Dominic drilled arithmetic and scientific reasoning. Brother Thomas taught them the cultivation and use of herbs, and Brother José the care of animals.

While some looked upon the children as foundlings and hopeless souls, she saw children rich in promise. She fondly remembered her own days of schooling here at the mission. She had thrived on the learning, though Blake had found it too tedious.

Pain seared her chest at the unexpected memory. Would the ache of her grief ever pass? It was less constant, but no less severe.

Here in the chapel Abbie and Blake had stolen glances and wicked giggles on many occasions: when Blake had released a horned toad in the aisle, when Brother Thomas had fallen asleep and snored. . . . She seemed to feel the ache more here. Maybe he was closer since he now abided with Jesus in heaven. Abbie glanced at the cross again. It was important to remember the sacrifice but even more to know there was hope beyond death.

How else to bear the memory of Blake's face blackened and swollen, his skull shot away by the outlaw Buck Hollister? Blake and his brother Mack. She turned and saw Mary McConnel beside Wes. Did they sense their sons closer here, too? Davy and Mariah sat silently beside their parents. Abbie turned back. She was fidgeting.

Mama nudged her, and she returned her attention to the mass. Father Dominic intoned the words in a clear tenor voice. She would have guessed him a bass or a baritone. He looked too stern to be a tenor, but then his gentleness was a surprise, as well.

Abbie tried to focus on the worship, but . . . what trouble was there at the Lucky Star? That was no chance stampede—Monte's face had shown her that much. Was that why he had been scarce before and again this past week? But no gossip had reached town other than the usual grumblings of a disgruntled cowboy or two.

She could get answers from Cole if she dared, but ever since his marriage proposal, he had not come to visit. *Visit.* He hadn't been visiting, he'd been courting, and she had put an end to that. On the occasion or two that they met in town, he was cordial enough, and she hoped he didn't bear her ill will. She didn't think so. That wouldn't be like him.

But what was Monte hiding? And why wouldn't he tell her? There was a time when they had spoken freely together, too freely maybe. Monte had shared some of his past, but had he ever really told her of his doings? It wasn't natural for him to include her. His was a society of masters and slaves, men who owned men, and women who feigned weakness to please men who desired them that way.

Monte wasn't like that. Abbie knew he admired courage and

strength in women. But there were areas, business particularly, where he excluded her. Well, what right was it of hers to know his business? Even Sharlyn, his wife, had been excluded. Monte had thought her simple, and in book learning she had been.

But Sharlyn had possessed more raw wisdom and strength than he had realized. And Abbie was anything but unlearned. She wasn't about to pretend she couldn't grasp the intricacies and demands of life.

Abbie squirmed, eager to get out this morning. She had tied Shiloh to the wagon in order to ride the plains a bit after mass and see for herself what might be brewing. Monte would be furious, of course, especially if there were troublemakers about, but he needn't know. By the time he came for her tonight, she would be washed and fresh, and he none the wiser.

She startled when Pa nudged her to go kneel at the wooden altar rail and receive the Holy Eucharist. A guilty twinge twisted her stomach when she realized how little she had prepared. In silence she offered her apology as she dropped to her knees on the stone floor, and Father Dominic laid the unleavened bread on her tongue. Surely God understood her shortcomings by now. She remained penitent through the benediction and forced her feet to a restrained pace as she made her way into the sunshine.

After a quick hug for Mama, Abbie unwound Shiloh's reins and mounted, heading south across the grassy expanse. At the draw she saw the start of the land Monte had fenced. He used fences not to contain the animals on the open range but to barricade them from dangerous sections and mark off choice grazing.

Several pastures he had fenced nearer the house to contain the horses and calving cows. She had to admit the fences were few and far between and didn't truly hinder the coyotes, rabbits, antelope, and other wild things. She kicked Shiloh to a gallop, lay down close to the mare's neck, and jumped the fence.

What were the ranchers' concerns? Rustlers, certainly ... as well as drought, disease, and disputes over water rights and boundaries. There was little she could do about the latter, but as for rustlers . . . Well, she could track as well as any man in town, thanks to Blake. If someone was causing Monte trouble, she'd find out.

After riding some distance with the mountains to her right and the fence line on her left, she angled southwest. If there were rustlers in the area, they'd try to hide evidence of their presence. An uncleared camp probably belonged to the cowboys in charge of the herd. A camp scattered and brushed meant stealth. She saw no sign of either.

There was a triangular piece of shade beneath a cut, and she made for that to lunch. Dismounting, she slid the saddlebag from Shiloh's back and allowed the mare to wander free and graze. The pork sandwich was from the end of last season's smoked meat and tasted wonderful in the open air. Once again she was thankful for Monte showing Pa how to build the smokehouse. . . . Was it only two years ago?

It seemed she had been a child watching Pa clap Monte's shoulder at the completion of the smokehouse and wondering if her family filled Monte's void. She had been brimming with dreams and questions about the wonders of life. And she had not yet discovered the mystery of love that Monte alone awakened.

But that was before. Before he married Sharlyn, before Blake was murdered, before she was taken by Hollister . . . before Sharlyn was taken in death. Abbie had made peace with God, forgiven Monte, and resolved to make her own way. Then he had returned and begged to court her. He had roused hopes and emotions with which she no longer felt comfortable.

She shook her hair back over her shoulders. No matter. The sun was shining, the air was fresh, the day was new, and she had a task ahead. She drank from the canteen, then popped the last of the dried apples into her mouth, relishing the satisfaction of a simple meal.

She gathered Shiloh's reins and remounted. A profusion of pronghorn marks crossed her path, and she guessed at least forty traveled together. There were mule deer, coyote, and fox tracks. A cottontail darted from one clump of sagebrush to another, but beyond that the land was still.

The sun was high, and until it made its descent toward the mountains, most of the wild things rested. She could hear grasshoppers and bees, the call of a lark bunting, and the squawk of a starling. A quail flushed out of the growth beside her and fluttered clumsily into the air.

She crested the low rise. Just ahead, a herd grazed lazily—Monte's, she guessed. They were Texas longhorn. For all the disparagement the longhorns received, she thought they looked the most natural to the plain. With their long legs and horns and their high bony backs, they were a breed suited to the territory.

Abbie hoped Monte would not attempt to crossbreed them again with the slower, beefier cattle. When he'd tried before, the shorthorns had succumbed to the Texas fever. Cole said it was carried by a tick the longhorns could withstand, but not other breeds. She'd had the distinct impression Cole had tried to tell Monte that, but Monte had gone ahead with the venture and reaped the results.

She raised her head at the sound of hooves. A cowboy cantered toward her. Abbie bit her lip. She hadn't meant to draw attention from one of Monte's men. The cowboy drew up, and she saw it was the same man who had come upon them after the stampede. She could tell he recognized her, too.

He swiped his hat from his head. "Howdy, ma'am."

"John Mason, isn't it?"

He blushed to the fair roots of his hair. "Yes, ma'am."

Another cowboy reined in beside him. *Wonderful.* Any moment now, she'd have a whole contingent to escort her to Monte's door. The new cowboy tipped his hat but didn't remove it. He had several years on John. "Afternoon, ma'am. Name's Breck Thompson. What can I do fer you?"

"I . . ."

"This's the lady ridin' with Mr. Farrel when the herd stampeded last week."

Breck glanced at John, nodded him back to the herd, then returned his attention to her. "I reckon you're lookin' fer Mr. Farrel?"

"No, I was just riding. I didn't mean to come so close to the herd." She was actually a good step from the farthest fringe. They must be watching sharply indeed.

He turned and spat tobacco juice to the far side of his horse. "Well, ma'am, it'd be better if you kept a good distance. As you saw the other day, if somethin' sets them off, they're a chore to stop."

Abbie recalled the demolished buggy, the crushed and bleeding cows. "Any idea what made them spook?" Since she was already seen, she would just make the most of it.

Breck's face might have been stone. "No, ma'am." He jutted his chin. "The house is up that way."

"Thank you." She knew very well which way the house was and had no intention of going there. She urged Shiloh into a canter and continued west, skirting the herd. What had she thought to accomplish? Maybe if it had been Cole on the herd . . . but she suspected she'd get no more from him.

Perhaps the men wouldn't mention her coming. Perhaps they believed her, although they had to realize she'd jumped the fence. At any rate, Abbie would hurry home and be sweet innocence by Monte's arrival.

She urged Shiloh to a gallop with pressure from her knees and eased into the motion. She breathed easier after she'd put a rise or two between the herd and herself, but she did not slacken her pace. Suddenly the horse stumbled.

Abbie leaped free as the mare went down. She rolled to break her fall, then got to her knees, a little shaken, but she seemed sound. Nothing hurt . . . much. She stood as Shiloh staggered up, as well. Abbie brushed the dirt from her dress and sleeves. She was all right. Was Shiloh?

The horse held up the offending hoof. The shoe hung by one nail. From the looks of things, she'd be walking back. Abbie closed her eyes and dropped her forehead to the mare's neck.

Was this penance for her meddling, or perhaps God keeping

her honest? She winced. He certainly had a way of turning her from sin. But she hadn't meant to deceive Monte, only to . . . avoid being confronted. Well, yes, she had intended to learn things he chose to keep from her, but . . .

She sighed. Running her hand down Shiloh's leg, she felt for damage. A small swelling already bloomed at the ankle, and the knee was scraped. She yanked the shoe from the hoof, and Shiloh tried her weight. It held, but painfully. Shiloh tossed her head and snorted. It would be slow going.

Abbie took the reins and led the horse forward. At this rate Mama would have searchers out for her . . . and with good reason. The last year she'd seen trouble enough. Pa and Cole and Monte and most of the townsmen had searched day after day for her when Hollister and his outlaws had abducted her. She could still remember the hollow weariness in their eyes.

And she could just imagine Mama's face when Monte arrived for her this evening to find she hadn't yet returned. Oh, what a commotion there would be! She plodded on. The dust climbed her skirts, and she kicked at a young yucca plant not yet sporting the sharp, stiff spikes of the others in her path.

Abbie swiped the beading perspiration from her forehead with her sleeve. The sun was well on its descending arch and the baked land radiated the heat. Maybe she should have made for town. If she had continued southwest instead of heading directly for the spur of mountain, beneath which her father's homestead nestled . . . She heard hooves from behind and hardly dared to turn. Was it Monte catching her in the act? *Thank you very much, Lord.*

The rider came alongside, and she looked up to find Cole Jasper astride his palomino. He tipped his hat up with his fingertips, releasing a riot of blond hair beneath, and grinned. "Afternoon, Abbie. Lamed yer horse?"

"She threw a shoe."

"And you, by the looks of it."

"I jumped clear, thank you."

"And took a roll. Yer hair's sportin' sagebrush."

Abbie reached a hand to her hair and found the sprig. She tugged it free and tossed it.

"You hurt?"

Abbie swallowed her pride. After all, Cole had found her unconscious and nearly frozen as a result of her last fall. "No. I'm not hurt."

Cole dismounted and bent before Shiloh, feeling the leg. "Bit sore, is she?"

"Yes."

"Why don't you leave her with me and take Scotch."

"How will you get back?"

"Breck's just behind me. He'll be along soon enough." He stood. "What're you doin' out here?"

"I . . ." Abbie expelled her breath. "I wanted to know what's going on."

His green eyes sobered. "This ain't the time to meddle, Abbie. If you're lookin' to git yer pa a newspaper story . . ."

So there *was* something happening. "I'm not. I just wanted to know."

"Ain't nothin' to know yet. Just watchin' and waitin'."

"For the rustlers to make their move?"

Cole removed his hat and scratched behind his ear, then replaced it and appraised her. "I don't know what Mr. Farrel's told you."

"Precious little."

Cole hung his head and grinned. "Well, now, Abbie, I am in his employ."

"Oh, Cole. You won't hold back on me."

He shook his head. "Ain't nothin' certain yet. Maybe rustlers, maybe not. Sure wouldn't be the first time. Once word gets out there's a profitable herd . . ." He swung his arm. "Lots of empty country round about."

"Have you seen them?"

He hesitated. "Might've."

"At the stampede?"

He narrowed his eyes, and she didn't give him time to deny it.

"Monte asked if the men had seen anyone. I guessed if you were on the herd ..."

"Look, Abbie. Like I said before, ain't nothin' certain. You keep quiet on that stampede. Mr. Farrel's of a mind to watch and wait, keep his cards close to the vest."

"So I've seen."

"Well, in this case it's wise. Don't want to tip our hand till we got somethin' fer sure."

"But you think it's rustlers."

"Now, there you go trippin' me into sayin' more than I should. Look, here's Breck comin' now." He held out his hand. "Climb up on Scotch. He'll git you home."

Abbie mounted. The horse was a good two hands taller than Shiloh and broader, too. She took the reins from Cole as he slid them over the horse's head.

"I'll git yer mare back soon as she's able."

"Thank you, Cole." Abbie nodded to Breck who came alongside, then clicked her tongue and heeled Scotch. He responded immediately. Short of any further catastrophe, she had a chance of beating Monte to her homestead. But she knew not to count on it.

Three

Abbie arrived home as the sun reached the still snow-streaked Pikes Peak. The sharp brilliance forced her to avert her eyes. Once it sank beneath the ridge, the sky would burst with color, each string of cloud set aflame in hues of gold and orange, then blushing pink, as though ashamed of calling such attention to themselves.

She had made good time on Scotch and silently thanked Cole for his consideration. But for his happening upon her when he did, she'd still be trudging the plain and tonight's plans would be ruined. She didn't want to think how often she narrowly escaped ruin.

Abbie led Scotch to the barn and stabled him in Shiloh's stall. Cole's saddle must outweigh hers by twenty pounds. She struggled to slide it from the horse's back and hook it over the rail. Scotch tossed his huge head when she removed the bit and filled his box with fodder. She blew the curling tendrils of hair from her forehead as she quit the barn and started across the yard.

Monte was just driving Chance and the old buggy through the gate. As Abbie slipped unnoticed into the kitchen from the lean-to, Mama spun around. "Abbie, where on earth . . ."

"Shiloh threw a shoe. And Monte's at the gate. Have you some water heated?"

"Yes, and I was about to add the beans." Mama sighed. "Well, take it and get washed. I'll have Pa keep Monte."

"Thank you, Mama."

"Toss your dirty things outside the door."

"Yes, Mama."

In the small lean-to, Abbie poured the pot's contents into the metal tub and added two pails of cold, as well. She quickly shed her dusty, bur-covered outer clothing and dropped it outside the door and onto the kitchen floor as Mama had directed. She dropped her underclothing into the water to wash with her, then she stepped into the tub. With more haste than care, she scrubbed herself with the sweet bar of chamomile soap, then rinsed her hair with lavender water.

She stepped out, toweled her arms, legs, and head, and panicked. She had neglected to get a change of clothes before bathing. She could hear Pa's laughter in the front room and guessed Monte's wit was the cause. She cracked the door to the kitchen. Mama was nowhere in sight. Neither were her clothes. "Mama?" she whispered.

No answer. Monte was praising Pa's editorial on education in the Rockies. She pushed the door open further. "Mama?" Nothing. She retrieved and squeezed out her wet chemise and drawers, then pulled them on.

Mama was still not there. She crept out onto the smooth wood floor. With her arms wrapped tightly around her wet chemise and her drawers running streams down her legs, she tiptoed across the kitchen, nearing the doorway to the front room.

Pa was laughing again. "And if I put that in print I'd have half the territory on my neck."

"That hasn't stopped you before."

"All depends what I mean to accomplish. Leading folks to a higher place is one thing, pointing out the planks in their eyes is another. I don't mind taking on a splinter or two, but you have to lead into the bigger things little by little."

"I suppose you're right. If there's . . ."

Abbie streaked across the doorway and rushed for her room. She closed the door behind her and felt the laughter boil up from her chest. She clamped a hand to her mouth and took deep breaths. Monte's expression was one she would not soon forget. She should be appalled, humiliated, but his face . . .

Not that he got much of a look, but all the same. Heavens, if Mama found out! Abbie shivered. Stripping off her wet underthings, she tied on the corset she rarely wore, pulled on the bustle she detested, and dressed in the blue cotton dress she'd been fitted for last month. Monte hadn't seen it yet, and he was taking her to town.

She brushed her hair up at the sides and held it with combs. The bulk she left loose down her back. It would dry as they rode. Drawing herself up, she took a quick survey in the mirror. In stockings and leather slippers, and with her breath constricted by the corset, she felt like a lady. Both Pa and Monte stood when she entered.

"Pretty as a picture," Pa said.

"Thank you, Pa." Abbie walked calmly over to Monte. "I'm sorry I kept you waiting."

He bowed. His white gabardine shirt with pleated yoke and ivory buttons, gray trousers, and matching vest were impeccable. Her heart skipped a beat when he reached for her hand and brushed her fingers with his lips. "It was well worth the wait, I assure you." His voice softened with the drawl.

Monte curled her fingers into the crook of his arm and led her out. The sky's fire had passed. Lavender deepened to indigo in the east and paled to pink over the mountains. The peaks themselves were a flat silhouette, like a paper cutting stood up inside the bowl of sky. "Oh, Monte, isn't it lovely?"

"It is. The western skies rival anything South Carolina could produce and make up for much of the dry expanse."

Abbie laughed. "It's creeping in."

He helped her into his older buggy. "What is?"

"This place. You said you have yet to find a love for it, but it's starting, I can tell."

Standing beside her as she settled in, Monte laid a hand on her knee. "Were it not for seeing things through your eyes, Abbie, I doubt I would ever come to it." He walked around and climbed up beside her. Clicking his tongue to Chance, he flicked the reins.

Abbie held her breath, waiting for him to mention her wet

dash. She didn't know whether to laugh or deny it. But it seemed he would be the gentleman tonight. He said nothing about it at all.

An owl hooted in the dusk from a clump of scrub oak as they passed. Monte searched for it. "That's a singularly lonely sound, isn't it?"

"Plaintive, yes. But I don't suppose he's any lonelier than the other wild things. Do you think animals long for companionship?"

"I don't know. Some more than others, I'd guess. Pack animals, for instance."

"Is it companionship they desire or simple need that keeps them together? Protection and survival."

Monte laughed softly. "I don't know. Take cattle, for instance. They huddle together and move as a herd, but I'll wager with the exception of cows and their calves, they haven't really an inkling the others are there. Nor a thought for those who aren't. It's enough to fill their bellies each day and lie safe each night from prowling coyotes and wildcats."

"Birds and creatures that mate for life, though—there might be something there."

"There might." He rounded the bend and flicked the reins lightly to return Chance to speed. "But still, you can't attribute human commitment to animal nature."

"Some humans can't be attributed even animal nature."

Monte glanced over. "I'm afraid that's true. That's why we strive for honor."

Abbie half smiled. She would not debate the merits of honor with him tonight. "Yet the wild things have a code of their own. A code we violate without a thought."

"In what way?"

"By fencing the land and overrunning their homes."

"Oh yes, the poor mangy coyote and the lithe pronghorn that leap fences in a single bound."

"And the great herds of buffalo and the Indian tribes, driven off to make way for settlements."

"Of course, you'd rather live in a tepee than have a ranch and a fine upcoming town such as Rocky Bluffs. Perhaps you'd prefer a savage brave to a southern gentleman seeking your favor. How many horses are you worth, Abbie?" He reached over and raised her chin. "Let me see your teeth and feel the meat on your bones."

He squeezed her arm. "Hmm. Not much extra to get you through a thin winter. Still, you might be a good breeder."

"Monte!"

He shrugged. "Be careful what you wish for."

"I wasn't wishing." Abbie settled her skirts around her. "What are we doing tonight?"

"Don't tell me you haven't heard?"

"Heard what?"

"Is it possible I'm possessed of knowledge you've not acquired?"

"How can I say when I've no inkling what you're talking about?"

"Why, the whole town was buzzing over it today."

"I wasn't in town today."

"No, you weren't, were you?"

Abbie bit her lip. How cleverly he had led her along, trapped her up in her enthusiasm. She tried to hide her discomfort. "I was riding."

"So I heard."

"Did you?"

"Don't play the innocent with me, Abbie. When three of my men feel compelled to report your presence, I pay attention. You couldn't have come near the herd without jumping the fence."

Abbie winced. All three of them. Had Cole told him her purpose? "Well, you know how I feel about fences."

He reined in and turned to her. "Fences can be for protection."

"Goodness, Monte. I was in no need of protection."

"Then you learned nothing from being stampeded by four hundred head of raging cattle?"

Abbie slouched. "You needn't scold. Nothing worse came of it than Shiloh throwing a shoe."

"Yes, I left Cole tending her."

"How is she?"

"She'll mend." He leaned forward and took her shoulders. "I want the truth, Abbie. Why were you canvassing my pastureland?"

"Canvassing?"

He gave her a little shake. "Though both Breck and John believed you'd gone astray, I know well enough your propensities. And Cole was amazingly vague for a man who can detail to me every action of the men in his charge."

So Cole hadn't told him. Somehow his keeping her secret made her feel twice as guilty. "If you must know, I was looking for the rustlers."

"The deuce!" Monte dropped his hands from her shoulders. "Who said anything about rustlers? And if there are rustlers, the last person I need involved is you."

Abbie shrank from the intensity in his eyes. "Monte, I . . ."

"Don't say it, Abbie. Whatever excuse you offer is worthless. I want to know you will desist from any such activity. Give me your word."

"What am I pledging? That I won't ride free and keep my eyes open?"

"Do you live to plague me with concern for you?"

Something in his tone quenched her indignation. "No, I . . ."

"Then promise me you'll not interfere."

"All right, I promise, but . . ."

"Nothing more. Only your word given. I trust you'll keep it."

She bristled. "You're not the only one to honor your word, Monte."

His silence was a worse reproof than any retort. She should not have flung that at him. They both knew what keeping his word had cost them.

"Well, then, shall we?" He took up the reins and the buggy lurched forward.

Abbie stung with his rebuke, though she had brought it on herself. What had she thought to accomplish? To satisfy her curiosity? Did she think there was anything she could do against a gang of rustlers, men reckless enough to risk being lynched for their actions?

Still, Monte hadn't needed to be so ... heavy-handed. He hadn't given her the chance to explain. Explain what? That she deliberately defied what she knew he would want? It hadn't seemed wrong at the start. It was so confusing. It seemed her very nature betrayed her.

Monte spoke low. "Forgive my ire, Abbie. I had intended this evening to be ... congenial. I'm tired of sparring with you."

"I'm sorry, too, Monte. I didn't mean to worry you."

"No. You meant to keep it from me entirely."

Abbie started to protest, then stopped. He was right.

"I've had enough of secrets. I can't live that way."

His tone held both hurt and weariness. It reminded her of what he had suffered the last year and awakened her own loss: the two people precious to her heart who had died. Blake and Sharlyn. She pictured Sharlyn's face, white blond hair, delicate rose petal skin, green eyes as lacking in guile as a newborn babe's. "I mourn her, too, Monte."

She spoke without thinking, and he turned, started to reply, then closed his mouth in silence.

"I thought when you brought her here as your wife, I would hate her. But I couldn't. I loved her so."

"You did so better than I." In the gathering darkness, his face revealed an ache she could almost feel.

"No, Monte. You were faithful and kind."

He reined in. "Faithful and kind. Is that enough, Abbie? Enough to make up for what I felt for you, for the nights I closed my eyes and imagined it was you in my arms?"

Abbie felt her chest tighten. What was he saying? That all the time she had so resented his loving Sharlyn, he had thought of her? Felt some measure of the loss she knew? She recalled the burning of his eyes when she would catch his glance, then coldly turn her back. Something inside had known how that would pain him. Yet how could it, unless he still cared?

Had he spoken the truth—that his love for her had never

changed? The self-reproach in his expression said it was so. She felt a deep sadness for Sharlyn. "Sharlyn never knew. She loved you."

"She knew ... and she loved me." He stared straight ahead. "She was so fragile. Perhaps if I had cared for her better, loved her better ..."

"What more could you have done, Monte? Can you stop scarlet fever? Can you stop death? Sharlyn's at peace; you need to be, also."

He reached over and squeezed her hand. "Shall we call a truce and enjoy the night?"

"Yes, of course." Abbie wanted to throw her arms around his neck and hold him until the smile was back in his eyes. But he'd been so formal since his return, as though they were truly beginning together with no thought for what had passed before. With the exception of the kiss two months ago by which he had cajoled permission to court her, he had maintained a strained and difficult distance.

Abbie tried for a lighter mood. "You still haven't told me what we're doing. Or was all that to trap me into confessing?"

"It was not, though I daresay your guilty conscience did a good job of convicting you."

"I thought you said truce."

He smiled. "So I did." As they came to the edge of town, he pointed. "Look there."

Abbie stared through the dusk at the crowd gathering outside the hotel. "What is it? What's happening?"

"Theater, Abbie. Theater has come to Rocky Bluffs."

"What theater?"

"A traveling troupe. None other than Miss Carolina Diamond and her Troupe Comique."

"Monte!"

He smiled. "I thought you'd prefer it to tracking rustlers."

Abbie bristled. "And if you keep throwing that in my face, I'll take up with Miss Carolina and her troupe."

He threw back his head and laughed. "Have at it, then. I don't doubt for a moment they'd take you." He pulled the buggy to a stop a good two blocks down because of the crowd of horses, wagons, and buggies.

Abbie alighted, aglow with anticipation. "Why is everyone gathered at the hotel? Surely they're not playing in the restaurant?"

"They're probably waiting to escort them to the saloon. I've heard Miss Diamond is wont to take the arm of some lucky chap and allow him to hoist her right up onto the stage."

"I've no doubt you'll be fighting your way to the front then."

"No, thank you. I've waited long enough to have *you* on my arm." He bent and kissed her fingers. This time there was no mistaking the contact of his lips with her skin, not at all the obligatory courtly bow. Abbie's heart raced. If he had taken her into his arms right there in the street and kissed her, she would not have resisted. But of course he didn't.

Montgomery Farrel was bred of generations of gentlemen, rigid in their honor and respect for the fairer sex. He extended the crook of his arm, and Abbie slid her hand within the protective cocoon as he led her to the saloon. She had been inside two months ago when the political orator had held a rally to propose the cause of statehood. All the town had gone, even Mama.

This time the entire back section had been cleared to erect the traveling stage. In deference to the lady guests, the main shelves of liquor over the bar were hung with fabric, though it wouldn't stop it being served, she was sure. During the political speech the audience had used every dramatic pause to order up.

Abbie followed Monte to a small table directly before the stage. The two chairs were roped together and leaned onto the table. Monte worked the rope free.

"Do you think we should?" Abbie glanced around at the other tables. None were tied.

"It's reserved for us."

Well. But then, she was not used to being formally courted by Montgomery Farrel. That had been Sharlyn's delight. Abbie felt a pang. How bitter she had been. It didn't seem right for her to receive his attention now. She felt for a moment as though the floor would open and swallow her up.

"What is it, Abbie?"

She shook her head. "I'm not used to being fussed over."

Before he could answer, the doors swung open and the uproarious crowd burst upon them. Ethan Thomas proudly sported the jeweled hand of Miss Carolina Diamond on his arm. She literally glittered from head to foot; a sequined headpiece adorned her blond hair, a white sequined gown shirred over ruffled layers of fine, sheer taffeta. Abbie's dress might have been burlap.

"What do you think?" Monte whispered as she passed.

"She's beautiful." Abbie now studied the lady's face. It wasn't really true. She was glamorous, and the clothes sumptuous, but Miss Diamond herself was too hard, too . . . overstated for beauty. Abbie doubted a man in the room would agree with her. The red lips, the eyes outlined and glittering like the rest of her, the beauty mark to the right of her upper lip . . .

Ethan Thomas bent and lifted her into his arms, and she wrapped a hand around his neck, then flounced enough ruffle to reveal both calves as she was swung onto the stage. Applause filled the room. Abbie had to admit this was excitement they hadn't known in Rocky Bluffs. She glanced around and found Clara and Marty Franklin.

She smiled broadly and Clara waved, then raised her eyebrows toward Monte. Abbie hoped he hadn't seen and warned her off with a glare, but Clara laughed. She knew the condition of Abbie's heart at that moment. Monte pulled out the chair and Abbie sat, thankfully with her back to Clara.

Monte took his place beside her, his eyes glowing with the same admiration evident on every face there. Miss Diamond folded her hands at her chest and began to sing. Abbie felt her mouth drop in silent wonder. Carolina Diamond's voice was more rich and clear than the combination of all her jewels. Abbie forgot her initial impression and was swept up in the music.

She noticed the man at the piano, though when he had taken his place, she couldn't say. The song ended, and Abbie clapped vigorously. Turning to her left she saw Judge Wilson with his wife, and beside them, Marcy. She startled to realize Marcy Wilson was not watching the stage but had her eye intently on Monte.

Marcy noticed Abbie and, in typical fashion, put up her nose and turned away. Abbie was dying to know if Clara had seen but didn't dare turn or draw Monte's attention. Instead she stole a glance his way, and he smiled and leaned close. "Not a bad little songbird, hmm?"

"She's wonderful." Abbie didn't have to feign her enthusiasm, for Miss Diamond began to sing again, this time a rollicking, even bawdy, tune. She strode back and forth across the stage, working the crowd with a swing of her hips, a swish of her arm, a flash of creamy neck and more chest than Abbie thought could show without coming loose. She was fascinated. What would it be like to grace a stage with every adoring eye in the room fixed on you alone?

After the second song, the stage emptied, and props were slid into place. Abbie sat on the edge of her seat. She'd never seen a play, not with props and all. The music started up fast, an old man now at the piano. How his fingers could fly! A boy held up a sign painted in gilded letters: *"Watson's Gold"—An Original Comique.* Miss Diamond, now dressed in stockings and layered scarves, played a nymph who led the bemused miners to think of things other than gold.

Monte laughed heartily when the now ragged and starving Watson forsook the glaring vein in the rock wall to follow the nymph to his death. He leaned close and whispered, "Not a bad end, really."

Abbie frowned, and Monte laughed harder. Two of the men juggled knives while the stage was cleared again, then Miss Diamond reappeared, dressed all in black fur except for sheer black sleeves. The dress was fitted to her figure with the front of her skirt cut away to reveal the black stockinged leg beneath her knee.

Abbie stared at the fur. "What animal do you suppose that is?"

Monte never looked her way. "A siren, surely. She's utterly bewitching."

The song was low and sultry, and Carolina Diamond moved her arms in a sleek, suggestive way. Abbie was not surprised that the eyes of the star fixed on Monte and held. He had no doubt drawn them there. She held her breath and watched. Monte was clearly dazzled.

The song ended, the applause thundered, and the players took their bows. Abbie clapped, but with less ardor. Monte made up for her lack. He leaned close to her ear to be heard. "Have you supped? No, of course you haven't. I believe you were washing when I arrived."

Abbie felt the color burn in her cheeks, but he didn't follow up his remark with the expected teasing.

"Let's join the troupe at the hotel, shall we?"

Obviously the sight of her in wet underthings was no competition for Miss Diamond's glitter. Before Abbie could respond, he stood and pulled out her chair. She was crushed against him in the press of the crowd, but he kept her hand firmly in his arm. They had almost made it to the doors when a voice hissed in her ear, "Just try to compete with Miss Diamond, will you."

The jostling of the crowd gave Abbie the opportunity to land her heel squarely on the toe of Marcy Wilson's slipper. It was surely wicked to enjoy the gasp and muffled cry so much. But the taunting words had their effect. She wished Monte would take her to the buggy rather than lead the crowd to the hotel. The restaurant was not large enough for all of them, but Monte had no trouble acquiring a table.

By blind luck or other forces, shortly after Monte had seated her he turned and seated Miss Diamond to his other side. The lead player, who had portrayed Watson, took his place beside her to complete the foursome. He was not tall but well shaped and elegant in motion. He still wore his stage makeup. Abbie could smell the greasepaint.

For some time the two were occupied signing programs until those not actually paying for a meal were shooed out, and Abbie found herself directly opposite Carolina Diamond, still in her black fur and black stockinged legs. Under the chandelier, her made-up features were sharper still, the outline of her lips stark against the pale skin, the black fur exotic and extravagant.

Miss Diamond smiled. "Did you enjoy the show?"

"You have a beautiful voice." That was honest. "I've never heard anything like it." She turned to the male player. "And I enjoyed your performance, Mr . . ."

"Cunnings. Randolf Cunnings. I was introduced at the start, but people rarely notice."

Abbie was surprised. Had he been announced? Was it possible Miss Carolina Diamond had so entranced her she had missed anything else but the woman's dramatic entrance? No wonder Monte was smitten.

Mr. Cunnings stood. "Forgive me, and you are?"

"Abbie Martin." As surely as anything, Monte was out of his senses forgetting himself so much as to neglect introductions.

"And you, Mr. Farrel?" Miss Diamond turned to Monte. "Did we entertain you?"

He reached for and bowed over her hand. "I cannot express the extent."

"Now there's an accent I can't mistake. Don't tell me . . . North, no, South Carolina."

"Madam, you are a marvel. How. . . ?"

She laughed. "Don't ask my secrets. It dissolves the mystery."

Abbie would bet her last dollar Miss Diamond had asked someone. All the town knew from where Monte hailed.

"Well, then . . ." He cleared his throat. "Shall we order?"

"Indeed. I'm absolutely famished." Miss Diamond ran her hand over his arm. "I can't eat a thing before I perform."

"Not nerves, surely."

"Oh yes. To this day I'm petrified the moment my feet touch the stage."

"You hide it masterfully."

"Oh." She gave a little shrug. "With the first note it . . . poof! Vanishes away. Do you know my secret?"

"I thought you weren't telling."

"This one I'll share. I find a good, strong face in the crowd and focus on that. I think to myself, if I can find pleasure on that one face, then I've succeeded." She smiled. "I have you to thank for getting me through tonight."

"Ah." Monte glanced at Abbie. Before she could feign a smile, he turned back. "Let me see if I can hail a waiter."

Hail a waiter? With Rudy Brown hovering behind him, red-faced and nervous as a new fawn? Monte raised his hand and Rudy rushed to his side.

"Mr. Farrel, sir." He turned to Miss Diamond. "Are you ready to order, ma'am . . . miss . . . uh, Miss Diamond?"

"What would you recommend?"

"The game hen with raspberry sauce is fine tonight."

She tipped her head, glittering the thin tiara tucked into her very blond hair. "Hmm. What do you do, Mr. Farrel?"

"I beg your pardon?"

"Your line of work. Your profession."

"At present, I raise cattle."

"Do you provide the beef for the hotel?"

Monte bowed slightly. "Yes, ma'am, I do."

Abbie stared in disbelief. How perfectly she set him up, and how easily he followed. Monte, who saw through Abbie's every move.

Miss Diamond turned to Rudy. "I'd like a steak. Rare."

Rudy looked at Abbie.

She folded the menu shut and held it to him. "I'll take your recommendation on the game hen, thank you." She hoped Miss Diamond choked on her meat. Mr. Cunnings ordered a steak, as did Monte. Abbie fumed as they waited for the food to come.

Mr. Cunnings tried to draw her in, but mainly Miss Diamond spoke of places both she and Monte had visited. Abbie wasn't about to admit she'd only read of them. Miss Diamond had plenty of anecdotes and told of her experiences and the wild enthusiasm of her audiences. "I had a young man follow me from Philadelphia to Chicago and attend every performance in between. It was truly pathetic." She laughed.

Abbie wanted to slap her. Randolf Cunnings was watching,

and she wondered if it was his job to distract her while Miss Diamond entertained her escort. He leaned forward once again to engage her, but the arrival of the food provided a worthier distraction.

The game hen was delicious, tender yet crisp, and the sauce sweetly tangy. The sage dressing and scalloped potatoes, steamed string beans, and apricots made up for a lot. If Monte was fool enough to let their evening together be dominated by that woman, Abbie at least would enjoy her meal. If it were to anyone other than Monte, she would almost find Miss Diamond's blatant ploys amusing.

She would imitate them to Clara, the fingers brushing accidentally against his arm, the fluttering eyelashes, the low, earthy laugh that shook her chest and drew Monte's eyes to her décolletage. And no wonder she put out such effort. Monte was splendid himself. How could she not choose him from all the crowd?

"Is your steak not satisfactory?"

Abbie heard more than courtesy in Monte's tone. His professional pride was also at risk.

"Oh, it's marvelous."

"You've hardly touched it."

"I couldn't eat another bite."

Abbie choked back the snicker with her napkin. Was she playing the southern belle? Too bad she didn't know he spurned the false protests of frail appetites.

For almost the first time, Monte turned her way. "Dessert, Abbie?"

"I'd love a slice of apple cake." She faced Miss Diamond. "You've never tasted anything like the caramel sauce."

"And I surely never will." Miss Diamond spoke in mock dismay. She slid her hands over the fur.

"What animal is that?"

Carolina Diamond showed her teeth. "Panther. Black panther from Africa. Feel it." She held out her arm where the wrist was wrapped with fur around the sheer fabric of the sleeve.

Abbie was certain the woman's perfume wafted up to Monte's

nose. She stroked it reluctantly. *Poor beasts.* "I wonder how many it took to make the whole dress."

"I don't know. Several, I suppose, though they're monstrously big cats. Have you been to Africa, Monte?"

When had they gone to first-name informality? She must have been dozing. But how like Monte to put her at ease.

"No. I haven't."

"Perhaps we'll do a safari someday."

He gave a genteel nod. His expression was unreadable. Abbie's apple cake arrived, and she dug in defiantly.

Monte turned to Miss Diamond. "Are you certain you won't try some? Nothing gives a healthy glow quite like a hearty appetite."

Miss Carolina Diamond's mouth opened and closed. She shook her head slightly and stiffened. Abbie actually felt sorry for her. What a lonely, heartbreaking life it must be to set your hat for a new fellow in each place you went. Sure enough, she probably won plenty of them, but the disappointments must remind her that she was, after all, no better than the rest of them.

The night air felt cold after the stuffiness of the restaurant as Abbie walked beside Monte to the buggy. He released her hand from his arm. "Let me get the top up."

"Oh, leave it down. The night is so beautiful." And she could finally breathe.

He paused. "It'll be chilly."

"That's all right." She walked around to the side and leaned back against the buggy. A profusion of stars lit the moonless night sky. She felt Monte stop beside her.

"Rather takes the glint from Miss Diamond's gown, doesn't it?"

Abbie kept her eyes on the stars.

He turned her face and commanded her view. "I believe I played the fool."

"Not completely. You escaped the web before she sank the poison."

"Are you very angry?"

Angry? What she felt was too confusing to give a name. Part of her wanted to laugh in his face and say she didn't care a fig. Part wanted to run until her lungs cried out. Why, why, why was she standing here hurting for him again?

"Come, Abbie. I've had more than a taste of your temper before."

"I'm not angry."

Monte looked at her a long moment. "I keep company with Marcy Wilson for political reasons, and you put up your nose. I marry Sharlyn because my honor is called upon, and you make my life torture. Now I play into the hands of a skilled temptress right before your eyes, and you say you're not angry?"

"It's not a matter of . . ."

"Have you no affection for me?" His voice was husky, and Abbie's heart beat suddenly against her ribs. He gripped her arms. "Have I estranged you, then?"

The rise of emotion choked her.

"Tell me, Abbie. Tell me you can love me as you once did."

She fought the pressure in her chest. "No, Monte. Nothing is as it was. You've changed . . . and I've changed."

He withdrew his hands, and her arms grew cold.

She searched for the words she needed. "I was a child, full of ignorance and dreams. I'm not a child now." But she felt very young and uncertain.

He smiled wryly. "No, you're not. How I fretted for you to grow up."

Abbie straightened. "I have. And you can't expect me to be as I was, any more than you can again be the man you were two years ago."

The smile wilted, and he turned away. Abbie's heart sank at the defeat in his stance. She had not meant to hurt him. Where was his fight? Had the past year taken more of a toll than she realized? She touched his shoulder.

She had never reached out to him before, and he turned in surprise, then clasped her hands to his chest. "Abbie, I love you. Can you return it in even the smallest way?"

"You know I do. You know I've refused others. I told you there was only one who would claim my heart." She searched his face. "Oh, Monte, could you really think it had passed?"

"You've done a devil of a job concealing it."

"Have I?"

With one hand he raised her chin. "Indeed you have, and I've been ravaged with doubt. Abbie Martin, you're a cruel mistress."

"I'm no mistress..."

He pressed her against the buggy. "Marry me." His voice was rough, full of emotion. She had never seen him so, nor were the words the genteel entreaty she had once imagined. They were spoken as though wrenched from him without thought. This again was a Monte she did not know.

Her breath came short and shallow, an ache gripping her chest. How long she had waited, how deeply she had despaired of hearing those words. She fought the ache and searched for an answer, she who had never before failed to say what she thought.

Monte slid his hand from her chin to the back of her neck. His breath was warm on her cheek. "If you refuse me, I'll hound you unmercifully. I'll chase you until you haven't an argument left." He bent and kissed her mouth.

Abbie responded with frightening ardor as though her body and spirit recognized their match. No other kiss, not Blake's nor Cole's, had moved her so. Dear God, did she dare? Was this at last His plan for them? What of all that had passed?

Passed. It was past. She whispered against his lips, "Yes, Monte."

He kissed her again, softly, tenderly, then pressed her head to his chest. The racing of his heart matched hers. She loved this man. Her need to show him rose up, but he stepped back and released her. "I'll speak with your father at the earliest opportunity."

"When?"

"I don't..."

"Tomorrow?"

He laughed. "Yes, Abbie, tomorrow, and we'll set a date. Perhaps August..."

"That's two months!"

"If you need longer..."

"Longer!" She almost stamped her foot.

"My dear Abbie..." He pressed her hands together between his. "Plans must be made, your trousseau ordered and fitted, travel arrangements made for your relatives and mine."

She hadn't thought of that. Her sister, Sadie, and Grant. Of course, Grant must come all the way from Boston. She smiled at an impish thought. "Perhaps Gray Wolf will come with his people."

Monte frowned. "I know he saved your life, and I am eternally grateful, but ... if it's all the same to you, we'll not have Comanches to the wedding."

"It would be distinctively western."

"And my southern relatives would never get over the shock of it. Especially my sister, Frances."

"Oh, Monte, two months is forever."

"No, Abbie. I've looked at forever. Two months is hardly a breath." He rested his hand on her cheek, and she raised her face. "Oh, Abbie, don't look at me like that. I intend to be a gentleman until August."

"And then?"

He pressed his lips to her forehead before stepping back and lifting her into the buggy, his restraint exemplary. Abbie sighed. She had a sudden urge to run and tell Clara. But that would wait until morning. For now, she savored the strength of Monte's arm around her as they drove. His warmth cut the night's chill.

Four

The following evening Monte rode home through the growing darkness. Sirocco was sure in his step, and Monte gave him his head. It had gone better than he had hoped. Not that he had expected Joshua Martin to refuse him his daughter, but the waters had been muddied. Now he saw again the caliber of man Joshua was.

It felt amazingly good to be once more embraced by the Martins. He would count it a privilege to be part of the family. Abbie came from good, wholesome stock. No bloodlines traced to the founding fathers, no decades of duty and debts of honor. Only honest, hardworking people. It was his good fortune Abbie was also maddeningly lovely.

It warmed him to see the glow in her face and know it was he who put it there. Beyond his hopes, God had restored her affection, he was certain. It had shone in her glance and rung in her voice throughout the meal he had shared at their table.

It had been a little touchy when Monte offered his compliments to Selena, and she suggested Abbie would feed him well. She did not realize that was his cook's job. Wild fowl was not Pearl's specialty, and Abbie had no doubt learned Selena's secret, but Abbie fighting Pearl for kitchen rights was not something he cared to witness.

Still, those things would be worked out. Monte pulled up at the stable, dismounted, and handed the reins to Will. "He's had hay. Just a rubdown and a little mash tonight."

"Yes, sir."

Monte strode to the bunkhouse across the yard and opened the door. The cowboys straightened at his entrance, except for Cole, who sat with a poker hand and a face that matched. "May I have a word with you, Cole?"

"Soon as I fleece this sheep," Cole replied without looking his way.

Across from him Skeeter MacCarthy turned and spat. "All right, I call."

Cole laid down his hand. Three jacks. Skeeter swore and threw down eights and fours. Laughing, Cole scooped the money his way and stood. "Better luck next time, Skeeter."

"No such thing as luck against you."

"Ain't that the truth." Breck Thompson shoved his cards to the center.

Cole swaggered past and joined Monte outside the door. "Mr. Farrel?"

Monte eyed him. Since signing on in his employ, Cole had lost none of his disrespectful pluck. Though he accepted the subordinate position, his maverick attitude rankled. Monte would not let it tonight.

"I remember an evening you informed me that you intended to ask for Abbie's hand in marriage."

"Yeah?"

"I've come to give you the same courtesy."

"I figured you'd be askin'." Cole leaned against the wall.

Monte paused. "I've asked, and she's accepted."

"Shoot, I figured that, too." Pulling a paper from his pocket, Cole shook tobacco from a pouch, then licked the edge and rolled it tight. He struck the match on the wall and lit the cigarette. "You lookin' for congratulations?"

"You know better than that, Cole. I value your skills. I'm asking if this will affect your work for me."

Cole brought up his knee and rested his boot against the bunkhouse wall. "Well, I don't rightly know." He drew on the cigarette again. "I guess we'll wait and see."

Monte nodded. "I appreciate your honesty."

"Ain't no good pretendin'. And I ain't exactly surprised. What puzzles me is why you didn't just marry Abbie in the first place. No offense to the late Mrs. Farrel."

"Well, Cole, God's truth is I did what I had to do."

"Yeah. Sure, marry Abbie. She's so crazy in love with you she'd a spent her life alone, rather'n settle for anyone else."

"You're a good man, Cole."

He tossed the butt and crushed it under his heel. "Anything else?"

"No."

"Then I'll git back to my game. My luck's a whole lot better in there."

Monte headed for the house. Bounding up the front stairs, he opened the door and James came forward to take his hat. "Nice evenin', Mastuh Monte?"

"I'd say." Monte smiled and went to the library. He pulled open the drawer of the walnut desk and took out a sheet of paper. Sitting down, he allowed Abbie's image to form in his mind, her blue eyes with their thick drooping lashes, her mouth soft and full, her silky brown curls in enough disarray to arouse him like nothing else.

In this past year her features had refined from her girlish softness. She was a woman now, and his pulse quickened. How many times had he sat here and forced her from his thoughts? It seemed impossible that he could not only think of her now, but that he soon would have her as his wife.

Dipping the pen, he began to write name after name. Likely they would not travel to the Colorado Territory for the wedding, but they would be invited. This would be no rushed and silent deathbed ceremony. He wanted all the world to know that he was marrying Abigail Martin.

✦✦✦✦✦✦✦

Abbie pulled on the reins and slid to the ground almost before Shiloh stopped, leaving the mare sweating and stamping in the July heat. In the past month she and Monte had covered the ground between their ranches frequently enough to wear a trail in the scrubby golden grasses.

She flung the leather strands around the hitch and skipped up the stairs where Monte stood, tall and darkly handsome, in the doorway. She was bursting with her news. "Grant's coming!"

"And here I thought your exuberance was for me."

Abbie brushed back the curls that clung to her forehead. "Don't tease, Monte. I haven't seen Grant in four years! I can't wait for you to meet him."

"Did you think your brother wouldn't come?"

"Well, they let him finish early on condition he pass at a level of excellence, and he has!"

"Of course he has. If he's anything like his little sister, he's smart as a whip."

"Oh, he's smarter than I am. You'll like him, Monte. I know you will. And he'll like you, too."

"Kind of you to think so." He smiled. "Come in and get yourself cooled off. You're in as much of a lather as your mare."

Abbie's spirits ebbed. "You're not as excited as I wanted you to be."

He ushered her through the door. "James, see that Will tends Miss Martin's horse."

"Yessuh."

Monte stopped at the base of the stairs. "Run up and freshen yourself, Abbie. I'll be in the parlor."

Abbie fought her disappointment as she walked up the stairs into the first bedroom. She hated it when he acted the lord of the manor.

A Negro girl, perhaps a year or so younger than she, rushed in with fresh water and a towel. The water sloshed from the pitcher when she curtsied, then again when she slid the bowl onto the stand.

Abbie smiled. Here was someone after her own heart. "Hello."

The girl curtsied again, wringing her wet hands on her skirt, but she smiled broadly. "Afternoon, Mizz Martin."

"Well, I'm at a disadvantage. You know my name, but . . ."

"I'm Zena, Pearl's niece. Mistuh Farrel took me on last week."

"Oh. Did you come in on the stage?"

"No'm. Mistuh Farrel's foreman brung me in from Denver, but I traveled on the train all the way from Macon, Georgia."

"That must have been a long and difficult trip."

"Oh, no'm." She squeezed her hands again. "It was worth it. Now I have a real position."

Abbie felt ashamed for thinking ill of Monte. His kindness had brought Zena there. "Well, thank you for the water."

"Yes'm. I wanted a look at you. Aunt Pearl said Mistuh Farrel's goin' marry hisself a real beauty, an' she was right."

Abbie stood still, unsure how to respond.

"You wants me to unbutton you?"

She hid her surprise. "No . . . thank you. I can manage."

The girl backed out, again grinning broadly. Abbie dipped the towel into the cool water and squeezed it out, then applied it to her face. Her hot skin tingled with the chill of it, and she ran it over her neck, as well. Gazing at her reflection, she mused. Soon she would be mistress of this house, and James and Pearl and Zena and Will and all the cowboys would answer to her.

She groaned. Sharlyn, of course, had been born into the southern world of servants and masters, as Monte had. But this was the Colorado Territory, and Abbie knew nothing of all that. No matter. She would learn. She hung the towel on the rack and flipped her hair back, then swung around, her skirts swirling behind. She found Monte in the parlor.

"Better?" He handed her a glass of lemonade.

"Yes, but you needn't scold me. I know when I need a wash." She drank thirstily.

Monte laughed. "I wasn't suggesting any such thing. But your face was flushed, and I didn't want to risk a sunstroke."

"Then thank you for your concern." She drained the glass and set it on the corner table. "Now will you respond to my news?"

"Abbie, I'm thrilled your brother is coming to the wedding. And as far as that goes, my sister and her husband are making the trip also, though Kendal will no doubt have to sedate her."

"Why on earth?"

"I'm afraid I embellished a tale or two when I saw them last, and she believes her very life to be at stake."

"Oh, Monte. How could you?"

"It was altogether too tempting." He reached out for her hands. "But I wish now I hadn't. The trip will not be pleasant for her. If only the railroad were through."

Abbie sighed. "It's close. Sadie's husband, Joe, works for the Denver Rio Grande. He said they're looking to send a spur through anytime now. Why didn't you tell me you hired a new girl?"

He raised an eyebrow. "I didn't know I had to."

"I just mean it was a surprise to meet Zena."

"Ah. Well, Pearl's sister wrote that things were hard, and with Pearl getting up in age . . . and you'll need a lady's maid. Not that Pearl would stand for just any help, mind you, but her own niece . . ."

"That's kind of you, Monte."

"This is a large home." He drew her close. "And soon I expect it will be housing a family."

Abbie raised her eyes to his face. "Oh, Monte, August is too far."

"It's not so far, now. Would you like to walk with me awhile?"

"I would, but I have to go to town. I promised Mama I'd post her letters at once. But you can come for dinner. Mama said to ask."

"I'm afraid not tonight. Cole and I are making preparations for the herd he's taking east."

"Will he be gone long?"

"Does the absence of my foreman concern you?"

She startled at his tone. Why was he so snappish? "I just wondered."

"Several weeks, I'd guess." He walked her back through the hall and out into the dazzling brightness. "Don't rush your mare this time, Abbie. It's too hot to ride her hard."

Abbie bristled. "Thank you, Monte. I do know how to care for her." She started down the stairs, then turned. "Tell Cole I wish him a good journey."

His smile stiffened. "I'll tell him."

She was instantly ashamed. What was it that made them spar? She mounted Shiloh and waved sheepishly. He raised his hand in response. She could feel his eyes on her as she cantered down the drive, and when she turned at the gate, he was still on the porch.

Monte watched Abbie canter off. The horse had mended well, but at times Abbie was careless—even reckless—though it annoyed her to be corrected. Still, it wasn't the horse that had set him off. It was the fear he had felt when she galloped up as though the hounds of hell were on her.

After finding the poisoned calf this morning, he was jumping at shadows. It was no accident. All that he had was in jeopardy. He didn't know why; he didn't know whom. And he didn't want Abbie in the middle of it.

He wearily dropped his forehead against the pillar. Whom should he suspect? Whom could he trust? Cole? The memory of Abbie in Cole's arms still stung. Why would she ask after him? Why not; it was innocent enough. Abbie had no way of knowing the turmoil it stirred in him.

Monte felt an inner probing that he did not want to acknowledge. Yes, he had submitted his will to God's guidance, and by God's hand won back Abbie's affection. But some things a man handled himself. He started across the yard. The sooner Cole was on his way, the better.

Five

Abbie waved away the dust kicked up by the stage as it careened to a halt in the street. Gus always came in with a show of speed, if not comfort. Beside her on the boardwalk, Eleanor Bailey stopped midsentence, mouth open, while her sister, Ruth, fluttered her hand and choked. The memory of Buck Hollister's stage robbery that had terrified their aunt and killed Gus's partner still put them in a tizzy, but Abbie was only interested in seeing the passengers. She raised up on her toes, not caring that it amused Monte. But she could not see in the window.

Gus jumped down from the box, smacked the dust from his shirt, and opened the door. He pulled down the step. A tall man with waxed mustache and sandy hair climbed out. He turned and held a hand to a striking, dark-haired woman.

Abbie squeezed Monte's arm. "I know that's Frances. Her likeness is unmistakable!"

Monte laughed. "You're right. Now behave yourself, and I'll introduce you."

Behave herself, indeed. She'd been looking forward to this almost as though it were her own sister coming from Denver City. She'd wondered about Frances ever since Monte had spoken so heartbreakingly of protecting her during the war. Even now, there was a certain . . . carefulness when he spoke of her.

Monte swept her forward, and the man caught sight of them. "Monte!"

Abbie stared at Frances. She looked like a dressmaker's doll in the newest fashion. Every hair on her head was perfectly coifed, and there was not a wrinkle on her sumptuous dress. She must not have moved the entire trip.

Monte shook Kendal's hand. "I see you've made it safely through with no fire, stampede, or Indian attack." He bent and kissed his sister's cheek. "Permit me to present to you my fiancée, Abigail Martin."

Frances turned, graceful as a doe. "How do you do, Abigail."

"Oh, I prefer Abbie. I'm only Abigail when I'm in trouble."

Monte squeezed her elbow. "Abbie, my sister, Frances, and her husband, Kendal Stevens."

Kendal bowed over her hand. "I'm delighted to meet you."

"And you."

"Yes." Frances waved a delicate ivory fan. "We've been so eager." She looked past her. "What a quaint little place."

Abbie turned. "It's grown tremendously over the last year. What on earth we need with two grocers and three saloons, I'm sure I don't know."

"Competition, my dear," Kendal said. "The lifeblood of commerce."

"I'd think they'd do better going somewhere they were needed."

Kendal chuckled. "Don't have her keep your books, Monte."

"Abbie's not going to run my business, only my home."

Frances fanned herself again. "Then by all means let's hasten out of this scathing sunshine. It's a mercy you don't come out in freckles with no bonnet, Abbie. But then, your complexion is darker."

Abbie put a hand to her cheek. "I hardly notice it, but come stand in the shade. Have you a parasol?"

"In my trunk." Frances stepped under the eaves and made no move toward the trunk. Instead, Kendal searched until he pulled out a ruffled yellow parasol. He snapped it open and handed it to her.

Monte lifted two of the bags into the wagon. Together he and Kendal hoisted up the trunk and tossed in the remaining bags.

Abbie had laughed when Monte brought the wagon instead of the buggy. Now she knew why.

Kendal handed Frances up to the buckboard, and Monte lifted Abbie in beside her, then climbed into the front seat with Kendal. They passed through town, and at the end of the street the wagon lurched, then settled into the twin ruts that led over the prairie. Frances grasped the side of the buckboard. "Is there no road to your ranch, Monte?"

"This is it."

Frances sighed. "You warned us it was rustic. But you never said primitive."

Abbie tried not to stare as they rode. Frances was the most beautiful lady she had ever seen. Unlike Miss Carolina Diamond, her beauty was natural. She looked like the miniature of Monte's mother but more sophisticated and less . . . She couldn't put her finger on the difference. Something disdainful in the expression perhaps.

As they pulled past the gate, Kendal tipped back his hat and appraised the house. He turned to Frances. "Now you don't say primitive, do you, my dear?"

"This almost looks civilized."

Abbie bit her lip. What would Frances think of her family's small, neat farm house? Monte lifted her down from the wagon. Suddenly she spun around. "But where is your daughter?"

Frances stared at her. "Surely you didn't think we could bring her out here."

Abbie stared. "Why ever not?"

"She's with her mammy at my mother's home," Kendal said.

"But you'll be away so long!"

Frances pursed her lips. "Yes. And she'll be far better off in Charleston with her grandmother than out here in . . ."

"I'm sure Abbie's disappointed not to see the child." Monte waved Kendal toward the house. "We'd have both enjoyed meeting the little one. How old is she now?"

"A year and a half in October." Kendal gave Frances his hand at the stairs.

Abbie felt Monte's grip like a vise on her elbow as he breathed in her ear. "Abbie, please. Try not to insult Frances."

She looked up, her mouth falling open. "How on earth did I insult her?" she whispered back. He didn't answer, and drawing a deep breath, she followed him inside.

"It's very like the plantation," Frances said. "Especially this parlor." She stroked the red velvet drapes.

The room was baking from the heat trapped by the heavy velvet even though they were tied back at the sides, but Abbie didn't repeat her advice to remove the drapes. Monte and Frances obviously approved of them. Abbie felt the sweat trickle down the back of her neck. She wanted out of there. "Can I get you something to drink? Your trip was no doubt hot and dry."

Monte turned. "Pearl will see to that, Abbie."

"Oh, I don't mind . . ." His eyes silenced her.

The door opened, and Pearl brought in tall glasses of pale tea with sugared mint leaves and a plate of thin chocolate wafers. Not exactly the oatmeal cookies or honey muffins Abbie might have offered guests at home.

Abbie watched Pearl set down the tray and leave without acknowledgment even from Monte, then realized he was looking at her. What now? Oh goodness, he wanted her to serve. She reached immediately for the tray and handed a glass to Frances and Kendal, then gave one to Monte.

"Thank you." She heard the amusement in his tone, though his expression was merely pleasant. "Perhaps our guests would care for a sweet."

Abbie lifted the plate. As she did, the last glass of tea tipped off the tray. Frances leaped back too late, and it splashed down the skirt of her dress. Abbie felt the blood rush to her face. *Oh heavens!* All the way from Charleston without a wrinkle and now that. "I'm terribly sorry! Let me get a cloth for it."

Before Monte could stop her, she rushed from the room and down the hall to the narrow corridor that connected the kitchen. It was a relief to run. She wished she could keep going out the back door and all the way home.

In the kitchen Pearl spun at Abbie's unexpected arrival.

"I need a wet cloth for Mrs. Stevens' dress."

Squaring herself, Pearl put her hands to her hips. "Mizz Martin. Mr. Farrel uses the bell if he needs he'p. Ain't no cause to run like a chicken on account of a spill."

Abbie stopped short, and the color rose in her cheeks. "I didn't know about the bell. But since I'm here I may as well get the cloth and go before Mrs. Stevens' dress is stained."

"Ah'll see to her, miss. You go on now."

She felt scolded and dismissed. There was nothing for it but to go back to the parlor. Her feet were reluctant. She stood a moment at the door, then squared her shoulders and went in. Only Kendal and Monte were there.

Monte turned from the window. "Frances has retired to change and rest."

Zena came into the room with a towel, dropped to her knees, and blotted the spill from the rug. Abbie wasn't surprised that neither man acknowledged her.

Well, she wasn't so constrained. "I'm sorry I was careless."

Zena's eyes flickered up, then returned to her task without answer.

"Don't worry." Monte raised his glass. "I'll have Pearl fix you another."

He must be mortified, though he didn't show it. And she wished Kendal would stop looking at her like that. The best she could hope for was a graceful exit. "Please don't bother. I think I'll go home now, if that's all right. You must have catching up to do, and Mama's canning today."

"All right." Monte brushed his lips on her hand as he bowed. "I'll call for you tomorrow."

Monte watched her leave. Kendal sent him a crooked grin. "I think your nights will not be dull."

Monte set his tea down and walked to the window. "Abbie is not a southern belle."

Kendal laughed. "You don't have to tell me that or apologize.

I find her utterly charming. Frances may have a different opinion, but then, it doesn't really matter out here, does it?"

Monte turned back. "I don't know if it matters. I do know Abbie is in my blood. From the first time I saw her two years ago, she had a hold on me."

"You knew her before marrying Sharlyn?"

Monte felt a shadow of the old shame. "Yes."

Kendal whistled. "Forgive me, Monte, but why did you choose Sharlyn?"

"Her father asked it of me on his deathbed . . . for reasons I felt I could not refuse."

"She wasn't compromised?"

"No. But the danger was real."

Kendal shook his head. "Did Abbie know of your feelings?"

"Unfortunately. That's why it's so important to me now to bear with the little infractions. I tell you, Kendal, Abbie is my life."

"I can understand that passion. She is remarkable."

✦✦✦✦✦✦✦

Abbie rode Shiloh along the edge of Pa's ranch. She couldn't go home just yet. Mama would see her humiliation. She stopped the horse and dismounted. The scrub oaks arched twelve feet over the track where she led the horse.

Pa's plot was only forty acres, not a true ranch, really—only enough to keep their few sheep, two horses, the cow, and chickens. Pa had paid a dollar and a quarter an acre, but to Abbie it was worth more than any gold field.

Monte's ranch comprised nearly a thousand acres of grazing land, the two purchased claims, and the open range he used. The house and yard, stable, bunkhouse, and barn occupied a full nine acres. But it lacked the beauty of the foothills.

His was prairie land and trees were scarce, with just a few ponderosas and spiky junipers, scattered mounds of scrub oak, and the cottonwoods that lined the river and surrounded the house. Yet its vastness, bare but teeming with life, the smell of sage, the circling hawks, the broken hills, and arroyos moved her. The mountains might hold her heart, but the plains reflected her spirit.

Soon she would call it home. It was a bittersweet feeling. She sighed. Why couldn't Frances have been like Sharlyn? Or even like Monte? Well, she was in a way. They both carried themselves with impeccable ease and natural poise. But Monte never made her feel ... low, as Frances had.

She put a hand to her cheek. It was warmed like tallow by the sun. Was she dark and coarse? Frances's skin was a soft pearly white even in August. She frowned.

Beside her a squirrel chattered from the branches of a ponderosa. Abbie raised her chin. "What do you think of this, Frances?" She grabbed up her skirts and ran to the tree. Her muscles tightened and stretched as she mounted higher and higher until the branches could no longer support her. "Bet you can't do that, Mrs. Stevens! I'd like to see you escape a stampede."

Perching on the branch, she felt the breeze in her hair and closed her eyes. *Oh, Lord, I want Monte to be proud of me.* She leaned her head against the trunk. How could she make up to Frances? How could she undo the impression she had made? She started down but her foot slipped, and she slid against the trunk. Crying out, she gripped a branch and stopped her fall, then painfully lowered herself to the ground.

Her knee and chin were scraped, and two fingernails, torn jaggedly, began to bleed. "Oh, God, I know. Pride goeth before a fall." She touched her chin. "A fine display I'll make now, thank you."

She flounced into the yard and stopped at the pump. Working the lever, she forced out the cold water, splashed it over her face, then grimly stuck her head beneath. It served her right.

Inside the house Mama had her back turned, standing at the stove. Abbie wanted to grab her around the middle and bury her face on Mama's chest.

"Monte's sister made it in all right?"

"Yes."

"How is she?"

"Fine. Very fine." Impossibly, unmatchably fine.

Mama turned. "Well, that's ... gracious, what did you do to your face?"

"I slipped."

"Get the salve from the shelf."

"Yes, Mama."

The sting brought tears to her eyes, but Abbie dutifully applied it, then replaced the jar. Beside it stood the fine cream Pa had given Mama. *For the maintaining of smooth, youthful skin.* Abbie took it down. She dipped a finger in and spread it over her cheek. It was a soft, cool delight.

Her skin felt velvety. She imagined Monte resting his hand there. Had Sharlyn used cream? Of course she had. And she knew better than to let the sun bronze her skin. Abbie looked at her reflection in the polished tin nailed to the wall over the washstand. She jutted her damaged chin. She looked five years old. What a Jonah day.

"Better?" Mama strained the beans and scooped a spoonful into the steaming jar.

"Yes." Abbie tied on her apron.

"You may as well tell me what's on your heart. It'll only trouble you until you do." Mama saw everything.

"I'm afraid I won't know how to be Monte's wife."

"Are you meaning ... personal things?"

Abbie flushed. "No, Mama. Practical things."

"He'll let you know your duties."

"He just smiles and waits to see if I'll embarrass him. I never knew keeping house for him would be so complicated. I thought it would be like you and Pa. I could keep a fine house for someone like Pa."

"And you'll keep a fine house for Monte. He'll be patient. He loves you so."

"I don't want to disappoint him." Sharlyn had managed his home with perfection. Abbie's throat tightened. She didn't want to compete with that image.

"Don't borrow trouble, Abbie. Today has enough of its own."

Six

The late afternoon shadows stretched across the land as Monte drove the phaeton toward Abbie's homestead. Its springs were good, the ride gentler than the wagon's, and he was glad to see Frances look about her with interest as they headed to Abbie's birthday party.

"This is pleasant over here, Monte. There are trees in the hills."

"Yes, but you can't graze cattle on scrub oak and ponderosas. Cole would have a devil of a time keeping track of the herd on this terrain."

"How does Abbie's father manage?" Kendal asked.

"He doesn't ranch. Joshua runs the newspaper. He's a remarkable man, very quick-witted . . . like his daughter." He winked at Frances.

"I make up my own mind, Monte."

"How well I know that." He waited for Kendal and Frances to climb down, then pulled up to the barn and unhitched Chance. Other neighbors' horses were tethered inside the barn, but they had kept the back stall free for Chance. He was growing accustomed to that space.

Back outside, he saw that Abbie had already shown Kendal and Frances to the refreshment table. Her back was to him as she shared some pleasantry with his sister. It would take more than that to thaw Frances, he was afraid. He caught Abbie's eye, and she hurried to meet him. He squelched the desire to catch her up into his arms and instead brought her outstretched hand to his lips. "You don't look a day over nineteen."

"I'm not yet. Not for another hour. Are you thirsty? There's tea and sarsaparilla at the table."

"All in good time." He tucked a finger under her chin and eyed her. "What did you do to yourself?"

"I slipped."

"Slipped! Fell headlong, more like."

"Don't scold, Monte. I feel conspicuous enough as it is."

He killed his laugh and pressed her hand. "You can't help that, my love. No one with eyes like yours could ever blend into the scenery."

"Well, thank you for the compliment."

"And what is this piece of finery?" He fingered the amethyst brooch at her throat.

"From Mama and Pa. Isn't it lovely?"

"As lovely as the neck that holds it."

She tucked her hand into his arm. "Pa's not home yet. I can't imagine what's keeping him. Would you mind acting as host till he gets here?"

"Not a bit."

While Abbie flitted between the house and yard, Monte introduced Frances and Kendal to the other guests: Ethan Thomas, Frank and Mildred Simms, Becky Linde, and Mary Beth Walker, whose wandering eye made it difficult to know where to look when one addressed her. He couldn't help noticing Frances's increasing disdain. Perhaps it was a mistake to bring her here tonight. It almost made him ashamed of his neighbors.

As the sun crowned the summits and edged behind, it shot fire to the clouds, then disappeared. That at least was a blessing as the occasion had warranted his black coat. He envied Ethan his cotton shirt sleeves. This heat was sharp. Not as pervasive as South Carolina's but more insistent. It didn't linger, though. Already he felt a coolness descending.

Abbie joined them again, as vibrant as always. If she was aware of Frances's mood, she hid it completely. Nor was there the awkwardness of the previous day, but then this was her element, her home, her day. She fairly bubbled with good spirits.

"Oh, Clara, I'm so glad you're here! You must meet Monte's sister." She rattled off the introductions. "And this..." she reached a hand to cup the toddler's plump cheek, "is baby Del. Frances and Kendal have a daughter just about Del's age."

"Oh, Del will be thrilled to see someone his size."

Frances stiffened. "We left her in Charleston."

Monte wished Abbie would leave it alone. What was she thinking, bringing that up again? Did she think it unnatural for Frances to have left the child? Abbie didn't understand mammies.

"Oh." Clara shrugged. "Well, Del will just have to wait for Melissa's baby to walk."

Monte didn't miss the glance Clara shot to Abbie, nor the answering rise of Abbie's eyebrows. So she wasn't as oblivious as she let on. Well, she was playing a dangerous game. She left Clara to greet the coming wagon. It was Blake McConnel's mother and sister. Mary McConnel climbed down and hugged Abbie close. "Happy birthday, my dear."

Monte wondered how the woman would feel about their announcement tonight. Had things worked out differently, it might have been her son that Abbie married. He went to the wagon and reached a hand to Mariah, who scuttled down before he could assist her, then stood pressed against the wooden side, shifting her weight from one foot to the other.

It was deucedly uncomfortable, and he was relieved when Abbie swept in and took Mariah's hand. "Come, Mariah, let me introduce you to Monte's sister."

Monte winced.

Mariah shoved her hand out and gave Frances a hard pump, then turned on her heels. "I gotta get the beans." She scurried back to the wagon.

Monte choked, caught between chagrin and the horrible hilarity of Frances's expression as she stared at her hand, then headed for the pump with a look that demanded Kendal assist her. Monte wished it otherwise but knew his duty. He, too, went to offer comfort.

He came up behind as Frances gripped Kendal's arm. "How can he stand it?"

"What?"

"This place, these people? Is that girl simple? Did you hear what she said? 'I gotta get the beans.' My days! I feel contaminated." She lathered her hands furiously.

Kendal worked the pump handle. "It's not so bad. And Abbie is delightful."

Frances held her palms under the flow. "I fail to see the attraction."

"That, my dear, is because you are a woman."

Monte cleared his throat.

Frances faced him. "How do you remain here, Monte? Poor Sharlyn . . . this place alone could cause anyone's death."

He felt it like a slap, and it must have shown.

"I'm sorry." She looked anything but contrite. "It's just . . . so rough and . . ."

"Sharlyn was happy here." He spoke fixedly, containing his anger.

"Of course she was. She loved you. She would have borne anything."

That hit too closely to the truth. His sister's contempt was wearing on him. He'd expected it, but he hadn't thought how it would cloud his own impressions. Monte watched Abbie with her arm tucked through Clara's, giggling. Coiled wisps of hair escaped her ribbon and blew across her face. She brushed the hair back absently but did not bother to contain it, unlike Frances, who regimented every strand.

Laughing, Abbie chattered fiercely and gesticulated. She was a wild thing sprung up on the mountainside, and even as his pulse quickened at the thought, he felt a twinge. Would he ever bring her to his childhood home and present her there? How would women such as Frances receive her? Blast them anyway. He didn't care.

Wes McConnel arrived with the hay wain. Monte hoisted Abbie up and pulled himself up beside her. Frances refused the ride, and in a rare act of defiance, Kendal climbed up without her. Monte couldn't half blame him. If he stayed behind he'd be subjected to a diatribe that no man should have to endure. He sent him a sympathetic smile, and Kendal raised an eyebrow in response.

As the wain started, Abbie wiggled deeper into the hay, grabbed up two handfuls and tossed it into the air. "Don't you love the smell of it, fresh cut like this?" She dropped back onto the heap, oblivious to the straw clinging to her hair and dress.

Monte saw Kendal's eyes on her. He knew what Kendal saw, though Abbie herself was ignorant of her allure. She acted without premeditation, unlike southern girls trained to calculate the effect of every glance. It pleased him to see Kendal's appreciation. Perhaps that would help with Frances, and at any rate, he need hardly feel jealous of his own sister's husband.

Abbie rolled to her elbow. "I wonder what's keeping Pa. He should have been home ages ago."

Monte shrugged. "He won't miss your party, if I know Joshua." The wain dipped, and Abbie jostled against him. Monte caught her arm. "Don't tumble off now. You're battered enough for one day. And you still haven't told me what you did."

"I don't intend to."

"Come, Abbie."

"I spit into the wind."

"What!"

"It's an expression, like laughing at fate or thumbing your nose. It frequently comes back on you."

"Oh?"

"You'll only laugh."

"I won't. My word of honor."

She put her mouth to his ear. "I fell down a tree."

Monte threw back his head and laughed, and Abbie hissed, "Your word is forever tarnished!"

"Forgive me, Abbie. But what were you doing in the tree?"

"Hush! If you think I'll give you one more detail . . ."

At the head of the wain, Marty's voice sang out into the

gloaming and was joined by others as Abbie sank back into the mound of hay. One tune led to another as his clear tenor urged them. Abbie did not sing but closed her eyes and rocked with the motion of the wain.

The first faint star appeared above them, and Monte watched it flicker until it dominated its spot of night sky and shone steadily. He was achingly aware of Abbie beside him. He leaned close. "I wish we were alone."

"It wouldn't do you any good," she replied without opening her eyes.

"Come, Abbie, I begged your forgiveness. I truly meant to not laugh."

They were nearing the house again, and the lanterns had been lit over the tables set out in the yard. The wain lolloped to a stop. Monte leaped down and reached up for Abbie. She placed her hands on his shoulders and slid, landing in a cascade of hay before him.

He did not release his hold. "Forgive me, Abbie?" Pressing her against the wain, he bent his head and kissed her. If he possessed one shred less decorum he would kiss her as he was certain she had never been kissed before. A throat being cleared behind him brought Monte's head up immediately.

Abbie squealed, "Grant!" She dived past Monte and sailed into her brother's arms. Lifted into the air, she squealed again. "Oh, Grant, I didn't know you'd make it here today! This is the finest surprise!"

Behind them stood Joshua. He smiled indulgently when Monte caught his eye.

Grant set Abbie on the ground. "I expect this is the man you intend to marry? Or does he have me to face for stealing a kiss from my sister right out in plain sight?" Grant stretched out his hand.

Monte gripped it. "Sometimes extreme measures are required. It's a pleasure. I've heard much about you—all glowing."

"I'm sure I'll have my earful coming."

Abbie hooked her arm through her brother's. "You must see

Marty and Clara and their little son. She'll be delighted that . . ."

Her chatter faded as she dragged him off. Monte watched their retreating backs and felt irrationally bereft. Joshua shrugged, and Monte shook his head, then sought out his sister and Kendal. Frances was seated on the rough bench along the split rail fence, her skirts arranged around her and her plate held precariously. She didn't appear to have taken a bite.

Kendal slouched beside her against the post. "You know, there is an appeal to this place, the way everyone's come together to enjoy the event under the stars. There's something very attractive in its simplicity. I can see why it agrees with you, Monte."

Frances sighed. "I cannot. At least with Sharlyn, you maintained some dignity, some breeding."

"I'm sure he intends to maintain breeding with Abbie, as well." Kendal chuckled, and Monte took his elbow in the ribs.

Frances frowned. "I'll thank you to keep your coarse remarks to yourself."

"I apologize. That was distasteful." But he chuckled again. "I see you've been deposed, Monte."

Monte nodded. "Abbie's brother. She'll no doubt drag him this way in her grand presentation. He's been at Harvard the last four years. Just passed for a lawyer."

"There you see, Frances, there is sophistication in this wilderness."

"Indeed there is." Monte balanced his plate on the fence post. "Abbie is better read than any lady I've known. She speaks intelligently on most any subject."

"That does not mean she can take on the responsibilities of your home."

"No. And I fear she has some to learn in that area, but she's quick and willing. And . . . by far the most entrancing creature."

Frances tossed her head. "I might easily believe you bewitched. You showed good sense when you married Sharlyn, even if it was rushed and mysterious. She was the kind of lady to make a home for someone of your standing, Monte."

"Frances . . ." Kendal frowned.

"Monte and I have always been honest with each other, Kendal. I would do him a disservice if I didn't speak my concerns."

Monte laid a hand on her shoulder. "Indeed you would. But I think you haven't given Abbie a chance. Sharlyn herself was devoted to her. Most of her days were spent in Abbie's company. Were she here to do so, Sharlyn would tell you how wrong you are."

"Would she? When she saw how Abbie plays up to you? It appears to me that she's very brazen—"

"Not brazen, I think." Kendal stroked his mustache. "Just innocent of her charm."

Frances sniffed. "I see you've fallen under the spell, too. But I fear you will regret this hasty decision, Monte."

His temper flared. "There is nothing hasty about it. It's been nearly a year since Sharlyn's death. That's longer than most widowers maintain that status out here."

"I don't expect you to be alone. But I think you should come home and choose a wife, as you did the last time."

"There's no one I would choose over Abbie. Had I my way, she would have been my first wife."

Frances opened her mouth, then closed it.

Abbie approached with Grant still on her arm. "Mr. and Mrs. Stevens, may I present my brother, Grant Martin."

Kendal extended his hand. "I understand you intend to practice law."

"That's right."

"Where?"

Grant glanced at Abbie. "Well, I'm considering Rocky Bluffs."

Abbie gasped. "Here? You're going to stay here?"

He tweaked her chin. "I need to meet with Judge Wilson and confer, but I'm considering it."

Monte leaned on the fence. "You'd be Rocky Bluffs' first lawyer."

"And only." Grant laughed. "But from what I've heard, it's grown enough to support one. I've not decided yet."

Monte touched Abbie's sleeve. "Your father's calling us."

Abbie caught his arm as they walked. "I do."

"You do what?"

"Forgive you for laughing. If it hadn't hurt so much at the time, I might have laughed, too. I'm sure it was quite a spectacle, though only the squirrel who lured me up there observed it. I promise my tree-climbing days are done."

He laughed low. "I'm glad to hear that. It's rather time, don't you think?"

Joshua climbed onto the crate in front of the house and called for attention. "Now, I know you've all probably heard, but this is the official announcement of the engagement between my daughter Abbie and Montgomery Farrel. May their life together be rich and filled with blessing."

"Hear, hear!" Marty yelled.

Monte took Abbie's hand and gave a slight bow. "I know I've spoiled the hopes of many of you, but I don't regret it one bit." He waited through the laughter and cheers. "And you can all come to the wedding." He stepped back and received the congratulations and backslapping from those around him.

There was an appeal to this place, these people. Monte felt more at home in that moment than he had yet. Whatever Frances may think, these people were there to stay, to make something of the town, the territory . . . and maybe in time, the state. While the South was decaying, new life was springing up here. And he was part of it. And so was Abbie.

Frank Simms took up the fiddle, and Monte used the moment to escape. Bending close to Abbie, he whispered, "Come with me."

He clasped her hand and led her away from the lanterns, across the yard to the barn. He eased the door open and pulled her inside.

"Monte, what are you doing?"

He took the lantern from the wall, but did not light it. They moved through the inky space until he felt a stall and got his bearings. "I don't want to be interrupted by anyone seeing the light."

"Interrupted from what?"

"I promised to be a gentleman, remember."

They reached the back of the barn, and he struck a match and lit the lantern, then turned the wick down low. "There, now." He set it on the shelf. "I have something for you." He lifted her chin with his fingers. "Shall I give it to you now?"

"How can I say when you're being so mysterious?"

He pulled a silver-hinged box from his pocket and handed it to her. She ran a finger over the filigreed leaves and vines. "It's beautiful."

"Open it."

Abbie obeyed and found earrings, a single garnet on a gold wire with a teardrop pearl suspended beneath. "Oh, Monte ... they're so fine ..."

"They were my mother's. You'll have to have Selena put a needle through your ears to wear them."

Her eyes met his, and her lips trembled.

Monte drew her into his arms. "One week, Abbie ..." He found her mouth with his, and she responded.

Suddenly a figure moved behind him, and before he could react they were slammed against the wall. Abbie's jaw smacked Monte's chest as they tumbled down and he fought to break her fall. The lantern toppled and smashed.

He rolled, shielding Abbie from the burst of flame, then leaped to his feet and pulled off his coat as fire rushed up the post and across the hay-strewn floor. The acrid smoke caught his breath as he smacked the coat against the flames. They roared into the adjacent stall and up the far wall. He dropped the coat and gripped Abbie's arm. "Go!"

"The animals!" She choked.

"I'll get them."

"You can't manage, not by yourself—"

"Go."

"No, I ..."

He rushed toward the front and shoved her. "Go!"

The door was already open, and she ran through. He turned back. The barn was dry, and there was little time. He plunged into the smoke, opened the stalls, and sent the horses out. Those tethered to the posts he cut loose and shooed. He wrapped his arm across his eyes and fought his way back through the flames. Chance was back there.

Behind him he heard voices, the thumps of bags and shovels and the sizzle of water on flames. It was no good. Even had they a lake, their efforts would be wasted. He had to reach Chance. There. The horse's eyes were wide, nostrils distended. He pulled back his lips and whinnied.

Monte spoke softly. "Steady. Steady."

Chance reared up, both walls of his stall ablaze. Monte gripped the bar. The heat of it seared his flesh as it burst to flame in his hands. Chance screamed, reared up, and his hoof caught Monte in the shoulder.

He went down, only half aware of Chance leaping over him through the smoke. He writhed, kicked at the pant leg aflame, but his hands . . . the pain . . . then nothing.

Seven

Abbie fought against Kendal's hold. "Let me go!" She wrenched one arm free and beat against him.

"You can't go back. It won't hold now." As his words faded, the corner of the roof collapsed.

"Please, God!"

"Don't faint, Frances! I've only one pair of arms."

Abbie saw her chance. She dropped and twisted. His hold broke, and she ran for the barn. The heat sucked her breath and she fell, regained her feet, and rushed through the door. No vision of hell compared to the raw force inside the barn.

"Monte!" She dropped to her knees and crawled.

Grant loomed up in the smoke, dragging Monte. No! She stood and ran toward them. Others rushed in and pulled Monte free. The smoke. The flames. She hit the floor hard. Someone . . . Grant . . . beat her legs, then pulled her up and ran. The horrible roar that followed sent flames rushing to the sky.

She yanked free of Grant and pushed through her neighbors to Monte's side. The strength left her legs. She dropped to her knees beside him. "Monte?"

He moaned.

Oh, dear God, he was alive. She felt her tears, though she had no knowledge of crying.

Pa spoke at her elbow. "Ethan's gone for Doctor Barrow. Don't try to move, Monte."

Monte rasped, "Abbie?"

"I'm here." She bent close.

73

He sucked in a strangled breath.

"Here is water for him." Mama handed Pa the cup, and he lifted Monte's head. Monte gulped, then choked and spewed it over his blackened chin. Closing his eyes, he dropped back.

Abbie swiped the tears from her nose. "Can we take him in, Pa?"

"I don't know that we should move him."

People suddenly rushed past, there was a crash, and a flaming geyser shot to the sky. The furious activity ceased. They were beaten. Abbie watched the flames soar and dance with fiendish fury. Held within the break, the fire consumed the barn but did not spread to the house or the land. The walls crumpled. Smoke blotted out the stars. She turned away.

Monte shivered even through the blanket.

"He's cold." She wanted to cover him with her body, hold him to her chest, feel the beat of his heart. "Pa, he's cold."

"All right. Wes, help me lift him." He slipped his arms under Monte's shoulders, and Wes grabbed his ankles. Monte cried out as they lifted him.

"No, stop, you're hurting him!"

Mama put a hand to her arm. They carried him limp and unresisting into the house as Abbie followed weakly. Placing him on the clean sheets Mama spread on the bed, Monte moaned again. His shoulder bled from a gash, but it seemed his hands pained him more. He held them like claws.

Pa tore the shirt free, and Mama pressed a cloth to his wounded shoulder. Without thought, Abbie soaked a towel and laid it across his forehead. A memory of Blake lying just so seized her. *No! Monte won't die!* She felt the hysteria filling her mind. A hand touched her shoulder and she lashed out, then met the eyes of Doctor Barrow. Relief rushed in.

"Joshua, stay. Everyone else out."

Abbie moved one foot after the other. It would be all right now. The doctor knew what to do. Hadn't he nursed her back from shock and pneumonia? He hadn't saved Sharlyn. But Monte was strong!

She could hear voices and commotion outside, but immediately around her all was still. She was in a cottony shell. There was no feeling but a dull numbness and something pressing her chest. Someone took her arm and led her to a chair. It was Kendal.

Frances was seated beside her. "What were you doing in the barn?"

Frances's voice sounded so queer and far away. Something more insistent was trying to penetrate her fog. But she couldn't quite . . .

"Frances." Kendal put a hand on his wife's shoulder, but she shrugged him off.

Her eyes were dangerously bright. "I warned you. I told you what she was. No lady would . . ."

No lady. What were they doing in the barn? Suddenly Abbie remembered the shadowy form that lunged at them. She shot up from the seat. "There was someone in there! Someone hit us, and we fell against the shelf!" She rushed for the kitchen. "Mama, I must get Marshal Haggerty!"

Mama turned from boiling the cloths. "You're not going anywhere."

"Then Grant, one of the men . . ."

"The men are containing the fire, searching for the horses, and taking their families home."

"But Mama, there was someone in the barn. Someone hit Monte and caused the fire. I have to get the marshal before it's too late."

"Listen to me." Mama gripped her arms. "If there was someone, either he's dead in the barn, or he's out there somewhere. And if he had malicious intentions, you're not going anywhere. Do you hear me, Abbie!"

Abbie hadn't the energy to fight. She felt so terribly helpless as she sank to a chair. The voices outside faded and stopped. Grant pushed open the door, spun a chair around, and straddled it. He leaned his elbows on the back and appraised Abbie. "You okay?"

She nodded.

"I didn't mean to hit you so hard, but your skirt..."

"I know. Did you get the horses?"

"Most of 'em. A handful headed for home, I guess. We'll find them in the morning."

But the morning would be too late to find the man who hit them. "Grant..."

The bedroom door opened, and Pa came out, closing it behind him. "We're ready for the cloths now, Selena."

Abbie leapt up. "Pa?"

"His lungs and throat are damaged, but Doctor Barrow says that should pass. Must have caught a hoof in the shoulder, but the bone is whole. I'm not sure of the burns."

Abbie's chest constricted as Pa took the cloths and returned to the room. Mama held her, stroking her head, and Abbie allowed the touch to soothe her. She turned her face to Mama's neck.

How could God let this happen? Why hadn't Monte come out? Why hadn't someone helped him? She should have stayed, should have helped. What were horses to his life? It was Chance he tried to reach. She knew it. He sent the others out, but Chance would have been behind the fire. Oh, dear Lord ... why?

"Abbie, offer Frances and Kendal your room for the night." Mama's voice was low, calm. "We'll keep Monte where he is, and the rest of us can sleep in the front room."

Abbie didn't want to move. She wanted Mama to hold her until Monte walked out of the room, strong and whole. She didn't want to think about Kendal or Frances with the accusing eyes. She sniffed.

"Abbie..."

She straightened, wiped her tears, then walked to the other room. They sat as she had left them. She steadied her voice. "You're welcome to stay the night here. I don't know if you could find your way back..."

Kendal looked up. "Likely not."

"I'll show you to a room."

Kendal took Frances's hand. "Go with Abbie. I'll join you later."

Abbie was surprised that Frances obeyed without argument. She led her to the room at the back. "In the chest at the foot of the bed you'll find a gown to use."

Frances said nothing and closed the door.

Abbie stood staring at the wooden panels. What could she say, what could she do to reach Monte's sister? There was a wall as solid as the wood of the door between them. And now, when they could be a comfort to each other, she felt only condemnation.

Was this her fault? Had she somehow caused it, as the spilled tea, the scraped chin? Who had hit them and why?

Pa stepped into the hall. "He's asking for you."

She rushed past to Monte's side. His face was pale in the dim light. With it washed of the grime, she could see his face was not burned except for the edge of his forehead, which was dressed and bandaged. Also bandaged were his shoulder and his hands that lay above the blanket.

"Oh, Monte," she breathed.

He swallowed, and his voice came out thick and hoarse. "Don't worry. Tell Frances."

"She's gone to bed. I'll tell her in the morning."

He closed his eyes and seemed to try to speak again, but did not.

"I've given him laudanum for the pain." Doctor Barrow snapped the bag shut on the bedside table. "He'll sleep now."

Abbie nodded.

"You can sit with him if you like." He looked up at Pa. "I'll be back in the morning. We'll need to rewrap the burns every day with fresh salve."

The deep voices continued down the hall, but Abbie kept her eyes on Monte. Sleeping, he seemed peaceful. He was alive. She laid her head on the bed beside him. "Thank you, Lord, for sparing his life."

◆◆◆◆◆◆◆

Jip Crocker stared at the crackling embers surrounded by rough stones and spat a long string of brown spittle. He readjusted the lump inside his lower lip and threw a stick at the fire. "What's keepin' the kid!"

Across the fire Emmet guffawed. "Gittin' soft over yer kid brother, Jip? He prob'ly got lost and wet hisself."

Jip kicked a bootful of dirt into the paunchy, pimpled face. "You're a pig, Emmet."

Emmet spit the dirt. "Sheez, I know that. What's funny is you think you're not." He swiped his mouth with his sleeve.

Jip huddled back against the tree. "I knew trouble would come o' this. You shoulda never put him up to it."

"Me? The whelp had his own ideas."

"You dared 'im. I heard you clear as day. Why don't you swipe you a real horse, kid. That's what you said." Jip sent Emmet a killer look. He'd like to squeeze that fat neck till it popped. If anything had happened to Spence, he would. Behind him a twig snapped, and he spun to his feet, his rifle ready in his grip. The boy stepped into the glow of the campfire and tethered three horses to the tree.

Jip caught him by the collar. "Where the heck you been, Spence?"

Spence shrugged him loose and sat down at the fire ring. He grabbed the coffeepot and poured it into a bent tin cup. "Started me a fire."

Jip stuck his nose into the night air and whiffed. "What'd you do thet fer?"

"I was in the barn like Emmet said, waitin' fer night. First I thought it weren't worth it, no corral, one cow, two middlin' horses. Then I saw they was havin' some big shindig. Ever'one brung their horses to the barn. I'd have my pick if I could git out unseen. I settled in fer dark, but then this guy come in actin' real strange ... didn't light the lantern till he'd stumbled his way to the back in the dark. He was almost on top o' me 'fore he lit up, an' I saw he had his girl with 'im."

"Ya learn somethin', kid?" Emmet poked him with a stick.

Spence shoved the stick aside. "I didn't wait ta see. Any minute they'd'a spotted me. I charged 'em, and they fell aginst the wall. The lantern smashed and flames was ever'where. I got out while he was arguin' with the girl to run."

Spence drank again. "Soon the whole place is goin' up like the Fourth o' July. I figured I better scoot, when all the horses come runnin' one after 'nother. Shoot, I says, this is better'n I planned. I grabbed the ones come my way an' looked 'em over. One wasn't worth nothin' so I left it an' brung these three. An' take a look at the black one. It ain't no common horse."

Jip strode to the horses and ran his hands over the black's coat, then down its legs. The horse shivered and widened its eyes. Then he examined the flank. "This here's the Farrel brand."

"Now, ain't that lucky?" Emmet stood and wiped the dirt from his britches.

Jip spun as another horse entered the circle, this one directed by its master. First Jip could make out nothing but the glow of his cigar. Then the fire lit the edges of his face, the auburn lambchop whiskers and the scar from his scalp to his left eyebrow.

"Captain Jake."

The captain shifted the cigar in his teeth but didn't speak.

Jip cleared his throat and looked from Emmet to Spence. He'd like to knock their skulls together. Why couldn't they keep to the work set for them? He stepped to the campfire. "Coffee?"

The captain swung down from his horse. He let the reins hang and the horse never moved. Military trained. Or something else. Jip had heard yarns of dogs turning tail when Captain Jake came, and other stories, too. Sweat started down his neck.

Captain Jake swigged the coffee, then poured the dregs in the dirt. "You men are a good step from the ranch."

Emmet stood up and hiked his pants. "We got some horses."

Captain Jake did not answer.

"You can look 'em over."

"Whose are they?"

Spence joined Emmet. "One of 'em's got the Farrel brand. It's a . . ."

"And the others?" The captain strode past him to the tied horses. He moved the black aside with a hand on its back, then checked the other flanks. He turned. "Horse stealing's a hanging offense."

Emmet rubbed his chin.

Captain Jake took off his gloves and slapped them against his palm. "I'm a rancher. I don't deal in stolen livestock."

"Then what about them cattle—" the argument died in Emmet's throat.

Jip shook his head. Emmet had more gall than brains.

"Spoils." The captain eyed each of them in turn. "Spoils, gentlemen. I suggest you learn the difference. There's only room for one boss in this territory, and it won't be Johnny Reb."

Emmet shut up. Spence had eyes like an owl. Jip hoped he learned from this.

The captain waved toward the horses. "Turn them loose."

Jip reached for the rope.

"Not . . . the black. That one is commandeered." Captain Jake took the black's rope and drew on his cigar until it glowed red. "I'll expect you at the ranch. Don't make me look for you again." He led the black across the circle, mounted his own horse, and swung them around together. He touched his boots to the horse's sides and disappeared into the darkness.

"Durn him." Emmet spat.

"He's the boss." Jip untied the other two horses and sent them off, then turned to Spence. "Did thet fella make it outta the barn?"

"I didn't wait ta see." Spence's voice cracked.

Another time Jip would have reassured him. Not now. A healthy fear of Captain Jake might keep the kid in line. If only Emmet had brains enough to feel the same. He shook his head. "We better git. Pack it up."

◆◆◆◆◆◆

Pain penetrated the woozy lethargy, and Monte cracked his eyes open. The ceiling above seemed low and shrunken as his vision cleared, then blurred and cleared again. This was not his room. He squeezed tears from his eyes and lifted a hand to wipe them clear. What met his face was a white, bandaged mound, and he stared at it, then lifted and scrutinized the other. Memory rushed in. Nerves no longer silenced by the drug began to scream, and he grimaced as he fought back the low moan that would not be contained.

Beside him Abbie raised her head. He turned to her slowly, eyes swimming again. "Abbie." His throat burned. She was seated in a chair directly beside the bed, still dressed in the flame-defiled dress she had worn yesterday. Evidently she had not left his side since his eyes closed last night. He cracked his parched lips, then fought another wave of pain.

"Can you drink, Monte?" Abbie lifted a cup of water.

He closed his eyes. His thoughts were fuzzy, and his tongue felt thick and foul. The skin on the back of his leg and the palms of his hands roared pain to his brain. He opened his eyes and rasped, "Yes, water."

Tucking her arm behind his head, she tipped it forward and held the cup to his lips. He allowed the cool liquid to soothe his tongue before swallowing it down. He did not choke and drank again before closing his lips against any more. Setting the cup down, Abbie gently released his head.

The door opened, and Joshua stepped in with Doctor Barrow beside him. Selena followed with an armful of fresh cloths. "Awake, eh?" Doctor Barrow moved to the bedside. "I'm not sure you're glad for that. Are you in pain?"

Monte nodded.

"We'll need to rebandage your burns."

Monte whispered, "Frances..."

Abbie leaned close. "I'll go to her, Monte. I'll tell her not to worry."

He nodded, following her with his eyes as she slipped from the room.

There was no sound yet from the bedroom, so Abbie did not

awaken Frances to deliver Monte's assurances. Instead she washed in the lean-to, pulled on a dress of her mother's, and slipped outside. The ashes and blackened fragments still smoldered.

The horrid smell of burned flesh clogged her breath, and she stared at the mound. Oh . . . sweet, gentle Buttercup. Her breath caught in her chest, but she trapped the tears with an angry sniff. What good was crying? Would it bring anything back? Heal Monte? Help her find the man responsible? Hot anger filled her.

She knew better than to step amid the smoking remains of the barn, but she did it anyway. Kicking aside a half-torched beam, she made her way to the area that had been the back beneath the loft. With the hem of her skirts held up over the devastation, she searched the ground.

There, lying among the ashes, she found what she sought, grabbed it up, and clasped it to her chest. The silver box was blackened, but intact. Like Monte. Injured but alive . . . yes, alive. Even in her fatigue she had been aware of every wheezing breath he took last night. She opened the box and the morning light caught the blood red stones, the white teardrops.

His mother's earrings. She recalled the portrait of the beautiful woman and the softness of Monte's voice when he spoke of her with the low gentleness he reserved for those he held dear. And now his voice was a tortured croak he forced like air through a reed. She closed the box, then retraced her steps.

Pa waited at the edge of blackened ground. "You know better than that."

"I know, Pa. But I had to find it." She held out the silver box, opened to reveal the earrings. "Monte's gift."

Pa brushed her cheek lightly with his ink-stained thumb. "Our guests are awake."

Abbie nodded. Perhaps a night's sleep had soothed Frances. Perhaps their shared concern would unite them. But Frances was paler than before, and blue-gray circles underscored her eyes. Nothing Abbie said changed the tight line of her lips. She refused breakfast, and when Pa said they'd keep Monte, Kendal took her home with Pa's gelding, Sandy, pulling the phaeton.

◆◆◆◆◆◆◆

In the front room of his ranch house, Captain Jake Gifford ran the cloth over the blade of the sword. Its sheen glittered in the lamplight, the filigreed tracery tossing fragments of light to the ceiling. He laid the sword beside the cleaned pistol and the oiled rifle. A man's weapons were his responsibility. Order, cleanliness, and discipline kept a soldier sharp.

Captain Jake stood and examined himself in the mirror. No extra flesh, shoulders back, straight spine. He was a weapon himself, as sharp and deadly as any saber. He would not allow civilian life to soften him, though he must admit he took to the amenities. That was the worst part of the war: the discomfort of it.

He took a cigar from the box on the mantle, snipped the end, and placed it between his teeth. He scrutinized his face. No hint of softness, no glimpse of mercy. He lit the cigar and drew the smoke to his lungs. It felt good to face an adversary again.

Montgomery Farrel. No matter that he had not fought on the fields. Captain Jake knew well enough his efforts to thwart the Union men on his father's land and that of his neighbors. He had heard his men speak of the coward southern boy that gave the soldiers sport. But until he came west, he had not had the opportunity to meet Major William Jackson Farrel's son. His face hardened.

Montgomery Farrel was no coward. It took more courage and strength of will to do what he did for the helpless at home than to go armed to war. Captain Jake did not underestimate him. Underneath his glowing southern charm, he was as uncompromising as his father before him.

Montgomery Farrel was an honorable man. Nowhere had he found anyone who spoke against him. He stood tall in the community, as had his father. His was a voice that held clout, that persuaded, that received respect. A voice to be silenced.

He would take Farrel down. Even were he not the son of Major Farrel, he would take him down—on principle alone. Were it in his power, he would take down every one of those southern slave owners who had . . . Captain Jake tightened his grip on the hilt of his sword.

He turned again to the mirror and studied himself. Sent behind enemy lines in stealth and darkness, had he even once failed to carry out his order? His own troops called him a spy. But it was the other camps, the enemy camps who feared him. They greeted the dawn only to find a man silently slain, the deadly sign that revealed he had been among them, had sniffed out their secrets and left betrayal in his wake.

He turned from the mirror. Betrayal. What to do about Jip Crocker and his kin? He would not tolerate insubordination. On the other hand, their escapade had maimed Montgomery Farrel, no matter unintentionally. Captain Jake drew on the cigar. Very well. For now he would let the incident pass.

He took up the saber and went out to the yard. Farrel's gelding stood tethered to the fence. Captain Jake took another rope, circled the horse's head, and fixed it to the opposite post, trapping the horse in the center of the corral. The animal balked at the constraint, nostrils snorting and eyes widening. Captain Jake came close, sensed the creature's fear, then drew his saber and slit its throat.

He leaped back from the gush of blood, watched the horse buckle and drop, suspended by the ropes. They would have looked for the animal. He could not risk being connected to that business. With the cloth he wiped the blade and sheathed it, then returned to the house. Emmet snapped to attention as he approached the door.

The captain eyed him. Emmet was shifty and unpredictable. Without Jip he would be worthless. He needed a lesson. Let him see what became of his thieving. "There's a carcass in the corral. Burn it. But before you do . . . bring me the head."

◆◆◆◆◆◆◆

Monte awoke to a room cast in sunset hues. The pain seemed less sharp, his chest less heavy. He breathed without wheezing and felt his mind clear. He turned his head, sensing that Abbie was there. "Evening already?" His throat felt full of rust.

Abbie smiled. "Evening of the third day. Doctor Barrow says no more laudanum."

Three days. No wonder he felt stronger. He tried to smile with cracked lips. "Mighty high price for one stolen kiss." He coughed.

"Oh, Monte."

"What was lost?"

She smoothed the coverlet over his chest. "It doesn't matter. You're better, that's all."

"The horses? Chance?"

She shook her head. "He got out of the barn but hasn't been found. All the others but Chance were recovered."

Monte frowned. "He would have gone to my stable."

"Monte, did you see who it was that hit us?"

So that had happened. After the crazy, undefined dreams, he wasn't sure what was real. "No. Not clearly. Perhaps I broke a heart worse than I thought."

"Don't, please."

He forced another smile. The pain was sharpening as his senses wakened, but not unbearably.

"Are you hungry?"

"Famished." He would be lucky to get anything down, but he saw her need.

Abbie sprang to her feet, swept through the door, then called, "Monte's ready for broth, Mama."

Monte stared at the empty doorway. Why was Chance lost? Why Chance alone? A thought pierced his consciousness. Had the attack been intentional? Had his harrasser threatened Abbie's home because of him? She returned with the bowl, set it on the table beside the bed, and tucked in extra pillows to raise him up.

He lifted his hands and stared at the thick bandages. "How bad are they?"

"Doctor Barrow said we'll see tomorrow. The scarring won't be bad if the burns are not too deep." Abbie dipped the spoon into the broth and brought it to his lips.

He recoiled at the thought of being spoon fed. She held it there insistently. He parted his lips, and the broth coursed warmly down his throat and awakened his hunger. She brought another spoonful and another to him. This was not how it was supposed to be. It was his place to care for her, to keep her safe, to . . . She again held the spoon until he accepted it.

"I had to remove a beam to free Chance. It burst into flame in my hands."

Abbie set the bowl down. "You saved all the horses. Not one burned." Her face suddenly crumpled, and tears filled her eyes.

He saw now how thin her cheerful veneer truly was, and that told him more than her words. Was he a cripple? He reached a bandaged hand toward her, touched the back of it to her cheek. "Abbie." He wanted to hold her.

"When you didn't come out, I wished I had stayed in there with you."

"Don't say that."

"It's true."

He pulled her head to his chest. Everything was spoiled. Everything changed. How he wanted her, but . . . "When do the bandages come off?"

"I don't know."

Or wouldn't tell. He released her. "I won't marry you until I'm healed."

She looked as though he had struck her. "Why?"

"We'll wait until my hands are restored."

"Oh, Monte, I don't care!"

"I do." He looked away. Memories of his father returning from the war assailed him. He had put behind him the images of his father, the sleeve that hung slack, the limping gait . . . the broken man.

How could he bring Abbie into the danger escalating around him? How could he keep her safe, with his own body maimed? If his hands did not heal . . . He clenched his jaw. He would not take Abbie as a wife while crippled and dependent.

Eight

Monte stood in the deepening dusk. The September chill seemed premature. Surely autumn had not arrived so soon. It must be that he did not yet gauge the temperature well. Though new skin covered the burns on his leg and back, it was tender still, more sensitive to cold and heat. He went inside to the library and closed the door behind him. He had just settled into his chair when James knocked and admitted Cole.

As always, Cole removed his hat, but it did little to show respect. "How much longer you gonna wait? There's at least thirty head missin'."

Monte straightened. "Good evening, Cole. Pour yourself a drink."

Cole went to the cabinet that held the decanters. He chose whiskey over brandy. Monte was inclined to have one, too, but refrained. He'd come close enough to following his father's footsteps after Sharlyn died. Now, in light of his injury, it was too potent a temptation to take lightly.

Nor did he wish for Cole to see him struggle to hold a glass. Each day proved more strongly Doctor Barrow's fears that the healing would be slow—if it came at all—and that he would never regain full use of his hands. "How do you know the animals haven't strayed?"

"I've looked. Cattle stray, but as a rule they graze close to their home range."

Monte couldn't argue with Cole's expertise. "How are they getting them?"

"Just helpin' themselves. Don't matter how many men're on the herd, if they're ordered not to act." Cole shot the whiskey down his throat and set the glass on a table.

Monte watched him. "I don't want to start anything."

"It's started already. You've watched and you've waited. Now you're givin' 'em leave."

Monte bristled. "What would you have me do?"

"Let the word out to the men they're lookin' for rustlers. They know it already. Tell 'em to shoot what they see."

"And if it's one of our neighbors?"

"You're stuck on that thought. Who do you suspect?"

"I don't—"

"No, you don't."

Monte bridled at the interruption.

Cole leaned on the desk. "Fact is, we got a small operation that only wants stompin', and it's time to stomp it."

Monte stood, then walked to the window. Yes, he had waited, hoped to hear from another rancher that they were likewise besieged, hoped for some sign that the molestation was not directed to him alone. But no word had come. All his feelers had returned empty. The attacks were on him alone. Why?

Perhaps Cole was right. Perhaps it was time to act. All it took was his word. His men would handle the situation while he stayed at the house and waited, while he himself did nothing . . . could do nothing.

"Who's on the herd?"

"Skeeter and Curtis. Breck and Forbes are watchin' the bluff. But it's time . . ."

"I heard you." He turned and fixed Cole in his gaze. "Do you expect trouble tonight?"

"Tonight, tomorrow. Who's to know? The herd's restless, but somethin's movin' in. Could be the storm's got them anxious."

Monte returned to his desk and sat. "Alert the men. Put them on shifts." He could see the relief on Cole's face.

"Yes, sir. You want one kept with Will, also?"

"Why?"

Cole picked up his hat. "Thought I saw someone skulkin' about the other night. I didn't want to say nothin' till I was sure, but it's been botherin' me."

"You think the rustlers are also horse thieves?"

"Might be. Might be they're the ones got off with Chance."

Monte leaned back and rested his hands on his thighs. Unconsciously he stretched the fingers and winced again. "You think they're brazen enough to risk coming to the yard?" He could tell Cole held back what he would say. Would he say they could do anything they liked as long as the cripple refused to act?

Cole shrugged. "Word's gone round about the new horse."

"Abbie's mare."

"How's that?"

"The new Arabian. She's my wedding gift for Abbie." Monte watched Cole's reaction. The man wasn't easy to read.

"Seems to me a weddin' gift wants a weddin'."

That was straight. Cole didn't pull any punches, and right now Monte appreciated that more than the restraint and pitying glances he got from the others. He held his palms out. "You see this?"

"Yeah, I see it."

"When you get a newborn foal that's just struggled to its feet and nuzzled for the first time, you take your hands and go over it, soft and gentle, stroking just so and letting it catch your scent and hear your voice. One spook, one rough or hurried motion, and you've put fear into it. But if you do it right, after that it recognizes your touch every time." He turned his hands palms down. "I'll wait until I have a touch I want her to recognize."

Cole's temple pulsed. He put his hat on. "You don't know Abbie as well as you think."

Kendal knocked on the open door and sauntered in a little unsteadily.

Monte stood. "Put two men in the stable with Will. As many as you need on the herd. We'll see what we catch."

"Yes, sir." Cole strode from the room.

"Trouble?" Kendal went to the cabinet and poured a whiskey.

"It appears we have rustlers. Cole thinks they may also be horse thieves."

Kendal sat and stretched his legs out before him. His fingers worked the waxed end of his mustache. "Doesn't the law handle that sort of thing?"

"If it can. In this case, I have the men to see to it. Marshal Haggerty and Deputy Davis are only two."

"Don't tell Frances of this, will you?" Kendal leaned forward. "Her *nerves* won't take it."

"Perhaps you should take her home."

Kendal sipped the whiskey. "She wants to see you wed or hear that it's off altogether. She'd prefer the latter."

"I'm sorry she feels that way."

Kendal shrugged. "We breed it into them, you know. From the time they learn to distinguish white from black, rich from poor, we set it into their minds to despise those beneath them, those different, just as we do."

"I'm glad I'm removed from that." Monte took his seat again.

"Are you?" Kendal's eyes were bright. "I don't see you so removed. So James and Pearl receive a pension. They're still your darkies, just as they always were. Your hired men jump to your beck. And Abbie now . . ."

Monte didn't like the way he said her name.

" . . . she's a cut above anyone out here. You still skim the cream and throw the rest to the hogs."

Monte frowned. "I admit I am well off. But I don't share your opinions."

"No? Then why don't we invite James in for a drink with us?"

Monte leaned back. "He's an old man. He would not understand a different way."

Kendal threw back his head and laughed. "How well you deceive yourself, my brother by law. But I know better. You would no more drink with a slave than bed one."

Monte seethed. "I find you distasteful." He'd seen Kendal like this before.

"Have you?"

"Have I what?"

"Bedded a slave?"

Monte stood. "You're drunk, Kendal."

Kendal laughed. "You keep a fine whiskey in this house. Whiskey of a quality I've not afforded for some time."

"If you're in financial trouble, we'll discuss it when you're sober. Good night." He left Kendal sitting alone and went upstairs. With both hands he worked the knob until it turned, then entered his room and closed the door behind him.

Kendal was out of his head, was all. They were growing fretful, Frances especially. She took every opportunity to remind him of women back home, women whose beaus and husbands were lost in the war. Some were the sisters and cousins of friends, some the very same he had protected and hidden during the Yankee raids.

He was tired of it. He should marry Abbie and send his sister home. He slowly closed his hands into claws then stretched them out again. They were improving, the skin growing more supple, the nerves less tender.

He walked to the drawer of his dresser, pulled out the jar, and lifted the lid. He rubbed the linament over the scars. The hands were not wholly useless, yet he chafed his infirmity. Why now when he needed to be strong? What was God about?

◆◆◆◆◆◆◆

Abbie stood in the yard in the cool, foggy morning, her shawl snug around her shoulders. She glanced at Monte beside her, but he seemed miles away. He watched, though she wondered if he saw. The men pulled the ropes. The wooden frame swung up perpendicular to the ground. Others sprang forward and braced it firmly.

They cheered, and Abbie clapped her hands. "First wall up! Is there anything like a barn raising?"

Monte's smile was thin.

"All yesterday they built the frames, but it's never so grand as when they stand the walls up. It was good of you, Monte, to provide the lumber. I don't know how Pa . . ."

"It was nothing."

Abbie almost stamped her foot. They'd spent a month now speaking polite assurances, ever since the morning he'd gone home after the bandages were removed. Where was he? Why had he withdrawn from her?

"What is it, Monte?"

He surprised her by not shrugging off her question. "I wish I could help." His voice was strained.

"You have helped! All the wood and the new cow..."

"You know what I mean. I'm tired of watching." He held his hands up. The red skin was fading but still stretched thick and tight over his palms. The fingers curled in, though less than they had. How helpless he must feel, so used to being in control. But she felt helpless, too . . . helpless to reach him, to show her love, her faith that he was still the man he had been.

She took his hands and brushed her lips over the palms. He groaned and grabbed her close with his arms. "Stop, Abbie. You push me past the bounds of decency."

"I won't stop. I don't care that the healing is slow, it will come."

He eased her back, and there was warmth in his eyes. His smile was even amused. Oh, how good it looked.

"I suppose God reports to you now?"

She put up her chin. "If He did, I'd have something to say about His timing."

He actually laughed. Abbie's heart soared.

"I just bet you would." He kissed her forehead. "Let's walk."

Abbie slipped her hand into his arm. The fog was lifting, though no breath of wind stirred. She breathed the dampness. "Why did Frances and Kendal not come this morning?"

Not that Frances would appreciate a barn raising, but she had not left Monte's side since his return home. Not once had she visited without Frances hovering, and Monte had made no move to change it. But James had driven him over today, and having Monte to herself this morning was pure heaven.

"Kendal was not feeling well."

"I hope it's not serious."

"A case of too much whiskey in too short a time."

"Oh." Abbie stepped over the wet gully. "I didn't take him for a drinker." Though she didn't doubt Frances could drive any man to drink.

"I expect he's facing troubles of some sort."

"There are no answers in a bottle."

"I doubt it was answers he sought."

"What then?"

"Escape."

She stole a glance. Had he read her thoughts? She couldn't resist probing. "Escape from what?"

"Abbie, I don't know."

"You must have an idea."

He turned suddenly. "And if I do?"

"Then I want to know."

"I never took you for a gossip."

"It's not gossip when it's family."

He smiled. "You have an answer for everything, haven't you?"

"Not everything."

Monte led her forward again. "I suspect it was the liquor talking more than anything, but I fear he may be in some financial strait. I wondered about his associates when I went there to close on the sale of the plantation." He sighed. "And I'm concerned about his happiness with Frances. There, you can say you knew it."

Abbie felt the blood rush to her face. "I didn't think . . ."

"Oh yes, you did. I know Frances is not easy to live with. But . . ." He shook his head. "I thought they were happy, especially with baby Jeanette."

"Don't get me going on that subject."

He squeezed her hand between his arm and side. "You have been intractable."

"I haven't said half what I think."

"How well I know that. Frances knows it, too."

Abbie sighed. "If only she thought better of me. . . ."

"Now, Abbie."

"Oh, Monte, I'm not blind or stupid. I know what she thinks. It's just that I thought I could . . . I don't know."

"Frances can be petty. Don't take it to heart."

"I don't blame her. She's a fine lady and . . ."

"You are, as well."

Abbie smiled. "That's kind, but you know my shortcomings." He turned and took her into his arms. "No." He bent close. "I don't know of any." He kissed her for the first time since the fire. Tears sprang to her eyes, and she clung to him. "Oh, Monte."

"No tears, Abbie. It's not like you."

Maybe not. But how much longer could she hold them back?

◆◆◆◆◆◆◆

When Monte returned he found Kendal slumped in a chair in the parlor. The dim noonday light hardly penetrated the velvet drapes. Monte crossed the room and pulled them aside. Kendal raised his head, greeting the light with a groan.

"Where's Frances?"

"Indisposed."

"Shall I get you coffee?"

"That wouldn't be my first choice, but I'll settle for it."

Monte tugged the bellpull on the wall, and James appeared. "Coffee for Mr. Stevens, please, James."

"Yessuh."

A few minutes later Pearl came in with a blue-enameled pot and two cups. She set them on the table and turned to go. "Thank you, Pearl."

"Yessuh."

Kendal's eyes had raised at Monte's thanks, and he grinned. "Determined to prove me wrong, eh?"

Monte shrugged. "Do you mind pouring? It's still a little awkward."

Kendal filled the two cups, then sat back and sipped. He grimaced. "Now that's a rude awakening. Not nearly as satisfying as last night's venture."

"Nor will it carry the price." Monte sipped the coffee and nearly choked. Pearl must have intended to tar Kendal's insides. He set the cup on the table. "So what were you telling me last night?"

Kendal chuckled, but it sounded false. "You should have seen your eyes widen."

Monte waited.

"I spoke with Frances about staying out here."

"What!"

"Why do you think I've tried to make her see the good things? I thought if she . . ."

"Kendal, have you gone mad?"

Kendal dropped his head into his hands. "There's nothing to go home to, you see. I've lost it all."

Monte's stomach pitched. "What? How?"

"My . . . partners. It's far too complicated to give you all the details. Suffice it to say, I was duped."

Monte stood, paced to the window, then back. "Why here?"

"Where else?"

"What will you set up with?"

"Perhaps a loan from my brother-in-law?"

Monte sank again into the chair. "What did Frances say?"

"What do you expect? She'd rather die than live here. She'll go back with my mother and raise Jeanette to be just like her."

"She'll not. Her place and duty is beside her husband."

Kendal smirked. "Tell *her* that."

"I will."

Releasing a deep breath, Kendal said, "Perhaps it's better for her to go. If something happened . . ."

"Frances will not leave you. If you're determined to stay here, she will also."

"And what of Jeanette?"

"What of the children I'll have? What of any of the children being raised here?"

Kendal shook his head. "I'm afraid her mind's made up."

"She's not heard from me yet."

Kendal sagged and looked at him. "Monte, the things I said last night..."

"I understand, Kendal. I told you I would forget them."

Kendal nodded. His cheeks were slack and lined, his eyes red rimmed. But there was something more ... something indefinable but more consuming. Failure. It clung to him. And now Monte wondered about other things. Had the plantation gone down by Kendal's fault?

Others had lost, as well, but Monte had left it to Frances in good shape. Yet not so long after, they had sold it for little enough. What would Kendal do here? Had he the mettle to forge his way in the West? God help him if he did not.

◆◆◆◆◆◆◆

Monte walked alone after leaving Kendal. He would not judge him. It was not his place to condemn. He walked to the cottonwood path behind the house and followed it along the stream. The morning mist had thickened to a solid cap, but no rain fell as yet. The air was chill, but he needed the silence to think.

His duty was clear. He must aid Kendal, but the manner to do so was not so clear. He stooped to pass under the branches and cut up the grassy slope away from the water and the house. He reached and followed the fence line that separated the yard from the back pasture.

The clouds would not hold much longer. That was good. The land needed moisture. The straw-colored grass was brittle underfoot. And the men should have Joshua's barn roofed by now, at least the base wood down.

He looked up. What was that on the corner post? He had not intended to go up that far. He strained to make it out. It was no good. He quickened his pace. As he neared, he narrowed his eyes. He should—it seemed he should know it, but...

With a sudden sickening jolt his mind made the leap. He did know it—the shape, the color ... Dear God, it couldn't be ... No blood ran from the severed horse head, but the fur was grizzly with it and the eyes had been eaten out of the skull. Chance.

Monte's chest heaved as rage and grief engulfed him.

Here was the reason Marshal Haggerty had found no sign of the stolen horse. Monte's hands clenched. All he had risked, suffered, to save Chance . . . for this! He felt the blood pulsing in his temples.

Teeth clenched, he turned from the head of his horse impaled on the post. He stared at his hands. He could not even hold a shovel to bury it. Who would do such a thing? Who would kill a fine animal only to torment its owner? To terrify him alone? He raised his face to the first drops of rain.

"Whoever it is, Lord, I will not succumb. I will not bend beneath his threats. Reveal him to me, and I will bring him down. He will not drive me from my land!" What else could it mean? No rustler would sacrifice a valuable horse like Chance. This was a warning. He'd seen its sort before.

He needed to find Cole. One of the men could bury the head, but Cole was right. The time of waiting was over. Vigilance and action would put an end to this business. He wiped the back of his sleeve over his face and slowed to a solid stride. And it was time for other things as well. Damaged hands or not, he would get on with his life.

Nine

Abbie could hardly contain herself as she rode to Monte's ranch. That he had sent and not come himself didn't matter at all. Chandler's coming had to mean something, portend some good. Monte had delayed him, but now ... maybe, just maybe, the waiting was over.

Sharlyn's brother. Surely this meeting would be different. How cheerfully Monte spoke of Chandler, of their long friendship. Chandler, whom he had chosen above all his friends here, even above Kendal, to stand up for him at the wedding. Chandler and his wife. She urged Shiloh on, heedless of the dust that rose from the hooves and gathered in her skirts.

She halted the mare at the stable where Will took the reins. She swiped the dust from her skirts and started for the house. *Please, Lord, don't let Maimie be like Frances.* Oh, that was unkind. She crossed the yard and started up the steps. She stopped before the door and looked at the knocker. Heavens, what was she waiting for? She knocked.

James opened to her with a nod. She smiled. "How are you, James?"

"Middlin', Mizz Martin." He ushered her in. She didn't wait for him to show her to the parlor. The door stood open, and she could hear the voices inside and Monte's laughter. Her heart jumped, and she stopped for a moment to listen. He was in rare good spirits by the sound of it.

"Go on in, Mizz. Mastuh Monte's expectin' you."

"Thank you." Abbie drew a deep breath and stepped into the

doorway. Monte's back was to her, but she got a clear look at Chandler. Her chest seized. She had not thought how like Sharlyn he might be, how it would recall to her Sharlyn herself. Fair and slight like his sister, Chandler was as impeccably dressed as Monte but with the same understated ease.

He glanced up and caught Monte's arm. Monte turned. "Ah, Abbie." He came forward, arms outstretched, and caught her hands in his. She was surprised by the firmness of his grasp. If it pained him, he made no sign. "Chandler, permit me to present to you Abbie Martin."

At least he didn't say Abigail. Abbie reached her hand to Chandler.

He grasped it warmly. "How do you do? I cannot tell you the pleasure this gives me."

His vehemence surprised her. She half expected the same shyness as Sharlyn, they were so similar in looks. "It's equally mine. I've looked so forward to your coming." Her voice softened. "Sharlyn was very dear to me."

He pressed her hand. "Thank you. I know she shared your affection."

Behind them she heard motion and turned. Frances was unspeakably elegant in blue silk, her waist corsetted tightly and the skirts billowing to the floor. Abbie's heart sank. Beside her, the petite lady who must be Chandler's wife was equally elegant. Her hair was pulled back from her heart-shaped face and wrapped neatly in a beaded snood, and her dress was impeccable. Abbie was suddenly aware of every dust speck on her plain linen dress, and her thoughtless rejection of corset and bustle.

Maimie clapped her hands together, her face breaking suddenly into delight. "Monte, you should be flogged for withholding. You never said your intended was so lovely."

"Not exactly, my dear." Chandler said. "He held forth at length over breakfast. Only you and Frances were still primping and missed the half of it."

Maimie swept forward, her rose-colored train swishing on the floor. She took Abbie's hands. "I'm so happy to meet you. I see Monte is as fortunate as he deserves to be."

Abbie was surprised by the tears that stung behind her eyes. Maimie's round, brown eyes and frank smile dissolved her unease. Of course she should have dressed for the meeting. But Monte's message had so excited her, she had hugged Mama and run for the barn as she was. Maimie's acceptance was an unwarranted kindness.

She ought to say something, but tears choked her throat. When had she become such a crybaby? "I hope your trip was not too difficult."

"She missed the whole thing with her head in a book." Chandler rested his hand on his wife's back.

"The trip was fine, though I was glad that Monte met us in town, else Chad said we'd have had an Indian guide. Imagine."

Abbie smiled. No wonder Monte got on so well with him. "I'm afraid you'd have looked a long way to find one."

Frances passed by in a swish of silk. "Do sit, Maimie. I'm starved for gossip." She settled onto the settee and patted the seat beside her. "You must tell me everything. You have no idea how I've missed polite company."

Abbie stood frozen. Had Frances poured a bucket of stream water over her head, it could hardly have felt worse. All the elation of Maimie's greeting was lost, and something dangerous stirred in its place. Monte touched her arm and motioned her to the wing chair beside the settee.

Frances hardly looked up. "Maimie, dear, I set to rights the melodeon in the great hall."

Maimie clasped her hands in delight. "Wonderful!"

"I knew you would want to play, though I'm afraid Monte hasn't kept it in the best tune . . ."

"It's a rarity for a tuner to pass through here, and I haven't much use for it." He leaned on the frame of Abbie's chair. She was glad to have him near. It reminded her to guard her tongue.

Frances turned. "I'm certain you play, Abbie?"

It seemed every eye turned to her. Frances had orchestrated that. "No."

"What a pity. Monte loved it so when Sharlyn played, didn't you, Monte? She played almost as well as you, Maimie. Do you remember the duet you played for Mrs. Baldwin's soiree?"

Kendal walked in. He smelled of the stable, and his hair was windblown. "Ah." He reached a hand to Chandler. "Good to see you, man." He bent over Maimie's hand. "You're a muse in pink, Maimie dear." He turned to Abbie, grasped her hand and lingered. "Fresh as a mountain rose."

Abbie felt her cheeks flush. Thankfully Chandler spoke up. "Kendal, where have you been?"

"Enjoying Monte's horseflesh."

"You missed breakfast."

"And I'm famished."

Monte straightened. "I'll order refreshments."

"I've already done so." Frances smiled sweetly. "I ordered early luncheon on the veranda since it's such a pleasant day. I hope you don't mind?"

Monte nodded. "That's fine."

Abbie bit her tongue. Of course it was fine. Everything Frances did was fine. Monte held out a hand and his sister took it, stood, and arranged her skirts. The light played on the silk like gossamer.

Abbie felt like a lump of lead. What was she to do? If Monte was escorting Frances . . . Chandler stepped forward and offered her his arm. "May I?"

Relief washed over her as she stood.

"Maimie and I were so pleased to learn of Monte's engagement. Wild horses could not have kept us away, and only his insistence made us delay."

"Thank you, Mr. Bridges."

"Please. Chandler." He pulled out a chair at the table for her and took the one beside it.

Kendal likewise seated Maimie across from them. Pearl carried out a tray of tiny wild capons boned and roasted with blackberry sauce, while James followed with mashed potatoes, bowls of tossed greens, stewed tomatoes, and fresh rolls. Nothing that needed cutting, Abbie noticed. Monte could not have managed. Either Pearl or Frances had seen to that.

Frances looked at Monte, and he nodded his approval. When James stood beside her, Abbie could hardly tell him what she would like. She was sure every bite would stick in her throat.

She watched Maimie to see which utensil to use when. She was almost certain Maimie intentionally rested her finger on each fork or spoon before lifting it, but she never let on by sharing even a glance.

"I can't get over how clean the air feels out here. Everything seems fresh and new." Maimie took a dainty bite of greens, and Abbie followed.

Monte answered, "It is fresh and new. That is the excitement of it."

"There is much lacking." Frances dabbed her lips. "Culture, gentility, tradition."

"We're making our own traditions, Frances. A new gentility free from the bonds of the past."

"I have yet to see it, Monte dear." She smiled. "What I see is . . . coarse and primitive. Survival, but no more."

Coarse and primitive. Abbie would love to prove her right. The desire to fling her plate down the front of Frances's gown seized her.

Chandler turned to her. "Certainly it's not a matter of survival still?"

Abbie mimicked Frances with the soft linen napkin and laid it in her lap. Wickedness filled her thoughts and found her lips. "Well . . . it is when the Indians attack."

Monte choked into his cup.

"Indians!" Chandler laid down his fork. "Oh, come, Abbie. Have they not been settled on the reservations?"

"Not the wild bands of Comanche, Ute, and Jicarilla Apache, though they rarely come in war paint. It's mainly raids on farms and livestock, though men have been scalped just crossing the street. You see, we've overrun their hunting grounds. They feel it's their right to take what they can. Luckily, this doesn't ordinarily include captives."

Abbie speared a bite of tomato but did not take it. "A worse concern are the bears that come down from the mountains to fatten before hibernation. One year a giant grizzly tried to carry off our hog. You have never heard such a squealing and bawling, but Pa got him—the bear, that is—right between the eyes."

She ran the tomato through the sauce. "The other wild things are more simply a nuisance. Coyotes and mountain lions are frightened by gunshots. If you're a good enough aim you can shoo them away before they eat something they shouldn't."

She took the bite and allowed herself only a quick glance at Frances's pale face.

Kendal banged his hands on the table. "Now tell us about the outlaw, Buck Hollister."

Abbie shrank. Lord only knew how he had heard about that. Well, it served her right. She shook her head. "If it's all the same to you, I can't think of him while eating."

Kendal threw back his head and laughed. He raised his cup. "Here's to Abbie Martin, the new breed of lady!"

Abbie hazarded one look at Monte. She could not guess whether it was pride or fury that lit his eyes. She glanced back at Frances. Perhaps it was, after all, a matter of survival.

◆◆◆◆◆◆◆

Monte rested his hand on Abbie's back as he walked her to the stable. He could feel her spine through the dress and realized what Frances no doubt had noticed at once. No hoop or corset. The new brand of lady. Kendal had hit on it.

Abbie turned so suddenly he stumbled into her. "I'm sorry, Monte."

He tucked up her chin and drank in her eyes. In the daylight, he could hardly believe their blue. "Sorry for what?"

"What I said about the Indians."

He raised an eyebrow.

"And the rest . . . though we did have a bear try to steal our hog once, only it was a runt suckling . . . and the coyotes are a nuisance. You've said so yourself. It's just that . . ."

"It was time you defended yourself."

"Then you're not angry? You were so quiet."

He did not dare tell her it took all his will not to laugh. Frances would never have borne it. "If you only knew the cruelty of your trick."

"What do you mean?"

"Kendal intends to stay here with Frances."

"What!"

"They are not going home. He claims they've lost everything."

"Oh, Monte, I'm so terribly sorry! I never would have . . ."

He put a hand to her lips and drew her into the shade away from the stable door. "I know. Frances will have to learn her place, but . . . I would consider it a favor if you didn't scare the breath from her again."

"Of course I won't. I feel dreadful. Oh, when will I ever learn to hold my tongue?"

"What you need is looking after. Someone to keep you in line. I see I'll just have to marry you." He watched his words sink in.

"Monte, do you mean . . . ?" She quivered in his hold.

"Friday, Abbie. I trust you have your things in order?"

"Yes. And I'll ride today—now—to tell Father Dominic."

"Father Dom . . . Abbie, I've already spoken with Reverend Shields." She stared, and he raised his hands helplessly. "I had no idea you'd want the mission priest."

"But Monte, we have to be married in the church."

He suspected she did not refer to the small white building in town. It hadn't even occurred to him that Abbie's ties to the mission went so deeply. A circuit rider would have served as far as he was concerned. But Frances . . . She would never forgive him pledging his vows before a Roman Catholic priest.

He groaned inside. Would nothing be easy? "Abbie . . ."

"You don't understand. Father Dominic administers all the sacraments. I've been to the mission since I was small. How can I be married by anyone else?"

Monte felt helpless in the wave of her emotion. How could he not have anticipated this? Of course she would expect her priest to marry them. But Frances would never set foot in the mission church, and her behavior today had shown how desperately she needed control. He was walking an impossible line.

Though he made light of Abbie's affront, in truth he was terribly concerned for his sister. Still . . . he would give his life for Abbie. Things had conspired against them for too long now. A sudden urgent longing for her seized him. He took her shoulders, wincing with the grip. "All right, Abbie. Your Father Dominic will join us, but here in the great room. Our guests won't fit in the mission chapel."

Her relief showed in her face, and he kissed her lips, not caring that Will stood in the doorway with her horse.

Ten

Abbie stood transformed before the mirror. The pale gray silk gown pinched in around her corsetted waist, and the white lace overlay billowed to the long train. Monte's taste was exquisite. He could not have chosen a color that better enhanced her eyes and paled her skin.

Mama had pulled her hair into a thick twist behind her head with a fringe of curls around her face. Pa's string of pearls at her throat complemented the pearl and garnet earrings in her ears.

As Mama placed the veil on the crown of her head and pulled the blusher forward, an indescribable thrill passed through her. She was no longer herself. Where was the tree-climbing girl? She felt so beautiful. The thought surprised her.

Mama held her at arm's length. "My little girl . . ."

"Oh, Mama." She squeezed her. "I'm so happy!"

Abbie turned at the knock on the door. Pa stood in his Sunday suit, black-ribbon tie crisp at his throat. He gazed at her. "You're the prettiest bride I've ever seen, along with your mama and sister." His blue eyes swam.

"Pa." Abbie pressed her face to his chest, and he patted her back.

"There's someone waiting for you even more eagerly."

Abbie let go. "I'm ready."

"Here." Mama pressed a handkerchief into her palm. "Sadie sent this."

Abbie recognized her great-grandmother's handiwork. Her

sister had carried the handkerchief on her wedding day. "I wish she could have come."

"She's too near her time."

"If we hadn't delayed . . ."

Grant pushed in and held his arm for Mama. "At this rate she'll have the baby before you reach the priest." He kissed Abbie's cheek and tweaked her nose, then tugged Mama out to escort her to her place. Abbie held her breath.

She heard the melodeon begin and caught Pa's arm, the same arm that had held her when she took her first tottering steps, that had steadied her on the back of a horse, that had walloped her when her naughtiness deserved it . . . though never hard enough to feel through her skirts. She felt no shame at the tears in his eyes. He was her pa, the best pa a girl could have. And he knew how happy she was. He knew what Monte meant to her.

He led her down the stairs, through the foyer, and past the parlor to the great hall. The room was filled and some even stood outside the French doors. Abbie saw Mary and Wes McConnel with Davy and Mariah beside them. Mary's eyes were wet with tears, and she nodded her blessing. Reverend Winthrop Shields also nodded from his place in the crowd.

Clara beamed at her from the back where she sat beside Marty with Del in her arms. Face after face passed by, but then she had eyes only for Monte. Had he ever looked so splendid? In his long, cutaway coat and cummerbund, starched white collar, and gray cravat he looked every inch the aristocrat, yet the warmth in his eyes captured her breath.

How could she ever have doubted his love? It was as though the past years never happened. They were alone in this moment as it was meant to be. *Dear Lord, you knew. You made him for me. Let me be worthy.*

She hardly noticed when Pa let go of her hand. Together Monte and Abbie turned to face Father Dominic. The music stopped, but within Abbie it played on and on. She felt buoyant with joy. Monte loved her. She could hear it in his voice as he spoke his vows, feel it in his fingers as he touched the ring to her thumb, *in the name of the Father,* to her first finger, *and of the Son,* the next finger, *and of the Holy Spirit . . . amen.* He slid it home.

Light streamed through the long windows, and her heart raced when he lifted the veil. Looking into his warm, dark eyes, Abbie trembled, unable to believe they were at last man and wife. Monte bent and kissed her, then grabbed her hand and swept her past the cheering crowd. As they went, her eyes landed briefly on Cole standing in the corner, then they were in the hall and through the doors.

The phaeton was at the bottom of the stairs, and Monte lifted her in. "What are you doing? Where are we going?"

He smiled and took up the reins, wrapped the end around his wrist, and slapped the horse.

"What about everyone else?"

"They're not invited."

She saw him wince as the reins tugged, but she said nothing. This was his moment, their moment. The October sun was rich and golden, gleaming on the grass, the horse's sleek back, the ring on her finger. The single gold band was beautiful in its simplicity, and Monte's was identical, save larger for his larger hand. He had smiled when she slid it on, making no sign of pain.

He turned the horse out toward the plain. The wheels bumped and lurched, but the springs cushioned them. They climbed the rise and slowed. The horse tossed its head, and Monte swung around a low clump of scrub oak and reined in.

A harvest smell was in the air, and Abbie wished her corset would allow her to breathe it more deeply. Monte took quilts from under the seat and layered them on the ground.

Then he came back and gave her his arm. She caught up her skirts so they wouldn't drag on the ground. What was he thinking, taking her out here dressed in such finery? Before she sat, he took her arms and turned her away from him. He pointed across the land. "This, Abbie, is the future. Our land, our home. The Lucky Star."

A thrill passed through her. "Oh yes, Monte."

He seated her, and she arranged the bustle and layers of the gown. It was like a frothy pool around her.

Monte smiled. "You look the perfect southern belle."

"I'll try to act it."

His laugh was expected.

"Monte, why did you name the ranch the Lucky Star?"

He pulled off his coat and folded it on the edge of the quilt, then sat beside her. "It was Pearl, really. She always said I was born under a lucky star, and when we came out here, she looked around her and said I'd found it—my lucky star." He took her hand. "Now I believe her."

The quiet enclosed them. With one hand he cupped her face, and she rested her cheek on his palm. She hardly felt the scarring.

"It didn't seem right to know you first anywhere but here."

Abbie felt the ground beneath her, looked up into the mackerel sky, and knew that he was right. This was God's land, their land. Here they would make their life. Here she would give him all she had to give, consummate the love he had awakened.

His voice was thick. "I have never in my life known a love like this. Do you understand?"

She knew what he was saying. There was still apology in him, but there was no need for it. She wrapped her arms around his neck and kissed him as he eased her to the quilt.

◆◆◆◆◆◆◆

"I don't like it." Jip kicked the dirt at his feet and leaned on the split rail of the corral.

"You're squeamish." Emmet spat. "With Farrel married t'day an' his cowboys havin' them a good time, it's the chance we been waitin' fer."

"Maybe."

"We can get in on the herd an' take what we like, make our break from Cap'n Jake, an' clear out."

"It ain't that easy."

"Heck it ain't."

"You don't know the captain. Not like I do, or did 'fore he was a big shot rancher. He's not like other men. He don't..." Jip shook his head.

"He don't what? Bleed?" Emmet laughed at his own joke. "I ain't afeared of him. We can be across the border 'fore Cap'n Jake knows we're gone."

Jip felt the sweat trickle down his neck. Captain Jake knew things other men didn't. The grim reaper. That's what the men of Company D called him. He had the feel of death about him, and one look at him on the battlefield proved he wasn't human. Jip swore he'd seen him smile in the midst of the screams and the dying.

Spence jacked up his pants. "I think we oughta git the horses an' never mind the cattle."

Jip frowned. Spence hadn't any more sense than Emmet.

Emmet knuckled him in the head. "Yup, it's hollow. You know the stable's up right next to the house. They're guardin' them horses like they're yeller gold. We take the cattle. We'll get a good price fer them down in Mexico."

"We'd never make it that far. You know the captain'll be watchin'."

"He'll be coverin' his hide so's no one can connect him with us."

"He'll come after us."

"Let 'im come."

Jip studied the flames. For all his arguments, he'd like nothing more than to cut loose from Captain Jake. He didn't owe him anything. Leastwise not anymore. So the captain had seen him heist the haversack and watch from a fallen comrade. That didn't mean he owed him for life.

Jip tossed a stick at the fire. "A'right, listen up. We'll take a look around, an' if there's no guard on the herd, we git 'em."

"If they're short o' guards we git 'em." Emmet rubbed a purple lump on his neck. "We can take out one or two."

Jip spat, then wiped the brown spittle from his chin with the back of his hand. "Yup, we can take out one or two, an' have a posse on our tail soon's we do. Ain't no use causin' thet kinda trouble. We got lucky no one died in Spence's fire. So far we ain't killed no one. There's no cause ta start now."

"You're soft, Jip. Thet's what it is. You're jest soft."

Jip threw his coffee on the fire and tucked the cup into his pack. With the least excuse he'd show Emmet just how hard his fists and boot could be. "Git goin'."

◆◆◆◆◆◆◆

Stars wavered in the indigo sky as they drove back. Monte rested his hands in his lap. Abbie had insisted on taking the reins, and he allowed her. It wasn't likely he'd deny her anything. He felt more complete, more satisfied than he had ever before. She was meant for him, made for him. All that remained was to make her as happy as he could.

They climbed down outside the stable. "Come." He ushered her inside. Will went out to unharness the horse, and Monte led Abbie to a stall in the back, to the gray dappled mare with the black mane and tail. Her velvety muzzle tossed as they approached, her eyes widened, and she stamped nervously.

Abbie reached a hand automatically to soothe her. The mare shied, then grew curious and sniffled her hand.

Monte smiled. "What will you call her?"

Abbie turned. "She's mine, Monte?"

"She's yours."

"Oh, she's beautiful."

He watched her stroke the mare's neck and smooth the rippled mane. He had chosen well. Give Abbie a choice between this horse or jewels, he knew well what she would take. "She's of the same line as Sirocco."

"Well, since Sirocco means a hot desert wind, I'll name her Zephyr. She looks like a storm, a powerful one." Her eyes shone. "Now I can ride the wind."

Monte laughed. "Soon, perhaps, when she's gentled some. Right now she's still half wild."

"Monte, she's wonderful."

He bent and kissed her forehead. "There's nothing I won't give you, Abbie. Anything that's in my power." He held her close.

"You've given me all I want."

He led her to the house and motioned for her to open the door. "Mrs. Farrel, you may take possession of your home. You are mistress here."

Abbie turned the knob and stopped. "You've no idea how frightening that is."

"Frightening! To the one who faced Buck Hollister, who hobnobs with Comanches?"

"I'd rather face Comanches than Frances, and I don't know what it means to be mistress here."

"It means whatever you want it to. You may do any—" He spun at the gunshot that echoed, followed by another of the same caliber, then answering shots. They were far, but not far enough. His land, certainly. What now? He pushed open the door and turned back to the yard.

Abbie caught his arm. "What are you doing?"

"Go into the house." He shook her loose, ran down the stairs, and across the yard.

Abbie stepped in but held the door and waited, her heart beating her ribs. What would he do? Get his men, of course. They should have heard the shot already. Who was on the herd? Cole? Breck? Monte came out from the bunkhouse alone and ran for the stable. He had a gun belt slung over his shoulder.

No one ran with him. Were they all with the herd? A moment later Monte plunged from the stable, bareback on Sirocco with the rein wrapped on his wrist. He cropped the horse's flank. Abbie stared. She had never before seen him use a crop.

She clutched the doorjamb, then ran for the bunkhouse and pulled open the door. The smell of whiskey and sour breath and something worse assailed her. Snores and grunts. Every bed but one was full. Skeeter hung over the side, head to the floor. They were drunk. Passed out drunk.

She spun as hooves beat the yard. Monte? No. Scotch veered and dropped his rider to the dirt. She ran to where Cole lay. Blood soaked his pant leg. Scotch snorted and tossed his head. Cole tried to sit, then fell back.

Oh, dear Lord. "Be still." Abbie tore open the pant at the thigh. Blood pulsed from the hole. The bullet must have nicked an artery. She pulled up her skirt and tore the edge off her petticoat, then tied it around his thigh above the wound and tugged it tight. "Put your arm around my shoulders."

"Thought you'd never ask."

She heaved him up. Cole was not a small man, and Abbie staggered but eventually got him across the yard and up the stairs. She pushed open the door and helped him inside. Cole collapsed against the wall and sank to the entry floor.

"James! Quickly!"

James came running, half dressed. He must have heard the commotion already.

"Send Will for Doctor Barrow."

Upstairs a door opened. Abbie looked up. Maimie would be welcome, but she saw both Maimie and Frances. If Frances fainted she'd personally slap her.

Maimie tightened her robe and started down with Frances following. Her voice was calm. "What can I do?"

"I need water boiled. Tell Pearl to find clean linen for bandages. He's losing too much blood to wait for Doctor Barrow. The bullet must have caught an artery." She lifted the folds of petticoat pressed to the wound. It spattered the gray satin and white lace of her gown.

Frances muffled a cry as she rushed out the front door. The sound of her retching followed. Abbie felt little compassion for her.

James returned and hovered about until Abbie instructed him, "Get me cushions from the parlor." Did she have to tell him everything? Had everyone gone simple? She'd have to keep Cole where he was. The leg had gushed terribly while getting him inside. "Where are Kendal and Chandler?"

"They gone to town. Playin' cards, Mistuh Stevens said."

Abbie tucked the cushions under Cole's head.

He groaned. "Sure could use some whiskey..."

"Whiskey, James."

He quickly brought her the decanter, then hesitated until Abbie said, "Now see what Pearl needs."

He loped off. She had never ordered anyone about so. Well, as Monte said, she was mistress, and it seemed she'd have no time to work into it gently. She poured a glass of whiskey.

Cole gulped it down. "Guess you didn't reckon on spendin' yer weddin' night with me." His mouth twisted into a crooked grin. "Sure wouldn't mind another glass to kill the pain. Both kinds, if ya know what I mean."

"Don't, Cole."

"You sure are a purty sight with yer hair all down like that." He raised a hand and stroked it.

Frances came in, and Abbie straightened. "You may as well go to bed, Frances. I can handle this."

"So I see."

Abbie heard the stairs creak as she mounted, then the door close behind her. That was one less worry.

"She's a fine 'un, ain't she? Guess I got ya in trouble."

"No more than always."

"Gimme the bottle, Abbie. Don't be shy." He pulled the stopper and drank.

Maimie knelt beside her with a bowl of water and strips of cloth. "Pearl's making coffee."

Abbie bathed the wound, then wrapped the cloth tightly around Cole's leg and tied it off. The bandage reddened. Though she knew it could jeopardize his leg, she couldn't remove the tourniquet until Doctor Barrow could cauterize. She plunged her hand into the bowl and the water swirled red.

Cole closed his eyes. She didn't know what else to do for him. If Chandler and Kendal were back, they could carry him. "Cole, was no one out there with you?"

He spoke without looking. "The men're in bad shape after yer little party. You better git Mr. Farrel."

"He's out there already. Didn't you see him?"

Cole opened his eyes. "No."

"Maimie, will you sit with him?"

"Of course, but..."

"Which way is the herd, Cole?" She pulled the gun from its holster at his hip.

He gripped her wrist. "What're you doin'!"

"Which way, Cole?"

"Farrel will shoot me hisself if I tell you."

"He might not live to."

He locked her eyes with his. She didn't flinch.

"They're runnin' the herd down Templeton Gap. He can't stop them."

She rushed for the stable. Will had gone for the doctor. She flashed a glance at Zephyr but bridled Lady Belle and swung up bareback as Monte had. She kicked in her heels and headed for Templeton Gap.

If Monte didn't know of Cole's condition, he'd have no idea what he was up against. Her chest tightened at the thought of Monte out alone with his hands still stiff and weak. She pictured the reins wrapped around his wrist. If he could not grip the reins, how could he shoot?

She urged the horse faster and shivered. The wind penetrated her wrap, and she wished she had grabbed one of Monte's coats instead. The weather was changing. She strained to see through the darkness. She had to be getting near; she could smell the cattle. Then she heard them.

They were driving along the base of the gap. She could make out two, no three men on horseback. She galloped along the ridge. If she could get ahead... Where was Monte?

Lady Belle reared, and Abbie seized the mane and clung with her thighs. A hand gripped her arm and dragged her down. Monte hissed, "Abbie! What are you doing here?"

"I came to help."

He caught her arms and turned her back to the horse. "You get right back on and go home."

"I can't leave you here alone. Cole..."

" . . . ought to be shot for letting you come."

"He is shot."

"What do you mean? How. . . ?"

"In the leg, but it's bad. He made it to the house. I . . ."

A gunshot burst past them and Lady Belle shied, yanked the reins free, and ran. Abbie fell beside Monte as the bullets flew. The squat scrub oaks behind them were no protection but offered concealment. Monte pulled her to the edge of the clump. Below, the panicked cattle charged on, but Abbie could no longer see the men on horseback.

Monte spoke in her ear. "They know where we are. They'll circle around."

Abbie nodded.

"You stay here." He edged forward.

She caught the movement of one man climbing the gap on foot. Did Monte see? The moonlight glinted on the gun in his hand. Monte crouched while she pulled Cole's gun from her pocket and slowly cocked it.

The man came closer. No . . . there were two, one farther down. Where was the third? She turned and searched through the scraggy growth behind her. She saw no one. Abbie strained to hear any sound . . . a twig, a rustle of grass. She looked back to the gulch. The man crept closer.

Monte stood. "Hold it right there."

Abbie saw the flash of gunfire. Monte caught his arm and rolled as the men fired from the gap. Didn't he know this was no time for gentlemen's negotiations? A bullet scattered the earth at Monte's side. He'd never make it back to cover. She raised her gun, aimed for the flashes, and shot. The kickback jolted her arm, but she pulled back the hammer and fired again.

Her bullet hit. The man buckled and fell, screaming, as the other rushed to his side. Abbie froze. It was a horrible sound. Inhuman. The agony in the screams chilled her blood. She pressed her forearms to her ears. Stop. Stop! Time stood still.

A bullet struck a branch at her head, yet she hardly noticed. The third man leaped up from the edge of the gap and shot again.

Dimly she saw Monte rise to his knee. With both hands he held his gun and fired. The man toppled over the edge and rolled.

The last of the trio ran, firing behind him as he went. He gained his horse and veered away. The hoofbeats grew silent. All around was silent.

Monte rasped. "Don't move, do you hear me!"

She nodded, her body quaking. She watched Monte creep over to the man at the edge of the gap. He bent and felt for a pulse, then went down the slope and checked the other, whose screaming had stopped. Neither moved.

Oh, God, what had they done? She wanted to run . . . run away, run to Monte. He came back up the slope and stood over her. She could not move. She needed his strength, his touch. With the moon behind the cloud, she could not see his face.

He took the gun from her hand. "Let's go." His voice was flat, emotionless.

"Are they dead?"

"Yes." He raised her to her feet and led her over the flat and into a gully. Sirocco waited there, and Monte helped her onto the stallion's back. He mounted stiffly behind.

Abbie sank back against his chest. "Why did he scream so, Monte?"

"Where he was hit, I guess."

She closed her eyes against the hot tears. She didn't ask him where her bullet had hit the man. She did not want to know.

The windows of the house were lit up, and Doctor Barrow's horse stood in front. Monte let her down at the stairs and rode on to the stable. She waited, but after a time realized he must be caring for the horse himself. She went in alone.

Maimie and Pearl and James stood like sheep in the corner of the parlor where Cole had been moved. Doctor Barrow was at Cole's side just finishing with the bandage. Beside him the slug lay in a pan. Abbie shuddered at the smell of burned flesh and looked away from the probe cooling on the hearth. Who had held Cole down for the doctor?

Doctor Barrow spoke without turning. "You did a good job on the leg, Mrs. Farrel."

Her throat was too tight to answer.

Cole stirred and opened his eyes. "They were gone?"

She had to speak. She owed him an answer. "No," she whispered. "They were there." Her mouth felt like cotton. "Two of them are dead." She sank to the chair. Maimie hurried over and put an arm around her. Abbie scarcely noticed.

"You shoulda never gone out there." Cole tried to rise, but the doctor kept him down.

"I had to. Monte could not have stood alone."

"I could." Monte came through the door. "Get me something to drink, James. And where the devil is Chandler?"

"They haven't returned from town." Maimie held Abbie's hand. "Shall we send?"

Monte shook his head. He emptied the glass James brought him and turned. "Cole, I hold you responsible for sending Abbie out there."

"I figured that."

Abbie squirmed. "It wasn't Cole, Monte. I gave him no choice."

Doctor Barrow stood. "The leg'll mend. The bullet didn't catch much bone. But he's lucky Mrs. Farrel stanched the blood." He tucked the cooled probe into the bag and turned to Monte. "Let me see that arm."

Abbie stared at the blood on Monte's sleeve.

"It's only grazed. I'll clean it up myself."

Doctor Barrow pulled apart Monte's shirt sleeve in spite of his argument, then swabbed and wrapped the wound. "Now I guess I'd better have a look at the bodies."

Abbie's gorge rose up. Bodies. Dead shells. She thought for a moment Monte would go back out, but he said, "My man's bringing them in."

He must have roused someone before coming inside. Oh, thank God. She needed him.

Cole tried to rise again, then sank back into the cushions. "Sheez."

"You're not going anywhere for a while. You've lost too much blood." Doctor Barrow closed the bag and straightened. "I'll have a glass of that whiskey while I wait. Mr. Farrel, why don't you see your wife to bed."

Abbie leaned on Monte's arm up the stairs. His hold was firm and steady, and she felt weaker than when she had learned he was married to Sharlyn. The sound and smell of death overwhelmed her. The violence, the horror. But once inside the room, he released her.

"They'll expect me to stay here tonight. You have no objections?"

Objections? Abbie's legs felt liquid. Dear Lord, the look in his eyes. "Monte?"

He walked into the dressing room and got out of his clothes. She stood stiffly where he left her. If she moved, if she took a step . . .

He came back in, went to the bed, and lay down. She waited until he turned down the lamp before she undressed and put on her nightgown. She crept to the bed and slid into the sheets. Monte lay on his back, unmoving. She waited.

His words were low and clipped. "I don't need you to protect me, Abbie. I am not so much a cripple that I cannot defend myself."

"I didn't think you were! It's just that . . ."

"You thought you could handle things better than I."

"No . . . no, it's . . ."

"How does it feel to have killed a man?"

Her whole body shook. A wave of nausea rose bitter in her throat and clamped her stomach into a tight ball. She rolled to her side and fought wretched sobs trapped by her will. How could he? She closed her eyes against the tears. She would not cry. She would not let him know how it hurt.

The darkness seemed endless. The screams echoed on and on in her head, and she gripped the pillow to silence them. The grandfather clock in the hall chimed eleven, twelve, then one, two.

Monte lay still, but his breathing was shallow. She was sure he did not sleep. She wanted to bury her face in his chest and feel his arms gentle and strong around her, but she did not move. She kept her back rigidly toward him as weariness overcame her.

♦♦♦♦♦♦♦

Jip dropped from the horse, both of them too exhausted to go on. He balled his fists to his forehead, and buried his face in the ground. He smelled his brother's blood on his hands, on his shirt. His jaw clenched and he groaned. He slammed his fists into the dirt, shouting every vulgarity that presented itself.

Emmet deserved to die. He had started the shooting; he had wanted to kill. But not Spence. Spence was too young to know, too young to choose . . . too young to die. Gut shot! *Oh no, no.* Jip sobbed brokenly. He smeared Spence's blood across his face when he swiped the tears away. He suddenly felt hard and grim. He would pay back the death of his brother if it was the last thing he ever did. And he'd see Captain Jake in hell.

Eleven

When Abbie woke, the space beside her in bed was empty. She looked around the sumptuous room, surveying the fine furniture and the grand mirror that stood in the corner. What was she doing there? She didn't belong in this house, in this bed . . . Monte's bed.

The breath left her chest, and she bent forward, holding her stomach. A murderer. She was a murderer. She closed her eyes, whispering, "Dear God, help me." Rolling out of bed, she went to the washstand and bathed. She held out her hands, hands that had killed last night, that ended a life. And Monte hated her for it. Oh, how he hated her.

She walked to the wardrobe, passed over the gowns Monte had commissioned for her, and found her cotton skirt and shirtwaist. She tied her hair back and went downstairs. She heard voices in the morning room but went on to the parlor. Cole lay awake on the settee, his leg up on the end. He looked roguish and uncomfortable.

"How are you?"

"Can't say I haven't been better. How about you?"

She looked away. "I guess the same."

"Look, Abbie, I know how ya feel, but you only did what you had to."

"How do you know what I did?"

"I saw it all over yer face when you come in last night."

Abbie sank into the chair. "I don't even know how it

121

happened. They shot at us, and I just fired. I just pointed the gun and fired."

"Everyone's got the right to defend himself—or herself—and yer property. You done what you had to."

She dropped her forehead to her hand. "Monte doesn't think so."

"He'll come around."

"I don't think so. I think this will stand between us."

"Don't let it. And don't let him cow you."

She nodded limply. It was easy to say. He hadn't seen the loathing in Monte's face, heard the tone of his cruel words. "Have you eaten?"

"Nope."

"I'll make you breakfast."

"You?"

"It's my kitchen. I'll use it if I like."

He chuckled. "Heaven help you."

Abbie found Pearl in the pantry. "I'll make Mr. Jasper's breakfast. He's hungry now."

Pearl puffed out her cheeks and put her hands to her hips. "Yes'um, Mizz Farrel." She waited without moving while Abbie browned the pork and fried the eggs.

Zena came in. "Aunt Pearl, I . . ." She looked from Abbie to her aunt, then backed out.

It was a mistake. Again. She had forced her way where she didn't belong. She tightened her jaw as she scooped the eggs onto a plate and laid the meat beside them, then smeared a chunk of bread with butter. She poured a cup of coffee and set it all on a tray. Without looking at Pearl, she carried it to Cole. She set the tray on the table, propped him up with cushions, then lifted it into his lap.

"Nothin' like breakfast in bed. You wanna join me? To eat, I mean."

She didn't even blush. She heard hooves and rushed to the window to see Deputy Davis rein in beside the wagon. Monte was there to greet him.

A moment later he entered the parlor. "Deputy Davis needs a statement, Abbie. Will you come outside?" He was gentle and polite, but he did not offer his arm. She followed him out.

"Mornin' Miss Mar . . . Mrs. Farrel." Deputy Davis tipped his hat. "I need a statement about last night's shootin'."

Abbie felt Monte's hand on her elbow as she slowly stepped down. "What do you need to know?"

"Can you tell me what happened? What you saw and did?"

Abbie tried to stop the sudden heaving of her chest, and she looked involuntarily to the bed of the wagon. "Three men . . . were down with the herd, running them off. They shot at us . . ."

"You and Mr. Farrel?"

"Yes."

"And why were you out there, Mrs. Farrel?"

"I . . . needed Monte. I was afraid for Cole. He'd been shot." Monte stiffened beside her. Did he expect her to say she'd gone to protect him?

"And why did you have a gun?"

"I took it from Cole to protect myself."

"Thank you, ma'am. That's all I need to know. It's pretty clear self-defense. I won't ask you to identify the men. Only thing is . . . Mr. Farrel believes one might be the man in your pa's barn the night of the fire."

Abbie turned and found Monte's eyes on her. They told her nothing, and he said no word. She swallowed the hurt. "I'll look." She walked to the end of the wagon. She knew immediately which one she had shot. His belly was caked with blood, and his face was distorted into a freakish grimace. He was young. So young.

She caught the side of the wagon as a wave of horror passed through her. His shape was familiar, and the face under the fair hair could have been the face in the barn, but she had not known he was a boy. Her knuckles whitened on the side of the wagon, and she closed her eyes. "I think it could be."

"Thank you, ma'am. That's all I need. I'm sorry about all that happenin' on yer weddin' day." He tipped his hat.

She left the wagon and walked past the house. Not for anything could she enter those walls and face Frances and Maimie, Kendal and Chandler. Most of all, she could not face Monte. She sped up, and as she rounded the stable, she lifted her skirts and ran. Mounds of pale golden grass muffled her feet as she left the house and all of them behind.

The wind carried a chill that matched the one inside her. The mountain summits were shrouded in gray. How different they looked than yesterday. Everything looked different since yesterday. Everything *was* different. She pushed on and on until she reached the top of a hill and staggered.

She dropped to her knees, and dry heaves shook her, since she had nothing inside. Not even bile. The stone angel over Sharlyn's grave waited, fingers outstretched. She had not intended to end up here but had come blindly. She dropped her face to her hands and wept.

She pictured the face of another boy—Blake's face, as she had swabbed the vinegar water over it and helped his mother prepare the body for burial. Now she had killed . . . same as Hollister. She shuddered. Even Monte blamed her. *Even Monte.*

The little stone angel smiled down at her. The tiny hands stretched out to her. If she could just grasp them and be lifted from this earth, from this loathing. "Oh, Sharlyn, if only you hadn't died. You were so good. You should be here beside Monte. You would have known not to dishonor him. That boy would be alive." But would Monte?

The wind gusted and blew pellets of corn snow. Her hair worked loose and whipped her eyes. She let it fly. "Oh, God, what am I to do?" Her voice was whisked away on the wind, and she knew God hadn't heard. There was nothing she could do.

The cold felt good. Let it numb her. Her neck stiffened with the ice that lodged in the collar of her dress. Her wet cheeks chapped, and her fingers reddened. If she were stone like the angel, she'd feel none of it. Oh, if only she were stone.

◆◆◆◆◆◆◆

Beside Monte, Chandler hollered over the wind buffeting their faces with white pellets. "How far can she have gone?"

"I don't know. With Abbie I never know."

"Perhaps she went to her parents."

"I've sent a man to check, but I don't think so. It's more likely she headed off across the land."

"Surely she knows the area and the weather."

Oh, she knew it all right. But whether she would heed it was another thing. It was his fault. He should have stopped her when she walked past. He should have known, but how could he? He didn't know her at all.

The damaged skin of his hands throbbed from the cold even through the gloves. If the wind would only stop. Where would she go? He scanned the land, shielding his eyes with his arm, then stopped. Of course.

"I have an idea where she might be." He changed course, loping over the ground, then hurried to the hill. The trees at the top waved in the wind, and Abbie huddled beneath, knees wrapped in her arms. Her hair was clotted with corn snow, her skin red and raw.

Chandler came up behind and glanced from Abbie to the angel that marked his sister's grave.

Abbie looked up. Her eyes were red rimmed, her lashes icy.

A pang of remorse stung him, and Monte pulled off his coat and wrapped it around her. "Abbie, what are you thinking? You'll catch your death." He raised her to her feet. "Come on, now."

Between them, he and Chandler shielded her from the wind. But Monte could feel the chill of her skin. What was she doing, sitting there freezing? Did she think to punish him?

Abbie felt the life returning to her fingers and toes as she was hurried into the warmth of the house. Monte led her straight upstairs to her room, then waited outside. A fire burned, and she could smell the pot of cider spiced with cinnamon. She stood near it as Zena peeled the wet clothing from her and rubbed her skin before wrapping her in the robe.

"Lawdy, Mizz Farrel. You's cold as ice."

Abbie wished she could reassure her, but she felt as frozen inside as out.

"If you gets in that bed and drinks yo' cider, you get warm."

Abbie didn't want to get into the bed. She never wanted to get in it again. She wanted her own bed. She wanted Mama and Pa. Her throat tightened. Had they heard? What would Mama think? Oh, what would they think?

Zena pulled the covers up around her. Monte tapped on the door, and Zena admitted him. "She's all dry now."

"Thank you." He waited until Zena left, then came to the bedside and took Abbie's hand between his. "Forgive me, Abbie. I should not have said what I did last night."

"You only said what you thought."

He did not gainsay her. "Nevertheless, I apologize, and I hope you will accept it."

He was formal, sincere . . . but so distant. Abbie felt the lump harden in her throat. "Of course."

He poured a cup of cider and brought it to her. "Drink this, and I'll have Pearl bring your dinner up since you missed it."

"Thank you, but I'm not hungry." Abbie held the cup in her lap.

Monte stood a moment, then nodded and left the room. As the door closed behind him, Abbie set the cup aside and sank into the covers. The tips of her fingers throbbed as the blood returned. She closed her eyes and wept before fitful sleep overcame her.

✦✦✦✦✦✦✦

The fire had burned low and the room was dim when she awoke. The first thing she saw was a tray of soup and bread. She rose to one elbow, and Monte turned from the fire. His presence startled her.

"Ah, you're awake. I trust you're warm?"

"Yes."

"You can manage the soup?"

"I can manage."

He nodded. "Then I'll check in again."

She looked away from his leaving. Duty required his attendance . . . or maybe honor. As it had with Sharlyn. What was it he had said? Did kindness and faithfulness replace love? The thought of soup turned her stomach. The cider had been removed. Zena could take the food, too.

She felt desolate. Nothing would bring life back to that boy, nor to the man Monte had shot, for that matter. And nothing would restore Monte's opinion of her. She had dishonored him. She rested her head back on the pillow. Well, they had lived estranged before. There was some small comfort in its familiarity.

A tap came at the door, and Maimie tucked her head in. "I hoped you were awake. May I come in?"

"Yes."

She came and sat on the end of the bed. "Are you warm?"

"Yes, thank you."

"I'm so terribly sorry for all of this. If Chad and Kendal had only been here. . . . Chad feels terrible."

"He needn't."

"Would it help to talk?"

"I don't know." Abbie ran her fingers over the quilted coverlet. "I . . . I didn't know he was so young. He was only a boy."

"How could you know? Even if you had, you did what you must."

Did she? Abbie passed a hand over her eyes. "I had a friend . . . a very dear friend who was killed when he was seventeen. He was killed for his gold . . . and this one for our cattle."

"No. In defense of your lives."

Abbie shook her head. "I should never have gone out there."

"Then it might be Monte buried today. He tries to hide it, but I've seen his hands, and I doubt very much he could have fought them all."

Abbie stared at her.

"It's his pride that blames you, not his heart."

"It doesn't matter which it is."

"Yes, it does. One's pride is more easily mended than one's heart." Maimie took Abbie's hand between hers. "You don't know what it was for him not to fight the war."

Abbie searched her face. "He was too young."

"At the start maybe. But later, others as young went to fight. Chad . . ."

"No."

"Yes. And Chad was there when his father pulled Monte's father from the field, bleeding from the ball that cost him his arm. The war did horrible things to our men, but at least they could say they fought for what they believed. Monte was not allowed that."

"I don't understand. Why would he want. . . ?"

"Honor, Abbie."

Abbie wanted to scream. "Who knows how many lives he saved? Surely Frances's more than once. And the girls he hid and the livestock that kept them all alive when the raiders would have left them nothing. . . . Was there no honor in that?"

"But it's not the same."

Abbie shook her head. How could killing men on the battlefield be more honorable than what Monte had done?

Maimie's voice was gentle. "His father was willing to lose his life for the confederacy but not his son's life. Monte honored his father's order, but it cost him dearly."

"How do you know this?"

"Chad. He and Monte were closer than brothers. It nearly killed Monte when Chad went to fight. It was all Chad could do to hold him to his promise. Monte went out last night to fight for his own. He was ready to lose his life if it came to it."

"Oh, Maimie, I'll never understand. I despair of being a good wife to him. I thought to protect him, but I defied him . . . and look what has come of it."

"Monte won't hold his anger forever. One day he'll face the sacrifice you made and love you all the more for it."

If only that were true. Abbie squeezed her hand. "Thank you."

Maimie stood. "If you're feeling up to it, why don't you put on something pretty and come down."

Yes, Abbie thought. There may be no way to change things,

but she would not hide any longer. She had no control over Monte's thoughts and feelings. All she could do was face this. Maimie sent Zena in, and Abbie allowed her to pull the corset tight. She slipped the bustle on and donned a blue velvet dress. Monte had wonderful taste. Zena wound her hair into a chignon, and she hung the earrings from her newly pierced earlobes. At least she would look the part.

♦♦♦♦♦♦♦

Monte stopped midsentence when he saw Abbie gliding down. He was surprised and annoyingly overwhelmed. How could she be so infuriating and so incredible at once?

"You were saying?" Frances touched his arm.

"I'm ... I'm sorry ..."

Abbie walked into the great room, and Kendal's jaw fell slack. Monte met his eye, then turned to her. "Well." He kissed her hand. It was warm and soft. "Feeling better, I see."

"Yes, thank you."

"Wonderful," Chandler said. "Maimie, why don't you play?"

Maimie smiled. "Of course I will."

"Your fingers would be permanently connected if they could," Chandler proclaimed as Maimie began playing a Chopin nocturne.

Abbie turned to Chandler. "That's lovely, isn't it? It stirs my soul."

Chandler bowed. "May I?"

She took his hand. Monte stepped back as Chandler spun her past. His mouth twitched as he watched Abbie murmur something that set Chandler chuckling, then in a lower voice added whatever brought his laugh full force. It was hard to believe this was the same girl who had stood beside him last night with a smoking gun in her hand. Who was this person he had married?

Chandler released her, but before Monte stepped forward, Kendal was at her side. "May I have the honor? A waltz, Maimie."

Chandler took Frances's hand. Monte stepped back again as both couples swept by him. Kendal spun Abbie in wide graceful circles. Did she have to look so deucedly happy about it?

Her lashes drooped, and Monte's fingers tightened into his palms. The pain increased the anger. Kendal pulled her close. Monte stepped in, but Maimie stopped playing, and Kendal bowed and released her.

Frances slipped her arm into Kendal's. "I declare, Abbie, you look as natural with Kendal as you did with Monte's foreman last night."

Abbie flushed. Monte frowned. *What was this?* He turned to her, but she drew herself up.

"If you'll excuse me." She swept out of the room without even a glance his way.

She had to go. One more minute and she'd have clawed Frances. And Monte, with his eyes burning into her, yet so aloof. Abbie pushed the door open and peeked in. Cole was awake.

"Purty music. Puts me in the mind for dancin'."

"I hope this injury won't keep you from it."

"Not much point."

"Nonsense. Every girl will be heartbroken if you don't show up with dancing feet."

Cole shook his head. "You know I don't care about that."

"So you say. I think you're as flattered by the attention as the next man. And you know what else I think, Cole Jasper?"

"What?"

"I think one day you'll settle down and raise sons and . . ."

"You're wrong, Abbie. I had me one notion to settle down in all my life. It ain't gonna happen again."

The look in his eyes silenced her argument. Oh, why had she said anything?

Monte tapped on the door and stuck his head in. "Supper is served, Abbie."

She turned. "I'll have a tray brought in for you, Cole."

"I've already seen to that," Monte said.

Her gown brushed against the doorframe as she passed through. She was surprised Monte extended his elbow. She tucked her fingers into the crook and sat in the chair he held. He lingered a moment, then took his place at the head.

Abbie forced herself to eat. She would not give Frances the satisfaction of costing her appetite. And she'd eaten nothing all day. Laced up as she was, it wasn't long before she was full, though Monte's superb cuisine was lost on her. The conversation was stiff and false, but she smiled and nodded as required.

Monte stood. "I believe I'll retire directly." He bowed slightly. "Good night."

Abbie made her excuses and went up to their room. Monte was not there. She walked around it. It was larger than two bedrooms at home. Home. This was her home, but she was a stranger here.

She looked at her reflection in the long mirror. Not even Frances could fault her appearance tonight. Monte had provided a trousseau worthy of her position. She reached up and let her hair down. Even so she did not know the girl in the mirror.

Monte knocked on the door adjacent to the dressing room.

"Come in."

He came to stand behind her. "I wanted to tell you how lovely you looked tonight."

"Thank you."

He reached a hand to her hair. Abbie's heart quickened.

"I didn't get a dance."

"You didn't ask."

"No, I . . . well, I'll be in the next room if you need anything. Good night, Abbie." He kissed the back of her head and left. Abbie dropped her face into her hands.

Twelve

The hand outstretched before her was delicate and long fingered, pale in the starlight, and Abbie studied its form, trying to place it. It seemed familiar as she looked up the arm to her own shoulder. *It's my hand*, she thought with surprise, and looked back at it. The stars glinted on the metal of the gun that it clutched, and with horror she watched the finger squeeze the trigger.

The smell of gunsmoke was acrid in her nostrils. Screams exploded into the night, and a figure staggered toward her. She did not want to look, did not want to see, but a face drew close, and it was the boy in the wagon, spattered with blood and beseeching her. Then it became Blake's face. Abbie cried out and jolted up in bed.

Her forehead was damp, her fists still clenched. Her chest heaved. She pressed her hands to her eyes, but the horrible images remained. "I didn't want to kill him. But I can't undo it. God, I can't undo it." Sinking back down, she buried her head in the softness of the pillow and closed her eyes. If only the rustlers hadn't come. . . .

◆◆◆◆◆◆◆

In the dim that preceded the dawn, Monte crept like a thief into Abbie's room. Her features were soft as she slept, though the bedclothes were tangled as though she had thrashed. A long moment he looked at her, then went to the window. He raised his hands and studied them, slowly squeezing and straightening the fingers, then pressing hard and wincing. The truth was that if Abbie had not fired when she did, he could not have stood against those men. At one time, yes . . . but not now.

Closing his eyes, he remembered the woods that had surrounded the plantation house and the long cut beyond it where he had practiced with a gun in his father's absence. Daily he had honed his skills with bullets from melted farm implements, thinking maybe, maybe he would go yet and fight.

He did not long for bloodshed or imagine glory on the field. But honor had its price. In his sixteenth year, he could have outdrawn most men and fired accurately, as well, but he never had. No one had even known of his skill. When he came to live here where everyone wore a gun, he did also. He was prepared to defend himself and his own, but he had never needed to . . . until now.

Had God made him weak for a purpose? Had He destroyed his human strength to make him know his frailty? Monte chafed at the thought, but it would not go away. Had he taken back the control he had surrendered? But how did a man live in surrender?

He peered through the organdy curtains to the coming day. He pictured Abbie's arm, bouncing with the kickback of the shots. This was not some frail and delicate creature to be protected as Sharlyn had been. He had known how to husband Sharlyn. It had been natural to guard and govern her, and she had responded with feminine tranquillity.

Abbie did not beg his strength. She had done what he should have been able to do, though her whole being trembled afterward as he held her on the horse. His hands had been stiff and awkward in the cold. He could not have taken three. If not for Abbie, he could not have taken them.

She stirred, and he looked back over his shoulder, then left the room.

◆◆◆◆◆◆◆

Abbie washed and allowed Zena to dress her. The house was quiet when she went down except for the faint, soulful humming of Pearl in the kitchen. She would not offend her again by invading her territory. She went instead to the library and breathed in the scent. Three things drew that response: the mountain air, the sage of the prairie, and the leather of books.

Abbie closed her eyes and pictured Pa in his chair, book laid across his knees. A wave of homesickness washed over her, but she couldn't go. She couldn't face them. She opened her eyes. Monte's library was extensive, he being such an avid reader. Dickens, Shakespeare, Tennyson. She pulled down *Idylls of the King*.

Sharlyn had loved that one. Sitting demurely, hands folded in her lap, she had listened with rapt attention as Abbie read to her out in the hills. She did not sense Sharlyn here, not in this room. In other parts of the house, yes, but not here in a room of books. Sharlyn could barely read.

She took the book and went out. Cole glanced up at her entrance and halted the knife on the wood in his hand.

"Good morning, Cole. How is your leg?"

"I'm ready to be up."

"Not according to Doctor Barrow. You have to give the healing time if you want the leg restored."

"Meanwhile, the rest of me is rottin' away."

Abbie smiled. She sat on the chair beside the settee and laid the book on the table. "The doctor said one more day before you try your weight on it. You can manage one more day, surely?"

"I ain't used to bein' coddled, and it's so dim in here I feel like sleepin' all the time."

Abbie looked at the windows. "You're right." She stood, shoved the secretary to the window, and climbed up.

Cole snickered. "You're givin' me more than a glimpse of petticoat, Abbie."

"Then be a gentleman and look away." She balanced herself and lifted the rod, slipping the velvet drapes loose and letting them fall.

Pearl came in with Cole's breakfast tray and gasped. "Mizz Farrel! You get down 'fore you falls!"

"Nonsense, Pearl. I'm not going to fall, and I want these curtains off."

"Them curtains is the crowning glory of this room. You don' know what you's doin'."

Abbie climbed down off the secretary, shoved it over to the next window, then climbed up again. "The lace is perfectly sufficient. The view is the crowning glory of this room."

From the corner of her eye, she saw Pearl's jaw jut, her hands on her hips. "Mastuh Monte had them drapes sent all the way from Cha'leston. You got no cause . . ."

"Honestly, Pearl." Abbie sent the next ones to the floor.

"Them drapes was good enough for Mizz Sharlyn. She knowed what her husband—"

"If Mrs. Farrel prefers the windows without the drapes, we'll have them without the drapes, Pearl." Abbie spun and caught herself when Monte spoke. He walked over and handed her down. "You might ask for assistance the next time. James could manage that better, I think."

"That's debatable." Kendal entered with Frances on his arm. "Redecorating?"

Monte picked up the curtain and handed it to Pearl. "Abbie, Kendal and I are going to Charleston with Chandler and Maimie."

Frances wilted into the chair. "Monte . . ."

"We'll fetch Jeanette, settle affairs, and be back before you know it."

Frances sniffed into her handkerchief. "Please let me come."

He shook his head. "It's better if we go alone. You'll be fine here with Abbie."

That meant she wasn't invited, either, Abbie supposed. She was hardly surprised. He was no doubt eager to put distance between them. She swallowed the ache. "When will you go?"

"We'll be on tomorrow's stage." He turned to Cole. "I wish you were not incapacitated. Breck is a good cowboy, but he lacks your judgment."

"There's nothin' keepin' me from givin' the orders. I'm ready to be up."

"Breck and the men have recovered the herd. They're keeping the animals close for the time being. I've alerted Marshal Haggerty to my absence, and the men can take shifts watching the house."

"We'll keep things in hand."

"Yes. Well." Monte bowed slightly to Abbie. "I've things to put in order now. Kendal."

Kendal followed him out. Abbie glanced at Frances, who looked smugly satisfied even in her misery. Abbie turned and went out. Frances could entertain Cole.

Abbie found Maimie in her room. "I'm sorry you're leaving so soon."

"Oh, come sit, Abbie." Maimie tucked the gloves into the trunk.

"I don't know what I'll do without you. Frances . . ."

"Don't mind about Frances. This has been a terrible shock to her, poor dear. I only hope Monte can salvage something of it all."

"Is it as bad as that?"

Maimie closed the trunk. "Kendal's not to blame. It's all too easy to come to ruin with the Yankee scoundrels preying on decent people. There's no honor, Abbie. And our men don't know how to fight that . . . or even recognize it."

"I wish I understood."

"You do. Honesty, integrity, ingenuity. The honor of the West . . . and you possess them all. Ours is complicated by a chivalry that no longer exists except in men like Monte, Chad, and Kendal. Be patient with Frances."

"Of course I will. But I despair of ever meeting her approval."

Maimie sighed. "You can't blame her. Monte was everything to her, especially through the bad times. In her eyes no one is entirely suitable for him."

"I'm entirely unsuitable."

Maimie pressed her hand. "You're exactly what Monte needs. And Frances, as well, if she only knew it."

Abbie left her to pack. The house was more peaceful with Frances spending the day in bed. At least she could go about without fear of condemnation. Why couldn't she let it go? What did it matter if Frances disapproved?

It mattered because Monte loved Frances. It was another way she had failed him.

"Abbie."

She jumped.

"I'm sorry I startled you." Monte touched her shoulder.

Oh, if only he would hold me.

"I have a favor to ask."

Anything. Doesn't he know?

"Look after Frances. She's not strong, not emotionally. In truth, I'm afraid for her."

"Of course I will. I . . ."

"And another thing. I want you both to stay close to the house. I don't expect trouble, but I've given Pearl and James leave to make any purchases, and the men can see to anything else you need. I've arranged for Breck to keep a man in the house at all times."

Abbie's throat tightened. She wanted to keep him, beg him as Frances had. *Please don't go. Please don't leave with so much unspoken between us.* She nodded.

He bent and kissed her forehead. "James will see us to the stage in the morning."

So she would not even have a good-bye. She refused to cling to him and kept her arms at her sides. "Don't worry about us. We'll be fine."

He almost smiled. "I know you will."

◆◆◆◆◆◆◆

Monte bumped shoulders with Kendal in the stage. He glanced at Chandler and Maimie sitting across from him. They were a glum company, silent and brooding. That was his fault as much as any.

He was more concerned about leaving than he had let on. If not for Frances, he would have left Kendal to settle matters himself, but Monte was determined to salvage what he could for her sake, and time was of the essence. Cole knew what they were up against. He would keep the men lively, and Marshal Haggerty had his eye out for the rustler who got away.

Truth be told, Monte hoped distance would ease his wrath and confusion. He did not want to hurt Abbie, but his chagrin left him no peace. He felt impotent.

Maimie sighed. "I envy you all. I've fallen in love with your West."

Kendal frowned. "I wish Frances felt that way. She thinks I've sentenced her to death."

"She'll recover." Monte watched the endless prairie out the window. Would she? Would any of them?

"I don't know what you said that convinced her to stay. But I am grateful."

Monte nodded. He did not tell Kendal that Frances had clung to him and wept, bemoaned Kendal's failings, and begged to be released from her duty. He had refused, of course. She would see in the end that it was best.

"I so enjoyed Abbie," Maimie said. "She's a wonderful girl, Monte. I know you'll be happy together."

He smiled with his lips. Yes, she was wonderful—wonderful, incredible, and dangerous. She threatened everything he knew, his understanding of the feminine nature, his own manhood, his code of honor as a gentleman. Maybe he was not so removed from the old ways as he had thought.

♦♦♦♦♦♦♦

Abbie wished it was Zephyr she galloped over the field, but it was disobedience enough to be sneaking away. She pulled up and slid to the ground, wound the reins, and ran inside. "Mama?"

The house was empty. Abbie found her in the garden and threw her arms around her, hoe and all. Mama squeezed back. "I was hoping you'd come."

"I would have come sooner, but . . ."

Mama held her at arm's length. "I know about your trouble. It's a terrible business."

She didn't know the half of it. "I don't want to talk about that." She looked at the ground. The garden was nearly finished, the last of the pumpkin vines shriveled and bare, only the potatoes and carrots left in the earth. "Where's Grant?"

"Out riding with Judge Wilson's daughter."

"Marcy Wilson?"

"Yes."

"Oh, Mama."

"He's met with the judge and received a very favorable welcome."

"I just bet." Abbie kicked a wrinkled pod onto the pile of vines Mama had hoed. "I hope he isn't duped by Marcy's pretty face. She hasn't the spirit to match."

"Shame, Abbie."

Abbie turned as the horses cantered to the edge of the garden.

"Abbie!" Grant leaped down and helped Marcy dismount her sidesaddle. "This is a surprise."

She smelled the wind and sweat on him as he kissed her cheek. If Marcy weren't looking so smug, she'd squeeze the breath from him. "Monte's gone to Charleston with Kendal to settle affairs. Oh, Grant, can you believe it—Kendal and Frances are staying."

He pinched her chin. "You know Miss Wilson, of course."

"Hello, Marcy."

Marcy tipped her head adorned in a sweet little riding bonnet. "Abbie."

Grant gathered the reins. "I'll stable the horses. Abbie, show Miss Wilson into the house."

For Grant she would do it.

Marcy lifted her skirts so as not to touch them to the dust and walked beside her. "Your wedding was lovely. I thought maybe it would be a hushed little affair, being Mr. Farrel's second and all. But then, second choice isn't always second rate, is it?"

Abbie didn't dignify her with a response.

"I suppose it was inevitable, the way you pandered to him."

Abbie clenched her skirt. "If Monte fell for pandering, he would have chosen the leech that attached every time he came near. I'm not surprised to find you a poor loser, however. I surely hope you haven't any fantasies about my brother."

Marcy paled. "I was never in the least interested in Montgomery Farrel. And I'm—"

"Oh, stow it, Marcy." Abbie pushed open the door. "But I warn you, Grant is no pushover." She set out milk and molasses cookies.

The minute Grant joined them, Abbie escaped. *Merciful God, open his eyes!* She stalked across the yard, then suddenly stopped short. Is that how Frances felt about her? It turned Abbie's stomach to think of Marcy for a sister. How wretched did she make Frances?

She tried to imagine things from Frances's side and winced. But what could she do? She dropped to her knees beside Mama and worked a potato out of the mound. She brushed it off and dropped it into the bushel. Mama's nails were brown and broken, the knuckles red. Abbie wanted to grasp her hand and kiss it, to tell her how much she missed working beside her, missed the simple, honest labor.

"There's nothing to stop you having your own garden."

Abbie laughed. "Heaven help me if I think something really awful next to you."

Mama laughed with her, then put an arm around her shoulders.

Abbie rested her head. "Pearl has the vegetable garden . . . and the kitchen. I'm not allowed."

"Have an ornamental garden."

"I could." She held Mama's hand between hers. It was warm and dry, the creases more distinct. She stroked the fingers. "How bad are things?"

Abbie sighed. "What have you heard?"

"Everything from you and Monte fighting off an army of rustlers, to you single-handedly saving the ranch."

"It wasn't like that."

"It doesn't matter. People are more interested in might-have-beens."

"I offended Monte . . . grievously."

Mama nodded slowly. "Well, it's been a difficult time."

"If you only knew. I'll never please Frances, Pearl treats me like a guest or a nuisance. At least when Monte . . . oh, Mama, will he ever forgive me?"

Mama stroked her hair. "So much is bound up in the heart of a man. He loves you, I know that."

"I don't know anymore. I just don't know." She was ashamed of her tears and wiped them away.

"When things seem overwhelming, it's best to take on one problem at a time."

"I wouldn't know where to start."

"Start with Frances."

"Frances? How?"

"Ask her to teach you what she knows, to train you as she was trained."

"Oh, Mama . . ."

"Now listen, Abbie." Mama raised Abbie's chin as she had when she was a child. "As much as you need to learn, she needs a purpose. Think how it would be, uprooted and wondering if all that you know means anything. Sometimes it's easier to be bitter than afraid."

Abbie didn't want to hear it, to think of debasing herself to Monte's sister now that she had just gained the upper hand. "I don't know, Mama. It won't be easy to be alone with her as it is."

"When have the best lessons ever been easy?"

Mama was right, but Abbie was not at all certain she could do it. She rode back to the ranch more discouraged than before. Grant keeping company with Marcy. Mama's directive. Monte gone. It seemed the hole inside would swallow her up. She pushed open the door.

Pearl descended the stairs with a tray. "Mizz Frances won' eat. I done tempted, begged, and hollered till I got no breath left. But she won' eat."

Abbie untied her hat and hung it on the rack. "She'll eat when she gets hungry, Pearl. I'll take my supper in the parlor with Cole."

Muttering, Pearl carried the tray away. Abbie brushed the dust from her dress and went to the parlor. Cole sat in a pile of shavings with his leg up and a herd of miniature animals on the table.

She clapped her hands together. "Cole, they're wonderful!" She dropped down and examined the tiny horse.

"Just keepin' sane. I ain't stayin' on this couch one more day, even if the doc says that artery's gonna burst."

"Don't be crabby, Cole. Did you like the book?"

"What book?"

"The one I brought you. *Idylls of the King.*"

He shook his head. "It don't do me no good. I cain't read."

Abbie stared at him. "Not at all?"

"Never had no schoolin'. Not that kind."

She sat down in the wing chair. "Would you like to hear it? It's wonderful—heroes and all."

He set down the knife. "A'right."

Abbie opened the book. " '*Idylls of the King,* by Alfred Lord Tennyson. These to his memory—since he held them dear, perchance as finding there unconsciously some image of himself . . .' "

"That's poetry."

Abbie smiled.

"Sheez." Cole sank down on the couch and adjusted his leg.

She continued to read and, through her lashes, watched his expressions—sometimes scoffing, sometimes puzzling. " 'Leodogran, the king of Cameliard, had one fair child, and none other child; and she was fairest of all flesh on earth, Guinevere, and in her his one delight . . .' " She glanced up and bit her lip at the faraway look in his eyes.

Pearl came in with pursed lips, set down the supper tray, and went back out.

Cole chuckled. "You're ridin' herd on a sour bunch, ain't you?"

"I can't seem to please anyone."

"Just keep doin' things yer way. They'll give in sooner or later."

She closed the book and set it on the table. "I'm a stranger in my own home."

Cole looked to the window. "I ain't the one to be hearin' that, Abbie."

"I'm sorry."

He picked up his fork. "Sure do eat good in here. Old Charlie could take some lessons from that huffy cook o' yers."

Abbie smiled. "Sometimes I wish I could take Old Charlie's place, hear the sizzle of a skillet, feel the steam in my face. I wonder what Sharlyn did with herself."

"That's one thing I couldn't figure."

"What?"

"How you and the late Mrs. Farrel got so tight."

"Sharlyn was special."

"I s'pose. Not my type, though. Kinda like them china dolls in the store. You don't wanna touch 'em. Same for that sister. She cleans up real nice, but you wonder if there's blood in her veins."

Abbie giggled.

"The one ta keep yer eye on is that Mr. Stevens."

"Kendal? Why?"

"Cain't say exactly. Somethin' in the eyes."

"Oh, Cole."

"You mark my words. I been around enough ta know. And if you was my wife, I'd keep you clear of him."

A rustle behind her brought Abbie around. Her heart sank. Frances certainly picked her times. "Come in, Frances. I hope you're feeling better?"

"I wondered if we could go into town tomorrow. I want to purchase some things for Jeanette."

"As long as we take an escort, I don't think Monte would mind."

"Good. Well, don't let me detain you." Frances's skirt swirled behind as she left.

Abbie released her breath. She caught Cole's glance.

"I shouldn't've said any of that. Look, Abbie, I gotta git outta here. It's addlin' my wits sittin' around all day. Run down the bunkhouse and get Breck to gimme me a hand, will you?"

"Tonight?"

"The sooner, the better."

Thirteen

Abbie sat up in bed, chest heaving, cheeks wet. Would she never be free of it? The face, the groping hands . . . the screams. If only Monte were there. No. Even if he were, she would be alone. There was only One who was with her always, who knew her innermost thoughts. But she couldn't hear Him anymore.

She slipped out from under the covers. The floor was cold, and she quickly dressed without a corset or bustle. Zena was sleeping, and Abbie wouldn't wake her. She pulled the smart woolen coat over her skirt and shirtwaist, then crept down the stairs.

Matt Weston slept in the alcove off the entry. She crept past him, slowly cracked the door open, and stepped outside into the dark morning. She made her way to the stable. Lady Belle nickered softly, but no sound came from Will's room.

She saddled the mare and led her outside. Enough light shone to guide her way, and its intensity grew with the coming dawn. She crossed the flat grassland with nothing to block the fiery sliver of sun that crested the horizon. She raised an elbow against it but kept on.

The small group of buildings and trees rose up like an oasis before her. She stopped in the mission yard, left Lady Belle at the trough, and slipped like a shadow into the chapel. The brothers had finished the morning Mass, and the chapel was empty. She crept forward and dropped to her knees before the altar.

Candles flickered, sending dancing shadows into the alcove above. She raised her eyes to the wooden crucifix, fixed them on the gaping wound in the side of the Christ. Her mind flashed to the blood-caked torso of the boy. She had put the hole there even as her sin had opened the side of Jesus.

"Oh, God. Sweet Jesus, help me." Her hands trembled. "What was I to do?" She dropped her face and sobbed. Her knees hurt from the stone floor, but she remained, unmoving, draped over the rail. The silence settled upon her.

At the hand laid gently on her head, Abbie looked up to Father Dominic.

"You are in torment, little sister."

"I can never undo what I've done."

"None can." He looked up to the cross above them. "But there is where your sin is hung. There upon the body of our Lord."

"But I've taken a life. The life of a boy not yet a man."

"I have heard."

"I thought it was right to go out there and stand by my husband. I thought..." She shook her head, tears starting again in her eyes.

"We can only seek God's way and trust Him to make right our failures."

Abbie's head spun. How could even God make it right?

"Do you seek absolution for your sin?"

She nodded. She spoke the words of contrition and signed herself with the cross. Father Dominic raised his hand in benediction. "*Indulgéntiam, absolutiónem, et remissiónem...*"

Abbie felt Father Dominic's presence, but it was the touch of God she needed. As the priest spoke, she opened her heart and welcomed the sweet presence, more real than living flesh. God's peace and forgiveness washed over her.

"... *et miséricors Dominus. Amen.*" Father Dominic signed the cross over her, then folded his long hands. "Look to the living and go in peace."

The sun was white in the clear, frigid sky, but Abbie's back was to it as she rode home. She felt charged with new purpose, fresh and vibrantly alive. God was no longer silent but walked with her ... amazing as that was.

Will came out of the stable. "I thought I'd catch it good. Next time you swipe a horse, wake me."

Abbie almost laughed, it felt so good to be treated like a real person. "I'm sorry. I'll unsaddle her."

"No need." He led the mare inside and loosened the cinch. He looked like a scarecrow in his outgrown clothes. He must have shot up three inches this last year. Who looked out for him?

Abbie followed him in. "How old are you, Will?"

"Thirteen. Fourteen in January."

"Why aren't you in school?"

"Got a job to do." He hoisted the saddle onto the rail.

Abbie rested her elbows on the top of the stall. "How long have you worked for my husband?"

"Since I was seven. I started muckin' stalls under his groom in South Carolina. He died, so I lucked into the job." He took out the bit and removed the bridle.

"But have you never been to school, then?"

"Sure I have. I went a whole year once. I like this better."

"Can you read and write, do numbers?"

"Don't need to." He rested one hand on the horse's back and looked at her.

Abbie wasn't sure she had ever seen his face straight on. But now he held her gaze defiantly.

"My pa was shot in a brawl, and my ma sells herself for money. When Mr. Farrel gave me a room in the stable, it was the nicest place I ever lived. I don't need more than that."

His young face was fierce, daring her to jeer or maybe to show pity. She did neither. "Would you like to learn?"

He stared at her. "I got a job that needs doing."

"I just thought..." Abbie rubbed the rail. "Maybe I could teach you. I worked with the children at the mission a long time, and I'm a good teacher."

He took the cloth and rubbed the horse down. "I'll think about it."

She watched him still. He was large for his age, with the kind of looks the eye passed over without a second thought. Nothing to set him apart, and yet ... she couldn't walk away. "That boy was not much older than you." Her voice was hoarse.

Will glanced up, tossing the straight, mousy hair back from his eyes. "He deserved what he got, if that's what's on your mind. Just like my pa . . . he deserved what he got."

◆◆◆◆◆◆◆

In the Charleston assessor's office, Monte frowned. It was worse than he had imagined, and he glanced at Kendal, who sat crumpled in the chair. He wanted to kick him and say, "Sit up and act like a man!" But Kendal's head was again aching from last night's excess, and Monte wondered if the assessor's words were penetrating his fog. Monte heard, though. They would be lucky to return with the clothes on their backs.

When he stepped outside the door, Kendal at last looked up and stared around him. "One minute you have everything, the next it's all gone."

"You should never have gambled like that on a venture so shady and unpredictable. At the very least you should not have risked Frances's holdings, as well."

"I know." Kendal dropped his head. "That's the worst of it, really."

They walked down the cobbled street and turned onto a crushed oyster shell path.

"I don't mind starting over. It's what it will do to Frances that I fear. She despises me for this."

"It was your responsibility to see to her interests."

Kendal glowered. "I don't need you to tell me that," he snapped, then sagged again. "I can't see her living in a cabin on borrowed land. Maybe if she had Abbie's spirit . . ." Shaking his head, he suddenly swore. "If I ever get my hands on those two . . ."

"I doubt you'll ever see them again. And right now our concern is salvaging what we can from the house before it forecloses."

"Monte." Kendal straightened and stopped. "I will make it back. I will keep Frances in the style she desires."

Monte faced him. "How, Kendal? How can you possibly hope to regain what you've lost?"

"I'm moving to the land of opportunity, remember?"

"That requires work. Real work. The kind of work I think you've never done."

"Nor you, and look where you are."

"You're starting from nothing."

Kendal swallowed and grabbed Monte's shoulder. "If you give me something to work with, Monte—something to get me on my feet—I'll multiply it and pay you back in no time."

Monte walked on. "That would require a substantial investment."

"Yes, but I would make it worth your while, pay you interest on the loan . . ."

Monte clenched his fists. The pain countered his temper. "You sound like a snake oil salesman, Kendal. I do not require interest from my brother-in-law. Nor will I hesitate to help in any manner that I can. But I must know that you will not again risk what you have so recklessly. It won't come quickly if you hope to gain your feet for good."

"Of course. But with ingenuity and—"

"Common sense and restraint . . ."

Kendal chuckled. "I'm not a schoolboy."

"I thought different last night."

"I was fortifying myself for today. Now that it's past me, I'll no longer depend on the bottle, no matter how sweetly it beckons."

"I certainly hope you mean that."

Kendal squared his shoulders. "Now, to retrieve my daughter. Mother will be heartbroken, of course, to learn of my intentions. I'll not tell her of the necessity, if you don't mind. It would only cause her to lose sleep."

♦♦♦♦♦♦♦

The mid-November wind smelled of snow, and Abbie looked up at the lowering sky. What was the weather like in Charleston, and what was Monte doing? She ached for him to come home, then quailed at the thought. Would he still be courteous and distant? That was worse than his anger by far.

She pressed the mare with her thighs, then gripped the horn and leaped the fence. She slowly approached the herd. John Mason turned on his mount, straightened up, and pulled off his hat. "Mrs. Farrel."

Abbie smiled. The cowboys were kind in their respect. *Some of them anyway.* Behind him, Cole rode up and tipped his hat back. His injured leg hung slack, but he managed the horse with no difficulty and pulled up next to her. "What's up?"

"I'm not sure about this, Cole, but last night I thought I saw someone sneak around the back of the stable. I started to follow..."

"You what! Doggone it, Abbie..."

She brought her chin up. "I beg your pardon?"

"Don't play mistress of the manor with me. I'll tan yer backside if you try that again, and Mr. Farrel will thank me for it."

John hid his snicker with a cough.

Abbie fumed. "Do you want to hear what I have to say or not?"

"A'right, tell me."

"I went as far as the corner of the stable, and I swear there was someone disappearing through the corral. I *didn't* follow. But I think someone should stay with Will tonight. I don't like him to be alone."

"Yes, ma'am. But we look after young Will just fine."

"Nevertheless..."

"I'll see to it."

"Thank you, Cole." Abbie turned back for home. He was ornerier than a mule with a toothache. And not only Cole. All the men were on edge, and she was certain they were keeping things from her. What was going on? If the rustlers were gone ... but then whom had she seen? She reined in at the stable and dismounted.

Will took the reins from her and hesitated. "Mrs. Farrel ... I've been thinkin' on what you said the other day. Do you think I could learn a little and still keep up in the stables?"

"I'm sure you could. If you'd keep my secret, I'd love to curry the horses myself. We could make it a trade."

He grinned. "You're sure a lot different than I thought you'd be."

She laughed. "You're not the first to think that. Shall we start today?"

"Yeah."

"Put an *s* on the end."

"Yes . . . ma'am."

She went to the house and found her primer, tucked it under her arm, and returned to the stable. "Let's sit outside in the light."

Will sat down beside her, back to the wall. "I know my letters some."

"Good. Show me what you know, and we'll go from there."

Nearly an hour later Abbie sank back against the stable wall, laughing so hard that tears came to her eyes. "I'm sorry, Will. But you see why it's important to pronounce things correctly if you want it to mean what you thought."

Will shrugged, still grinning. "I wish you'd been my teacher from the start. Maybe I'd've stayed in school."

Abbie smiled. "Thank you, Will."

He glanced up. "Guess I'd better get back to work."

"I'll help."

"There's no need."

"I miss caring for the animals. How will I get to know Zephyr if I never touch her?"

"Suit yourself, then."

Fourteen

Snow blew through a knothole in the stable wall, and Cole turned and stuffed a rag into the gap, then settled back down in the hay and pulled the blanket close. Will's breathing from the room at the back was heavy. Cole rubbed his thigh. The wound was aching from the cold. The small stove that warmed the boy did little out here.

Grunting, he tucked his arms under his head. The soft grating of the door latch brought him up suddenly, and he peered through the darkness. The door cracked, and Cole slid his pistol from its holster. Snow swirled in as the door widened. "Hold it right there."

The figure bolted back out into the night, slamming the door against the wall. Swearing, Cole staggered to his feet and lumbered across the distance. Empty, swirling darkness filled the yard. Sliding the gun home, he limped back in and smacked his palm on the post. "Doggone it!" The horse tossed its head.

Will called out. "Cole?"

"Go back to sleep. Excitement's over." He frowned, then rolled and lit a cigarette. He should have been on his feet. What kind of fool sets an ambush lying down? Well, he'd be ready next time. He blew the smoke and wished he had a whiskey to go with it.

When the sun shone pale into the stable, Cole stood. He brushed the hay from his clothes, strode out to the yard, and washed at the pump. His breath came white as the thin covering on the ground. He shook the water from his hair, then mounted the steps to the house. James admitted him to the library.

Abbie sat penning a letter. She looked fresh and cheerful like he hadn't seen for a while. Not since her wedding, since before the shooting. Maybe she was getting over that business at last.

She looked up. "Cole, you look positively frozen. James, bring coffee, please." She motioned him to stand by the fire.

"You were right, Abbie. There was someone out there last night." He hated to see her smile fade.

"Who do you think?"

"I dunno. He scampered away 'fore I was even on my feet."

She stood and walked to the window. Her voice was small. "Could it be the rustler that got away?"

Had she read his thoughts? Or maybe they just thought alike. "Could be anyone. If he's back tonight, we'll know."

She turned back to him. "Please don't do it alone, Cole."

"I ain't stupid, and I know my limits. Till this leg heals I ain't exactly lightnin' on my feet." He took the coffee James brought and drank. The heat felt good in his belly.

She folded her hands. "I'm taking Frances for tea at Clara's today. Would you escort us to town? Frances is ... concerned about traveling alone."

"Don't she know yet how you can shoot?"

"That's probably what she's worried about—whether her reputation can stand being seen alone with me."

"She don't know what an honor it is."

Abbie smiled. "Thank you, Cole. You always did pay a pretty compliment."

He smacked his hat. "Not that it did me no good. Anyhow, don't you worry none. We'll get this feller and make things safe again."

"Monte is lucky to have you."

"Not near so lucky as to have you." Cole's mouth twisted wryly. "I'm awful useful, but you're a good sight purtier. And don't bother blushin' cuz you know it, too. What time're you needin' my service?"

She raised her chin. "Maybe I'll take Breck. You're too ornery."

"Comes from bein' up most of the night. Now if you'll tell me what time you want to go, I can git some sleep first."

"One o'clock."

Cole replaced his hat and left. *Dang, she is purty with her hackles up.*

◆◆◆◆◆◆◆

Frances was elegance itself as she descended the stairs in tiered layers of white crepe, and Abbie stared. "Frances, that's the prettiest dress I've ever seen!"

"It's just an afternoon gown. But it is rather nice."

"You look just like the miniature of your mother."

Frances stopped. "Do you think so?"

"I do. I've always thought Monte favored her, but you ... you could be the woman in the picture."

Frances swept past her into the parlor and looked at the portrait in its silver frame. Her voice was soft. "I was so young when she died I don't remember her at all. But I wanted to grow up just like her. Everyone spoke of her beauty and charm ... usually when I had been less than charming." She cast a slight smile Abbie's way. "I don't believe you would flatter me falsely."

"I wouldn't."

"Then you've paid me the highest compliment."

"I only say what's true."

"That's why Monte loves you." Frances turned away. "He never could stand anything less than the absolute truth." She lifted down the portrait. "Do you know why he married Sharlyn?"

"No."

"I only learned it myself after she died, when Monte came to stay."

Abbie did not press her to tell. She felt a faint disquiet at having Monte's secret opened.

"Her father asked it of him on his deathbed."

"Why?"

"She was entangled in a romance with a man who meant to ruin her family. Monte had given his pledge to marry her when Father went to war, but he never expected it to be called on."

Abbie felt weak. So that was it. What a terrible thing for Monte—torn between a need thrust upon him and the need of his own heart. She pictured Sharlyn, so outwardly frail, yet noble and brave. Would she have been that way had the destructive romance ensnared her?

How like Monte to accept the duty no matter the personal cost. And he had done his best by Sharlyn, though Abbie had resented him for it. How badly she had treated him, how cruelly she had misjudged him. *A matter of honor.* He had tried to make her understand without revealing anything that would dishonor Sharlyn. Her chest tightened.

Frances's eyes glittered. "He kept his pledge . . . but he loved you, didn't he?"

Abbie forced her voice to stay calm. "He was very good to Sharlyn. She was happy."

Frances raised an eyebrow. "I never questioned that. I know my brother. But how that must have tortured him." She replaced the portrait. "My husband . . . has no such scruples."

"Oh, surely . . ."

"You're very naïve. At first I thought you were intentionally enticing him . . . and Monte's foreman, as well. Now I think you don't realize what you do."

Abbie was stunned.

"Well, we should go, shouldn't we? Fetch the foreman."

She wished she'd asked anyone but Cole. How could Frances think . . . and just when she hoped that Frances was opening up to her. How had it twisted again?

Abbie went to the bunkhouse and knocked on the door, but no one answered. She went in. Cole slept, stretched out on his bunk. But for his breathing, the room was silent. She almost turned back, but instead she reached out and touched his shoulder. He sprang up and gripped her wrist. She cried out.

"Shoot, Abbie. Never touch me like that. Feels like someone goin' for my throat."

Abbie's heart pounded. "You scared the wits out of me. I swear you're faster than a rattlesnake."

"Sheez. Next time just kick me." He stood. "Tea time, eh?"

"If you don't mind."

"You're the boss, ain't ya? Leastwise the boss's wife." He snatched up his hat. "You know what I cain't figure? What in God's name I'm still doin' here."

Abbie stiffened.

"I mean it's pure torture every time you sweep by, yer skirts swirlin' just so, and you smellin' so sweet."

"Cole . . ."

"But hang it all, I cain't make m'self leave. Maybe I ain't sure Farrel can take care of you. Maybe I'm just plain stupid."

Abbie spun, but Cole caught her back.

"I'm sorry." He spoke hoarsely. "I always wake up meaner'n a bear in spring. Doggone . . . Abbie, don't cry. I feel so low."

"I didn't mean for . . ."

"'Course you didn't. It's my own durn fault. Just ferget I said any of that."

Abbie blinked back the tears. "Cole, I . . ."

"Don't say nothin', Abbie. Get yer sweet sister-in-law, and we'll go."

Abbie hurried out. Oh, how could things be worse? Was Frances right? Was it something she did without even knowing?

Frances stood at the door wrapped in her fur-lined cape.

Abbie couldn't look at her. "Cole is bringing the buggy."

He came out of the stable in his sheepskin coat and Stetson. Abbie was sure his bow-legged swagger was exaggerated.

"He is handsome. Did he really propose marriage to you?"

"Yes."

"Does Monte know?"

"Of course."

Cole stopped the buggy and handed them in. He gave Abbie the reins. "I'll ride alongside."

Frances stared at the wet, brown countryside left behind by the melted snow. "I can't believe Maimie liked this dreary place. The sight alone could cause consumption."

"Consumption is healed by this climate. And it's the most beautiful place in the world."

"How would you know?"

Abbie smiled. "Maybe I wouldn't. But no place else matters. This is my home and Monte's. I'll make him happy here."

Frances turned away. "Then I suggest you stay away from Kendal."

Abbie sucked in her breath. "You're wrong, Frances. Kendal loves you. He . . ." She fell silent. What did she know?

Cole pulled his horse even. "Looks like we might get some weather. Don't you ladies dawdle over tea."

Abbie glanced toward the mountains. Already the clouds poured over the summits. "Fetch us from Clara's at three, will you?"

"Yup." Cole circled his horse around the buggy, then rode on up ahead.

"He's devoted, isn't he?"

Abbie refused to answer.

Frances snickered. "At least I won't die of ennui. There's certainly enough intrigue."

Abbie clenched the reins. "There's no intrigue, Frances."

"I don't doubt your fidelity. You're quite simple in devotion to my brother."

"Then leave it alone."

Frances waved her hand. "Fine. You're the lady of the house. I'm simply the poor relation."

Abbie forced her voice to steady. "You are my sister. Nothing more and nothing less, though . . . I hope in time you will also be my friend."

Frances said nothing, and Abbie hid her disappointment. She could have laughed aloud when Clara pulled the door open. Hers was the face of a friend, a true friend who didn't judge or demean her. Abbie wished terribly she had come alone.

Clara bustled them in. "When I saw the clouds I was afraid you wouldn't come. And I have the most delicious scandal to share."

"What are you talking about?"

Clara took their wraps. "Come and sit. Oh, Frances, your dress is marvelous. Tea or coffee?"

"Tea." Frances draped her skirts perfectly about her on the settee, and Clara joined her.

Abbie sat across from them. "So tell."

"You recall the new schoolmarm, Miss Plochman? And how her contract states that no male callers are allowed for the duration of this term and any terms thereafter?"

"Clara, don't tell me she received a caller and it's now considered a scandal."

Clara poured the hot tea into their cups. "Well, you decide for yourself. It would seem Miss Plochman had no intention of rebuffing any male overtures that came her way. Secretly, she's entertained at least seven men in the three months she's been here." Clara handed Frances the sugar bowl.

Abbie shrugged. "I imagine she was beset. Any halfway acceptable female is hard put to ward off the overtures, and she's quite attractive."

"Well, that's not all. This morning when the children showed up for class, there was no Miss Plochman."

"What do you mean?"

"The word is Mitchell Pike crept up to her room at the boarding house and carried her off."

"No."

"They've gone to get married." Clara giggled.

"That's dreadful," Frances said.

"So now the town has no schoolteacher, and it's too late to try the other applicants." Clara looked pointedly at Abbie.

Abbie sipped her tea. Well. She'd even started with Will, and she dreadfully missed working with the children at the mission.

Clara spread her hands. "Someone has to teach the children until they can find a replacement. We can't let them fall behind."

Frances turned to Abbie. "You're not considering . . ."

"Why not? Clara and Melissa have little babies at home. Neither Mary Beth Walker nor Becky Linde are qualified, and Marcy

Wilson would never accept the responsibility. . . ."

"Nor can you! Monte wouldn't hear of it."

"Why on earth not?"

Frances's lips tightened. "You are his wife."

"Under the circumstances, I can't see that he would mind."

"It's not proper for you to take employment."

"It wouldn't be employment. I'd volunteer my services. It's my civic duty." Abbie set her cup and saucer down. "Do you think I'd find Mr. Lowe at the store?"

"I've no doubt." Clara smiled.

Abbie wrapped herself in her cape. "I won't be long." She ignored the protests of her sister-in-law and stepped out into the wind. Here was an opportunity handed her, a God-given chance to serve, and she would not miss it because Frances was too prissy to consider both sides.

Oh, she'd have plenty to say on it, Abbie was sure, but it didn't matter. She'd made up her mind. She hurried to the saddlery. "Good afternoon, Mr. Lowe." The wind banged the door shut behind her.

He rubbed his hands on his vest. "Mrs. Farrel."

"I hear you have need of a temporary schoolteacher."

"That's how it looks."

"I'd like to offer my services to the board."

He set down the saddle he was rubbing. "That right?"

"I'm not officially certified, but my husband is back East for a bit, and I'd be happy to teach the children until a replacement can be found."

"We know how qualified you are, Mrs. Farrel, but I don't know if the board will hire . . ."

"I'm not looking for hire. I'm volunteering."

He rubbed his cheek. "Well, then. I'll bring it to the board members tonight."

"I'll wait to hear."

She had just made Clara's door when Cole rode up. "I know it's early, Abbie, but the wind's whippin' up. I don't think the weather's gonna hold."

"All right. Let me get Frances."

Abbie squeezed Clara's hand. "I'm sorry to run, but the storm's moving in. I'll likely see you soon." She gave her the slightest wink.

Thank goodness the wind made conversation difficult as they rode back.

◆◆◆◆◆◆◆

Mr. Lowe came himself two days later. "You're being hailed as a heroine by the parents."

Abbie offered him a cup of hot coffee. "I'm happy to serve."

"I'm a little concerned about your distance from town. It was a good forty minutes out here today."

"I'm used to the drive."

"I was thinking more of your safety. Suppose we say if it's bad you don't come in."

"I think that's wise."

He smiled. "My son's looking forward to your teaching."

"Thank you."

"The job you did with the foundlings was remarkable."

Abbie frowned. "It was the children who were remarkable. I hope the town children can do as well."

"Er . . . yes, I'm sure." Mr. Lowe took up his hat. "Well, then. You'll start tomorrow? Weather permitting?"

"Tomorrow."

◆◆◆◆◆◆◆

"I won't have it." Cole stood, legs spread in the stable door. "Mr. Farrel said for you to stay put."

Abbie bristled. "Cole, I'm not sixteen. I'll thank you not to use that tone with me."

"Like it or not, your husband charged me with yer care, and you ain't makin' this easy."

"I didn't ask anything of you. I merely informed you that—"

"And I won't have it."

Abbie pulled herself to her full height. "Well, it's not up to

you. Please step aside so I can get my horse and be on my way."
Didn't he realize she had to do this? Not only could she not bear
to be cooped up another day, but she had to serve—whenever the
opportunity arose. It was the only way she could live with herself.

"Maybe ya haven't noticed it's snowin'."

"I've noticed. It won't amount to much. It's more a blow and
bother."

Will led Lady Belle out to her.

"Thank you, Will." Abbie took the reins and mounted.

"I don't suppose you've given thought to this horse standin'
in the weather while you're teachin'?"

"I'm putting her in Marty Franklin's stable."

Cole frowned. "Sheez. If you're stubborn on this, I'll see ya in."

"I can find my own way to town, thank you. I've lived here
longer than you."

"That ain't the concern." He said nothing more as they rode
into sight of town. Then Cole reined in, and let her proceed alone.
She could tell he was anxious to get back. Everyone was anxious.
She shook her head and urged Lady Belle to a canter.

By the time she reached Marty's stable, the snow had stopped
completely. But with the school at the end of town, the children
were all waiting outside by the time she arrived.

"I'm sorry I'm late," Abbie said to the children. "I hadn't
counted on the time it would take to stable the horse and walk
here. Tomorrow I'll start earlier." She opened the door and waited
as they filed past. Parker Bates went to the front and lit the fire
in the stove, then ambled to his seat in the back.

Eight little faces and two nearly manly ones looked at her cu-
riously. She knew them all, but the relationship was different
now. One of the older boys smirked and whispered to Parker.
"Would you share that with the class, Todd Loewe?"

Todd dropped his face and mumbled.

"I don't believe the class heard you. Could you stand and repeat it?"

Todd stood and towered over Abbie, his fourteen-year-old

frame already a match to his father's in height. "I said we're havin' the foundling teacher now."

"Thank you, Todd Loewe. You may sit." Abbie walked forward. "Now, class, who can tell me the correct word for foundling?"

Mary Driscoll raised her small hand. "Orphan, ma'am."

"That's right. Though some people consider orphans an object of sport and ridicule, I'd like to remind each of you that only by God's grace are you not in that position. I pray He will give you compassion for those less fortunate. Now, primer class please open your books and print your letters. . . ."

The day grew dimmer rather than brightening. Abbie hardly noticed, so full was her time. She loved instructing them, listening to them read and recite. All that was missing were the faces of the mission children that she knew and loved so well. She had not been to teach them since before her wedding. Things had become so complicated.

She checked the time on Monte's pocket watch and stood. "You're dismissed. I'll see you all tomorrow." She followed them to the back and helped bundle the little ones. Only a thin layer of snow covered the ground, but it was enough to make tracks, and she smiled when they gleefully did so.

Abbie hurried down the street. The wind was cruel, though dry so far. She saddled Lady Belle, her eyes tearing as she rode. Maybe she should have listened to Cole, but the thought of spending the day with Frances haranguing her . . .

She saw Cole riding in and straightened in the saddle. "Business in town, Cole?"

"You know my business."

"Honestly." He was keeping Monte's orders to the letter, as far as he was able. Had Monte reinforced the need? Were things worse than even she knew? Cole turned about and rode at her side. They were halfway home when another horse cantered toward them.

Abbie shielded her eyes and made out the fourteen-year-old orphan from the mission. "Why, that's Silas." She urged Lady Belle. "Silas, what is it?"

"Miss Abbie . . . I mean, Mrs. Farrel. It's Father Dominic. He's . . . he's passed on."

Abbie clutched the saddle horn, and Cole reached for her elbow.

"When?"

"This morning, but . . . it's been coming. And . . . well, Brother Thomas says the brothers have been called back to their order in the East and could you come talk to him."

"*Look to the living*," Father Dominic had said and given her hope. Had he known? Was it near even then? Cole's grip tightened on her elbow. She shook herself.

"Yes, of course I'll come."

Cole held fast. "No, you—"

"Cole, those children need me. Go back and tell Frances where I've gone."

"The heck I will."

"Come, Silas." Abbie turned the mare.

"Mrs. Farrel, yer a regular thorn in my side." Cole drew up with them. "But I reckon the snow might hold off awhile yet."

The children were more solemn than she could have imagined. Poor things. Not only did they have the loss of Father Dominic, but if the other brothers were leaving . . . what would become of them? Abbie didn't want to think how things would change without the mission, but right now her job was to comfort. She opened her arms and they came to her.

They took some small solace in each other before she went to see Brother Thomas. They had laid Father Dominic in the ground behind the trees. Abbie was glad she had not viewed him. Too many dead faces filled her memory, and she chose to remember him as she had seen him last. "*Go in peace*."

Yes. And he, too, had gone in peace. She returned her thoughts to Brother Thomas and realized with a start what he was saying to her.

"They haven't another to send, and we can't remain here without a priest. The children could come with us. The bishop expects it, but you don't know what things are like in the cities. The sisters do their best, but the homes are filled to overflowing. That's why I hoped you . . ."

He had more confidence in her than Abbie could muster. How could she possibly arrange for eighteen children? Where would she find homes and families? They were already scorned and avoided. Dear heavenly Father, she was only one person.

See to the living.

Yes, but she was already doing that. Wasn't she teaching Will and the town children?

Feed my sheep.

Yes, she could provide shelter and food for some short time, but . . .

Look to the living.

She raised her head. "Yes, Brother Thomas. When you go, the children may stay with me until I can find another way."

"Thank you, sister. You ease my heart."

Abbie stood and walked out. Cole did not say a word on the ride home.

Fifteen

Monte woke at the sound of the brakes and looked out the steam-clouded window. Kendal still slept with Jeanette beside him, and across from them her mammy. It seemed she had only just stopped the child's crying. Rubbing a hand through his hair, he leaned forward and touched Kendal's shoulder. "Denver."

Kendal worked at the crick in his neck. "Where are we putting up tonight?"

"Hightower Inn. We'll get a late supper and start by stage in the morning."

Kendal nudged Mammy, and she lifted Jeanette. He turned as Monte reached overhead for their bags. "Can you manage?"

Monte gripped the handles. "Yes."

The hotel glittered. But what mattered more was that it had two rooms available, one for Mammy and the child, one for Kendal and himself. Top-end rooms, naturally. Monte paid. "Go on up. I'll see about having supper sent."

Kendal lingered. "Couple of fancies there." He nodded toward the ladies on the couch in the corner. "But then you're not in the market, are you?"

"Nor are you," Monte answered without turning.

"Did I tell you Frances locked me out the night before we left?"

Monte turned the bags over to the bellhop and told him where to find the trunks. "You'll be back soon enough."

"You think that'll matter?"

"Kendal, I'm tired and I'm hungry. Take Jeanette up and forget those two in the corner."

◆◆◆◆◆◆◆

Abbie bundled into her coat in the dark. It was long before dawn, but she could not sleep thinking of the men huddled in the stable. It was too cold for a night-long vigil. She lifted the pot of coffee and slipped past John Mason sleeping in the alcove. She made her way through the flurries to the stable. "Don't anyone shoot." She said it just loudly enough for them, then pulled open the door and stepped in.

Cole, Breck, and Skeeter slouched in the back of the stable. "I brought you some coffee."

Breck blew on his hands. "Must be an angel from heaven."

Cole glared as Abbie went forward, set the pot on the ground, and pulled the cups from her cape pockets. The steam rose up when Breck poured.

Cole shook his head. "Guess I gotta escort you back and spoil whatever surprise we had." He started to rise.

Abbie pushed him back down. "I don't need an escort."

"Sure wish you'd stop meddlin'."

"Quit yer complainin'." Breck elbowed him. "This here coffee's puttin' life back in me. Thank you, ma'am."

Abbie turned and slipped out. She closed the door silently. If that wasn't just like Cole to—She gasped as a hand covered her mouth and a frigid gun barrel touched her throat.

"One sound and you're dead. Understand?"

She nodded. She smelled liquor on his breath, but with the cloud cover and no moon she could see nothing of him. His palm was cracked and rough and he was not much taller than she, but his arm was thick and the gun insistent.

He half led, half dragged her away from the stable to the edge of the corral, then bent her down and ordered her through the fence. Gripping the ice-coated rail, she pulled herself through, and he pressed through with her.

"How many men in the stable?"

"Who are you?"

"I ask the questions." He tightened his grip on her arm and raised the gun to her face. "How many?"

Abbie brought up her chin.

"Look, lady..." He dug his fingers into her arm. "I ain't playin' games."

"I've dealt with worse than you."

He shook her.

She kept silent.

"A'right. You come along with me then. Soon's I have you where you ain't causin' trouble, I'll git back ta business."

"If your business is stealing horses, you ought to ride out right now and forget about it."

"Got a welcomin' committee, eh?" He dragged her on.

"I'm perfectly capable of walking, if you'd stop shoving." Abbie searched the darkness. It was a good while until dawn and the coldest part of the night. She had not dressed for an extended stay. She felt his grip loosen. If she could just...

He pressed the gun to her neck. "This here's the business end, lady. Git movin'."

They kept on. Abbie felt a change in the air, and the darkness thinned almost imperceptibly. At last he stopped. "Thet's far 'nough." He sat her at the base of a ponderosa. She knew where she was. This stand of trees was north of the house and a bit west. He pulled a rope from his coat. "Sit up nice an' straight, now, and I won't hurt ya."

"Yes, I know the rules. Do you plan to leave me here to freeze?"

"You got yerself into it."

He tied the rope around her wrists and pulled it tight, then lashed her to the tree. "Why are you doing this? What can you possibly gain?"

"Thet's my business."

"There's honest labor to be found. No one has to steal."

"Ain't nothin' to do with stealin'."

"What then?"

"Avengin'."

"Avenging what?"

"None o' yer business. Now listen, missie, I don't mean ta hurt ya, but if you cause me any trouble, I'll kill ya, got it?"

"Exactly what trouble could I cause tied to a tree?"

"Only the kind I mean to take care of now." He stuffed a rag into her mouth, and she gagged as he tied it. He walked away.

Furiously she pulled against her bonds, but they held fast as she knew they would. She leaned her head back against the tree. *Lord, please . . . help Cole.*

◆◆◆◆◆◆◆

The first paling of the dawn filtered into the stable as Cole rolled a cigarette.

"Farrel would have yer hide if he saw you smokin' in here," Skeeter said.

"Mind yer own business."

"Sure was nice o' Mrs. Farrel ta bring the coffee."

"Durn foolish is what it was."

Skeeter shrugged. "Guess I'm just more appreciative than you."

"Guess you're just stupider. I oughta thrash Mason for letting her slip out when we're waitin' to catch us a horse thief. I don't reckon we'll see hide nor hair of 'im now."

"That's just as good, ain't it? I mean . . ."

"You don't know what ya mean."

"You're awful cranky."

"And don't you ferget it." Cole ground the cigarette butt out with the heel of his boot. He stood and stretched. "I'm gonna have a look around 'fore we call it a night."

He pulled open the door and stepped out. All was quiet. The main house was dark. Abbie must be back in bed. The bunkhouse, the yard . . . he caught the motion only a moment before the handle of the gun crashed against his skull.

He collapsed with a groan. As his own gun was pulled from his hand, a voice rasped in his ear. "Which one o' yer men killed my brother?"

"What're you talkin' 'bout?" Cole gripped his head, felt the lump, and played stupid. The man's breath was foul with liquor. The hammer clicked against his temple. Not enough liquor.

"I know it wasn't you, cuz you was shot. Who was it?"

Cole took a kick in the ribs.

"Who shot the kid?"

So that was it. The boot caught his belly, and he tensed too late. The pain took his breath. The stable door burst open. Skeeter kicked the gun from the man's hand and swung a punch that doubled him.

Breck ran past, grabbed the gun, and spun. "A'right, hold it." He planted his feet and braced his arms. "You okay, Cole?"

Cole rolled to his knees and stood slowly. "Tie 'im up in the bunkhouse."

"You're makin' a big mistake."

"That right?" Cole rubbed his ribs. "Maybe we should just shoot ya."

The man chuckled. "Ya could. But then ya'd never find the young lady till she was good an' froze."

Cole stiffened, then gripped the collar of the man's coat. "What young lady?" he asked, as if he didn't know. "You got one minute ta tell me where she is 'fore I throttle you with my bare hands."

"You ain't gonna kill me. Only I know where I left 'er."

"Start walkin'."

"No, sir."

"You don't value yer life too good." Cole lifted him from the ground by his coat.

"You . . . don't . . . value hers."

Cole's chest heaved. He could tear this man apart. He could . . . The cold cut to the back of his neck. They'd find Abbie. But if they didn't . . . He released him. "Wha'd'ya want?"

"The girl fer the man who killed Spence."

"You're crazy."

"Templeton Gap. You got till daybreak. Send 'im unarmed."

"What about the girl?"

"You'll git 'er home alive. It ain't her I want."

Cole kept his face blank. "A'right, git out o' here."

The man went to the edge of the corral and mounted a horse tethered behind the oaks. "Don't follow, or she'll freeze long before we're anywhere near."

Cole clenched his hands and watched until the rider disappeared.

"Guess we're in it now," Breck said low.

Skeeter picked up his hat. "What're we gonna do?"

Cole glanced at him. "I dunno ... yet. First make sure he's really got her." He strode to the house and banged on the knocker to raise the dead, then opened it himself. She hadn't locked it behind her if she went back inside. James hurried forward in his nightclothes.

Cole shoved past, walked to the alcove, and kicked John Mason awake. Then without a word, he took the stairs two at a time to the bedroom. He banged the door.

"What you doin', Mistuh Jazzper? You can't wake the Missus like that."

Cole grabbed the knob and pushed the door open. The bed was empty. He leaned on the jamb and swore.

White-faced, Frances cracked open her door.

"Git yer head back in and keep it there."

She shoved the door closed, and Cole strode down the stairs and back out to the yard where Breck waited.

"Do we search?"

"And git Mrs. Farrel killed?"

"What else can we do?"

"What he said."

Breck stared. "What're you talkin' about? He's got the one who killed his brother."

"He don't know that."

"But who's gonna go?"

"I am."

"He knows it wasn't you. You was shot."

"He won't know it's me. Most likely he'll shoot before he looks close. I'm gonna have me a shave an' git me some bootblack."

"Are you crazy, Cole? You'll git yerself killed!"

"Maybe. Maybe not. Either way he'll let Abbie go."

Breck blocked him. "You're takin' that chance fer Farrel's wife?"

Cole shoved him aside and went to the bunkhouse. Inside, he clipped then shaved his mustache. He hadn't taken that off since he had whiskers enough to grow it. He shaved the rest of his face. "May as well make a job of it, save the undertaker the trouble." He grinned at Skeeter's solemn eyes.

Breck handed him the bootblack. "You really goin', or you got another plan?"

"Ain't no other plan." He smeared the black over his hair and down his side whiskers. "Purty now, ain't I?" He slopped his hands in the wash tub, then shook them dry. "Guess I'll have me some breakfast." He shook the cook. "Git up, Charlie. I need some grub."

Charlie grunted. "Git it yerself, then."

Grabbing him by the shirt, Cole dumped him out of bed. "Don't make me ask twice."

After eating, Cole saddled a spare horse. He would not take Scotch and risk recognition. "You're in charge, Breck. I don't want no one leavin' the yard, goin' for the marshal, nothin' stupid. And keep a watch on them in the house. No one goes anywhere, got it?"

"Cole . . ."

"I know. I'm a durn fool." He tipped his hat at Breck's salute.

◆◆◆◆◆◆◆

Abbie stiffened at the sound of hooves approaching. Her limbs ached with cold, and the folds of her wrap had stiffened under the frost. The gag in her mouth was soggy and foul. Her jaw hurt. Up over the rise a rider appeared, and seeing him in the dawning light, she started. His thick shape . . . and his face. She'd seen the face too often in her dreams to miss the likeness.

He dismounted and began to work the ropes loose. They had

frozen tight. She moaned against the gag.

"Sorry. Cain't risk any noise now. We're changin' camp."

He did not remove the rope from her wrists, and held the end of it as he raised her to her feet. Her limbs were so stiff she staggered, but he held her up and lifted her onto the horse. Abbie's pulse raced. At last. If she just . . .

He put one foot in the stirrup. Abbie kicked in her heels, and the horse bolted forward. The man sprawled to the ground but held the rope. She was yanked from the saddle and fell squarely. She gasped, fighting for breath through the gag.

In a moment he was on her. He sat her up. "Lost yer wind, thet's all." He pulled her to her feet and her chest heaved with returning breath. "Cain't say as I blame ya fer tryin'. Wouldn't do it agin, though." The horse had stopped some yards away. He shoved her up into the saddle.

She could see the rope coiled around his arm. He was no fool. He had anticipated her. He climbed up behind and urged the horse. The sun crested the horizon to her right, dazzling the frost. She knew this ground. They were heading for Templeton Gap. She began to tremble.

"If you're cold, you'll be home soon. If you're scared, I ain't gonna hurt ya, not unless ya make me."

Abbie closed her eyes as they passed the place she had waited with Monte, then dipped steeply into the gulch. She gripped the saddle horn with her tied hands as they went down, then climbed the far side. This rim had heavier growth, and he pulled the horse into a clump of oaks and slid down.

He lifted her off and untied the gag.

"Why have you taken me? Who are you?"

"It wasn't my first intention, if you recall. But turns out fortunate." He pushed her to sit. "In trade fer you, I git the man who killed my brother."

Abbie's stomach pitched. She had guessed they were kin. They were similar, though this one was a man, a good number of years older than the one she shot.

"He was fifteen years old. Jest a kid."

Abbie closed her eyes. She wished she could stop her ears. Fifteen. The screams, the blood, his young face. "How do you know who killed him?"

"I don't. But yer foreman does. I expect you're the missus?"

Abbie felt his eyes go over her.

His voice changed. "Maybe you know, too? Maybe yer fine husband told ya?"

Her chest seized.

"Don't matter. I don't need a name. After today he's a dead man."

Abbie struggled against the rope. "Will killing him bring your brother back?"

"Eye fer an eye."

He pulled a knife from his pocket and ran it over a twig, curling shavings off like wax. Abbie watched them fall. She thought of Cole's little wooden animals. Where was he? What had happened? How could he agree to a trade? He had no one to trade. Was he getting Marshal Haggerty?

The man scanned the gap. "Sure hope they don't try nothin' stupid."

"Why are you doing this?"

"Got to."

Abbie heard the hooves before he did, but a moment later, he tossed the stick and craned forward. A rider came along the gap, riding the base rather than the ridge. Her chest constricted. Cole. Only he rode like he was attached to the horse with every sinew.

The man pulled his gun and eased back the hammer.

She wanted to scream. Instead she whispered, "If it's an eye for an eye, then I'm the one you want."

"Hush, now," he hissed.

"Killing Cole won't avenge your brother."

"That ain't Cole. He ain't dark like thet fella."

"He knows it was my bullet that killed your brother."

She saw his knuckles whiten on the gun.

"I didn't mean to kill him. It was so dark . . ." Tears started in her eyes. "I didn't know he was just a boy. But . . ."

He spun and gripped her shoulder. "You're lyin'! You think I won't shoot a woman."

Abbie didn't dare look back to Cole. He must be in shooting range now.

"You came onto our land to steal our cattle, and you shot first. I did what I had to do, but if you want vengeance, then I'm the one to kill, as God is my witness."

He stared, his throat working, his breath shallow. He brought the gun to her face, the cold barrel inches from her cheek. His eyes burned. He believed her. "I swore revenge on him . . . when he died in my arms I swore revenge on him."

"Then have it." Abbie felt suddenly peaceful. She would not go to her grave with Cole's death on her soul.

He grabbed her face and pressed the gun to her temple. Her breath stopped. Every moment lingered. Oh, Monte, if only . . .

He groaned and shoved her back. She fell against the branches, her breath rushing in, her mind slowly comprehending. He holstered the gun, looked down at the rider, then once again at her. Then he swore and ran to his horse. He mounted and kicked in his spurs.

Abbie saw Cole stiffen at the sound, but he never looked up. He expected the bullet. The lump in her throat choked her. She made a hoarse croak, scrambled to her feet, and shoved her way through the oaks to the edge of the gap. "Cole!"

He dived from the horse and rolled.

Abbie then slid down the slope, groping with her tied hands. Cole leaped up and ran, grabbed her down, and braced himself over her. He searched the ridge, body tense.

"He's gone." Her voice was hardly a whisper.

Cole did not move. He held her hard to the ground.

"Cole, he's gone." She felt his tension slacken.

He looked at her.

"He left when I . . . told him . . . I killed his brother."

He searched her face. "What'd you do a durn fool thing like that for?"

"He would have killed you in my place."

Cole sat her up roughly. "You had no business doin' that."

The calm she'd felt with the gun to her head deserted her. "Oh, Cole, why did you come?"

"How'd ya know it was me?"

"I know how you sit a horse."

"Sheez." He searched the upper bank again, then slid an arm under her knees and carried her to the horse. She gripped the horn when he hoisted her up and mounted behind. Relief flooded her, and she blinked back the tears. He turned the horse and started back down the gap.

"Cole?"

"Yeah?"

"Would you mind untying my hands?"

"Yeah, I mind. Tied up you just might stay outta trouble. But I ain't countin' on it."

Abbie leaned back against his chest. "Have it your way then."

He reined in, hooked the reins on the saddle horn, and reached for her wrists. He worked the rope free and tossed it down. She bit back a whimper.

He touched the raw mark on her skin. "I'm sorry, Abbie."

She looked up at him. "You have nothing to be sorry for."

"Don't I?"

His voice was hoarse, and she searched his face, a sudden dull ache inside her. Cole loved her. He understood her. He had risked his life for her. Oh, dear Lord . . . had she made a mistake? Did she misunderstand? Did she think Monte . . . Monte. Oh, it hurt. She needed him. She loved him. And he . . . it didn't matter. She loved him with all that was in her.

Even if he despised her, hated her . . . she would love him. She couldn't help it. They were one flesh.

♦♦♦♦♦♦♦

Monte grimaced as he helped Kendal lift the trunks onto the boardwalk.

"I'll get it, Monte," Kendal said.

"I can manage." Monte reached for the handle of the next

trunk. Though it was painful, there was strength in his hands, if not dexterity. "I don't understand why Abbie didn't send a man out with the wagon as I asked. The wire should have reached her in plenty of time this morning."

"We'll hire a hack and send back for the trunks."

Monte nodded, but that did not explain Abbie's failure. He felt a deep disquiet. Was she punishing him for treating her so poorly? He wouldn't blame her if she were. He should never have left without reconciling. Had he not already caused her enough distress for a lifetime?

Kendal returned with the buggy and handed Jeanette into the back with her mammy. He seemed amazingly cheerful. "You're going to see where Uncle Monte lives, chicken. And you're going to see Mama."

Tear streaked and hollow eyed, Jeanette snuggled into her mammy's chest. She looked about the way Monte felt.

Monte climbed into the front as Kendal took the reins. Their breath misted the air as they drove. He glanced back at the child, nestled closely to the woman's chest. They should have a wrap in this cold, but it wasn't far now.

As they crested the rise, he made out the men standing in the yard. "That's odd. Why aren't they at work?"

"When the cat's away . . ."

"Nonsense. Go." He reached over and slapped the reins. This was trouble and he knew it. Breck and Matt Weston flanked the front door like sentries. What on earth . . .

Monte leaped down. "What's going on?"

Breck stepped forward. "Trouble, Mr. Farrel. That third rustler came back lookin' fer revenge. He's . . . got Mrs. Farrel."

Monte froze. His pulse throbbed in his temple. "Where?"

"Templeton Gap. Cole's . . ."

He didn't wait to hear.

"Monte," Kendal called.

"Take care of the women." He bolted for the stable, but stopped midway as Cole rode into the yard with Abbie cradled against him. Monte's throat tightened.

Cole pulled up beside him, slid Abbie down, then rode on. She stood there, less than an arm's length away . . . yet held back. Dear God, what damage had he done? Slowly he reached out, pulled her into his arms, and smelled Cole's tobacco in her hair. He pressed his cheek to her head. "Abbie, what on earth. . . ?"

"Just hold me."

She was cold and warm at once, her cheek where he kissed it like ice, her chest against his warm and throbbing. God help him, he loved her. *Tell her. Show her.*

Breck cleared his throat. "Uh, Mr. Farrel, if you're not needin' us now . . ."

Monte released her. "Tell Cole I'll see him inside." He led Abbie to the house. In the hall he took her wrap and handed it to James. He glanced at Pearl, and she heaved a sigh of relief. He could hear Frances and Kendal in the parlor with Jeanette. From the sound of it, Kendal would not be cheerful long.

He pressed Abbie's hand. "I'll be up shortly."

He went to the study and in a short while heard Cole's knock. Monte eyed him as he removed his hat and ran his hand through his scrubbed hair, still flecked with bootblack. "Well?"

"The last of them rustlers."

"So I heard. Why was Abbie involved?"

"Well, Mr. Farrel, I reckon it's cuz she's Abbie."

Monte listened to him relate the affair. It chilled him to think what might have happened had Cole not done his part. It chilled him more to think what had made Cole willing to do it. "The man is dead?"

"Nope. He high-tailed it before I got in."

"Why?"

"Abbie told him what she done. I reckon he's no lady killer."

Monte winced. Why had he not prevented this? All of it. He turned to the window. "I don't know how to repay you."

"No need."

"I'm in your debt."

"I just done what I could."

"Do you think this is the end of it?"

"I don't rightly know."

Monte stared at the yard, gray and brown like his soul. He had failed her again. He had not protected her. Because of his pride, he had wounded her, abandoned her, and Cole had been there to assuage the hurt. "That will be all."

He climbed the stairs, knocked on the door and opened before she could refuse him. She stood, clutching the dress to her chest. Zena ducked behind her.

"Zena, leave us."

She scurried out, and he closed the door and turned. In three steps he had Abbie in his arms. He found her mouth hungrily and felt her response. "How many times must I face losing you?"

"Oh, Monte . . ."

He lifted her into his arms.

Abbie lay with her head on Monte's chest. Every deep, satisfied breath he took as he slept was balm to her soul. *Lord, you have restored us, beyond my hope united us. Help me to guard this man's honor as my own.* But as she sank to sleep, she could not help but realize he had avoided any mention of the shooting.

Sixteen

Monte's face was stern. "I'm not running an orphanage."

Abbie hushed him. "It's only temporary."

He motioned toward the door. "There are eighteen scruffy children in my foyer."

"Seventeen. Silas took a room at the boardinghouse." She pressed his hand between hers. "Where else can they turn, Monte? I gave Brother Thomas my word."

"To turn my home..."

"Our home. You said as mistress I could do whatever I liked." She rested her hands on his chest.

"That's not fair. And don't use your eyes like that. It's bad enough this ... volunteering in the town school...."

Abbie caught his face in her hands and kissed him. "I know you won't have me turn them out, so stop your blustering. Where shall we put them?"

"I'll build a new wing."

Abbie clicked her tongue. "Monte..."

He released a long breath. "Will the lower guest rooms do?"

"They're used to sharing. Come, I'll introduce you." She tugged him toward the door and caught the knob. "Now, no sour expression."

"You're a minx." He spun her. "And I love you." He kissed her soundly.

Abbie's heart raced. Would she ever have enough of his love?

"Felicity Fenham, Jeremy Smith, Emmy and Pauline Barret..." She watched Monte bow over each little hand. How cordially he smiled, no hint of his disapproval. Oh, she could hug him herself. "And this is Tucker Finn. He'll have a birthday soon and be six years old."

Monte shook his hand. "How do you do, sir."

"Fine, thank you, sir." Tucker's eyes were sober until Monte ruffled his hair. Tucker displayed the gap in his teeth, and Monte's grin almost matched.

Abbie beamed. "And now, children, I'll show you to your rooms."

She led Tucker by the hand with the others trailing. It shamed her to see the awe in their eyes as they passed through the house. What on earth would she do? Could she find homes, families for them? The townspeople had rejected them once. Would they again?

Mama and Pa would help. Yes. She'd ride to Mama tomorrow. No, she'd be teaching school tomorrow. Well, she'd take them all with her. Thank goodness the brothers had left the wagons with her, as well.

✦✦✦✦✦✦✦

Monte waited outside the door. When it opened he removed his Panama straw hat. "Reverend Shields."

"Mr. Farrel. Come in."

He stepped into the double-roomed house and took a cursory glance. The minister was not as fastidious as he'd imagined.

"This is a pleasant surprise. I've not seen you at services, I don't believe."

Monte turned. "No ... well, my wife is Roman Catholic, you recall. She attends—or did attend—service at the mission."

"A sad business that. The priest dying, I mean, and the others pulling out. But you don't mention your attendance."

Monte half smiled. Was he going to be sermonized? "Ah well, I've made acquaintance with the Lord, but it's a private one."

"A private acquaintance is a doubtful one. Won't you sit?"

Monte took the wooden chair by the wall.

"Coffee?"

"No, thank you."

Reverend Shields sat on the edge of the cot. He had nervous hands, Monte noticed.

"Actually, it's the mission that brings me here."

"If you have questions of conversion . . ."

"No, no. It's about the children."

"Ah yes. The orphans." The minister brushed a hand through his thin blond hair. For all his youth, the good reverend would be bald soon. "I heard they were lodged with you."

"Yes, temporarily. But . . . I was hoping you would help find a solution. Surely there are families . . ."

"It's been tried. Did you not hear the difficulties of my predecessor?"

"Yes, I know. But there must be something."

Reverend Shields stood and walked to the small window. "Every human life is precious, we know. But the sad truth is, not every life is wanted. These poor souls have been cast on the mercy of men who lived . . . a foreign, if holy, life. People don't like what they don't know."

"That's outrageous. They're perfectly normal children." Especially in noise level and food consumption. "Why should not the families here. . . ."

"Are you adopting?"

Monte paused. The minister was clever, for all his washed-out bashfulness. He had caught him squarely. "I've only just married. I would expect with the natural course of things, we'll have children of our own."

Reverend Shields spread his hands. "Everyone has circumstances."

Who was this pup to tell him that? Monte felt a nudge inside. "Very well, I see your point. Is there no assistance you can offer?" He stood.

"I'll see what I can do." The reverend grasped his hand. It wasn't the limp clutch he expected. "And it would be a pleasure to see you and your wife in church on Sundays."

Monte straightened. "Well, there wouldn't be room for her entourage."

The reverend smiled. It was amazingly boyish. "You'd be surprised how tightly we can pack."

Monte left him still smiling. That had not gone as he had hoped. He took the ride home slowly. It was heavenly solitude. Between Jeanette crying, Frances weeping, and seventeen extra mouths and pairs of feet, there was precious little peace at home. If not for Abbie, he would . . .

He sighed. He would watch what he promised hereafter. The day was warm for December, but still a chill breeze caught his collar. He turned it up. Sirocco fought the bit. He wanted to run.

Monte looked at the reins wrapped on his wrist. No more of that. He uncoiled the rein, tightened his hand in the black leather glove, and gave the horse his head.

✦✦✦✦✦✦✦

Abbie clapped her hands together. "You must have gone high to find a fir."

Kendal and James dragged in the tree. "Monte would settle for nothing less than perfection."

Monte laughed. "I was under orders. Call for cider, Abbie."

Abbie tugged the bellpull. "Isn't it funny to have a tree in the house, Jeanette?"

The child gripped her mother's fine chintz dress. Frances bent and extricated the fabric. Kendal had brought every one of Frances's fine gowns back with him. A peace offering, though it didn't seem to appease her.

She smoothed the skirt. "Come, Jeanette. Time for your nap."

Abbie wished Frances wouldn't whisk her off every time she paid her any attention. She was sure the child would feel more at home if they could all reach out to her. And heaven forbid she should play with the orphans. White trash, Frances had called them. White trash! Abbie still shook.

Kendal hammered the crosspieces to the trunk and stood the

tree at the end of the great room. It towered beneath the high ceiling.

"Oh, it's wonderful." Wouldn't the children be thrilled? Of course, they would only be allowed a glimpse when it was lit, then they would be hustled back to bed.

Monte smiled. "I have a surprise for you. I've hired a quartet from Denver. I daresay Marcy Wilson will never quite recover."

Abbie groaned. "You've no idea how difficult it is to keep a civil tongue. How can Grant not see through her as you did?"

"Love is blind."

"Infatuation is blind."

Monte laughed. "It amounts to the same."

James, Pearl, and Zena clipped the tiny candles to the branches. What a lighting it would be! Yet it could hardly compare with her buoyant heart. Abbie was happier this Christmas than she had believed possible. *Look to the living.* Father Dominic's words had filled her with hope. And now her home was filled, her heart overflowing.

Kendal went to the hearth and took down a box. He pulled out a pale sprig.

"What's that, Kendal?"

"Mistletoe."

"That parasite?" Now she recognized the leathery leaves and white berries from her botanical manual. "What for?"

He chuckled. "It's a custom. Quite pagan, I'm afraid. It originated with the Norsemen. Frigga, goddess of love, wished to protect her son, Balder, the sun god. So she drew a pledge from every plant not to harm him, but she overlooked the lowly mistletoe. Loki, god of evil, made an arrow tip of mistletoe which was shot by Hoder, the blind god of winter."

"Was Balder slain?"

"Yes, but Frigga restored him by the power of her love. Her tears became the berries, and in her joy she kissed all who passed beneath the mistletoe. Hung from the rafter, so . . ." He mounted the ladder and secured it. "It brings luck, and no lady caught beneath can refuse a kiss to her captor." Kendal raked her with his eyes.

Abbie looked at it hanging there, and it seemed to suck the joy from her. It wasn't Kendal's story so much as the look in his eyes. If only Frances would show him some small kindness.

But Mama was right. Frances was bitter, so bitter it stung all of them. She felt a guilty twinge. She had not heeded Mama's advice. How could she? But something had to be done. And not only for Kendal's sake.

Abbie swallowed her pride and found Frances in the parlor. "Is Jeanette sleeping?"

"Soon. Mammy's singing."

"Frances . . ." Abbie's tongue stuck, but she forced herself on. "I wondered . . . would you teach me . . . things I need to know?"

"What could you possibly need to know?" Her tightened lips did not help.

Oh, Mama . . . Abbie took a deep breath. "Well . . . how to be a lady."

Frances raised her eyebrows. There was almost a sneer, then she smoothed her features to their serene perfection. "I wouldn't presume."

"There is so much I lack, and . . . well . . ."

Frances's eyes glittered like black ice, frigid and brittle.

Abbie bristled. She'd like nothing better than to shake her. "I apologize. I shouldn't have asked." She swirled her skirts in her wake.

"There's more to being a lady than you know."

Abbie paused at the door. *Guard my lips, Lord.*

Frances continued. "But . . . we could begin with the art of conversation."

Abbie counted ten, then turned back.

"Come, sit." Frances patted the settee beside her.

With stubborn control, Abbie took the seat.

"There are general rules, of course, in how to conduct one's speech and govern one's voice. But you must know that the first rule is silence."

Silence in conversation. Abbie kept her face blank. If Frances were toying, she would not take the lure.

"By that, of course, I mean one should strive to listen more than speak. Always draw out the other person, that they may feel they have participated admirably. No man is interested in your strengths, but there is not a man alive who won't discourse on his. As La Bruyère says, 'The great charm of conversation consists less in the display of one's own wit and intelligence, than in the power to draw forth the resources of others.'"

Abbie felt a stirring inside, her irrepressible desire to learn. There was wisdom in Frances's teaching. She settled into the corner.

"Never quibble or in any way doubt the speaker's sincerity, or speak of things with which others are unacquainted or uninterested. Fluency of tongue and self assurance go a short way when conversing without substance."

Abbie nodded. Of course. Who wanted to discuss things that didn't matter?

"Never pose a direct question. Give an opinion and leave opportunity for the other to respond or not. A gentleman in polite company will avoid asking any question of a lady, and whereas a lady may have an opinion, she will not voice it in his presence."

Frances seemed to take great pleasure in providing that lesson. Abbie frowned. How silly. She and Pa had discussed everything from the time she was small, and Monte had no such qualms. But she listened, learning as much from Frances's delivery as from her words.

It was almost like music—or drama. While she lacked the accent, Abbie could imitate the inflection and expression—though why she'd ever want to, she didn't know. With all the "never do's," she'd be completely tongue-tied before Frances was through.

◆◆◆◆◆◆◆

Abbie winced as Zena tugged the strings of her corset tighter. "If this isn't the most ridiculous thing."

"Just you wait till you sees yo'self in that gown, Mizz Abbie. Lawd, you's gonna be beautiful."

"Well, that's tight enough. Good grief, my lungs can scarcely move. No wonder Frances goes faint at every provocation."

Zena slid the crinoline over her head. Abbie adjusted it and raised her arms for the gown. The emerald silk shimmered as it settled over her figure. Abbie stared at the glass.

Her shoulders were bare, the rim of the V-cut bodice trimmed with red satin roses. A generous flounce of ivory lace gushed from the center of the V where the roses clustered. It was the most exquisite dress she had ever seen, much less worn.

Zena took the brush and worked it through her hair. "This fine, thick hair, these curls . . . they's heaven to arrange."

Heaven for Zena, maybe. Abbie thought her neck would go stiff before it was done, but she had to admit the twists and plaits and ringlets transformed her. She put on the pearl and garnet earbobs.

"You looks like a queen, Mizz Abbie."

She felt like one—or something very near. What would Blake have said? The twinge in her chest told her clearly. But that was in the past. She had grown up and now was Monte's wife. And he had sent to Paris for this silk and stunned Mrs. Munson with the dress order. Abbie wondered how many orders she had turned down to complete his pattern. The fitting alone had taken days, or so it felt.

Monte's eyes showed his approval as Abbie swept into the room. He held her at arm's length. "You take my breath away. You'll have every eye on you tonight."

She smiled. "And you. You look splendid." And he did, in his black coat and satin sash. How was it everything he wore seemed personally designed for him? He was the most handsome man alive.

He reached into his pocket. "Here is something to wear with your dress."

She pulled open the ribbon-tied paper. "Oh, Monte . . ." She caressed the bracelet set with emeralds.

He took it out and clipped it on her wrist. "A perfect fit. You'll have to keep it."

"Wild horses couldn't get it away from me."

He laughed. "I'd hate to see them try."

"And I have a gift for you. In the library." Abbie tugged his elbow, and he followed. She fervently hoped he would like it. It was the first gift she had given him. He untied the string and pulled the paper off the smooth, wooden carving. The horse was rearing, the mane and tail arched and flying.

"It's Sirocco. I commissioned it from Cole."

"Cole carved this?"

"Don't you like it?"

"It's incredible."

Abbie smiled. "When I saw him whittling other animals, I asked him to make a horse for you. I had no idea it would turn out so well."

"I must say I'm impressed. He's a man of hidden talents." He stood the statue on the corner of the desk. "Thank you, Abbie."

Her spirits mounted as she stood in the hall with Monte, Kendal, and Frances to greet the guests. She looked around her at the windows and doors festooned with evergreens, some still bearing their pinecones. She had fallen into a fairy tale and was living it this moment . . . and here was the wicked witch.

Grant came down the hall with Marcy on his arm. Her claret velvet gown with an extravagant bustle perfectly set off her golden curls and green eyes. And she knew it.

Abbie extended her hand. "Marcy Wilson, you look lovely. What an attractive color on you."

"Why . . . thank you."

Abbie received Grant's kiss on her cheek. "And *you* are enchanting," he whispered.

"You must be sure to have the taffy, Grant. Pearl and Zena had a pull just as you and I used to."

"My mouth's watering already. Point me in the right direction."

Abbie laughed. "You're headed the right way."

He clasped Marcy's hand into the crook of his arm and she brushed by, elegantly poised.

Abbie glanced at Monte. "Why are you smiling like that?"

"I confess I overheard you and Frances in the parlor. You *are* a quick study."

"Not so quick as you think. I almost tripped Marcy as she passed." Abbie turned back as he stifled his laugh.

The musicians were playing, and the strains filled the house as the guests continued to arrive. Mama and Pa; the McConnels; Clara and Marty; the Simmses; the ranchers Ephart, Dunbar, and Hodge; Reverend Shields; and Ethan Thomas . . . "Are you certain the house can hold the entire town, Monte?"

"Only our friends and fellow ranchers . . . and hired help." He frowned slightly as Cole walked in with the men behind. All save Cole were slicked and looking bashful. Their suits were a motley assortment of tweeds and broadcloth. But Abbie was glad she had insisted on inviting them, despite Monte's protests.

They were like family. How could they be excluded on Christmas?

Cole was cleaned and combed, his mustache nearly full again, but he had not slicked his hair. He would never slick it again, Abbie guessed, after she'd called him pretty for it. He pulled off his hat and held it to his chest. "Merry Christmas, Abbie. You never looked purtier." He swaggered past.

She felt Monte stiffen beside her. Cole was a rogue indeed. The others filed through the line looking as awkward as schoolboys, but she could sense their high spirits, as well. A dance without cowboys was just no dance at all, whatever Monte may say.

Beside her, Abbie heard Frances gasp. She turned. A man with auburn side whiskers had given James his frock coat and stood at the door in full Union uniform down to the sword at his side. A pale scar ran down his forehead. His features were proud, cold.

"Oh my . . ." Frances swayed. "Take me out, Kendal. I won't stay in a room with a Yankee soldier."

"Monte . . ." Kendal turned to him.

Monte stood still. Abbie's throat tightened at the clench of his jaw. The man was upon them. Monte bowed stiffly. "Mr. Jake Gifford . . . Captain Gifford. My wife, Mrs. Farrel."

He bowed. "Good evening."

Abbie nodded. "Good evening."

Monte's tone was even. "Mr. and Mrs. Stevens."

She had to admire Frances. She nodded as required, but froze him to the bone, nonetheless. The moment he passed, she turned. "Take me out, Kendal. I'll spend the evening in my room." She stopped before Monte, and for the first time ever, Abbie saw disapproval of him, scathing disapproval. "How could you, Monte?"

"I didn't know."

She sagged against Kendal's arm. "You've contaminated your house and your honor."

Abbie felt Monte stiffen, but he said nothing. Kendal took Frances out.

Abbie touched his arm. "Who is he?"

"A rancher." He took her elbow and led her into the great room. "We'll lead the grand march."

"Monte . . ."

"Please, Abbie. If I say more it'll only be ugly."

They lined up and came together to bow and curtsy. She trembled for the fierce control in his face. He forced a smile. How she loved his courage. They started down the channel. The couples around them danced with gusto. If anyone was aware of the affront paid their host, they made no sign. Bright Christmas spirits, hearty smiles, and light steps abounded. She wished she could feel the same.

The music ended and they stood apart. Grant had signed her card for the quadrille and claimed her now, then Davy McConnel the first waltz, and Marty Franklin the caledonian. Abbie noticed Captain Gifford did not dance. He stood mainly at the end with the ranchers clustered about, though she did not see him converse once with Monte. Why had he come in uniform like that? Was it intentional, or did he not realize the insult?

Monte claimed her for the next waltz. It would never lose its magic when he took her in his arms and swirled her so. "Oh,

Monte, if I could only breathe we could dance without stopping until the sun comes up."

"I shudder to think how condemned I'd be for keeping you from the others."

"There's no one else in the room when you dance with me."

"Nevertheless, it would be decidedly poor manners." His crooked smile made her heart leap. He seemed recovered, cheerful even, if not entirely himself. Her concern eased. They stopped and did their courtesies.

"If you'll excuse me, my dear." He kissed her hand.

She danced the lanciers with Ethan Thomas, then stood, clapping, as Wes McConnel and Pa did the jig in the center of the floor. The cowboys whooped and whistled.

Abbie stepped back, laughing. They would go until one or the other gave in, she knew. Like two crazy leprechauns they grabbed hands and kicked wildly until both could barely lift their feet, then stumbled to the side, laughing and pounding their backs. Good heavens, they were a pair. Her heart swelled.

Kendal touched her elbow. "I was hoping to find you here."

She turned, and he pointed to the ceiling. She looked up to the white-berried mistletoe, and her chest lurched. "Oh, surely..."

"There's no escape. It's the rules." He claimed her mouth with unexpected ardor. She could taste the brandy on his breath and pulled back.

"Kendal, you snake." Monte scowled and brushed through those standing near. "Turnabout would have me kissing my sister, and that's hardly a fair exchange."

Kendal laughed. "When are things ever fair?" He bowed and walked off.

Monte took her hand and drew her away. "Let's not find yourself there again, my darling."

Abbie swallowed her distaste. "I certainly won't, though I'd swear Marcy's trying her best to lure Grant over." She directed his gaze to where Marcy pouted and tossed her curls at Grant's laughter.

"You have to admit she has style."

"A rattler has style."

He laughed. "Well, I'm signed on Mrs. Franklin's card. I trust you'll manage without me?"

That was the problem with protocol. She had to spend most of the time without the one who mattered. Never mind. Tomorrow was Christmas, and she'd have him all to herself. Abbie's hand was warm where he kissed it.

Cole stepped up and nodded. "I ain't signed on yer card . . ."

"This waltz is free."

"My lucky night." He held out his arm.

As Cole waltzed her, she caught Kendal watching from where he stood with two men. He responded to what one of them said, but his eyes were on her. She turned away.

"Wish you'd keep clear of him."

Abbie startled. Had she been so obvious? "It's the mistletoe. Some black magic of Kendal's."

"It ain't the mistletoe."

Cole turned so his back blocked Kendal, but her eye caught Captain Gifford.

"Cole, who is the man in uniform? Do you know him?"

"Jake Gifford. Owns a spread southwest of here. Big operation. Runs six hundred head so far. He set up headquarters this spring."

"Does he know . . . about Monte?"

Cole quirked an eyebrow.

"I mean about being from the South and all. His uniform gave Frances quite a scare, and . . ."

"I reckon it would." He shook his head. "I'm not familiar with the man, Abbie. It's to Mr. Farrel's credit that he's put that war business behind him. It's a lesser man can't pick up and go on." Cole bowed at the music's end.

Abbie dropped a curtsy. "Thank you, Cole. And Cole . . . would you keep your ears open?"

He nodded. "And both eyes."

Monte crossed to her. "It's nearly midnight."

"Oh . . . I must get the children."

"Hurry then. I should have hired the men to herd them in."

Abbie clicked her tongue, then left him and passed through the doors. To her surprise, Jeanette's mammy had them all up and dressed, and Jeanette looked like an angel perched on Felicity's knee. "Come. It's time to light the tree."

She stood the children to the side as she and Kendal and Monte took long tapers and lit the tiny candles. Frances would have participated, but for Captain Gifford. Abbie was aware of him at the fringe of the crowd. His presence filled her with foreboding. Something in his stance—in the way he held his shoulders, his hand resting on the hilt of his sword.

She stepped around the tree and stretched up. Kendal took her hand and gave her the needed inch to the candle's wick. His grip was warm and firm, and she wiggled her hand free. James had mounted the ladder and lit the upper candles. One by one the lamps in the room were extinguished until only the tree shone. Marty Franklin sang into the hush, "Silent night, holy night . . ."

Monte rested his hand on Abbie's back. Warmth filled her. It was a blessed night. Monte was beside her, the children's faces glowed, and the Christ Child would visit their home that night. Even though she would tuck the treats into the socks, she never doubted that it was all His gift.

✦✦✦✦✦✦✦

Sitting astride his charger, Captain Jake Gifford brushed his blue sleeves down to the yellow cuffs. He sucked on the thin cigar. What a passion he had for fine tobacco. Too bad the plantations in the South were so decreased. Still, Cuba provided for the lack.

He turned the horse and headed for home in the cold night air. Oh yes, he had enjoyed himself at Montgomery Farrel's Christmas gala. He enjoyed hearing the ranchers praise Farrel's hospitality, geniality, generosity. And he had enjoyed the stir he caused.

It was time to step up his efforts, though he was momentarily hobbled by the loss of Jip Crocker and his unfortunate kin. His mood darkened. Wherever Crocker was, he hoped it was hard and cold.

◆◆◆◆◆◆◆

Monte stood at the window as Abbie slept. He had loved her gently, passionately, but it had not soothed him. Frances's words burned inside. He had not exchanged a single word with Jake Gifford past the greeting, but he indeed felt tarnished.

The war was over. Long over. He had put it behind him. But the swagger of that man. What audacity for a neighbor to enter his home in uniform. And what was the purpose? To challenge him?

For what? Monte's breath fogged on the frosted window. Was Gifford behind the sabotage of the ranch, the fouled pond, the stampede, the poisoned calves ... Chance? Was it a gauntlet he had thrown down tonight?

Monte looked up to the stars, haloed through the glass. Cole believed their trouble had ended with the last rustler's departure. Certainly the harassment had stopped. But Monte felt uneasy. Too many things did not add up. He rubbed a hand over his eyes and glanced back at Abbie.

In sleep she looked so vulnerable. He ached to keep her safe. He climbed back into the bed and pressed into her warmth. He wished he could find abandon in sleep. Monte sighed. Would life always be a battle?

Seventeen

The afternoon sun dazzled the dusting of snow when Abbie opened the door to Reverend Shields. She scarcely contained her surprise. What could he want the day after Christmas? "Reverend, do come in."

James took his hat and coat, and Abbie showed him to the parlor. She stoked up the fire to chase the chill. "I'm afraid my husband has gone out."

"I'd be glad to give my news to you. In fact I've only just received answer to my inquiry and came as soon as I heard."

"Please sit." Abbie pulled the bell.

"Some time ago your husband asked my assistance with the orphans."

Abbie hid her surprise. Monte had said nothing to her.

"I believe I've found the solution."

"Solution, Reverend Shields?"

He twisted his hands. "Well, yes, of course. They can't all remain here, naturally."

Pearl brought tea and cakes. Abbie poured and offered him a cup. "You've found homes for them?"

"I've arranged an orphan train. At very little cost a Mrs. Beardsly from Denver takes the children from the city to outlying parts and . . ."

"And what, sir? Auctions them off?" He reddened, and Abbie bit off her indignation. "Forgive me, but these are children."

"Mrs. Beardsly disembarks at each township, and people in need of a child choose from those she brings. It's a blessed arrangement for all parties. The children have a home, and..."

He spoke on, and Abbie sank to a chair. A slave market. People the children had never seen, who want another pair of hands.... Oh, little Tucker, and Emmy and Pauline... How could Monte have thought... well, perhaps he didn't know the means by which Reverend Shields would remove the problem. And the minister—he was so young, so uncertain. But did no one think of the children?

"I'm sorry, Reverend Shields. These children will not be on any orphan train."

"But your husband said..."

"Do you know these children? Have you ever seen them?"

"Well, yes, at the Christmas recitation last year..."

"Do you know their names? Have you sat beside them and heard their letters and sums? Have you wiped their noses and cleaned their scrapes?"

"Mrs. Farrel. I understand your consternation. I have my own flock."

"Whose flock are these, Reverend?"

He removed his glasses and wiped the lenses, then replaced them. "The Lord's, I suppose."

"And what did he charge Peter?"

"Mrs. Farrel, I've worked hard to arrange..."

"I'm sure you did. But Reverend, if you saw these children, spoke to them... you must see that sending them to be picked over like—like produce or cattle..." She saw something ignite behind his eyes. Maybe it was anger, but perhaps a dose of anger would do him good.

What the minister needed was an awakening. He spoke his message well, as attested by his sermon last Sunday, but now she saw why Monte had brought her there. He was working with the minister to remove the children. Her own anger kindled.

It was time to more than speak the message. It was time to live it. "Have you spoken with the families in town?"

"My predecessor..."

"I know all about Reverend Peale. He was a wonderful help to the orphans. Yes, there were some troublemakers who made things difficult. But when his appeal didn't work, he found other ways to support the children—and the brothers in their work."

"I've never opposed . . ."

"But have you risked anything?"

"You forget yourself."

"Maybe I do. No doubt my husband would agree with you. But I know these children. I know which teeth Emmy lost last year. I held Jeremy when Father Dominic set his arm. I won't allow them to be sent off in that way, picked over and rejected. I won't subject them to that."

"Then what will you do?"

Abbie sat back in the chair and folded her hands. "I will accompany you to the homes of our neighbors and friends, your flock. And we will appeal to them to adopt the children."

The minister sat, unmoving. Then he smiled, his face becoming pleasant for the first time. "Very well, Mrs. Farrel. I'll make the appeal with you. And if I lose my congregation, no doubt you and Mr. Farrel and all the children who remain in your home will fill my church in their stead."

Abbie laughed and stuck out her hand. "It's a deal."

✦✦✦✦✦✦✦

With Monte in Denver two days later, it was the perfect opportunity to attempt her plan. Abbie stood in Pa's yard and hugged Mama around the neck. Little Tucker would have the best Mama and Pa alive. He'd be her own little brother. She climbed back up to the wagon with Reverend Shields.

He maintained a straight face. "Where to now?"

"The McConnels. If anyone knows how to rear a boy like Jeremy, it's Mary McConnel. Why, he's Blake all over."

"Don't count on such easy success."

But the reverend shook his head and smiled when she came from Mary McConnel's and nodded the affirmative. She didn't tell him it was her reference to Blake that decided Mary.

"Now, Pauline and Emmy must stay together. Let's try the

Franklins. Clara could use two willing helpers with that rascal, Del, and another on the way."

Clara was easy. Del was fretful with his first molar, and the thought of two little girls to distract him was welcome. Abbie's spirits soared, then plunged when the Simms refused her offer. They were past child rearing and had enough to do with the store. Never mind, there were others.

But the others were not so easily convinced. Many said they'd think on it, but she heard their reluctance. She had chosen families with whom she thought each child would respond well. Those families were her first hope, but if they refused, she would have to look further.

It was obvious this would not be accomplished in a day, and though Reverend Shields was gentleman enough not to press his point, she could see he doubted their ultimate success. What would she do if she couldn't place all of them?

Her back end was tired of sitting, but she was determined to see it through. "Will you attend me again tomorrow, Reverend Shields?"

"If you feel my presence is beneficial, I'll gladly do my part."

She climbed down from the buggy. "I'm certain Monte would appreciate your escorting me in his absence. And your influence is most helpful."

He bent his head. "Then I'll meet you here in the morning."

"Thank you."

◆◆◆◆◆◆◆

The morning came soon enough, and they first made the rounds of those couples who had asked to sleep on it. Abbie's spirits soared when four of them said they'd agreed to take a child. That was more than half of the orphans accounted for, and as she reached the side of the buggy, she glanced expectantly at the minister.

He smiled. "I rather suspect the Lord has his hand in this, Mrs. Farrel."

"I've always believed these children were close to His heart.

And nothing feels so good as accomplishing His plan."

"You are right about that. I've dedicated my life to that practice, but I always thought my strength was in words."

Abbie rested her hand in his as he helped her climb in. "If you'll forgive me, Reverend, out here actions mean more than words."

He dipped his head. "I believe there is need for both." He walked around and joined her.

By the time they had swept the outlying homesteads as far as the Dunbars' ranch, the sun had dropped behind the mountain crests, and the minister stopped the buggy in the yard. There were still three boys without homes. Abbie refused to feel discouraged, but she was at a loss of where to turn next. She was not willing to send even one on that horrible orphan train.

As though reading her thoughts, Reverend Shields spoke gently. "If you're willing, we'll try again tomorrow."

His words surprised her. She'd expected him to say they'd done the best they could and would have to settle for that. "Of course I'm willing, but ... I must admit I'm not sure whom to try."

"You've thought it through as well as you could. Now we'll leave it for the Lord to say."

She nodded and walked wearily up the stairs. The children greeted her, and she responded with a cheerful smile. She'd not told any of them, yet, that their fate was being decided. She must have a joyful report for all of them before she broached the news.

At first she had approached each family with the prospect of taking the particular child she felt best suited. When she'd exhausted those choices, she'd left it to the couples to indicate their preference for a boy or girl and what age. Now she looked at the three boys unaccounted for—Michael, quiet and studious, and Jacob and Fred, slow with their studies but quick with their hands.

Abbie didn't betray the concern she felt by her expression. Surely the Lord had a place for them, a place specially suited to them. On her knees that night, she turned over her efforts. Abbie could think of no one they hadn't asked whom she found acceptable. Now it was up to God to guide them.

The next afternoon Reverend Shields came for her and drove to town. Whatever they found would be right there in Rocky Bluffs or nowhere at all. Abbie looked about her. She had slept fitfully and was no closer to a solution than when she went to bed. "I'm at a loss this morning. I can't think where to start."

Reverend Shields glanced her way. "You've not tried the Wilsons."

Abbie cringed. That had not been oversight. "I don't dare."

The minister smiled and drove to the end of Wilson Road. He pulled up in front of the judge's fine house. There was certainly room for a child, and she must not let her personal dislike of the judge and his family stand in the way of opportunity for the boys.

"Coming?"

"I think I'll wait out here." She'd be a detriment to the cause. Darla Wilson's feelings for her were mutual.

He hooked the reins. "Then allow me. Any family with only a daughter ought to welcome a studious, comely lad like our Michael. Especially when Mrs. Wilson learns that Mrs. Faulks has taken a son, as well."

He winked, and Abbie raised her eyebrows. When he returned, his smile was broader than she had seen. He climbed up and took the reins. "I suggested the boy might have a leaning to the ministry. She agreed he must, then, have every advantage."

"Why, Reverend Shields . . ."

He bowed. "Mrs. Farrel."

He clicked to the horse. "You say the other two are clever with their hands."

"Yes. And I'd like to keep them together."

"What would you think of apprenticing them?"

She hadn't considered that. "Well, they are ten and twelve. Not so very young."

He pulled up outside the wagon shop. "For some reason, Mr. Garner was heavy on my mind last night."

She climbed down and went inside with him. It seemed this

was the reverend's day, and she allowed him to speak with the bent and gnarled wagonmaker. He wasn't so old, but the rheumatism made him appear so.

He rubbed his chin at the minister's words. "Can't say it wouldn't be good to have some young hands about. Especially when I'm ailing, and the orders won't wait."

Abbie looked around at the orderly shop and felt encouraged. It was a good place for two boys to learn and grow. And Silas was near, working at the livery. She turned back to the men. "They must still attend school."

Mr. Garner appraised her. "Of course. But I will expect them to do their job. It's a valuable skill I'm imparting."

"I know you'll find them hardworking and eager."

They stepped back outside. With Jacob and Fred apprenticed to Mr. Garner, the wagonmaker, Abbie's heart soared. Reverend Shields whistled as he drove her home, then climbed down and assisted her at the stairs. She caught sight of Sirocco in the yard.

"Do stay to supper, Reverend. Monte will be delighted."

"Thank you, I will."

Abbie mounted the stairs and reached for the door. She suddenly spun. "Oh, my goodness!"

"What is it, Mrs. Farrel?"

"Why, we've placed all the children. Every one."

"That was the intention."

"But . . . I had thought Monte and I . . . I intended to keep one for us."

Reverend Shields paused. "Well, I . . . suppose you could speak with one of the kind people who . . ."

"No, no. We've set up their hopes now. I can't go back on the promise."

"With all respect, Mrs. Farrel, Mr. Farrel has hopes for children of his own."

Of course he did. She opened the door. And she would have all the newly adopted in her school in town. She drew a long breath. "Reverend Shields, you've accomplished a great thing."

He bowed. "We have together, Mrs. Farrel."

◆◆◆◆◆◆◆

Monte looked from his wife to the minister. "Every one of them?"

Reverend Shields nodded, and Abbie smiled. An unlikelier alliance he had never seen.

"Well."

Abbie turned in a swirl of skirts. "I'll have Pearl set another place for supper."

Monte stared after her. "Yes, do." Then he turned back to Reverend Shields. "My hat is off to you, sir."

"It was Mrs. Farrel, really. She twists an arm with a silken touch and talks around any obstacle until it vanishes away. One is never quite certain how one got there, but the journey was utterly painless."

Monte smiled. How well he knew.

"She decided in advance the best possibilities for each child, then together we pursued them. Even when she received more regrets than acceptances, she was undaunted."

"A remarkable feat."

"A remarkable lady. With a heart like hers I don't doubt I'll find a willing help in any concern."

Monte chuckled. "No doubt. Mrs. Farrel is not one to contemplate when action will serve. Have you heard she's teaching the town children since the . . . loss of Miss Plochman?"

"Oh yes, I'd heard."

"She's also privately tutoring my stable boy, but don't let on that I know."

"She has a heart for knowledge."

"A heart for many things, not least this territory."

The reverend drew himself up. "That, sir, I can well believe."

Monte stifled his smile. After a few days with Abbie, the young reverend was clearly smitten.

◆◆◆◆◆◆◆

After dinner, Abbie saw the children to bed. They had taken

the news with general acceptance, if some trepidation. It would be an adjustment, but she was certain the families chosen would do their best for them. She tucked the covers up to Tucker's chin.

"Will you really be my sister?"

"Yes, Tucker. My Mama and Pa are going to be yours, too. And my brother, Grant, will be your brother and my sister, Sadie, another sister for you. What do you think of that?"

"Can I still come see you here?"

"Yes, you may. And I'll come see you, too." She turned down the wick and kissed his forehead. "Sleep, now. Tomorrow you all go to your new homes."

She went out and settled into the library. Reverend Shields had gone, and business of Cole's had taken Monte out. She was glad for the solitude. Though the day had been as successful as she could have hoped, she felt a mingled sadness. Things changed so swiftly.

The mission was gone. With the children no longer in her home, it would be truly over. Father Dominic had fulfilled his charge, and she, too, had done her part. But inside it left an emptiness. The board had hopes of a new permanent teacher for the town school come spring, and she would be relieved of that task, as well.

The door opened and Frances came in. Abbie sighed. Frances had a gift for appearing when Abbie's defenses were down, though at the moment she looked more fragile herself. No doubt Kendal's absence at supper disturbed her. Frances went to the shelf and took down a volume of Emily Dickinson, then sat in the leather wing chair.

Abbie glanced up to find Frances watching her with the book unopened in her lap. There was no contempt in her gaze. She looked quite frank and almost vulnerable. Her voice was low.

"I need poetry tonight. I always do when it's cold and dreary in the winter doldrums. Why is that, do you think?"

"Perhaps it brings thoughts of the coming spring and bolsters your hope."

Frances shook her head. "I have no hope."

"You mustn't despair, Frances. I know things seem bleak to you, but it's only a matter of time."

Frances smiled faintly. "I believed I had seen the worst through the war and what followed. But it wasn't. At least then everyone suffered the same. I wasn't alone. Here . . ." She spread her hands.

"But what are you suffering, Frances? Monte and I are happy to have you here, and Kendal is working to reestablish himself. You have Jeanette . . ."

Frances laughed softly. "I should be satisfied. Maybe I am. I don't know anymore. Nothing makes sense to me here."

"You'll get used to it."

"I don't want to get used to it. I want to go home."

What could she say? Frances's honesty deserved no less. "You will make a home here, Frances."

"I don't have what it takes."

"Look at yourself. How long has it been since Kendal produced your smelling salts or calmed a fit of vapors? You're stronger than you think."

Frances ran her finger over the book. "Did you know Sharlyn couldn't read?"

"Yes. I used to read to her."

"Monte detests ignorance."

"He was very patient with her."

"As only Monte can be." Frances laughed, but it was mirthless. "He was always one to overlook another's shortcomings but never his own. Kendal forgets only his own."

"He's trying very hard."

"He brought me here. I shall never forgive him that."

"Oh, Frances, don't say so! He only wants to make it up to you."

"You've no idea what he wants. Nor do I. Do you know why I married him?"

Abbie shook her head.

"He reminded me of my father before the war. Tall and handsome and a little reckless. I had no idea how reckless."

"He'll be more careful now."

"Does a leopard change its spots?"

"People learn from their mistakes."

Frances raised her chin. "Kendal is drawn to unsavory types. Were he not a gentleman, he would be a crook."

Abbie stared.

"Does that shock you? Of course it must. Your only connection to our world is Monte, true and wholly honorable. But I assure you, sometimes pedigree breeds decadence—not overtly, perhaps, but inwardly. Kendal is a gentleman, but he's also a rogue."

"I am sorry." Abbie met her eyes. What she saw made her ache.

"He called your name in his sleep last night." Frances looked away. "I wonder if Monte knows. . . ."

Abbie's chest tightened. Whatever denial she might speak seemed false and dishonest in light of Kendal's recent behavior. Words stuck in her throat. Frances opened the book, flipped the page, and read.

◆◆◆◆◆◆◆

Cole caught Monte by the wrist before he dipped his hand in the water. "It's strychnine. Look at the animals."

Monte stared at the fallen beasts. Eighteen of them collapsed at the edge of the half-frozen water hole. The moonlight shone on their hides. He felt his jaw tighten. "So much for rustlers."

"I reckon you're right."

"Who then?"

"I don't know."

Monte paced. "Have you seen anything like this before?"

"Like and worse."

"For what purpose?"

"Control."

Monte stared at the cow at his feet. He knew what Cole was saying, but he had not thought to find that sort of trouble here.

"I reckon we need more men," Cole tucked his thumbs into his belt, "to watch . . . and take care of business when it comes to it."

Business. Monte toed the cow's frothy muzzle. This was not business. But Cole was right. They could not afford to be careless. He had little spare after guaranteeing Kendal's debts, but there was no choice.

"Take on hands, then. Tell them only what's necessary."

"Yes, sir."

Eighteen

Abbie stared through the canvas flap at the tent city sprung up virtually overnight. The city of railroad men. But not only men—there were gaunt women and even children. A cold January drizzle kept the women and children in the tents, though the hammer blows and hollers of the men never ceased.

Abbie had ridden a good eighteen miles when she learned Sadie was among the workers at the front of the tracks. Within weeks, the rails would be through to town, but she couldn't wait that long to see her sister. Now she was glad she hadn't.

Sadie finished changing the baby, and Abbie turned. At least Joe and Sadie's tent had a wood plank floor and a real four-poster bed with quilts. For a kitchen she had a separate tent with a stove, not merely a fire pit chiseled from the frozen ground. Little Matthew had a bearskin on his cot, and baby Hannah's cradle was piled high with feather ticks and quilts.

"She's like the princess and the pea." Sadie brushed a strand of mousy brown hair from her forehead.

"Are you warm enough?" She couldn't hide the concern in her voice. "Won't you stay with me?"

"Joe needs to be here with the men, even though he is the foreman. The children and I could have stayed in Denver, but I didn't want to be apart."

"No, of course not. But . . ."

Sadie faced her. "I didn't marry into a mansion. But it doesn't mean we're not happy or well cared for."

Abbie flushed. "I didn't mean that."

"Joe's putting enough aside to build us a nice home—maybe when this line is through." Sadie bounced the baby on her hip. "I will be glad when we can settle, though, and stop worrying whether Joe will make it home each night."

"Why wouldn't he?"

"Rail wars. Different lines vying for the same passage. Some crews have seen violence—tracks and supplies blown up, laid again the next day, and blown up again the following night. Actual armies guard the workings day and night."

Abbie stared at her. "Sadie!"

"Don't worry. No one's fighting to get to Rocky Bluffs, being just a side spur and all." Sadie laughed. "And I always thought you'd be the one living the adventure, off with Blake somewhere."

The ache touched her. Abbie took baby Hannah and hugged her neck. It was the first she'd seen of the baby, as she had not seen Sadie since before Blake's death, and they hadn't corresponded as well as they should. How could she relate all the feelings and confusion? She sighed. "Blake was like a brother to me. I loved him as I do Grant."

Sadie smiled with Mama's warm brown eyes. Sometimes even her expressions looked like Mama's—especially now, with her I'm-not-sure-I-believe-you look.

"I miss him, but it was never like that. It was Monte I loved."

"And he's a fine man, Abbie. A true gentleman." She giggled.

"Don't."

"I can't help it. My little sister, the ruffian, married to a southern gentleman. How I wish I could have seen the wedding."

"I wish you could have, too, though I assure you I deported myself just fine, thank you." She would not discuss what happened after. If Sadie heard it from someone else, so be it.

Sadie laughed. "I'll check the water." She passed through the back to the other tent and returned with two cups. The coffee steam rose up. "Mmm. Puts heart into one, doesn't it?"

Abbie did not tell her she drank coffee only in the morning. She wondered how long it had been since Sadie had tasted tea. She set the baby down to crawl.

Sadie sipped. "What a treat to be together again. And Grant here, too."

"Oh yes, Grant." Abbie rolled her eyes.

"Now, Abbie . . ."

"I can't help it. I want to kick him every time I see Marcy Wilson on his arm. What can he be thinking?"

"That she has a pretty face, and she does; that her father's the judge; that it's high time he was married . . ."

"Don't even say that!" Abbie set down her cup with a clang on the trunk. "You don't have to live here. Can you imagine having to swallow that pill every time you wanted to see Grant?"

"Have you told him how you feel?"

"Only once. And I don't dare repeat it. Monte says it's a gentleman's natural inclination to defend his own. If I spoke my mind, I might drive Grant to it."

"You know how he defends the underdog."

"Underdog. Marcy's a coyote in pussycat fur. Makes my skin crawl. Do you suppose Grant's kissed her?"

"Abbie!"

Abbie brushed back her hair. "Well, I can't help wondering."

"I'm surprised at you, though why I should be, I don't know. You always did say whatever popped into your head."

"I am trying. Monte's sister, Frances, is taking great delight in pointing out all my improper speech. It's really impossible, you know. She'll never approve of me. What's so funny?"

"When have you ever cared what anyone—especially any lady—thought of you?"

"Of course I care."

"Oh, Abbie. From the time you were small you did whatever pleased you, and the devil take anyone who didn't like it. Remember Marcy Wilson making fun of your short skirt? Did you take it to heart? Indeed not. You intentionally hiked it an inch above your knee and asked Blake if he didn't like it better that way. Naturally, the scoundrel boy agreed he'd like it even shorter, and Marcy was perfectly scandalized. I was, too, but I couldn't bear to scold when you'd held your own so bravely."

Abbie laughed. "I don't remember that, but Marcy has always brought out my worst. It's a gift of hers."

"Then let's not speak of her. Tell me all the news."

"The biggest news is the railroad coming in. People are speculating how it will change things."

"And it will."

"I know. Even seeing the rails across the prairie shook me. It looked so . . . settled."

Sadie smiled. "It's progress."

"Noise and smoke. Hustle and bustle."

"That's not the worst of it. It's the vultures that follow."

"Vultures?"

"Gambling dens and dance halls."

"Not in Rocky Bluffs."

"Just wait and see."

After their visit Abbie rode back through town. She looked at the frame buildings, the folks on the boardwalks, the horses at the posts. The town had a pleasant bustle. She read the signs as she passed: *Peterson's Hardware, Simms General Mercantile, Mrs. Munson Clothier,* and *Men's Haberdashery,* which opened just last week. She passed three saloons, the post office, the hotel, and her pa's newspaper office with the Western Union telegraph inside.

Reverend Shields' small frame church, the school, the frame skeleton of the new courthouse, the scatter of houses on side lanes . . . Rocky Bluffs. It couldn't become a city. Not like what Sadie described. Why did the train have to come through?

She urged Shiloh past the last buildings. Monte expected her home when he returned from whatever business he was conducting. He would not allow her out past dark, and lately he seemed tense and troubled. He didn't tell her why, and she didn't ask. If he wouldn't trust her on his own, she would not interfere.

She sensed he would forbid her going anywhere if he thought she'd listen. He insisted on escorting her to town as long as she continued teaching, and he frowned at her solitary rides. He would not have approved the trip today. The distance to the railroad camp and her detour through town had pressed the limit of the short daylight.

She hurried home, but Monte had not yet returned. She settled down in the library with *Canterbury Tales*. The fire burned warm, and she sank into the leather chair. She looked around at the shelves of books, wooden paneling, and cut-glass lanterns.

Sadie's canvas walls would be wet tonight. But she was happy, she and her husband and her babies. They worked hard and had little, but they were happy. Sadie had always possessed a gift for contentment, and her life was simple, uncomplicated. Abbie sighed.

◆◆◆◆◆◆◆

The noise of new construction and the excitement of speculation filled the streets of Rocky Bluffs. Monte watched the hubbub from Reverend Shields' porch. He leaned against the wall and sipped the coffee the minister had provided. The day was unseasonably warm for February and fair.

"Big things are coming to Rocky Bluffs. With the railroad through, business will flourish, families will settle . . ."

"Vice will reign."

"Oh, come now."

"Look at it." Reverend Shields pointed to the two-story building taking shape just beyond the livery. The new hotel.

Monte knew it was not the lodging that disturbed Winthrop Shields. It was the tent of prostitutes set up behind it. Women waiting to take up residence in the upstairs rooms but already plying their wares in the tent. The objections of the town council did nothing to keep men away—not once word was out.

Across the street, the Gates of Paradise Dance Hall and Gambling Emporium had opened its doors. And just beyond that stood the raw pine railroad station, small but serviceable. Other businesses were coming, but Monte supposed Reverend Shields was right. The railroad was bringing more than progress.

"Still, the transfer of goods will improve. The train coming in this morning begins a new era for Rocky Bluffs. No more freighting by wagon, no more driving cattle over endless miles. Now only to the stockyards to be loaded onto the cars."

"That will help you, I know."

"And others—the smaller ranchers especially, who haven't the manpower for the drives."

"I've heard you're carrying a good number of hands."

"Have you?" Monte shifted on the bench. "Well, there's work to be done."

Monte stood as Abbie bounded up the walk to the porch, two paper-wrapped parcels in her arms. He relieved her of them. "Did you find what you wanted?"

"Yes."

"Will you drop off the cloth with Mrs. Munson?"

"Heavens, Monte. If I can't make a skirt and shirtwaist for gardening..." She spun suddenly at the sound of the train whistle. "It's coming."

"Shall we go and see?" Monte glanced at the minister who was beaming at Abbie's arrival. "Reverend?"

"By all means."

Monte held his arm to Abbie, and Reverend Shields followed. They joined the crowd at the end of the street and watched the engine, hung with banners and streamers, chug along the track to a steamy stop before the station.

Monte looked at the townsfolk, alight with excitement. Joshua stood at the front of the crowd, pad in hand. He'd have stories to last him a good while. Beside him Selena hugged Sadie, and Sadie's husband, Joe, stood tall. He and his crew had accomplished the task, bringing the railroad to Rocky Bluffs. The cheers and hoots as the first passengers disembarked rivaled anything Monte had heard.

He glanced at Abbie. She showed none of the gaiety of those around them. He patted her hand tucked into his arm. "Don't fret, Abbie. It'll become commonplace soon enough."

She gave him a halfhearted smile. Over her head he caught the eye of Captain Gifford. Involuntarily, Monte stiffened. Jake Gifford took the cigar from his teeth and nodded. Monte nodded back.

Marv Peterson, newly elected mayor, stepped onto the plat-

form. "Ladies and gentlemen. This is a great day for Rocky
Bluffs. . . ."

Abbie squeezed his arm, and Monte leaned his ear close.

"I've seen enough. Let's go."

Monte whispered his farewell to Reverend Shields and led her
out of the crowd. "What is it, Abbie?"

"I want to go to the mountains."

"Now?"

"Right now. I want to feel the wind in my face and hear the
birds and smell the pine."

"Abbie . . ."

"Please, Monte. Take me. Up behind Pa's ranch, where we pic-
nicked once. Do you remember?"

"Of course I do."

She tugged his hand, and Monte followed. He tossed her parcels under the seat and handed her into the buggy. They drove
into the hills and up the pine-clad slopes of the Rocky Mountains.
Monte could almost feel her trembling beside him.

When the slope became too steep, he stopped, and she jumped
down. "Come with me, Monte." Lifting her skirts, Abbie plunged
up the mountainside, panting and stumbling and leaping from
one rocky outcropping to another. They were higher than he'd
ever gone, and still she kept on.

"Abbie . . ."

She didn't listen. She scrambled over a ridge and cut up the
cleft. He could hear water, then presently saw the spring breaking
from the rocky wall and cascading down the side. Abbie reached
for the jutting rock and dug in the toe of her boot.

Monte caught her arm and held her back. "Stop, Abbie. You
can't go up there." He turned her, and there were tears in her eyes.
He closed her into his arms. "My darling, what is it?"

"I can't stand it."

He held her while she cried into his neck. He felt as though
he held a wild creature, somehow more connected to this mountain than the life he gave her. It hurt. Yet on some level it touched
him deeply. "Abbie." He stroked her hair. "Change is inevitable."

"I hate it."

He kissed the crown of her head, raised her face and kissed her wet cheeks, then her mouth, salty with tears. She kissed him back fiercely, and a warm urgency filled him. What was this woman? Would he ever understand her?

He kissed her throat and felt her pulse quicken. Never had he felt more one, yet so vastly different at once. He wanted her. He needed her. And God had given her to him. What he did with her on the mountain seemed more sacred than anything else in this life. She was bone of his bone, flesh of his flesh.

He cradled her head from the rough ground and gave her one last lingering kiss. He ran a finger over her cheek, and she smiled. "That's better." He eased her into his lap and leaned against the rocky mountain wall.

She cradled her head into his neck. "I'm sorry, Monte. I don't know what got into me."

He chuckled. "Don't apologize."

She pinched him. "I mean for leaving town."

He shrugged. "You see one train, you've seen them all. But this . . ." He swept his arm across the expansive view. "Now this is worth seeing."

He watched her take in the scene, her expression so acute it made him ache. He almost wished now that the train had never come. Yet as he looked down over the hills and out to the plain with the single line of track, he was amazed by the emptiness. He tugged a strand of her hair. "I think there's still room."

She turned. "Room for what?"

"Your dreams."

She leaned against him, smiling gently.

He kissed the corner of her mouth. "If we don't go down, we'll lose the daylight."

"I know. Thank you, Monte."

"For what?"

"Understanding."

He didn't tell her that as long as he lived, he'd only scratch the surface.

Nineteen

Monte surveyed the line of fence posts hacked down, the wire trampled and twisted on the ground.

Beside him, Cole rubbed the back of his neck. "Reckon we found our hole."

Breck Thompson rode up beside them. "I make the count sixty-five."

"Sixty-five!" Monte turned in the saddle. "Sixty-five cattle gone?"

"As well as I can make out. The men gathered in the stragglers."

"We can't afford these losses. See that it stops. I don't care what it takes." Monte turned Sirocco and took him through the breach.

"Where're you headin'?" Cole called.

"To see Ephart and Dunbar."

Monte rode hard across the plain. He made Dunbar's ranch within the hour and dismounted at the house. He led Sirocco to the trough, but before the horse finished, the door opened, and Mary Dunbar hailed him.

"Good afternoon, Mary. Is John in?"

"He's out with the men. But I've just baked a winter apple pie."

"That's a worthy temptation, but my errand won't keep."

"Well, I'm sorry to hear that. How's Abbie?"

"Still filling in at the school and getting ready for spring planting. She's planning an ornamental garden."

"I'll have to see it when she's done."

"I'm sure she'd like that." Monte tossed the reins over Sirocco's neck and remounted. "Can you tell me which way?" She pointed and he headed south. Dunbar's spread comprised his 160-acre homestead. It shouldn't be too hard to find the herd.

As Monte approached, John Dunbar pulled the wire tight and hammered in the clamp, then wiped his face with his kerchief and stood. "Monte." He reached up and shook the hand Monte extended. "What brings you down my way?"

"Sixty-five head stolen."

"Stolen?"

"It looks that way. I wanted to see how you and Brock are faring."

"I've lost no stock. I heard about the trouble you had with rustlers before. But I thought you'd run them off."

"I'm not certain it was rustlers."

"Not rustlers—but who else?"

"I don't know. I'd hoped maybe you'd heard something."

Dunbar shook his head. "I spoke with Brock Ephart just last week. He said nothing about losses."

"Well, I guess I'll see if anything's changed since then."

"Good luck."

Monte nodded. What did he expect? He had no doubt as he rode that Ephart would tell him the same as Dunbar. And when he rode south to Hodge's place and on to Bates' Lazy L, he'd hear the same there, too.

It was his ranch alone Captain Gifford wanted to take down, if indeed it were Gifford. Monte shook his head. If it was a fight Jake Gifford wanted, he'd learn what the Lucky Star was made of. And Montgomery Farrel, as well, so help him God. Monte closed his hands around the reins and felt the leather burn as Sirocco leaped forward at his word.

◆◆◆◆◆◆

Abbie felt stifled in the cozy warmth of the parlor. Where was Monte? What kept him so late? He was never absent from dinner, certainly not without word.

"Now, then." Frances held herself primly in the wing chair. "If you wish someone to notice you, don't rush at them. Rather position yourself in their way as though by accident."

Abbie walked to the mantle and studied the picture of Monte's father. "That's hardly honest. Why is subterfuge good manners?"

"Because that's the way it's done. Suppose you fling yourself at someone who doesn't want to speak with you. What choice have they? But put yourself in their path, and they can either notice you or change course."

Abbie could just picture Frances changing course. She saw the flicker in her eyes as she said it. *For Mama*, she reminded herself. And she had asked for the help. She sighed. Well, maybe one day all this silliness would come in handy.

"Ladies may show, but never show *off* their children, especially when introducing them to strangers. But then, you don't have to worry about that yet, do you?"

Abbie felt a burning in her chest. Was that an honest observation, or a barb sent right to her heart? The latter she supposed. She bit her lip. Why hadn't she conceived yet? It was surely not for lack of trying. Had Frances any idea how badly she wanted to bear Monte's child?

"Are you listening?"

Abbie startled. "I'm sorry. Please repeat that."

"I said it is unbecoming to exhibit petulance. No matter how angry you might be, your countenance must never show it."

How well Frances obeyed that one. Except for her eyes, she kept her face cool and serene even when Kendal staggered in late or Jeanette had a tantrum.

"Cleanliness of person is required at all times. Slovenly habits destroy character. And if . . ." She looked up at the tap on the door.

Monte came in. He had obviously changed into fresh pants and shirt, but his face was worn and tired. Relieved, Abbie almost hurried to him, then thought better of it and kept her place at the mantle. She was in his path.

He came directly to her, and she felt a rush of warmth. He kissed her forehead. "Forgive my missing supper."

"Where were you? I was worried." And it had been dull and difficult dining alone with Frances and her instructions on table etiquette. Frances was taking smug delight in her training.

"I needed to see some ranchers. It was a good long way." He turned. "Is Kendal home?"

"No." Frances's voice and face were smooth.

It sent a pang through Abbie to see her so. She brushed Monte's arm. "I'll have Pearl fetch your supper."

"Yes, thank you, Abbie."

♦♦♦♦♦♦♦

Kendal staggered back from the brass-edged bar. The room swam, then cleared. He stepped forward and banged his knee on a chair back.

"Watch it, mister."

Kendal steadied himself and passed through the crowd to the doors. They swung open, and he propelled himself onto the boardwalk and grasped the post. He had quite possibly exceeded himself tonight. But he had cause to celebrate. The deal presented him that night would make his fortune ... again. The stars streaked when he looked up, and where was his horse?

A hand gripped his shoulder. "Kendal?"

Kendal staggered as he turned. He couldn't place ... ah yes. Abbie's brother. The lawyer ... though his name eluded him at the moment.

"You're looking a little green."

"I s'pose I yam." Grant. That was the name.

Grant took him by the shoulder. "You won't make it to the ranch in this condition. You'd better stay the night in my room."

Kendal leaned on Grant along the boardwalk to the old hotel. It was quieter than its rival. The way he felt just now, that was fine with him. They crossed the lobby, sidestepping the dining room tables with the chairs upended atop.

"You're up late."

Grant steered him toward the stairs. "I had work to do."

Kendal clicked his tongue. " 'See saw, Margery Daw, Johnny shall 'ave a new master. He shall have but a penny a day, because ... he can't work any faster.' "

"Something like that."

Kendal slung his arm over Grant's shoulders, and they started up. The stairs would not hold steady. He caught his boot on the edge, and only Grant's strength kept him up. "I think ... I should not have had ... that last one. I'm afraid I am ... inebriated."

"Yeah."

Kendal swayed while Grant worked the key in the door and pushed it open.

"Go ahead and take the bed. But if your stomach wants emptying, hit the chamber pot and not my linens."

"You're a good friend." Kendal staggered to the bed and collapsed. One leg hung over the side, but it was altogether too much trouble to pull it up. He closed his eyes.

Grant sat down on the chair and pulled off his boot. Kendal started snoring before he'd removed the second one. He unbuttoned his vest and tossed it on the bureau, then his shirt and trousers, down to his long johns. With a good tug he freed a blanket from under Kendal and wrapped it around himself, then curled up in the chair.

This wasn't the first time he'd seen Kendal have too much. But he hadn't seen him so badly off as tonight. The man would have broken his neck if he had managed to mount his horse and start for home. Kendal might wish he had, come morning.

Grant pulled the blanket tighter and put his feet up on the end of the bed. Kendal's snoring gained strength. It was going to be a long night.

◆◆◆◆◆◆◆

"No, Kendal." Monte kept his voice low.

"But surely you see the advantage to getting in early. Why, with this information we can purchase railroad land low and sell at tremendous profit. You've already seen the stir the train has made in Rocky Bluffs. That will only continue wherever the rails run."

"I said no."

"The return on your loan would be more than doubled. It . . ."

"It smells."

"What are you suggesting?"

"I don't trust those men. Have you no judgment of character?"

"Of course they seem different. They're English." Kendal rubbed his hand through his hair. Though cleaned and meticulously dressed, Monte saw the bloodshot eyes, the skin of his face, pale and flaccid. If Kendal's head had stopped aching from his excess of last night, it had surely started again from the bite of Frances's tongue.

"Come, Kendal. I've been to England, as have you. Did you at any time have difficulty distinguishing the gentlemen from the lower classes?" Monte stood. "These two . . . they're not one and not the other. They remind me of the carpetbaggers—well dressed and spoken, but inside vulgar and corrupt."

"Some of the carpetbaggers are men like ourselves trying to make their way. We cannot spend the rest of our lives bemoaning the fate of the South."

"I have no intention of doing so. But have you learned nothing from it?"

"I've learned to take my opportunity as it comes."

"So I've seen. And at what price." Let Kendal take offense. "There is honest work and sound investing. Yes, buy land, Kendal. God knows, it's land that matters, the difference between free and bond. Purchase a spread and set yourself up. There's profit in ranching."

"Slow profit."

"Honest profit."

"Meaning?"

"Just what I said."

"Would you accuse me then of dishonesty?"

Monte drew a long breath. "I am not accusing you. But I'll

have no part in this venture. I warn you to stay free, as well."

Kendal's eyes narrowed. "When I need your advice, I'll ask for it."

"Just as you do my money?" Monte watched the blood rush to Kendal's face.

The door opened, and Abbie swept in. Her face was flushed and cold, her hair falling loose. "Oh, Monte, she's wonderful!"

He walked around the desk and took her hands. "Who is wonderful?"

"Zephyr."

"Abbie . . ."

"I know you said she's not ready, but truly, she's as smooth as silk. She carried me like I wasn't there and flew like the wind."

"She's skittish enough to throw you at any provocation, and she doesn't know the land."

"Well, I do."

He frowned. "Abbie, I don't want you to do this again. If you want to ride, take another horse."

Her lip jutted. "Come with me, then, and see for yourself."

Kendal stood. "He'd rather control you, my dear. It's his forte these days."

Abbie spun. "I'm sorry. I see I've interrupted you."

"We were finished," Monte said.

"Indeed we were. If you'll excuse me." Kendal strode from the room.

Abbie turned back. "I'm sorry, Monte. I didn't know you and Kendal . . ."

"It's all right. Listen, Abbie, this has nothing to do with control. Zephyr is not the kind of horse to which you're accustomed. Arabians are very high-spirited. Yes, she can fly like the wind, but she must first know that her wings are clipped."

She raised her hands to his chest. "Don't scold me. It was incredible! It's the first of March, and I've been cooped up all winter."

He took her in his arms. When she looked like that, how could he not? "My wild mountain girl! How can I hope to tame you?"

"I don't want to learn my wings are clipped. I just want to fly."
He shook his head. "Nor does Zephyr. But she will." He
brushed her cheek with his fingers. He would not say he wanted
her on a horse that would come home should anything happen,
nor that he'd prefer she stay close to the house altogether.

He did not expect that Captain Gifford would harm her. But
if she happened upon something . . . Monte would put nothing
past Gifford, not after Chance. Making Abbie understand that
would not be easy. He rested his cheek on her head. With any luck,
she would be with child soon. Perhaps motherhood would bring
her down to earth.

Twenty

The amber globe of the lamp yellowed the faces across the table from Kendal. They sat in the corner of the hotel, the noise around them sufficient for secrecy. "As I told you, gentlemen, Mr. Farrel is not a risk taker."

"Of course there's risk, Stevens. No venture worth pursuing is without risk." William Emmerson spoke in his horsy accent. Kendal noticed it more since Monte had pointed it out. Perhaps the man was not what he seemed, but who was?

"You're astute enough to see the possibilities, aren't you?"

The possibilities and the consequences. So far they had spoken in vague assurances. Now he wanted more. "I want details."

Emmerson exchanged a glance with Harris next to him. "We handle the details. Less chance of word getting out that way. One slip and our competitors will be on this deal like wasps on a honeycomb."

"Save your blather for the stooges you'll be selling to."

Emmerson narrowed his eyes. "We're only thinking of your welfare. The fewer in the know, the better chance of success. And you want to be part of that success, don't you, Mr. Stevens?"

Kendal sat back in his chair and ran his hand over the waxed end of his mustache. He glanced at Harris, silent as usual. "Maybe I do, maybe I don't. If I'm putting up the earnest money, I need more of a guarantee."

"Such as?"

"First, I want to know the deal."

Again the men shared a glance. "It's very simple, Mr. Stevens.

You buy the land low, we sell it high."

"Where and how?"

"Investors from London and New York."

"What's to keep me from doing the same without you?"

"Have you contacts in the North? What entrance do you have, sir, to the monied Yankees, if I might be so bold?"

Kendal's jaw tightened.

"Or perhaps you know of southern gentlemen who came off as well as your brother-in-law?"

That rankled. No one prospered like Monte. "And you have these contacts?"

Emmerson sat back magnanimously. "With our foot in the door, your success is guaranteed. Everywhere the railroad goes the land skyrockets."

"Not everywhere. These plots are stretches of barren country between townships. I checked. I rode them myself."

The man smiled indulgently. "Yes, but that's our little secret."

"What other secrets have you?"

Emmerson cracked his knuckles. Definitely not a gentlemanly sound. "How scrupulous are you, Mr. Stevens?"

"How lucrative is it?" Now he would get some answers.

Emmerson chuckled. "Oh, you won't be sorry."

Kendal leaned back and studied them in silence. So it wasn't on the up and up, as Monte had said. But Montgomery Farrel lived by a code that was as outdated and disarrayed as the southern dreams that had spawned it. Men dealt differently these days, and those with less scruples rose above others more tightly fettered, as he had seen with his last partners. This time he would not go in with his eyes closed. Still, he held his silence.

"All right, Stevens."

Kendal turned to Harris, surprised the man had spoken. Usually he let Emmerson spin the tale.

"We need front money to acquire the titles, pay our travel and expenses, advertise the goods, and pretty up the offering. It's a lay that requires each of us to play our part with discretion. After the sale you receive your share, we receive ours."

"And what's to keep you from disappearing with the lot?"

Emmerson drew himself up. "You have my word as a gentleman."

"Oh, come, Emmerson, even were you a gentleman, I would not take your word."

Sobering, the man asked, "What, then?"

"Your daughter."

Leaning forward, Emmerson glared at him. "What of 'er?" His sudden consternation caused the cockney slip, no doubt.

"Once I hand over the funds she goes into my custody until I receive my portion."

Emmerson glanced at Harris, who sat stone faced, then back to Kendal. "Where?"

"Here at the hotel, in comfortable accommodations. As long as all goes well, no harm comes to her."

Emmerson's fingers tightened on the glass. "Well, I don't . . ."

"Agreed." Harris said.

Kendal waited for Emmerson. His right eye twitched, but he nodded slowly.

Kendal finished his drink. "Very well. It'll take a day or so for me to acquire the funds."

Emmerson stood. He was clearly flustered.

Harris remained seated. "Contact us when you're ready, but . . . time is of the essence."

"I realize that." Kendal stood. He did not extend his hand. Now that they understood each other it was not necessary. He had lain down with the dogs.

When the doors swung closed behind Kendal Stevens, Emmerson turned on Harris. "What d'ya mean by lettin 'im 'ave my girl?

"That's not a concern."

"Well, it's a concern to me. She's but fourteen with no mother to care for her. She's not part of this."

"She is now, if that's what it takes to secure Mr. Stevens. Don't worry, Emmerson. There's more than one dog to set on a man."

"Meaning?"

Harris pulled a crumpled paper from his pocket and licked the end of his pencil, then carefully penned:

Mrs. Stevens
c/o Montgomery Farrel
Lucky Star Ranch

Dear Madame,
Be advised your husband strays.

Emmerson leaned forward. "What does it say?" Harris read it, and Emmerson sputtered, "That insinuates that my Patricia—"

"Insinuates only. I doubt Mr. Stevens goes in for children. And if he does ... well, she's bound to get the education sooner or later. I'll hold this until the time is right, then have it delivered. There is no fury like a woman scorned. We'll get Patricia easy enough."

He drained his glass. "Once we've multiplied Steven's offering, we'll retrieve the girl and be on our way with Mr. Stevens holding the bag." He sent Emmerson a sharp look until the man nodded. No doubt the mention of money went a long way toward easing his fears.

◆◆◆◆◆◆◆

The house was quiet when Kendal went in. He handed James his coat and hat, then made for the study. No doubt Monte had retired with Abbie. Frances would be in bed, not that it meant anything for him. Her intent was clear: to exclude him until he restored their wealth and standing.

And that he would do. He pushed open the door. He would not remain dependent. He would beg, borrow, or steal to get the funds for this deal, and then he would repay his self-righteous brother-in-law every cent. He strode to Monte's desk, pulled open the drawer, and paused.

There was a thick portfolio immediately on top. Did Monte keep his things so carelessly? Glancing up, he listened, then took out the folder. He struck a match to the lamp and swiftly scanned the documents. He looked closer at one and then the next two. "Hmm... in Abbie's name..." Now, what could he do with that?

He studied the corresponding figures. Well, well, well. If he played his hand right... and he was not without charm. Maybe, just maybe... He slid the papers back in place and closed the drawer.

◆◆◆◆◆◆◆

Abbie carried Jeanette on her hip through the knee-deep snow and pulled open the stable door. So far, so good. No one had seen her from the house. At least no one had stopped her. She searched in the dim light for the tin tub hanging from the wall, set the child down, and stretched for it.

"I'll help you," Will said, coming out of the back.

"Thank you, Will."

"What's this for?"

"I want to give Jeanette a slide on the hill."

He grinned. "I can do better than that." He went to the back, stooped, and pulled out a wooden toboggan.

"Where did you get that?"

"Made it. I pulled apart some old barrels and refitted the slats. Come on, I'll show you."

Abbie straightened Jeanette's muffler and made sure her mittens were snug, then lifted her and followed Will outside. "How are you enjoying *Robinson Crusoe*?"

"It's a little tough."

"The challenge is good. It sharpens your skills."

"I knew you'd say that."

She scanned the hill as he settled the toboggan. The slope behind the corral looked gentle, but steep enough to afford a good slide as long as they stayed out of the trees to the side. Abbie sat, then gathered Jeanette into her lap.

Will grabbed the back of the sled. "Ready?"

Abbie nodded.

He gave them a shove, then jumped onto the back. The slope

was faster than she thought. She should have tried it without the baby. But Jeanette laughed as she squeezed her tighter. She had never heard Jeanette laugh so. She snuggled her face close. The sled slowed as the land evened out.

"That was wonderful!"

Jeanette clapped her mittened hands and laughed again. It was an incredible sound. What did it matter that Frances would have vapors if she knew? This was the happiest she had ever seen the child.

Abbie grabbed her into her arms. "Let's do it again."

Will tugged the sled. "It'll go faster if we follow the same line, now the snow's packed some."

"I think that's all right. It runs straight."

"Long as you don't lean. Don't want to shoot into the trees there."

Abbie followed his point to the cottonwoods, bare of leaves but bushy with undergrowth. "I won't lean."

The next ride was faster, and the next faster yet. Her cheeks chapped in the cold, and her hair came loose, but Abbie had not been sledding since she and Blake took the hill behind the McConnel's barn. Each time she stood at the bottom, she rebundled Jeanette. "Enough?"

"More."

Abbie laughed aloud. "A girl after my own heart." She couldn't wait to tell Monte that Jeanette had spoken, though he'd laugh when he heard her first word. She trudged to the top, placing her feet in each of Will's tracks.

"Looks like fun."

Abbie jumped. Kendal stood just above them. She would catch it now.

"I hope you don't mind. March snow is the best of the season, and I hated for Jeanette to miss it."

"I'd have taken her myself if I'd known there was a toboggan."

Abbie smiled. "She's quite the scamp. Not a bit afraid."

"Mind if I have a run?"

Will shrugged. "Sure, if you want to."

"Keep the child, will you?" He took Jeanette from Abbie and placed her at Will's feet, then motioned. "After you."

Abbie glanced down. "Would you like to ride alone?"

"Now, where's the fun in that?"

Reluctantly she sat, and Kendal shoved off and jumped on. He wrapped his arms around Abbie.

"Don't lean. Kendal, don't lean!"

The sled skewed off the track. The unpacked snow flew up, powdery and choking. The toboggan shot into the air, then plunged into the fringe of cottonwoods. They crushed through the twiggy brush, and Abbie flung up her elbow as they banked off the roots of a cottonwood and flipped over.

Snow stung her neck beneath the scarf and clung to her hair. Lying back, she released her breath.

Kendal leaned over her. "Are you all right?"

"I think so."

"I'm sorry. It was entirely my fault."

She sat up and shook the snow from her hair. Will and Jeanette were lost to view, nor could Will climb down with the child. "Well, no harm done."

She started to rise, but Kendal pulled her up. "Are you certain you're all right?"

"Yes, quite . . ."

He suddenly closed her into his arms and covered her mouth with his.

There was no taste of brandy to excuse him. Abbie pressed her fists to his chest. "Kendal, how dare you!"

"How dare I not? Can't you see I'm sick with wanting you?"

The breath left Abbie's chest.

"My dear . . ."

"You would do well to stop now." She itched to slap him. She felt foul and guilty. If Monte knew . . .

Kendal trapped her against the tree trunk and leaned close. "I can be discreet."

Abbie's hand stung with the blow to his cheek as he staggered back. Her chest heaved. "And I can be dangerous." Will would hear if she screamed, but then Monte would know. What would his honor require? She dared not find out.

Kendal straightened. "I see I've shown an alarming lack of judgment."

"Lack of judgment?" She seethed.

He brushed off his coat. "Will you go to Monte with this?"

"Will I need to?"

He picked up his hat from the snow. "You've made your position clear. It won't happen again."

Will called from the top of the hill.

Abbie glared at Kendal, then called back, "It's all right, Will." She started up. "Bring the sled, Kendal."

Kendal stared after her. His pride stung more than his cheek, but the worst of it was how this might jeopardize his attaining the funds. How could he have judged her so poorly? With what Frances had told him about Abbie and Cole's intimacy, he assumed she would be an easy mark. Oh well. He reached for the sled. He would find another way.

♦♦♦♦♦♦♦

Inside the new courthouse, Abbie turned from the window and faced her brother. "Why do you ask?"

Grant smiled and laid down his pen on his desk. "Because I know you. And I can tell what you're thinking."

"I've not said anything at all against Marcy Wilson."

He stood and came around the desk. "That in itself is evidence enough. I've never known you to hold your tongue so extremely."

"It's not my business to tell you who to court or not to court ... however much I may wish to."

Grant laughed. "Now we'll get to the truth. Tell me why I should not woo the fair daughter of the judge."

"Oh, Grant!" Abbie stomped her foot. "What can I tell you that you can't see for yourself if you'd just open your eyes?"

"I don't know. I find her intelligent, attractive, and quite charming. I've gathered that you and she have not been close, but then, you are quite different. She is a lady, and you would flee any semblance of such if you could."

Abbie jutted her chin.

"I admit your marriage to Montgomery Farrel has improved your deportment. . . ."

"Oh, you're impossible! Marry Marcy, if you like. But you'll pay the price for the rest of your life."

He caught her arm as she spun past. "Abbie, don't be angry."

Abbie sighed. "I know there are fewer ladies here than in New York, but there are other choices."

"And maybe I'll explore them."

"If you get the chance. Once Marcy attaches she clings like a leech."

"Now, Abbie . . ."

"I won't say another word. Come for supper, and I'll keep any thought of Marcy so far from my mind even you won't know it's there."

"I will, then."

Abbie smiled. "Six o'clock." Her skirts swirled behind her as she swept out the door. She blew him a kiss over her shoulder, then rounded the corner. She caught her breath as she almost landed in Kendal's arms and sprang back.

He frowned. "You needn't look as though you've encountered a rattler in the dust."

"You startled me."

He bowed. "I apologize. Actually I was looking for you."

"What is it? Has something happened?"

"No, no. It's . . . I have a rather delicate matter to discuss."

More delicate than other matters they'd discussed? Abbie flushed angrily. He had made any encounter between them distressing, especially in Frances's presence. "I'm listening."

"Perhaps I could buy you lunch?"

"No, thank you. I'm having lunch with Clara."

Kendal glanced around them, then returned his eyes to her. "First, let me say that I regret my past indiscretion. My conduct was inexcusable, and I can only attribute it to the angst of my current difficulties."

Abbie dropped her eyes. He seemed sincere, and certainly it was a difficult time for him. "I accept your apology."

He hesitated. "The business I would speak of is . . . rather more sensitive."

She waited.

"I need a certain amount of earnest money for a business venture that I think will enable me to set Frances and myself up on our own. But I . . ." He released his breath. "I can't go to Monte with it. I don't want to ask for more than he's already done."

Abbie softened. "You want me to ask?"

"No. That would be one and the same. I don't want him to think that I cannot care for his sister." He took her arm and pulled her aside to the wall as a man started down the hall toward them. Waiting until he had passed by, Kendal said, "You can't imagine how difficult this is for me to ask . . . but . . . I was hoping you could help me yourself."

Abbie stared at him. "How?"

"There are certain stock certificates held in your name."

"In my name?"

"Yes. No doubt Monte has not divulged this to you. He keeps his business to himself, I've noticed. But he has invested in your name as well as his own, and it is this that I'm hoping to borrow against for this venture."

Abbie's stomach tightened. "I don't know anything about this, Kendal."

"It's very simple. You put up your stock as collateral and sign on a loan at the bank for me, and I will pay you back substantially more than you started with when the transaction is completed."

Abbie hesitated. Why could he not go to Monte? Surely they had settled the affairs together, and Monte knew the extent of his need. She should go to Monte herself, but perhaps it was again that southern honor that she understood so little that kept Kendal from seeking the money that way.

He sighed. "I know what you think of me." His eyes fell. "And by God you have every right."

"No, Kendal, it's not that . . ." Abbie's thoughts whirled. What should she do?

"You've no idea what it costs me to beg, but I want a chance to make up to Frances for all the ways I've failed her. This is my opportunity, the one I came out here hoping to find. What little pride I have left forbids my asking Monte, but I throw myself on your generosity. . . ."

Abbie glanced down the hall to Grant's office. Maybe he could help. He would certainly understand the workings of it all and . . .

Kendal cleared his throat. "Forgive me. I'll not trouble you again."

"Wait, Kendal. I . . . all right. I'll help you."

He paused a moment as though uncomprehending, then took her hand and kissed it with a low bow. "You are the finest lady."

If Grant could only hear that. But somehow, it didn't sound quite true. Kendal held out his elbow, and she slipped her fingers through. "I really don't know what's required."

"Don't worry. I have the certificates with me, and it's an amazingly simple process."

As he said, the transaction was completed in less than three-quarters of an hour. They stepped into the street, and Kendal bowed over her hand. "I am forever in your debt." Abbie nodded, then headed slowly for Clara's house.

Twenty-One

That evening Kendal stood, elbow on the mantel, when Emmerson and his daughter entered one of two suites the hotel boasted. He would not be accused of poor hospitality. She was a comely lass, with mousy hair and freckles, but a nice shape and pleasant features. He bowed. "Good evening."

Emmerson brought her forward. "Patricia, this is Mr. Stevens."

"How do you do, Patricia. I trust the accommodations suit you?"

Patricia nodded slightly and glanced at her father. Kendal turned to him, also. "Shall we discuss our affairs in the hall?"

Emmerson nodded, turned to his daughter with a dim smile, then went out.

Kendal closed the door. "Just so there's no confusion, I'll be guarding this room carefully." That was another reason he had chosen the suite with its access only from the hall.

"That's hardly necessary."

"I find it so." He pulled the wallet from his breast pocket. "Here it is in full. Make good use of it, but I warn you, if this does not come out as you say, I will not be easy to reckon with."

"You just see that my girl is safe."

"She'll be my highest priority."

Emmerson stuffed the wallet into his coat in silent response and left.

Kendal returned to Patricia. "I've had supper laid out for you in the other room. You've nothing to fear." She nodded without

232

moving from the spot. He turned. "Well, then, I'll be off to my own supper. Good night."

◆◆◆◆◆◆◆

Sitting on the floor of the parlor, Abbie carefully bent the stand and slid it into the slot, then stood the paper doll on the floor. "There, see?"

Jeanette snatched it up.

"Gently. Don't squeeze."

She watched the little fingers loosen as Jeanette examined the embossed paper of the ruffly hat and petticoat. "Now, then. The blue gown or the red? What do you think, Frances?"

Frances glanced down. "Redheads never wear red." She returned her attention to the fire.

"The blue, then." Abbie cut the paper dress and tucked the flaps over the doll's shoulders. "My, she's pretty."

"Pitty." Jeanette poked one small finger at the doll.

"Come, Jeanette. Time for your bath." Frances swooped over and took the child by the hand.

"No! Play Auntie."

Frances pulled her sternly, and Jeanette dug in her heels.

Abbie handed her the doll. "Go, Jeanette. We'll play again tomorrow."

The scathing look in Frances's eyes was quickly veiled as she took Jeanette out. It hurt less than the child's cries escalating to a tantrum. If only Frances would scoop her up in her arms and smother her with kisses. If only she would smile and say she loved her. No matter how Abbie tried to fill the gap, it was Frances Jeanette needed.

But Frances was untouchable, so removed she hardly seemed alive. And she seemed determined to make Jeanette the same. Abbie stole moments with the child, aching to do more, but Frances always separated them at the first opportunity. Only Mammy was allowed to hold Jeanette and soothe her temper.

Mammy would bathe her now, then tie up her hair in rags and rock her against her breast. For the life of her, Abbie would never understand. And if she did bear children of her own, no mammy of any color would take her place. Abbie closed her eyes and leaned against the settee.

She jumped when Monte stormed into the room in a rare temper and closed the door behind him. "What is it, Monte?" She scrambled up from the floor.

The muscles of his jaw clenched and rippled. "I want to discuss a matter with you."

"What matter?"

"Your loan to Kendal."

Her heart fluttered. "The bank made the loan, Monte. He needed the money for . . ."

"I know what he needed it for. I turned him down."

Her heart sank. Would she never learn?

He paced before her. "Do you know what it means to sign over your stock as collateral?"

"It guarantees the loan."

"Do you know what that means?"

"Not . . . exactly. I believe it means—"

"It means that if Kendal's venture fails, you lose your stock." Abbie nodded slowly. "He felt very confident—"

"Did you procure the certificates from my desk?"

"I didn't even know they existed. He had them with him."

"Did you not wonder at that?"

"I . . ."

"Why didn't you ask me!"

Abbie started. He had never raised his voice to her, nor to anyone in her recollection.

"I would have told you this 'deal' smacks of infamy! What guile did he use to dupe you?"

"He didn't dupe me, Monte. I wanted to help him. I didn't think—"

"You didn't think to consult your husband."

"Kendal didn't want to—"

"Be turned down again."

Abbie sat down on the settee. "I'm sorry."

Releasing his breath, Monte dropped to his knee before her. "What's done is done. But, Abbie, I must know this will not happen again. I've already stretched by investing in your name. I thought to protect you should anything happen to me and you remarry. But you are to make no financial decisions without me . . . especially if they concern Kendal. Is that understood?"

"Yes."

"Now come. I'm going to teach you somewhat of how the world works."

"A little knowledge can be a dangerous thing."

"Not near so dangerous as ignorance, I think."

◆◆◆◆◆◆◆

The next morning, Monte tapped the bell on the bank counter. "Mr. Driscoll, please."

"Certainly, Mr. Farrel." The teller hurried off.

Mr. Driscoll straightened his vest as he came forward and extended his hand. "Mr. Farrel."

"I'd like to follow up on our previous conversation."

"Ah . . . yes, of course. Come in, please." He ushered Monte into the small office in the back and closed the door. "Cigar?"

"No, thank you."

Mr. Driscoll closed the box and seated himself at the desk, motioning Monte to take the matching brass-studded wing chair across from him.

Monte sat. "When my wife and brother-in-law transacted their loan with you, did Mr. Stevens explain the nature of the business he was pursuing?"

"I . . . ah . . . regret that unfortunate business tremendously. . . ."

"You've already expressed your regrets. I assure you I hold neither you nor the bank responsible. I just want to understand the venture."

"Yes, well, it's . . . ah . . . very sound, I assure you. With the railroad coming through, the land developed along the line will be appreciated considerably. Mr. Stevens is financing the offering for two gentlemen from London working in conjunction with the railroad." He swallowed.

"The Denver Rio Grande?"

"Of course, though as I told you before, I did not require references . . . your standing with the bank and the presence of your wife . . ."

"But the gentlemen, Harris and Emmerson, were referenced."

Beads of sweat stood up on Donahue's forehead. "Well, yes. That is, their references were English, of course."

"But you checked them."

"With Mr. Stevens vouching . . . forgive me, Mr. Farrel, but as he is your brother-in-law I had no reason to doubt his word."

Monte stood. "Let's hope that's an oversight you won't pay for."

He then went directly to Sterling Jacobs' Western Union office in the front corner of the newspaper building. "I'd like to send a telegram to Denver, to the railroad office for the Denver Rio Grande."

"Certainly." Sterling Jacobs took out a pad and pencil.

"And another to New York to be posted to London. Inspector Pierce, Scotland Yard."

Sterling whistled. "No kiddin'?"

From his desk, Abbie's father looked up.

Monte shook his head. "If you don't mind, Joshua, I won't expound for the newspaper just yet."

Joshua cocked his head. "It's been a bit dry lately. I could use a good story."

"I'm hoping very much there's no story here at all. But Inspector Pierce is the one to know if there is."

After writing his inquiries, Monte left. He rode toward the ranch but dismounted out on the range. He walked Sirocco to an upended piñon stump and tied him firmly, then turned and slipped the pearl-handled revolver from its holster.

He centered the gun in his palm and raised it. He aimed for the oaks and fired, winced, then fired again and again, reloading and holstering and drawing. Wood splintered as the small branch shot from the tree. Monte breathed deeply.

♦♦♦♦♦♦

Kendal started up the hotel stairs for the eighth day in a row. He knocked, then turned the key in the lock and entered. Patricia sat by the fire, working the sampler as usual. The girl was certainly industrious. Glancing up as he entered, she set aside the sewing.

"And how are we tonight?"

"Fine, thank you." Her accent was clearly cockney.

"I trust you're comfortable?"

"Yes, sir."

"Not lonely?"

"Not too much."

"Good." He glanced casually at her work and nodded. "They've seen to your needs all right?" He always asked this.

"Yes, sir. Very well, sir."

Kendal paused, then followed through with his intention. "Shall I join you for supper?"

Her eyes widened. "If . . . if you like. The food is good here."

"Then I shouldn't miss it." He had already ordered for two, as supper at Monte's had become a decidedly chilled affair not only from Frances, but also Monte since he'd learned of Abbie's loan. He supposed he was lucky Monte hadn't shown him the door, but his disdain and fury were thinly concealed. Well, he'd expected that, but he needn't endure it.

In a moment the tray was brought up to the room. Kendal sat at the small table and motioned Patricia to the chair across. "Please." He would have seated her, but she seemed awkward with formalities.

She sat.

He flipped the napkin open onto his lap. She silently did likewise. He raised his fork and she raised hers. The silence stretched as they ate. It was scarcely better than supping at home. At least with Patricia there was no condemnation. She was certainly not a chatterbox, most likely scared witless by all of this. He could put her at her ease, or at least try. "Tell me of yourself, Patricia.

Your mother is dead?" He flaked the last strip of trout with his fork.

"Yes, sir."

"I'm very sorry. How do you like America?"

"Fine."

"You've no brothers or sisters?"

"My brother died of cholera."

"How very sad." Kendal glanced at her as he chewed slowly. "You and your father, you've not settled anywhere?"

She shook her head. She wasn't making this easy.

He tried a different tack. "Is there . . . a lad you cotton to?"

She dropped her gaze. "No, sir."

He sighed in exasperation. "How was the trout?"

"Good. I don't care much for fish, but this was good."

Kendal pushed aside the tray and stood. "I hope you've not found this time too tedious." There was more of a bite to his words than he intended.

"I don't mind sewing and reading some."

He half-smiled at her misunderstanding. "That's good. I wouldn't want you to be bored or lonely." He noted the flush that came to her cheeks.

He raised her to her feet, suddenly acutely aware of the warmth of her hand. "I wouldn't want you to be unhappy."

She shook her head a little stiffly and glanced back over her shoulder. He followed her gaze. The window was heavily shaded. Kendal's throat tightened. This was a treacherous path.

He reached up and stroked her hair, and she caught her breath. Her lips trembled. The danger beckoned him. He bent low and kissed her.

Her mouth was soft, uncertain. The mouth of a child. He could feel her fear. It was not what he expected, not what he wanted. He drew back, then bowed stiffly, and left.

Downstairs the bar beckoned, and he wasted no time finding a stool.

◆◆◆◆◆◆◆

Monte led Zephyr and Sirocco out to the yard where Abbie stood expectantly. "Before you mount, I'll have your word not to try anything foolish."

"I promise."

He tethered Sirocco to the post and helped Abbie up. Zephyr tossed her head, sidestepped, and flared her nostrils. Cole had worked with her some, but she was still fiery and unpredictable. Monte wished Abbie would wait, but patience did not come easily for her. He handed her the reins.

Besides, they all needed to get out. With the snow melted, the earth smelled damp and inviting, though the air was keen. He mounted Sirocco. "Ready?"

Abbie nodded. He nickered, and Sirocco set the pace. Zephyr vied with him, but Sirocco kept her back. So far Abbie allowed it. Monte glanced over his shoulder and smiled. She drew up beside him, and Sirocco quickened. Zephyr whinnied and broke into a trot.

"Abbie . . ."

Frowning, she reined the horse in. Monte smiled. His wife needed as much training as the horse. They entered the open range and Sirocco fought for his head. Monte looked at the reins in his hand, no longer wrapped on the wrist. It would be painful, but he glanced at Abbie sitting proudly on the equally proud mare. He couldn't hold them all back.

"All right, go then."

With a laugh, Abbie pressed in her knees and Zephyr bolted. Sirocco responded with no urging. Monte watched Abbie's motion on the mare. She sat her well, but then the horse's gait was smooth and even. The ground flew by beneath them until he called, then Abbie reined the mare in, and he allowed Sirocco to circle, establish himself.

"Oh, Monte, I've never felt such freedom!"

He chuckled. "Yes, I know."

They walked the horses down the slope and dismounted at the stream. He kicked away the edge of the ice and the animals drank, then he tethered them with two large rocks and took Abbie by the hand. They walked to the end of the cut, then stood together, the back of her head to his chest.

"Abbie, with you here by my side, I couldn't want for anything else. Do you remember when I told you this place held my destiny?"

"Yes."

"Now I've found it. You and I will raise up generations of Farrels who will tame this land and call it their own."

"God willing."

He stroked her hair. "Yes, God willing."

"I keep thinking to find myself with child."

"It will come."

"It's long in coming."

He turned her to face him. "Are you anxious?"

"Not anxious, really, but surprised. Mama conceived Sadie after two months of marriage. She was only eighteen, and Sadie had Matthew by nineteen."

"No matter, Abbie."

"I know how it was for you to lose your son when Sharlyn died. I want so much to give you children. I've thought of it since the first time you kissed me. Do you remember?"

His chest tightened. "Of course. I carried that moment in my heart through all the time that followed. At first it was a torturous thing, as I'm sure it was for you. I should never have presumed."

"Do you wish you hadn't?"

"I did for a time, knowing that I had hurt you so deeply. Even so, I played it again and again in my memory when I should not have."

Abbie pressed his hands in hers. "Do you think of your child still?"

"I think sometimes of what might have been had he lived, but more than that I think of what will be. Of the children you and I will have."

"I hope so, Monte."

"I know it will be so." He kissed the crown of her head.

Twenty-Two

Monte stared down at the bull. Two seasons ago he'd paid two hundred fifty dollars for it, and now it lay in the dirt, throat sliced. What manner of beast took down a Durham bull and emptied its jugular? He looked out across the land, then again to the ground at his feet. From the tracks, the bull had struggled. Its thrashing destroyed any other marks.

But nothing wild made a clean slice like the one across the bull's throat. Here again was wanton destruction. His stomach tightened. Gifford. He pictured the red lambchop whiskers, the cold, proud expression, the straight military bearing.

That they had served opposite causes was not enough to convict the man, nor the fact that he stood to gain the most should the Lucky Star fail. But something inside told Monte it was Gifford. He turned and walked to Sirocco.

The stallion would not come near the scene and scent of blood. Monte glanced back at the fouled ground, the mound of flesh. Was Gifford capable of such? He was a military man. It would not be the first time he dispatched appropriated stock, but for what? To leave it on the ground to rot? *God, what manner of man have you brought against me?*

Before Monte could mount, Cole rode up with Breck beside him. "Mr. Farrel, we got—" His glance fell on the bull. "Tarnation!"

Breck swayed in his saddle, then dismounted. He stopped beside the bull. "No coyote done this."

"No." Monte calmed Sirocco, who quivered under his hand.

Cole turned. "Mr. Farrel, word's gone round that Jake Gifford'll double the wages of any man in our operation who signs on with him."

"Who's going?"

"All the ones that just came on, and Skeeter and John Mason. He's too young to know better."

"Can't fault a man for wanting to improve his lot."

"If you call it that."

Monte straightened the stirrup and tucked in his boot.

"What're you doin'?" Cole questioned.

"I'm going to call on Captain Gifford," Monte replied as he mounted.

"I'm comin' with you."

"It's better if I go alone."

"No, it ain't."

Monte brought Sirocco around. "Trust me in this, Cole. If Gifford wants to kill me, your presence won't change that. And I have to let him know we won't stand for any more."

Cole rubbed his forehead with the back of his sleeve. "Tarnation," he muttered.

Monte urged Sirocco with a word. The horse was fresh and willing, more than willing to flee the scene. They headed southwest for the Double Diamond, headquarters of Captain Jake Gifford. He tethered Sirocco at the post before the long veranda of Captain Gifford's white stucco hacienda. A Mexican woman opened the door but said nothing.

"Good afternoon. Is Captain Gifford at home?"

"Sí, senor." She stood aside.

Monte removed his hat as he went in, then followed her through the large open room. Thick beams spanned the ceiling. Over the fireplace hung a rifle and sword and the head of an elk with a vast rack. Another Mexican girl rubbed oil into the chairs set around the long table. She neither looked nor spoke as they passed. They stopped before a heavy paneled door, and the woman knocked.

"What?"

"A man to see you, *Capitan*."

"Send him in."

She opened the door and backed away. Monte stepped in. The room was small with a single arched window. Other trophies—antelope, elk, even a buffalo—lined the walls. Captain Gifford turned from the window, and Monte caught his surprise before he masked it.

"Mr. Farrel. I didn't expect a social call."

"No doubt it was my men you expected."

Captain Gifford walked to the oak desk. "Cigar?" He held out the box.

"No, thank you."

Gifford clipped the end and lit one for himself. Then he took his seat without offering Monte a chair. "Your foreman's reputation is formidable. I can't do better than men he's handpicked."

"For the Lucky Star."

Gifford shrugged. "It's a free country, even in the territories. I'm taking on hands as I've acquired more cattle."

"Lucky Star stock?"

Captain Gifford drew himself up. "Are you accusing me of thievery?"

"Inquiring only."

"By God, for a reb you've got pluck."

"I know your record, Gifford. Special reconnaissance, captain in charge of 6th Company. Commendations for services rendered beyond your normal duties. I believe that means you were a spy."

"Correct on all counts. I'm flattered."

Monte held his anger in check. "In case you haven't heard, the war's over."

"Oh yes, I'd heard."

"Then have you no honor?"

"Honor? You, the son of William Jackson Farrel, speak to me of honor?"

"What has my father to do with it?"

"Elias Gifford."

Elias Gifford? "I don't—yes, I recall a man of that name. He was . . ."

"My father was an abolitionist."

"He was hung for rape and murder." Monte countered.

"Lies, propagated by your father and the other planters."

It was years ago, but Monte recalled the incident, the daughter of Wallace Bendar found in his field. He remembered the outcry, the horror at the brutality of the crime, the smug denial put forth by the troublemaker Elias Gifford. He now saw a smoldering fury in Captain Jake's eyes that prompted memories of the man on a scaffold, a man consumed by violence.

Did Gifford hold him responsible for his father's just demise? Was that behind the unwarranted attacks? An incident, however traumatic, in which his father had a hand? Of what was the off-spring of Elias Gifford capable? Monte clamped his will over the rage that rose inside. "Let there be no misunderstanding. I expect your harassment to stop."

"Harassment, Mr. Farrel? Business, rather."

"There's room in the territory for both of us."

"Well, now, I don't see it that way. Take that contract you have with Bent's fort."

"What about it?"

Gifford opened the drawer of the desk and pulled out a paper. "Seems the man in charge of purchasing livestock would rather buy from me."

"You undercut me?"

"Only slightly. I served with Lieutenant Beard in '63. In your native state, I believe."

Monte felt the rage pounding in his temple. "If I learn that you have one single head of Lucky Star stock, I'll bring you to court, Captain Gifford."

Gifford leaned back in his chair. "You don't think I'd be that careless, do you? Take that sixty-five head I had driven down to the fort last week. Fine Double Diamond stock, it was."

Monte grabbed him by the collar and dragged him up. "You

set foot on my land, just once, and I'll kill you." He saw the muscles ripple in Gifford's jaw.

"Why don't you have your wife do it for you?"

Monte smashed his fist into Gifford's nose and blood spurted. The door crashed open and three men were on him. He ducked as one swung for his head, but the fist of another caught him in the belly. He doubled and a boot cracked his jaw. The third smacked a stout club across his back. The blows came faster than he could defend, and he collapsed to the floor. Blood ran from his nose and mouth, and he could feel his ribs shift.

Captain Gifford came and stood over him. "Take him where the coyotes will find him."

The men dragged him from the room. Sirocco shied at the smell of his blood when they heaved him over the horse's back. Monte tried to speak to calm him, but they slapped the flank and Sirocco broke away, galloping heedlessly. Monte cried out with the pain in his ribs and clenched one hand in Sirocco's mane, fighting to get upright.

His palms were cracked and bleeding, and the strength left his fingers. Less than a mile from Gifford's ranch, he fell heavily to the ground. Sirocco kept running. Monte lay in the grass. One eye was swelling shut, and every part of him hurt. His breath came sharp and painfully.

God, what can I do against one so evil? I'm only a man. He closed his eyes. He felt utterly helpless.

Trust me.

It was almost as though Monte heard the voice. His mind said he was losing consciousness, but his heart suddenly burned with hope. Even the pain that grew keener every moment did not dim it.

He heard hooves and thought for a moment Sirocco had returned. But when he raised his head, inches from the ground, he saw the pale, heavy hooves of Cole's palomino. Cole jumped down and dropped to his side. "I trust you, Mr. Farrel. It's Jake Gifford I don't."

Monte groaned when Cole raised and half carried him to the

spare horse, tied behind Scotch. "I don't reckon you'll appreciate the ride just now, but it's a sight better than lyin' there till nightfall. Can you hold on?"

Monte nodded. He focused on staying astride, and not crying out with each jolt and jerk. By the time they reached home, he felt numb and exhausted. Cole eased him from the saddle, and he kept his legs with difficulty.

"Go ahead and lean." Cole hauled him to the house.

James opened the door. "Mastuh Monte."

"Monte!" Abbie rushed forward. "Cole, what happened!"

"Had a run in at Captain Gifford's place. Most likely his men." Cole helped him to the sofa.

Abbie turned on him. "Where were you?"

"Waitin' outside."

"Why weren't you with him? How could you let him go in alone?"

"Abbie . . ." Monte flinched from the effort.

"I'll get the doc." Cole put on his hat and left.

Monte turned when Abbie dropped to his side. "It looks worse than it is."

"You don't expect me to believe that." She dipped a towel into the basin Pearl brought and dabbed it over his face.

He could tell by her expression that he'd do better not to speak again. No reassurances would belie what her own eyes told her. He could make out Frances and Kendal standing over him, but his good eye teared as she washed him, and the throbbing in his ribs and head was draining his energy. He fell asleep before the doctor arrived.

◆◆◆◆◆◆◆

Abbie shook as she sat beside Monte after Doctor Barrow left. Fury and fear held sway inside her. They could have killed him. He had slept for two days now, waking only once for water and then drifting back to his heavy slumber. The doctor had wrapped his ribs and treated the cuts, but there was nothing he could do for the internal bruising, save check back as he had just now.

He said it was good Monte slept on his own. He did not want to sedate him. And he felt that there was likely no permanent damage. But why had Monte risked himself? She clenched her hands.

Abbie had not spoken to Cole since he brought Monte in. He of all people should have known. He had told her he'd keep a watch. So what if Monte ordered him away? It was foolishness and stubborn pride. Or maybe it was honor. She flounced up from her seat and paced the room.

Kendal came in. At least he'd been sober since the incident. "How is he?"

"Stronger. Doctor Barrow says he'll mend."

"I don't think I've seen a beating so bad. He must have been outnumbered."

"Of course he was outnumbered. He was alone. By his own order." She spun. "What is it with you men? Why must pride govern your sense?"

Kendal smiled. "Perhaps we haven't enough sense to govern our pride."

Abbie stalked to the sofa and stared down at Monte. The swelling was diminished, though the bruises were dark and ugly. She longed to take him in her arms and love him. Maybe by coming together she could share his pain.

Look to the living. How could she when life was so fragile and men so stubborn?

Kendal straightened. "I'm going to town. Will you tell Frances if she asks?"

Abbie didn't argue. She hadn't the strength to say he should tell her himself. She nodded and took her place again at Monte's side. He stirred, and she leaned close. "Monte?"

He opened his eyes. The diminished swelling allowed some movement in the bad one. "Well."

"Are you hungry?"

"It seems we've been here before."

"I think you like the attention."

He reached for her hand, and she brought his to her cheek.

"Why, Monte?" Tears stung her eyes.

"Perhaps it was not the best judgment."

"Not everyone is a gentleman. You can't wait for a man like Captain Gifford to remove his coat."

Monte smiled and winced. "Actually, I started it."

"You? Why?"

"I felt he had it coming."

Abbie sank back against her chair. All the times she had seen Monte refrain from action, hold back retribution, control his anger . . . what could have spurred him to attack Captain Gifford? She whispered, "Why, Monte?"

"He's behind all the trouble we've had at the ranch."

"And what is the trouble?"

"The rustlings, the stampede, the poisoned water holes, the slain and mutilated stock. He killed Chance."

Abbie gasped. "How do you know?"

"Never mind that. Where's Frances?"

"In her room."

"I don't want either one of you leaving the ranch."

"You're hardly one to talk."

He raised up slowly. "Don't give me trouble, Abbie."

"Oh no. You find enough of it on your own. Why didn't you take Cole?"

"I thought if I confronted Gifford, we could settle it."

Abbie shook her head.

"At any rate . . ." Monte raised up on his elbow. "At least now we know what we're up against."

"Skeeter, John, and the new men collected their wages."

Monte nodded. "I won't bid for their loyalty."

"That's what Cole said, so I paid them."

There was a knock on the door, and Abbie opened it to find Pearl with broth and bread. She brought the tray to Monte, and Abbie helped him sit.

"Thank you, Pearl." Monte's smile was gentle.

"You get that down, now, Mastuh Monte. Get yo' strength back."

He bowed his head briefly, then raised the spoon and took a sip. He smiled again, and Pearl left them. Abbie sank to her knees beside him while he ate. She did not dare ask him how she could help. But the need to help burned inside. Perhaps Cole . . . no, he would tell her not to meddle.

How could Monte expect her to stay in the house and do nothing? They were down to six men, not counting Will and James. Or Monte. "Have you told the marshal?"

"He's aware of some of it. I alerted him to the missing stock."

"Does he know it's Captain Gifford?"

"I have no proof."

"But, Monte—"

"Abbie, let me handle this my way."

"If he saw you like this—"

"He'd say Captain Gifford defended himself. I went to his home and accosted him there."

"But . . ."

Monte put his hand on her head. "Give me your word, Abbie."

"I won't."

"Then I'll have you guarded day and night."

She stood and stalked to the window. The last of the day's light faded to gray. "Then talk to Pa. And to Grant. And the McConnels and the others."

"I can't defame a man without proof."

"Defame?" She spun. "He tried to kill you."

"No, he didn't."

Helplessness washed over her. What chance had common sense against his southern honor? "I will stay on the ranch unless I've no other choice."

He smiled grimly. "I guess that's the best I'll get from you."

♦♦♦♦♦♦♦

Monte lay awake in the dark. One thing the beating had shown him was that Gifford would not shirk violence. They were all at risk—his men, his family. Monte was not foolish enough to think he had accomplished anything with his threats. Gifford knew he had him by the throat. He had but to hold on, and he'd drain the lifeblood from the Lucky Star.

Where do I turn, Lord?

The other cheek, Reverend Shields would say, as he had spoken eloquently on brotherly love during Sunday's service. Well, Monte had given Gifford both cheeks and the rest of him, as well. Though the bruising was healing, the anger was not.

"Trust me," the Lord had said—if indeed it had been Him. But how? What did Monte know of God and His ways? He rubbed a hand over his face. Gently, so as not to disturb Abbie, he slipped from the bed and pulled on his wrap.

Outside the room, he lit the lamp and went down to the library. He set the lamp on the table. Slowly, painfully he climbed the ladder to the top shelf and pulled out his father's Bible. He ran a hand over the leather, gilt lettered and tooled. Inside were chronicled all the generations of Farrels, but the rest of the book had not seen much use.

The Farrels lived by honor, not by faith. Monte climbed down the ladder and slid it back to the corner. He sat and opened the Bible. God's instructions, Winthrop Shields called it. Monte fanned the pages. Had he years, he would not learn all this book had to say. And he hadn't years. Time was running out already.

He tucked his fingertips in and opened the book. *Ecclesiastes.* He scanned the page. *To every thing there is a season and a time to every purpose under the heaven. A time to be born, and a time to die; a time to plant, a time to pluck up that which is planted; A time to kill, and a time to heal. . . .* Monte frowned as he read. What did it mean? *A time to love, and a time to hate; a time of war, and a time of peace.*

He sat back in the chair and stared at the rows of books on the wall. There was a plan larger than himself. Indeed, what place had he in it at all? Each season would come whether or not the Lucky Star remained. People would be born, people would die. Whether he lived or not was out of his hands.

And yet . . . *A time to love, and a time to hate.* Should he not hate evil when he found it? *A time of war.* Should he not fight that evil?

If he fell, if the Lucky Star failed, who would be next? How would his neighbors stand?

"God," Monte whispered. "I don't know if I've heard you right. But I pledge here and now to stand against the evil Jake Gifford would wrought with whatever weapons I have. Not for myself alone, but for those I love, for my neighbors, and for your righteousness."

✦✦✦✦✦✦✦

Captain Jake frowned at the men who stood awkwardly before him. "I told you to take care of it."

"We flung him on the horse. He was bleedin' bad, and the stallion took off crazy. There's no way he rode it home."

"His man got him home. Cole Jasper. That name mean anything to you?"

The man swallowed. "I didn't see no one around. We figured he'd fall and the coyotes would get him just as you said."

Captain Jake shook his head. "Get out of here. Send Skeeter to me." He ought to learn something from Farrel's man. Something he could use.

Twenty-Three

The day was almost balmy as Abbie strolled arm in arm with Sadie, leading their horses behind. They'd spent the last two days together since Joe's work was completed, and Sadie would leave before the week's end. They had ridden to the edge of Monte's land and dismounted for a walk.

Sadie drew a long breath. "You're very fortunate to have all this, your beautiful home . . . your handsome husband." She elbowed her.

"When he isn't black-and-blue." Abbie spun at the sound of gunshots. Her heart jumped to her throat. The reports brought the sickening feeling of death, the sound of screams, the smell of blood. Unconsciously she pressed her hands to her ears. Her breath came thin and weak.

Sadie gripped her arm. "What is it, Abbie?"

She fought the horror. "I don't know." Her voice was as clipped as her breath.

Sadie clutched her shawl. "Where's Monte? At the house?"

"No. He left for town early this morning." Abbie gathered herself and slowed her breath. This was no time to let past fears disable her. Gunshots meant trouble. "Sadie, do you think you could find Cole? He has the herd just south of here. Send him to me, then wait at the house."

"What are you going to do?"

Abbie swung up into the saddle. There was no time for explanations.

"Abbie!"

"I won't get close." Kicking her heels, she swung around. Abbie's heart raced every time the shots sounded, then stopped, then sounded again. They ricocheted off the bluffs with a double report that vibrated in her chest. She slid down from Zephyr but held the reins firmly as she climbed.

Topping the rise, she saw him below, back straight, legs apart, arms ready at his sides. Suddenly he flipped the gun from the holster at his hip and fired, stuffed the gun back, and shook his hand. Abbie didn't need Sirocco near to see that it was Monte.

She watched him reload and repeat the gunplay, the report of the shots echoing off the wall of the bluff to the right. She spun at the sound of hooves behind her as Cole reined in Scotch. His face was thunder and lightning, and Abbie knew he'd lay into her. She hushed him before he began, and he climbed up the rise on foot, then followed her gaze to the range below.

He stared as she had, until the firing stopped. "I'll be licked."

"What is he doing?" Abbie watched again as Monte drew and shot three times, then holstered the gun and gripped his hand tightly, bending low with the pain. He straightened, picked up his hat, and walked over to the horse.

Cole gripped her elbow. "Better git 'fore he sees us."

She nodded and led Zephyr down the slope. Once out of view they mounted. Abbie did not speak. What was Monte doing, shooting like . . . like a gunfighter? A terrible thought seized her. *Please, God . . . he didn't hope to fight Gifford that way!*

The *thunk, thunk* of the hooves on the prairie grass matched the thumping of her heart. A startled cottontail bounded away. A meadowlark sang from a clump of sage. The quiet seemed to have swallowed up the echoes. Abbie glanced at Cole. He glanced back.

"Was he fast, Cole?"

"His draw was. He was slow on the trigger. I guess his hand . . ."

"Why is he shooting like that?"

"I don't know."

Or wouldn't say. She glared. "I have a right to know. Has there been more trouble?"

"No. Things have been quiet since . . ."

"Since Monte nearly got himself killed?" Her fear became anger.

Cole kept his gaze ahead.

"How long are you going to wait and let him face this alone?"

"That wasn't my fault, Abbie."

She huffed and shook her head. She barely heard the rattle before Zephyr reared, hooves pawing the air. Abbie grasped for the saddle horn, but her hand slipped as the horse twisted and bucked. She fell to the ground. In the same moment Cole's bullets blew the snake in half. Zephyr ran.

Cole leapt from the saddle. "You okay?"

She sat up. "I think so." It had not been a good fall. Her ankle throbbed, and her elbow was scraped.

Cole reached a hand to her. She tried to stand, then collapsed with a cry.

"Yer ankle?"

She bit her lip.

"Let's have a look." He raised the edge of her skirt and removed her boot. He ran a hand over the ankle and she winced.

"Tender?"

Before she could answer Sirocco bore down on them and skidded to a stop, and Monte jumped down. "Take your hands off her, Cole." He dropped to the ground beside her, and Cole backed off.

Abbie brushed the hair from her eyes. "Zephyr was spooked by a rattler."

"Are you bitten?"

"No. Cole shot it."

Monte frowned. "I heard the shots. Where's Zephyr?"

"She ran." Abbie touched the swelling around her ankle.

Cole stood. "I'll fetch her back."

"Stable her. I'll take Abbie with me." Monte spoke without looking at Cole.

Abbie saw his jaw tighten as he bent and lifted her into his arms as Cole left them. She knew that look. "He was helping me."

Monte didn't answer. He carried her to Sirocco, lifted her into the saddle, and swung up behind. As he took up the reins, Abbie saw his cracked and bleeding palm. "Monte..." She reached down to it.

He jerked it away. "My hands are fine, Abbie."

His tone hurt and frightened her. "Why are you shooting like that out here alone?"

"I was obviously not alone."

"I heard the shots. I didn't know it was you."

"Then you had less business being there."

"Why are you so angry?"

"How am I supposed to respond when I find Cole with his hands on you?"

"He was checking the injury."

Monte looked away. Abbie shivered. His irrational anger frightened her more than his shooting. And he was excluding her completely. They rode in silence until the house came into view.

He released a slow breath. "Perhaps I overreacted."

Abbie raised her chin. "Not perhaps."

"I apologize. Hearing the gunshots ... and then seeing you down ... I asked you not to—"

"I didn't leave the ranch. Not until I heard *your* gunshots." She could feel the tension in him still. "Oh, Monte, what are you thinking? When did you learn to shoot like that?"

He didn't answer, but his arm around her tightened. He turned his hand on the reins, and she saw the raw and broken skin. His face was firm. "If there's trouble, I'll be the one to handle it ... not Cole, not you, not anyone else."

Abbie trembled.

He pulled up at the stable and took her down. "Will!"

Will rushed out. One look at Monte quenched his questions. "Did Cole return with Zephyr?"

"No, sir. I haven't seen him."

Monte frowned. "That's what I feared. She doesn't know to

come home." He walked swiftly into the house and laid Abbie on the sofa. "Pearl! See to her, will you?" He strode out.

Abbie sagged. She didn't think his anger was for her this time, but she felt estranged nonetheless.

"Lawdy girl, what you done to yo'sef now?" Pearl's face was a dark cloud.

"It's just a twisted ankle."

Pearl clicked her tongue. "It's swellin' bad." She bustled out and returned with a bandage and her medicine box.

Abbie bit her lip against the thorough ministration of Pearl's hands, firm and insistent. She sank into the couch when it was over.

"You's gotta be mo' careful, Mizz Abbie. Mastuh Monte already lost hisself one wife."

Abbie nodded. A lump came to her throat. It was the first time Pearl had used her given name.

Monte rode away from the house. How could he explain what God had charged him with? How could he tell her the responsibility that rested on his shoulders? He caught sight of Cole, watched him slide from his horse and walk slowly toward the restive mare.

Zephyr tossed her head and stomped, but did not run again. Gently, Cole reached out for her, ran his hands over her neck, then gripped the bridle and relaxed. Monte brought Sirocco over. "Quite a chase."

"Yup." Cole stroked the mare, then led her to Scotch and mounted.

"Cole . . ."

"Don't say nothin'. I know how it looked."

"Nevertheless, I apologize."

Cole grunted. "If you don't know already how Abbie feels about you, you're a durn fool. It ain't like any efforts on my part would change that."

Monte raised an eyebrow. "Are there efforts on your part?"

"No, there ain't. With all due respect, Mr. Stevens is the one you should be watchin'."

Monte eyed him keenly. "I'm aware of that."

Cole turned in the saddle. "You ain't thinkin' of callin' Gifford out?"

Monte stiffened, but there was no judgment in Cole's question, only honest concern. "No. But I won't be caught short. I'd appreciate knowing you're on my side."

"I been here three years. Whose side do you expect I'm on?"

Monte looked out over the land. Perhaps, just perhaps, he wasn't expected to do it alone. He released his breath. "Please excuse my misjudgment . . . with Abbie."

Cole shrugged. "Heck, if I thought there was a chance, you might have somethin' to worry on." He spurred Scotch to a canter, trailing Zephyr behind. Monte watched him go, then smiled. Cole Jasper wasn't exactly the sort he would choose to depend on, but it certainly felt good to know he could.

✦✦✦✦✦✦✦

Abbie felt barely a twinge in her ankle as she stood on the stool to reach the book. It had healed swiftly, as well it should with everyone insisting she stay off it completely. Frances tutored her needlework, and Abbie was sick to death of ripping stitches. Frances had an eye like a hawk for a single crooked or misshapen stitch. And like Cole, Abbie chafed the inactivity. She was ready to be up.

She turned as Frances slipped into the room and closed the door behind. Her countenance was anything but serene.

"What is it, Frances?"

"I need to speak with you."

Abbie replaced the book and climbed down. She waited as Frances walked slowly to the end of the room and turned. Whatever it was, Frances was clearly shaken.

She gathered herself. "I believe Kendal has taken a mistress."

Abbie caught her breath. The feel of Kendal's arms and his kiss rose unbidden to her mind. Did Frances suspect her? Was she here to confront, to accuse? "I know he's been distracted. He's working on a business venture."

Frances sniffed. "That's not what keeps him away." She held out the note, and Abbie took it. *Madame, Be advised your husband strays.*

"Where did you get this?"

"It was delivered to the house."

"By whom? It's unsigned."

"I don't know. It was given to James."

Abbie folded the note and handed it back. How could she deny the possibility? "Who do you suspect?"

Frances shook her head. "I don't know. I thought he could be watched."

Abbie's mouth dropped open. "You're not suggesting that I . . ."

"No. Someone he wouldn't notice."

"Oh, Frances. Are you sure you want to do this? Kendal will be furious if he finds out."

Frances straightened. She was perilously controlled. "I want to know."

Abbie hesitated. If only Frances had treated him more kindly. If only she could have relented, forgiven, reached out to him only once.

Suddenly Frances crumpled. Tears sparkled in her eyes. "I need to know. It doesn't matter the risk."

She loves him. The thought came with sudden clarity. Frances loved Kendal. It was her fear that estranged them, and now his betrayal had brought her to the edge. Oh, Lord, how could they reconcile? Even Monte's pride had been no obstacle compared to what Frances faced if Kendal . . .

She touched Frances's arm. "Grant lives at the hotel. He might know if Kendal frequents . . . someplace."

"Will you talk to him? Will you ask him?"

"Monte . . ."

"I don't want him to know." Her voice broke. "I couldn't bear it."

There it was again. Southern pride demanding silence. Abbie sighed. "All right."

"Will you go now?"

Abbie hesitated, but how could she not respond to the trust Frances placed in her? For the first time since she came, Frances was reaching out—of her own accord. She had made herself vulnerable. Abbie nodded. No sense putting it off. If Grant watched, maybe ... maybe he would find that something else occupied Kendal. She went out and wrapped up in her coat.

Surely even with their difficulties, Kendal would not run out on his wife and daughter, but perhaps he thought no one would know. She felt again the pressure of his hands on her shoulders. "*I can be discreet.*" She shook her head. Oh, Kendal.

♦♦♦♦♦♦♦

Kendal's throat worked as he reread the telegram. Short and to the point. *Deal turned bad. Get Patricia. Pine Creek ford. Thursday by six.* The deal turned bad. His chest felt hollow. He crumpled the paper and dropped it in the yard. He dug his fingers through his hair. The deal turned bad.

Closing his eyes, he tried to think. "Turned bad" could mean any number of things. Perhaps it had not worked out as profitably, or they had to stop before capitalizing on all of it. Perhaps they had overstepped themselves. All these could be remedied.

He smoothed his vest. He still held the trump card. Patricia. They would not dare cheat him as long as she was in his grasp. He would go to town, have a drink, think things through. Maybe he would not bring her to the meeting. Maybe he would hear them out first.

Yes. His tension eased. But he would make sure she was guarded. His bribes to the hotelier had vouchsafed her so far. There was little that could not be gained with a little gold crossing the palm.

♦♦♦♦♦♦♦

Abbie tethered Zephyr at the new pine courthouse. Grant

hugged her as she entered his office. "Now this makes for a good day. A visit from my sister . . . and the judge's daughter."

Abbie raised her chin. "I'll not comment."

He laughed.

"I've come to ask a favor."

"Anything at all."

"It's rather delicate."

"Oh?"

Abbie walked to the window. "Well, I don't know how to say it nicely. Frances suspects Kendal is . . ."

"Ah. And with good reason."

She spun to face him.

Grant shrugged. "His regular visits to room sixteen."

"Oh, Grant!"

He strode to his desk and tucked some papers into the drawer. "How about lunch? The hotel serves a fine meat loaf."

Abbie nodded as they crossed the street. Her stomach was in knots, but Grant would not talk once he got food on his mind. They took a table and ordered without seeing a menu.

Grant must have understood her need, because as soon as Rudy left to place their order, he leaned close. "At first I assumed he had business, perhaps an associate to meet. But the other night, Monday I guess it was, I met him in the hall on my way up. He seemed . . . agitated, and from behind the door, I heard someone crying."

Abbie closed her eyes. "So Frances is right."

"Well, in a court of law that's extremely circumstantial."

"What else could it mean?"

"Any number of things. But . . ." Grant shrugged. "I allow it is the most likely."

"Can you watch the room?"

He frowned.

"I know it's a dreadful thing to ask. But . . . Frances wants to know."

"I am not a spy. A man's private affairs are his own, however questionable."

Abbie took a bite of meat loaf without tasting it. She should have known better than to ask Grant to skulk around after someone. There was only one way to answer the question; confront it head on. "You're right, Grant. I'm sorry I asked. I'll go up and have a look."

Grant shook his head. "Not a good plan."

"Frances is trusting me. I won't let her down." Abbie wiped her mouth and laid the napkin aside.

"Then I'll come with you." He checked his watch. "But I have to meet a client now. Wait until later."

"There's no need. I'll simply pay a visit." She squeezed his hand, hushed his protest, then headed back to the hotel lobby and up to room sixteen. She tapped lightly on the door. There was no response, and she knocked again. This time there was a soft shuffling inside and the knob turned slowly. The face that appeared was younger than she had expected.

Abbie forced a smile. "Is your mother here?" The girl shook her head. "Your father?"

"No one else."

Abbie's heart sank. Surely Kendal . . . there must be some mistake. "My name is Abbie Farrel. May I come in?"

The girl shook her head and glanced swiftly down the hall. "No, I don't think so."

"If you're worried about Mr. Stevens . . ."

The girl's eyes widened, and the door narrowed. Abbie put up a hand to stop its closing. "Please let me talk to you. I want to help."

"You can't help."

"I can." Abbie stepped between the door and jamb. "You're alone here?"

"Mostly."

"Except when Mr. Stevens comes?"

The girl slowly nodded.

"What's your name?"

"Patricia."

"Now, Patricia, suppose you tell me about Mr. Stevens." Abbie hadn't meant to be so direct, but her growing anger ruled her tongue.

"My father brought me here. I must stay until their business is finished."

Abbie's chest eased. "Your father's in business with Mr. Stevens?" She dared to hope.

Patricia nodded. "Mr. Stevens ... required me to stay as a guarantee."

As awful as that sounded, Abbie felt relieved. If that was all, if he was acting as a guardian over the girl ... "So he comes to check on you?" She expected a quick nod, not the rushing of blood to the face and the mortification in her eyes. Abbie's hope evaporated as her anger rose again.

"Has Mr. Stevens ..."

"Please, I can't talk about it." Patricia squeezed her hands to her cheeks.

It was clear enough that Kendal was not acting the gentleman. Abbie recalled the stinging of her palm against his cheek. She wished he were there to receive it again. Well, she would take matters in hand. "Get your things. I'm taking you with me."

"Oh, but I can't."

"Of course, you can. Whatever business they're conducting does not involve you."

"I don't dare."

"Well, I do. And I'll answer for you when it comes to it." Abbie spun at the sound of Kendal's voice downstairs in the lobby. Another man spoke, and she could not make out Kendal's response. He sounded tense, impatient.

She would not get Patricia down that way. She had intended to take her home, bring the matter to Monte, and even if she must, confront Kendal with it. But not alone. Not here.

She turned to Patricia. The child was quaking. Again her anger gave her strength. "Come quickly." She led the girl by the hand, down the hall past Grant's door to the potted plant at the end. He kept his key there when he didn't want to carry it. With any luck ... she touched the metal nesting in the leaves and hurried to the door.

"This is my brother's room." Stepping in, she saw it was none too tidy. "You'll be safe here. Don't open to anyone. Grant has his own key, but I'll have him knock three times and then once more so you'll know it's him. If you hear any other knock, don't answer. Perhaps you should find a place to hide in case you need to."

Patricia nodded. "Mr. Stevens will be angry."

"Not nearly so angry as I." Abbie turned. "Lock the door behind me." She swept down the stairs, just as Kendal came up.

He raised his eyebrows. "Good afternoon, Abbie."

"Kendal." Abbie composed her features.

He spread his hands and feigned a smile. "What ..."

"I was running an errand for my brother." She didn't bother crossing her fingers. A lie was a lie. She'd confess it to Reverend Shields if he were inclined to listen. "Good day, Kendal." She tossed her cape over her shoulders and went outside.

She crossed swiftly to the courthouse and knocked on Grant's office door. She waited, knocked again, and tried the knob. It held fast. Of course. His appointment. But surely he conducted business from the office. Perhaps he had concluded that and gone elsewhere.

She hurried down the hall to the small courtroom. It was empty. Hastening back, she stopped outside Judge Wilson's door, lifted her hand, and hesitated. She didn't fancy facing him, the way the judge always looked at her as though she were guilty of something. But need drove her. She knocked. He beckoned.

"Excuse me, Judge Wilson." She cleared her throat. "Would you know where to find my brother?"

"Am I your brother's keeper?" His lowered brows alarmed her until he smiled, his goatee poking out stiffly. "A little joke."

Abbie formed a smile. "Yes, sir."

"No, I don't know where your brother is, but if you want to find him, I suggest you check with my daughter. He's not given her a moment's peace since he got here."

Abbie bit her tongue. As though that were Grant's doing.

"Thank you, sir." He nodded, and she backed out. If Grant was with Marcy, she could not speak with him, and in any event, she did not have time to search for him now. Kendal would have long since discovered Patricia's absence. She slipped out of the building and ran for Zephyr.

Sensing her need, Zephyr responded with wonderful speed, and Abbie raced for the ranch. The wind blew against her face, and her hair streamed out behind her as she rounded the hill. Suddenly Kendal's horse blocked her path and Zephyr veered. Abbie felt her hands wrench loose as she fell, and her head hit the ground. Stunned, she found Kendal bending over her.

He looked haggard and disheveled. "Where is she?"

Abbie pressed a hand to her forehead. "What on earth are you thinking, jumping out like that in front of my horse?"

Kendal shook her. "Where is Patricia?"

Her heart raced as she groped for an answer. "What are you talking about?"

Kendal's fingers dug into her shoulders. "The girl, Abbie."

"I must have hit my head harder than I thought. You're not making any sense at all." She struggled to rise.

Kendal held her firmly. "I swear you'll not continue this ruse."

"You're hurting me, Kendal. Have you gone mad?"

"Yes, maybe I have." Crushing her in his arms, he kissed her. Abbie beat her fists against him, and he laughed. "Not nearly so stunned now, are we?"

"Unhand me!"

"When you tell me what I want to know."

Abbie's anger flared. "I expect you have more to tell. How could you, Kendal? She's only a child."

"Oh, she told you about that, did she?"

Abbie's chest heaved with fury.

He shook her. "Where is she?"

"Why do you need her? What part has she in all of this?"

"Collateral."

"Like my certificates? Will you stop at nothing?"

"No, Abbie, nothing. I am holding a two-edged sword. One slip and I'm cut."

"Go to Monte, Kendal. He knows already."

"He doesn't know the half of it. No, Abbie, your husband is too much a man of honor to deal with this. I, on the other hand, have no honor left to hold me back. Nor have I time." His fingers dug into her shoulders like talons. "Where have you taken her?"

Abbie pushed against his chest, but could not match his strength.

His voice was low. "I won't touch you unless you force me to." He took a strand of hair and slowly twisted it around two fingers until his hand reached her neck. "Where is she?" He wrenched her face forward. "I swear I'll take you without a moment's regret."

She cried out as he pulled her close again. "All right! She's in Grant's . . . office." Her breath rasped. "In the courthouse."

Kendal's eyes narrowed. "What does he know?"

"Nothing. He wasn't there. I . . . I couldn't find him; he was out with Marcy." If she buried the lie in truth maybe . . .

He leaned close. "It was foolish of you to interfere."

Abbie trembled. Did he see her lie? Was it written clearly on her face?

"But I suppose I expected no less. In a different world, Abbie, you and I . . ." He released her so suddenly her head snapped back. He stood. "And for your information, I no more than kissed Patricia. I've no need to force any woman, and she was more reluctant even than you."

Abbie couldn't speak. He stood and reclaimed his horse, glanced back, then gave Zephyr a smack that sent her running. She had expected that. Kendal was no fool. He knew she'd go to Monte. And she would still. He had only bought time. She waited until he rounded the hill, then she cut away from the road in a direct line to the ranch.

Twenty-Four

Monte sat in the bank office and fought to control the fury boiling in his chest. Mr. Driscoll wore his most patronizing expression. "I'm terribly sorry. But the matter is out of my hands. The railroad has stepped in to investigate. It appears the business deal your brother-in-law and wife initiated . . ."

"They did not initiate the deal. They were approached. Kendal was approached. Mrs. Farrel had nothing to do with it."

Mr. Driscoll shook his head. "I'm afraid her signature on the loan says otherwise. No doubt you'll clear that up at the inquiry."

"You know as well as I do that my wife—"

"Mr. Farrel." Mr. Driscoll stood. "The good name of this bank has been jeopardized by the shady dealings of Mr. Stevens and his companions. I intend to follow whatever measures are required to clear my reputation. If you are concerned about your wife, I suggest you take her in hand."

Monte stood. Mr. Driscoll had certainly changed his tune now that things had fallen out as they had. He did not need a reply from Scotland Yard. The railroad had responded to his inquiry and stepped in. Abbie's holdings were as good as lost, and God only knew what he would salvage if the railroad sued for fraud in their name.

It was Kendal's affair, not his. Yet honor demanded he stand by him and right the wrong as far as he was able. This was ingrained in him, though it burned. But he would not stand for Abbie to be dragged through it. Her ignorance would cost them dearly, but that did not include her in Kendal's infamy.

Mr. Driscoll knew that, but he was covering his own backside. Monte would find no help there. He took up his black felt hat and left. Kendal must be somewhere in town, and Abbie, as well. He had left Frances alone at the house after divulging as much as he dared of Kendal's scheme. Frances had a right to know. As it was, they would all share the ruin.

He searched each business along the main street but found neither Kendal nor Abbie. He then went to the courthouse, where Marcy Wilson was taking leave of Abbie's brother at the door. Impatiently, he tipped his hat and bowed. "Good afternoon, Miss Wilson."

"Mr. Farrel." She deepened the dimple in her cheek and sashayed past.

"Monte. You're looking better." Grant extended his hand.

Monte shook it. "I'm quite recovered. Have you seen my wife?"

"I left her at the hotel, looking into that matter with Mr. Stevens."

"What matter?"

"With the girl . . . I assumed you knew."

"Knew what, Grant?"

Grant blew a slow breath. "Oh, brother."

Monte listened as Grant explained Abbie's visit. He fought to maintain control. Was Abbie set on destruction? "Where is she now?"

"Monte, I don't know. She can't be there still. Likely you'll find her at home."

Monte turned and strode for his horse. He had not passed her on the road, but he did not limit Abbie to the road. He would find Kendal later. Marshal Haggerty had agreed to question him quietly at the house, though he held warrants for Harris and Emmerson. That would all wait. Right now, Monte's concern was Abbie.

He rode home hard, leaped from Sirocco's back, and bounded up the front stairs. "James!"

"Yessuh."

"Is Mrs. Farrel at home?"

"No, suh."

Monte frowned. As he turned, Zephyr cantered into the yard empty saddled. She had learned to come home—but without Abbie. He remounted and hurried Sirocco to the eastern pasture. He found Cole kneeling beside a new calf entangled in the wire. He reined in. "Have you seen Abbie?"

Cole shook his head.

"Get the men and spread out to Templeton Gap. I'll take the west side."

"Mind my askin'..."

"The sky is falling, Cole. And Abbie's in the middle of it."

❖❖❖❖❖❖❖

Kendal clenched his hands. Abbie had lied to him. Patricia was not there. He had searched thoroughly. But he must find her. He stepped out of the courthouse. Activity in front of the marshal's office caught his attention, and he paused, then joined the crowd. The faces on the wanted poster chilled his blood. Harris and Emmerson. The deal had turned indeed. He slunk through the shadows for his horse.

His fear and fury drove him through the deepening dusk to where he'd left Abbie. Of course she was no longer there. Had he not expected as much? Perhaps he had even hoped. He gripped his head between his hands. What was he doing? Where had everything gone wrong? What now? What now!

Pulling the reins, he brought the horse around and searched the ground. Her footsteps showed in the loose gravel at the side. So she had left the road in the direction of the ranch. Still it was a long way. Perhaps he could intercept her.

The westering sun crowned the tip of Pikes Peak and illumined a ghostly half-moon in the pale eastern sky. The light would not hold. Even as he lingered, the edge of sun shrank away. He heeled the horse up the bank and followed her trail.

❖❖❖❖❖❖❖

Captain Jake spurred his charger. The men riding behind

would see that he did not shirk. He would do whatever it took to rid the territory of his rival. With what he had learned from Skeeter, he knew one more blow would sink Montgomery Farrel. And that blow would come at the heart of his operation.

The horses had been moved to the west pasture with the warmer weather. They were accessible now, as they had not been through the winter. Once he had marred the Lucky Star brand with his Double Diamond, he would drive the herd to the fort for the army's use. Lieutenant Beard was eager for horses. Especially fine horseflesh such as Montgomery Farrel raised.

They rode steadily as the night deepened. Soon they would be on Farrel land. Skeeter had directed them, describing where to find the horses, though he did not ride tonight. Captain Jake would not try his loyalty that far. And the kid, John Mason, was too wet behind the ears to be of any use. He was back at the ranch oiling saddles.

The night was clear and keen. They came to the fence line and reined in. Baker dismounted and cut the wire in three sections. They rode through. Captain Jake's charger sensed the herd. He watched the ears raise, the nostrils flare. But the horse made no sound. It was too well trained for that.

Captain Jake caught sight of the grazing animals. They would be guarded, but he could not make out any guards. He motioned his men to circle. As soon as they flanked the herd he would give the signal. He searched the darkness. Surely they would be detected.

Something was not right. It was too quiet. Where were Farrel's men? Was it a trap? Montgomery Farrel would not leave the horses unguarded. But his own men took their positions unchallenged. Captain Jake raised his arm, and they whistled and hollered. The horses shied and started to run. The men held them together and drove them back the way they had come, toward the breach in the fence.

Captain Jake waited for them to pass. His men would drive them to the ranch to be branded at first light while he made an appearance in town to establish his alibi. He cut across the pasture heading east.

◆◆◆◆◆◆◆

Abbie pushed on. Her indignation made her strong. What was happening that Kendal must keep a girl hostage? Even if he told the truth—that he had not forced his attention—she was frightened. He had no business using the child as a pawn.

Abbie would see that he did not continue, but she felt a sinking in her stomach. She had lied to his face. The deception had slipped out in spite of her, a cunning she had not known she possessed. Was it so easy to depart from the truth? Had Kendal taken one step so small?

How much time before he discovered her ruse and returned with a fury? Could she make the ranch before that? Everything in her cried out to run, but she knew if she did, she would soon tire and be forced to stop. It was better to maintain a steady progress.

The darkness was now complete. She thanked God for the stars. Without them she would lose all point of reference on the empty range. She had angled too far east and now cut back slightly west as she kept her northward progress. Pulling her coat close, Abbie kept on. She had to make it to the ranch, find Monte.

The memory of him standing legs apart, Colt blazing, seized her. What would he do? She shook her head. It no longer mattered. He would look for her. Maybe even now he searched. But he would not be alone in that. Kendal had yet to be reckoned with.

She searched the land around her. It was laced with dips and cuts, but none would shelter her, and there were no trees, only scattered low clumps of scrub oak and juniper. " 'The Lord is my light and my salvation . . .' " She forced herself on. " 'Of whom shall I be afraid?' "

If only she had told Monte. If only Frances . . . Oh, Frances. Well, at least she would know Kendal had not taken a mistress . . . if he spoke the truth. Somehow Abbie suspected he had. He seemed stripped of his bravado, bared to his essence. Maybe there was still a way for him to make amends. But she did not want to discuss it alone with him in the dark. She had to make it home. Suddenly a horned owl flapped from the grass before her, and she cried out, then shoved her fist between her teeth.

Kendal looked up. Shortening the reins in his hand, he headed toward the cry. Overhead, an owl circled against the star-filled sky. He peered around him with eyes as tuned as the winged scavenger. She was near. The cry could have only been hers. What would he do when he found her?

Monte straightened, head cocked, breath held. He strained to hear it again, but no sound came. Still, he turned his horse and headed in the direction he imagined he had heard the cry.

Cole drew up even and shook his head. "No word from anyone yet. Breck's headed for town."

Monte's jaw tightened. "I thought I heard something over this way." He kicked in his heels and Sirocco sprang forward, Cole on Scotch following right behind.

Lying motionless in the cut, Abbie held her breath until even the sound of Kendal's horse's hooves disappeared, then slowly gave release to her lungs. She forced her trembling to stop and swallowed down the fear. She counted the moments that passed. Her head against the rough ground throbbed.

Kendal had passed, but now he was between her and the ranch. She stood up. Suddenly a horse reared up before her, and she threw her arms over her head. The rider mastered the horse, but her heart thumped madly as she made out the brass buttons and yellow cuffs of Captain Gifford's uniform. His face looked inhuman by the moonlight. Her spirit recoiled.

She turned to run, but he slid from the horse and grabbed her. Abbie cried out.

"None of that." He clamped her mouth with his hand.

She wrenched free and screamed, but he grabbed her by the

hair. She beat him with her fists and screamed again before he got his hands on her throat and squeezed. She ripped at his wrists, desperate for air, but her mind grew fuzzy and her legs gave way.

Monte rode hard. The scream cut short spurred him on, and he unstrapped the gun in his holster. Cole had fallen behind, but Monte could hear him following. Through the darkness he could make out two figures on the ground ahead, and he pulled out his gun and fired into the sky.

One of them leaped up and ran, reached the horse, and wheeled away into the night. The other lay motionless.

"Abbie!" Monte dropped from Sirocco, grabbed her up into his arms.

She choked, then clung to him. "Captain Gifford," she rasped. "It was Captain Gifford."

Cole thundered past them. Monte didn't stop him. If anyone could chase Gifford down, it was Cole. Right now, all that mattered was that Abbie was safe. He pressed her to his chest.

"I'm sorry, Monte."

"Are you hurt?"

"No."

Monte stared up at the sky. Too many emotions clashed inside. "Where is Kendal?"

"He . . . oh, Monte, he didn't mean for it to turn out this way."

"He has betrayed us all."

"Not betrayed, Monte."

"Oh yes. More deeply than you know. One cannot abandon honor without a price. He knew that."

"He lost his way."

"He chose his way." Their breath mingled white in the moonlight. She raised her face, and he stroked her hair, then helped her stand and led her to the horse. "I'll get you home."

She spun. "Home! Monte, we can't."

Monte stared at her, incredulous. Did she know no limits?

"Patricia . . . Grant—we have to go to town. We—"

"Abbie!"

"But..."

He grabbed her close. "It's out of our hands, don't you see? The law, the railroad, and Almighty God will take it from here."

◆◆◆◆◆◆◆

Grant stood up from the table and gave a hand to Marcy. She'd seemed impatient throughout dinner, but for the life of him, he couldn't figure what peeved her now. She was harder to understand than any case he'd yet encountered. "Would you care to walk?"

"In the dark?"

"In the moonlight." Why did she make everything he said sound so awkward?

Her eyes went to the stairs. "You could just have me up..."

He nearly choked. Did she know what she was saying?

Her dimple deepened. "As long as you're a gentleman."

Grant's heart beat against his chest. He glanced up the stairs. "Uh...I don't think my room is exactly presentable."

Marcy laughed. "I didn't expect it would be. What bachelor has time to clean up after himself?" She started toward the stairs.

"Marcy." He caught her arm. "I don't think it's a good idea."

"What's the matter, Grant? Afraid to be alone with me?"

He released his breath. "Well, yes." That and his upbringing, his knowledge of right and wrong, not to mention societal conventions and her father's opinion. Did she want her reputation compromised? And his?

She pouted.

"Marcy..."

She hooked her fingers into his vest pockets. "I promise to behave." It was like whiskey to his blood.

"I'm not sure I can say the same."

She ignored him, started up the stairs, and he followed. He dug his key from the plant, opened the door and motioned her inside before anyone below could notice them. He lit the lamp and looked around in surprise. The room seemed strangely tidy.

Maybe he'd kept it better than he thought. He relaxed, then tensed again when Marcy came close.

"You know, Grant, I won't break if you kiss me."

"Oh boy. I have kissed you."

"Ye-es . . ." Marcy ran her fingers up his chest. "I mean really kissed me." She tipped her head up.

"Sheez, Marcy, don't do that." Grant grabbed her close, and she giggled.

"Kiss me, Grant."

He obeyed. Bending low, he kissed her with increased passion, and she melted against him. Her intent was clear, and it burned up inside him. Everything he knew, all he believed melted in the wake of it. She grabbed his shirt and tugged him toward the bed.

They dropped down together, and the bed creaked and sagged. He heard a stifled gasp and froze. It had not come from Marcy. She was as startled as he. Her eyes darted as her breath came quickly. Confused, Grant raised to his elbow and listened, then bent over the side and looked under the bed. The girl beneath began to cry, and he fell off the edge, then scrambled up.

Marcy flew to her feet, her hands at her throat. "Oh . . . I've never . . ." Grant turned to her, and she slapped him smartly.

"What . . . ?"

"Don't even try to explain!" Her face was crimson. "I've never been so insulted! How dare you!"

"I didn't . . ."

She pushed him aside and flung herself out the door. Grant watched her go. Then after a long moment, he turned. "Come out of there, whoever you are."

The scrappy girl climbed out from under the bed. Grant looked her over. "Suppose you tell me who you are and what you're doing under my bed."

"Patricia . . . Emmerson." She cleared her throat. "Your sister said . . ."

"Okay, okay. That tells me everything." Grant shook his head. "I almost believe she planted you there on purpose."

"She . . . said to wait here, that you'd have a special knock, and if I didn't hear it . . . I was to hide." Her face flamed crimson, and she bit her lip.

"Yeah. Well . . . I guess she forgot to tell me." He rubbed his hand over his cheek. He could just shake Abbie. But that was neither here nor there. He studied Patricia. Emmerson . . . the Englishman's daughter? Was that Kendal's game? He hadn't liked the look of those two. His instincts and training warned him against them. But that was hardly this slip of a girl's fault.

"Have you been here since this afternoon?"

She nodded.

"You've had no supper?"

She shook her head.

"Then we'll get you some. I just had the roast beef, and it was passable."

"Thank you." Patricia wrung her hands. "I'm sorry . . . about . . ."

"Yeah." He didn't want to think about Marcy yet. Lord only knew how he'd get past this one. He started for the door and turned back. "What was this knock I was supposed to use?"

"Three and then one."

"Wait until you hear it." Grant started down the hall, then stopped when he saw Emmerson and Harris walk in below. In the shadows of the hall he backed toward his door as Emmerson mounted the stairs with Harris behind him like a wary cur.

Behind them a door slowly opened and Marshal Haggerty stepped out, gun ready. "Stop right there, gentlemen."

Harris spun and fired. The marshal took it square in the chest, staggered and fell. Grant sprang to the banister as Harris and Emmerson jumped the railing and ran. People rushed to Haggerty's side.

Grant ran down the stairs. Someone grabbed his elbow. "Get Doctor Barrow!"

He pushed his way out the door. Only a miracle would save the marshal. A .45 at close range did not leave a man much chance. And somewhere out there were two desperate men . . . three, if he counted Kendal Stevens.

✦✦✦✦✦✦✦

Kendal heard the horse closing on him. His own mount—Monte's, rather—was spent. If he ran the horse to its death it would be one more debt, but what did it matter? He reined in beside the scrub oak.

The charger that bore down on him was large and powerful. He could see the whites of its eyes in the moonlight, and the sheen of the sword at the hip of its rider. Captain Gifford? What madness . . .

The captain was upon him, then passed. Another pursued him. Cole, leaving the smell of horse sweat and broken sod in his wake. Well, that was a turn. What was Gifford doing here on Monte's land, with Cole in hot pursuit? Kendal rubbed his hand over his forehead. It didn't matter. His only thought now was to get away. Escape. To where? He had not thought to run. A fugitive, with wife and child left behind. Frances.

He slumped in the saddle. It was over. What use in fooling himself longer? He had failed her. There was no hope. Perhaps there never had been. He had lost them. All of them. When Abbie told what she knew, they would align against him. The thought left him empty, hopeless.

He raised his head. The night was silent. The world seemed vast, endless. Where would he go? He had nothing, not even his honor.

Kendal dismounted, attached the reins to the saddle horn, and swatted the horse's flank. It trotted for home. He started on foot for town. What he had in his pocket would get him a drink. The morning could bring what it would.

The lights of town came into view, and he stopped a moment—some sense of self-preservation, perhaps. It waned as quickly as it came, and he took another step. Emmerson lunged from the brush and blocked his way while Harris flanked him.

Kendal stopped. "Gentlemen."

"Where are you off to?" Emmerson hissed.

"I should think that's evident."

"What are you after in town?"

"A drink. Perhaps more than one."

"Don't you know the game is up?"

"You alluded to that in your telegram." Kendal held himself straight. He had half a head on both of them. He had not noticed that before.

"Well, things are worse now. The marshal's dead."

"What do you mean?"

"There's a posse forming ... for us."

They killed the marshal? Kendal stiffened. "What's that to me?"

Emmerson came up chest to chest. He was shaking. "You're in this as deep as us. Don't forget it."

"I've had no part of murder."

Emmerson gripped his shirt. "You will have, if you mean to double-cross us now."

Kendal heard the cock of Harris's gun. He pried his shirt free. They didn't scare him. What did his life matter now? But he wanted a drink. "Out of my way, Emmerson. You want your daughter back, don't you?"

"Fool! If you walk in there, they'll be on you with a rope."

"And don't think of talking to save your neck." Harris's voice was low, menacing.

Kendal paused without turning. His body yearned for the liquor. One drink. His mouth watered. "Why don't you join me? I'll buy."

"He's daft, off his head," Emmerson muttered.

Kendal looked up at the sound of hooves. They were coming that way. The posse, no doubt.

Emmerson grabbed his collar again. "You get my girl and meet us ..."

"Where is the money? You must have made something off my investment."

Harris leaned from the horse and held the gun to Kendal's head.

Kendal raised his chin. "Do you think it matters if you kill me?" He felt the man's hesitation. It was terrifyingly heady to taunt death. "I'll take my part of the money now."

Harris clicked back the hammer. "You may not be afraid to die, but we know where to find your wife and child."

Kendal's body went cold. He swallowed against the cleaving in his throat. His legs felt suddenly useless, though he hardly moved. "I don't know where Patricia is. Mrs. Farrel interfered."

"You have till morning to find her." Emmerson released him. "Meet us at the creek down yonder."

The posse was closing. Emmerson mounted, and the two melted into the night. Kendal stood at the edge of the road. He had but to wait and the searchers would be upon him. What then? Do the honorable thing? He narrowed his eyes, gauging the distance, then slipped around the scrub oak and crouched.

The horsemen passed. Kendal remained crouching until the hooves were faint. They must be on their way to the ranch. He could just picture Monte's face, the stern dismay at learning of the marshal's death, the wondering at what part his brother-in-law had played, the honorable agreement to help in any way.

Kendal stood. At least the saloon would be clear. He wouldn't have to wait for a drink. His gait was swift, and he made it to town winded and weary. The light shone from the arched swinging doors where he paused, but inside was quiet.

He put one hand to the wood, then stopped. To his right, Patricia came out the door of the hotel with Abbie's brother supporting her. So Grant had her after all, but what was wrong with the girl? She looked like death. Kendal slipped into the shadow and watched him lift her to the saddle, then mount behind. They left town heading northeast. Patricia would soon meet Frances.

Kendal pushed through the saloon doors. The bartender raised his eyebrows briefly, then recovered himself. Kendal pointed to the top shelf whiskey. The man took it down and reached for a glass. Kendal brushed it away and took the bottle. He paid and left.

◆◆◆◆◆◆◆

Abbie sat down on the edge of the bed. The posse had gone on, Grant had returned to town, and she was weary and shaken. Marshal Haggerty murdered. Kendal missing and his companions on the run. Patricia was in the lower guest room, and down the hall Frances wept.

The clock struck eleven. The deal had been fraudulent, as Monte had suspected. If only she had spoken with him first. She closed her eyes. "Dear Lord, forgive my part in all this. Help us, please." Her voice trembled.

The door opened and Monte stepped in. His shirt was unfastened at the collar, his hair rumpled, his face haggard. There were circles beneath his eyes. Abbie tried to stand, but her legs shook from exhaustion. He sank to the bed beside her, hands limp in his lap. She had never seen him look so defeated.

"Monte..."

He reached for her hand and held it without speaking.

Abbie's heart ached. How could they have prevented this, any of it? How much had her silence and lack of judgment cost them? If only she had gone to him with everything—Kendal's affections, his plea for money, Frances's fears ... She dropped her chin to her chest.

"Don't blame yourself." Monte's voice was gentle.

"I should have told you. I should have told you everything. I was afraid ... afraid that honor would exact too high a price."

He squeezed her hand. "It might well have." He looked to the ceiling and released a slow breath. "Where is he now, Abbie? Hiding? Running?"

"I don't know."

"What of Frances, Jeanette?" Monte shook his head, and Abbie's heart ached.

She wished she had something to offer him. Hope? Faith? Trust? She had love, but could he accept it? Could he forgive her yet again? He spoke no blame, but it must be there, as it had before.

A knock came on the door, and he opened it. She heard Breck speaking low. Monte suddenly hardened. "No, Deputy Davis is with the posse looking for Harris and Emmerson. We'll have to take care of it ourselves."

Abbie jumped to her feet. "Monte?"

He turned, cold fire in his eyes. "Captain Gifford has made off with the horses."

She felt as though she'd been kicked. How much more? "But he was alone . . ."

"When you saw him, yes. Obviously the deed was done already, while the men were looking for you."

Abbie rushed to his side. "What do you mean to do?"

"Get them back before he's branded and transported them somewhere."

"You can't. You haven't the men."

"Perhaps not. But I have something more."

"What?"

"The right."

Abbie followed him with her eyes as he left. *Dear God in heaven, guard him now.* She dropped to her knees.

Twenty-Five

In the study Monte strapped on his gun. *A time for war.* He went out and gathered Breck and the men in the yard. "How many fresh mounts have we?"

Breck shook his head. "One horse each from the stable, counting your wife's."

"Get them saddled." He watched them go. Matt Weston, Breck, Curtis, Randy Gaines, and Drake. Cole had not returned yet. Monte wished now he had stopped him.

Sirocco was as spent as the men's mounts. Will led Zephyr out, and Monte climbed into the saddle. Well, maybe it was time for the storm. He brought her head around and pressed his knees to her sides. The men followed.

Breck came up even. "Any chance we'll run by Cole on the way?"

"I'm not depending on chance."

"What then?"

"God."

◆◆◆◆◆◆◆

Cole reined in. His chest was pumping almost as hard as Scotch's. Sweat ran down his forehead, and he brushed it from his eye with the back of his arm. He scanned the scrubby growth and ponderosas. Nothing moved. Scotch coughed and shook his head.

Cole stilled him with a hand. He turned and peered behind

281

him. Nothing. He took off his hat and raked his fingers through his hair, then replaced the hat and dismounted. He couldn't read the ground in the dark, but there were other ways. He listened. No cricket song. Nothing stirred. He climbed back up and nickered to Scotch.

Captain Jake took his hands from his charger's nostrils. The dark had been enough to conceal them in the dry stream bed, but one sound from the horse would have brought Farrel's man onto him. Cole Jasper was a man to be reckoned with.

His reputation in Texas had indeed been formidable. Captain Jake did not underestimate him. He raised to his elbow and sniffed the air, then murmured to the horse. Immediately it rose to its feet with very little commotion.

He stood and sheathed his sword. The sound of Cole's pursuit was past, the night quiet. But still he waited. He needed to think. Encountering Mrs. Farrel had been a shock and a mistake. What on earth was she doing on the range in the dark?

If only she had not recognized him. He felt again his fingers on her throat. He had stopped her air, but the pulse had throbbed still when he had to let go. He looked up. The sky was so clear the stars seemed as deep as the sea, layer after layer of tiny pricks of light. The air was sharp.

He could just keep riding. Any direction, any distance. Taking the reins, he led his horse up the side of the stream bed to the open range. He tossed the reins up and spun as something whooshed in his ears and slid over his head. Rope. It pulled tight on his neck as he grabbed for it. *Jasper.*

Cole yanked hard. Even as the man fell he reached for his gun, but Cole kicked it from his hand and yanked again. Captain Jake clawed and gasped for air. The veins in his head stood up like snakes. He writhed as Cole slid the sword from its scabbard and tossed it in the scrub, then rolled him face down in the dirt. He yanked his hands back and tied them, then loosened the rope on the man's neck.

"Git used to the feel of that. This ain't the last time a rope'll tickle yer neck. On yer feet."

Captain Jake struggled up. Cole tugged as he mounted Scotch. Captain Jake followed on foot, pulled by the neck. "How did you know I was there?"

"I smelled you."

"It doesn't have to be this way. I have gold. Enough to make you a rich man. You don't owe Montgomery Farrel anything."

Cole touched his spurs to Scotch's sides and the horse broke into a trot. Captain Jake ran behind. He stumbled. "All right! Stop. Please."

Cole drew on the reins, and Scotch dropped to a walk again. "I don't like the sound o' yer voice."

The captain made no response. Cole figured it was about two hours to town—less if Jake Gifford had a mind to talk.

◆◆◆◆◆◆◆

Monte reined in, and the others gathered around him. He could see the horses, penned in the corral behind Gifford's hacienda. He could also see the men with rifles standing watch. The ride had cooled his temper, and he now considered the situation. He did not want to risk his men—or for that matter, those who followed Gifford's orders.

"I count thirteen," Breck said beside him. "Eleven with the horses, and two on the porch."

"And likely more in the bunkhouse."

Breck rubbed his chin with the back of his hand. "Tall order."

"I'm guessing they're waiting for first light to brand them. The house is dark. I'd sure like to know if Gifford is inside."

"I reckon I could manage that."

Monte turned to him.

Breck shrugged. "Plenty of windows. All low down."

"There might be men inside. There are at least two women."

Breck grinned. "My lucky night."

Monte stared at the yard again. They were far outnumbered.

The more they knew before anything happened, the better. "All right, give it a try."

Breck walked the horse down as close as he dared, then tied it and continued on foot. Already the night was less deep. The chilled, premorning air stirred, but it was dark enough for Breck to get to the house unnoticed. Monte watched him creep along the side wall and try one window, then move to the next.

He pushed it open and crawled in. Monte held himself ready. At the first sign of trouble they would rush in. But everything stayed quiet. After a time, Breck crawled back through the window and, crouching low, scurried across to where he'd left the horse. He led it, then mounted and rode back.

"The two women are sleepin'. That's all."

"Good work." So Captain Jake had not returned. Perhaps his men would wait for his orders. But Monte couldn't count on that. "All right, circle round. When I see you're in position, I'm riding in."

"Ridin' in?" Curtis raised up in his stirrups. "Out in the open?"

"I must at least give them the chance to release the horses on their own."

Breck shook his head. "Mr. Farrel, with all due respect . . ."

"I won't ambush them."

"Then what chance do we got?"

"What chance have we shooting it out?" Monte held his gaze. "If I give the signal, make as much noise as you can and move about. They may think there are more of us than there are."

"You're makin' yerself a target."

"I don't believe anyone there wants to shoot me. At least not without Captain Gifford's order." Monte raised Zephyr's head. "Go on now."

Monte watched as the men drifted into the darkness beyond the corral. When he guessed they'd had time to seek cover, he started down at a crisp trot. It wasn't long before he was noticed.

"Stop right there."

He slowed but continued at a walk.

"Who are you? What's your business?"

It was one of the men on the porch. He could tell that as he approached. The man stood forward. In the paling darkness Monte could see it was the one who had wielded the stick. He stopped in front of him. "I've come for my horses."

The man guffawed. "He don't learn too good, does he, Dixon?"

The other man joined him. "We shoulda finished him off the last time."

"You ain't got no horses here. You better git back where you come from 'fore you git hurt. Again."

"I'll leave when I have my stock."

The man stepped forward. "Then you're a dead man."

Zephyr reared and caught him in the head with her hooves. The man crumpled. A bullet whizzed past his ear, and Monte fired back and caught the other man in the leg. A shot from the side of the house hit the man in the shoulder and he fell.

Gunfire broke out from the corral, and Monte spurred Zephyr around the side of the hacienda. It was chaos. His men were closing in. He could see them in the dawning light, firing from behind bushes and boulders. The horses rushed frantically in their confinement, and their guards were fighting as hard to avoid being trampled as shot.

Four men came running from the bunkhouse, but their shots were aimed at the men in the corral. Monte stared. It was Skeeter and John Mason, and two of the new men, Landis and Scott. This was help he hadn't expected. It evened the score somewhat and threw the guards into confusion.

John Mason made it to the gate and pulled the slats free. The horses ran out. Monte and his men closed in, and those in the corral dropped their guns and raised their hands high.

Breck came with rope, and they tied them in pairs, then took off their boots and left them sitting. The ground was none too inviting after hosting forty-six horses. Monte took in the scene with satisfaction, but no credit to himself. Through it all he'd felt a presence more potent than his human strength. He whispered a prayer of thanks then surveyed the situation.

John Mason came slowly to him. He pulled off his hat. "Mr. Farrel, I didn't know nothing about stealing them horses. I swear it. I'd've had no part in it, no matter what he offered."

Monte believed him. The young man's throat worked, but his eyes held steady. "Get your horse, John. Help the men round up my stock."

"Yes, sir!"

Monte turned and eyed Skeeter. The man looked chagrinned and uncomfortable.

"Mr. Farrel." Skeeter circled his hat in his hands. "I reckon I'm to blame for some of this. I told Captain Gifford where you kept the horses once the weather warmed."

"Why?"

"Well, I just figured it was my job to answer. I didn't know what he meant to do. Leastwise, I didn't want to know, so I didn't look too close."

Monte considered that. Skeeter could have made excuses, but he didn't. "That's honest, Skeeter."

"I'd sure be obliged to work for you again. At any wage."

"I'll consider that. For now, you can keep watch on the men in the corral." Monte walked around the porch. The man he had shot leaned against the post bleeding from the leg and shoulder. The man Zephyr had kicked still lay in the dirt.

Breck joined him as Monte bent and felt for a pulse. "Well, I suppose one casualty is better than I expected." He thumbed the man on the porch. "Take that one over with the others and send someone for the doctor."

The sky on the horizon was paling to a robin's egg blue. Monte rubbed the back of his neck, then turned as a half dozen horsemen rode in. Ethan Thomas wore a deputy star on his chest. He reined in and dismounted. "Monte."

"Ethan. I see you've been deputized."

Monte waited while Ethan surveyed the yard. "Looks like you don't need us after all."

"There are men in the corral wanting transportation."

Ethan grinned. "Yeah. They'll be wanting it more when the sun comes up and things get ripe."

Monte retrieved his hat from the ground where it had fallen when Zephyr reared. "It seemed appropriate."

"Did you get your horses?"

"The men are rounding them up. How did you know?"

"Cole. He brought in Captain Gifford." Ethan shook his head, chuckling. "Sure was a sight. Gifford was just about played out by the time he staggered in, tied by the neck behind Cole's horse. You know, I never liked that man. Gave me the creeps. Even my dog wouldn't tolerate him, and you know Brutus. He's a sap for everyone."

Monte smiled, and Ethan ran on. "When Gifford confessed to taking the horses, Cole said we'd find you here. Reckon he guessed right, only he thought you'd be mincemeat by now."

"Yes, he would." Monte put on his hat. "If you don't mind cleaning up the mess, it's a long ride home, and I've been up all night."

"We'll take it from here. I must say those horses would have been a sore loss. I'm hoping to have a look at your foals myself come spring."

"You do that, Ethan. I'll make you a fair deal."

"I know you will."

Monte climbed into the saddle. Breck came from the corral and climbed astride his horse. Together they started for home. The miles between seemed long indeed.

◆◆◆◆◆◆◆

Kendal sank down against the back of Monte's bunkhouse and uncorked the bottle. Fully a third of it remained yet, and he swigged a mouthful. The horse he had taken from the livery stood by the corral a short distance away, saddled and ready to convey Patricia.

Kendal frowned and drank from the bottle. He wanted no more part of this business. He had never intended it to go so far.

But Harris and Emmerson had threatened his family. He had no choice but to see it through.

His head sagged against the wall. He was tired, so bone tired even thinking made him groan. And his thoughts were senseless, pointless, futile. He closed his eyes and let his mouth hang open. A little sleep . . . just a little . . .

◆◆◆◆◆◆

Abbie raised her head from her arm on the windowsill. Her neck ached, and her limbs were stiff with cold. But that had not awakened her. The morning sun pierced her swollen eyelids when she opened them, and she couldn't think. Then memory rushed in, and she stared down at the yard.

Horses. One was Zephyr, bearing Monte. She sprang up and ran, her hair flying free and the ribbons on her wrap trailing behind. She yanked open the door as Monte dismounted wearily, and Will led Zephyr away. Without a thought for Breck, she dashed across the porch and down the stairs into Monte's arms.

He staggered back, then wrapped her close. Breck headed for the bunkhouse.

"Come inside, Monte. You're exhausted." She led him up the stairs and sat him on the edge of the bed. She systematically removed his clothes and brought him a damp cloth from the basin.

He smiled. "Let me wash properly. Then I'll tell you what happened so you won't die of wondering."

"I'm perfectly capable of waiting."

He went to the basin and plunged in his arms, then scrubbed his face and neck and toweled dry. He took her hands and kissed her.

"You got the horses?"

"A-ha-ha. I knew it."

"So tell me."

"We got the horses. One of Gifford's men was killed."

"And Captain Gifford?"

Monte pressed her hands to his chest. "Cole brought him in. He's in the jail at this moment awaiting trial. I daresay it won't go well with him, but that cell probably looked like paradise once Cole was through with him."

Abbie closed her eyes with relief.

"Any sign of Kendal?"

"No."

He rested his forehead on hers. "Well, now I must sleep."

She nodded and backed away, but he pulled her close and kissed her again, then let her go. He dropped to the bed like he'd never move again. Abbie leaned against the post and watched him sleep. Her heart rejoiced. He was home safe ... unlike Kendal.

••••••••

Kendal woke with his face on the ground. The grass and bracken dug into his cheek, and the sun pierced his eyes. His head throbbed and his mouth was foul. He looked around. Everything was quiet, a serene moment when all seemed right with the world.

He pulled himself up and made his way to the stream behind the house. He dipped his hands and splashed his face with the icy water until his senses cleared. The lives of Frances and Jeanette depended on his doing his task, though how he would secure Patricia he didn't know.

He leaned against the gray-brown trunk of a cottonwood and looked at the house. If he could just walk inside, take Frances in his arms, promise her ... promise her anything. If he could hear Jeanette's laughter, watch her tiny hands clap together. He smiled at the thought.

He even hoped for one more chance with Monte, clasping his hand in the man's scarred palm. Kendal had never given him much credit. It was easier to believe things just fell out well for him. But he saw now that wasn't so. Monte deserved what he had. He worked for it.

And Abbie. Better not to think of her. She had given him the benefit of the doubt, time and again kept her faith in him, though God knew he didn't deserve it. Frances had more sense. She saw him for what he was.

It had not always been that way. Once she had cherished the

ground he walked on. They had been happy; he would not forget that. Kendal hung his head. But that had been another life. He had sold it with his soul.

◆◆◆◆◆◆◆

Hearing Frances weeping softly, Abbie left Monte sleeping. She tied up her wrap and went down the hall, then tapped on the door. After a moment it opened. Frances looked as she expected, swollen-eyed and drawn. Her hair was carelessly braided down her back, as though her fingers had forgotten their skill.

She pushed the door wide, and Abbie stepped in. She was surprised to see Jeanette curled into the bedcovers. She was rosy with sleep.

"She was afraid," Frances murmured. "Mammy brought her in."

Abbie nodded.

Frances walked to the chest and lifted the brass-framed picture. She looked at it a moment, then handed it to Abbie. "Our wedding day."

Abbie looked at the stately couple: Kendal in his crisp coat and Frances, young and soft. Abbie was struck by the vulnerable bend of her mouth. It was not tight and bitter, nor were the eyes haughty or angry. Their hands were clasped between them, fingers interlocked.

"It was the happiest day of my life. Kendal was . . . so fine."

Abbie returned the picture to her.

She replaced it in the chest. "Tell me truthfully. Was he faithful to his vows?"

"To the best of my knowledge, yes."

Frances's hand trembled as she fumbled with the tie at the throat of her gown. "I can hardly fault him, if he wasn't. I drove him to all of it." A tear slipped from her eye and trailed down her cheek.

Abbie led her by the arm to the small sofa.

Frances dropped wearily beside her. "I don't know what I hoped for. I don't know if I hoped anything, only . . . to force his hand maybe, to take me home. And now I see he . . . could not face that. Of all things he could not bear . . . standing as a failure among those he knew . . ."

"It's too easy to see what's past."

"The past seems less bleak than the days to come."

"We don't know yet what will come."

"What hope is there?"

"God's hope."

"God." Frances shook her head. "He asks too much."

"Only that we forgive."

"How can I? How can I forgive what Kendal has done? He's brought us all to ruin, even Monte."

Abbie's chest tightened. "We don't know that."

"I hoped for plain speech from you."

"I will speak plainly. What God intends through this, I can't see. But I know—I *know*, Frances—that He has a plan if we trust Him."

Frances closed her eyes. "Abbie, I . . . I love Kendal."

"And you should. We've all strayed. God help us if love depends on goodness."

Frances smiled faintly. "God help us indeed." She dropped her face into her hands. "It's myself I can't forgive."

Abbie wrapped her arms around the woman, acutely aware of the fragile shoulders that shook with the sobs. When had Frances grown so thin? *How could I have been so blind to her suffering?*

"Oh, Abbie, what can I do?"

Abbie swallowed against the tightness in her throat. "Pray."

◆◆◆◆◆◆◆

When Frances had calmed, Abbie went down. Her limbs felt leaden, but there were others who needed her. She found Patricia in the hall looking dazed and forlorn. "Here, Patricia. This way." Abbie led her outside and pointed. "The privy is there."

Patricia nodded. Abbie watched her cross the yard to the outhouse. She had not spoken since Grant brought her. Was it shock or fear that kept her mute? If only she had not seen what her father or his partner had done.

Abbie recoiled at her own memories that sprung on her unawares: the contorted face, the blood-caked abdomen. She closed her eyes. Oh, Patricia. The poor child was terrified. For the hundredth time Abbie wondered if she had done right to interfere.

She could not blame Grant. He had found Patricia at the stairs when he came back with the doctor. All around her, people railed against Harris and her father. She had stared, stricken, at the marshal's body as Grant led her out. All this Grant had described when he came. He had done well to bring her here, but what would they do now?

Patricia came out and swung the door shut behind her. She stood uncertainly. Abbie walked to meet her, took her by the arm and started for the house.

"Please . . ." Patricia stopped. "May we stay out a minute? I feel . . . queer." Her voice trembled.

Abbie patted her arm, relieved to hear her speak. "Come walk along the stream with me. The air will refresh you." The stream ran freely, and its music was soothing. A blue jay chirped from the cottonwood branches, and a crow cawed loudly in response.

Suddenly a shadow loomed in the trees, and Abbie startled as Kendal stepped free of the growth. He looked as though he had slept in the ditch. His clothes were soiled, his hair tousled, and his expression grim. "Thank you, Abbie. I'll take Patricia now."

Abbie drew herself up. "You'll not, Kendal."

"I must return her to her father."

"She can't go to him. He's running from the law and is at the least an accomplice to murder. If there is decency in you, let this end here."

"I can't do that."

"Why not? If you turned yourself in and testified—I know Grant would defend you. . . ."

"It's too late for that now."

"It's not. Kendal, put things right. Frances loves and needs you . . . so does Jeanette."

He looked away. "That's impossible."

"I know it's so."

"She doesn't know..."

"She knows everything." Abbie took a step forward. "Come back to the house. Talk to her yourself. Talk to Monte."

Kendal shook his head. "I can't." He dropped his hands to his sides, then turned from her to Patricia.

Abbie felt the girl shrink behind her. She tried to reassure her with a grip on her arm. One move from Kendal and she'd send the girl running and fend him off the best she could. But she prayed it wouldn't come to that. Somewhere inside him Kendal knew what was right. He must.

Kendal slowly released his breath. "Very well, I'll leave her. But you must tell Monte..."

Abbie spun as four horses closed them in. Emmerson and Harris were flanked by two rough men who smelled, even at a distance. She'd never seen them before, but she'd remember them now. One wore a patch on his left eye.

Harris leveled his rifle. "All right, Stevens. You've done your part, now get out of the way."

Abbie held her breath as the patched man also aimed for Kendal's chest. She eased Patricia back behind her.

Emmerson glowered. "Come on, Patricia. We'll be on our way now."

The girl trembled. Abbie's anger kindled. "She'll stay here with us."

Emmerson narrowed his eyes. "I warn you not to interfere. Let her loose."

"I won't."

Emmerson pulled out his gun. "I've nothing to lose by killing you."

The barrel came up, and slowly his thumb pulled back the cock. Abbie raised her chin, though her heart quaked. Would they hear from the house? If she screamed, would they hear? She watched the knuckle of Emmerson's trigger finger whiten.

"No!" Kendal lunged in front of her with the report of the rifle.

Abbie heard the thud of the bullet and screamed as Kendal buckled and fell into the water. Gunfire exploded as she grabbed Patricia and half dragged her to cover. It took only moments to realize the shots were no longer directed at them. The men had turned and were answering gunfire from the trees on the right.

She could see Cole and two others in the undergrowth beyond them. She pressed Patricia down behind the boulder at the stream's edge and crouched. The patched man fell, and Emmerson went down with his horse spurting blood from the chest. He fired, then took a bullet in the throat and collapsed across the beast.

Abbie pressed Patricia's face to her chest. From the corner of her eye, she saw Monte running from the house. He took cover near Cole, and Abbie prayed he would stay there. Harris lunged but was shot from behind. Others must have come from the bunkhouse. The last man looked about him, eyes wild and chest heaving. He stood suddenly, rifle blasting, and Abbie ducked behind the rock as a volley of gunfire erupted. Then it was silent.

She raised her head. Gunsmoke hung in the air with its acrid sulfur smell. For a moment no one moved, then Monte left his cover and dropped to his knees at the water's edge. Grabbing Kendal up, he felt his neck for a pulse, then leaned slowly back, Kendal's body slack in his arms.

Abbie crept to his side.

"Take Patricia in, Abbie."

She didn't want to leave him. She looked at Kendal, soaked in blood from the bullet meant for her, then back to Monte. Tears choked her throat but did not fall. She tried to speak, but there was nothing to say. She obeyed. At the house, she gave Patricia over to Pearl, then found Frances in her room.

Frances must have heard the gunshots. Her head was bowed over her clasped hands as she knelt beside the couch. She did not weep, but Abbie saw her shoulders tremble as she prayed. Slowly she dropped down beside her.

"Frances," she whispered, "Kendal is dead."

✦✦✦✦✦✦✦

Abbie stood at the window. The house was strangely quiet, and she felt like a shell, emptied and useless. Kendal had been lowered into the ground for taking a bullet meant for her, and the knowledge left her bleak and desperate. Monte came and stood beside her, wrapping his arm about her shoulders.

She leaned against him. "Frances?"

"She's sleeping now."

Frances had not cried when Abbie told her. It was as though the tears had suddenly dried up, left her parched as the brown, barren land outside the window. Even when Monte had come in and taken his sister in his arms, she had not wept. Abbie glanced at him now. How much their lives pivoted around this man. How did he bear up under it?

He spoke low. "I entrusted Frances to him, knowing her fragility. I put her into his arms."

Abbie's chest ached.

"When Kendal first came to court her, he was so beside himself he could hardly speak. I took him aside and told him what to say. I even told him how to propose marriage to her. Oh, there were things we disagreed on, plenty of things. But one thing I knew ... he loved Frances, and he would do anything for her." His voice broke. "How does that change?"

"Maybe it doesn't. Sometimes loving can hurt as much as hating ever could."

He stroked her arm. "Perhaps they're irrevocably tied together."

Abbie felt the truth of that. Love and hate bound up in the heart together. Had it not been so between them? Had she not felt the extremities of each emotion for Monte? And he for her? Perhaps he did still.

She had betrayed his honor, broken her word, jeopardized their future. She had dishonored, disobeyed, and disillusioned him. Through her silence and bad judgment she had brought everything he worked for crashing down about him. If only she could start again. Her head sank to her chest.

"How bad are things, Monte?"

"No worse than I expected, barring further catastrophe. The railroad made no claim against us. Driscoll dare not do so. And at the very least he now holds stock worth as much as his bank."

Anguish washed over her. "I'm such a fool."

Monte tightened his arm on her shoulders. "At any rate we've both learned something." He turned and cupped her face with his hands. "To trust each other."

"I am so sorry."

"There's no need."

But Abbie felt the need. "Monte . . . about the other time . . . when the rustlers came . . ."

"You saved my life."

Sudden tears choked her throat and stung her eyes.

"I was too stubborn and prideful to admit or even believe it myself. But I acknowledge it now. And I thank you." He kissed her lips, and she let the tears flow.

Twenty-Six

Monte glanced once at Frances before he slid the stone into place. The gray speckled marble looked out of place against the red earth, but it settled in with an air of finality at the head of Kendal's grave. It had lain unmarked for three weeks while the stone was ordered, worked, and shipped. Now the grave was complete.

Death was irrevocable, and it took whom it would. Like his father before him, Captain Jake Gifford had dangled from a rope, kicking out his last moments. Monte had taken no pleasure in the sight, though his presence was required to make the statement that lawlessness would not be tolerated. Reverend Shields and the city council had made strong speeches warning of that, and some who had come in with the train cleared out.

Monte looked up. The breeze blew a strand of hair across Abbie's forehead. Beside her Frances stared down at the stone. She looked strangely strong. How queer for it to come now, her ability to cope.

Slowly Frances dropped to her knees and ran her fingers over the chiseled words. *Kendal Stevens. 1846–1873. There is no greater love than to give one's life for a friend.* Bowing her head, she laid her hand upon the mounded earth. If she wept, he couldn't tell.

He circled Abbie's waist with his arm and waited. At last Frances stood and came to them. Monte took her hands in his. "At the end he knew the price of honor, and he paid it."

She nodded, glancing once again at the stone.

"There's no reason for you to go, Frances. There's nothing for you to go back to, and you're welcome here with us—both you and Jeanette."

She smiled. "I know that, but . . . I don't belong here." She ran her eyes over the graves.

"In time . . ."

She squeezed his hands. "I need time away first. I need the South, the land in which I was born."

The waif, Patricia, had said much the same when Monte sent her back to England in the care of her aunt. But he had hoped to keep Frances close, at least until he was certain she had recovered from her grief. Now he wondered if recovery was possible for her here, where she'd experienced only trouble. He pressed her hand. "I understand."

"At least I'll have the train the whole way this time . . . free from pestilence, fire, and Indian attack." She smiled faintly. "Jeanette and I will stay with Kendal's mother. She's offered us her home."

"I intend to see to your expenses."

"Thank you, Monte." She turned to Abbie. "Thank you for everything. I know I was not kind."

Abbie embraced her.

Monte watched them walk away together, then looked down at the two graves on the hill, the little angel and the monument bearing witness to the lives that had been. His eye rested on the newly chiseled stone. Even with all Kendal's faults and the losses he had caused him, he could not despise him.

Kendal was a man like the rest of them—weak and fallible. But at the end he had shown his worth. In his last moments had Kendal surrendered his will along with his life? For Kendal's sake, Monte hoped it was so, but he'd never know. No . . . not never. One day he would see, when he, too, left this life and stood before God. There was no way but surrender, no strength but God's own, no hope but that won by the Savior. He knew that now, and he could only hope to live by that truth . . . with honor.

♦♦♦♦♦♦♦

Grant strode down the boardwalk and turned at the corner. He headed down the lane, mounted the three stairs that led to the Wilson's front door, and knocked. He had already caught the movement of the upstairs curtain.

Darla Wilson opened the door and frowned down her nose. "I'm sorry. Marcy is indisposed."

Grant removed his hat and held it before him. "I see. Well, I'll just sit here on the porch then, until she feels better."

"I don't think that's wise."

"Oh, Marcy's a hardy girl. She'll recover soon enough."

"*Well . . .*" Darla turned back in. "Please yourself." The door clicked behind her.

Grant sat on the rocker beside the door and tucked his hat down over his eyes. Rocking gently, he hummed along with the creaking of the boards beneath the chair. Somewhere a dog barked, and a wagon rolled heavily down the street. The shadows lengthened and paled, then vanished with the reds and coppers of the sunset. The evening chill settled over him.

He stood and paced slowly across the porch. He nodded when Judge Wilson came home, scrutinized him, then went inside. The sky deepened and stars dotted it. The crescent moon joined them. Grant rubbed his arms and strode back and forth, then settled again into the rocker. He dozed, felt his chin sink to his chest, then succumbed.

✦✦✦✦✦✦✦

Grant jolted stiffly. He squeezed his eyes against the sunlight until Marcy blocked the rays with her frowning countenance and hands on her hips.

"What on earth are you doing? Have you lost your mind, spending the entire night out here on our front porch?"

"I reckon so." Grant stretched.

Marcy turned to go in, but he caught her arm and pulled her back. "Not so fast."

"How dare you!"

"At least hear what I have to say."

"Whatever excuse you have is of no concern to me." She struggled to free her hand.

"Isn't a man innocent until proven guilty?"

"What more proof could be required than . . . than of a woman under your bed?"

"Now see, that's just it. A woman *in* my bed . . . now that would be incriminating."

Marcy's face reddened.

"Marcy. She was fourteen years old, and Abbie . . ."

"Abbie!" Marcy wrenched her hand away. "I might have known."

"Would you stop and listen? The girl was in trouble. Her father was one of the men who killed Marshal Haggerty. Abbie hid her in my room for safety—only I didn't know she was there. Do you think I'd have carried on as I did if I'd known?"

"I don't know how you'd have carried on." Marcy raised her chin and tossed back her ringlets. Grant guessed she knew exactly the way the sun would catch and shine on them. She walked over to the rail of the porch and leaned against the post.

He followed. "I guess there's only one thing to do." He turned her toward him. "Will you marry me?"

She stared. "Marry you?"

He took both her hands in his. "I'm asking for your hand in marriage." He watched her soften. Tears sparkled in her eyes, but that hardly surprised him. Marcy was not nearly as confident as she made out.

"I . . . I didn't think you'd ask. That's why I . . . thought if we were alone . . . if . . ."

"Maybe that little girl was put there to bring us both to our senses. I'm sorry I thought to compromise you." Grant brought her hand to his lips. "But you haven't answered me."

"Yes." Her voice trembled, then her smile broke out broadly. "Yes, I will marry you. Of course I'll marry you! It took you long enough to ask!"

Grant threw back his head and laughed. "Now look here. My back aches, my neck is stiff, and I'm hungry enough to eat a full-grown heifer. I guess I'll run along."

Marcy stuck up her nose. "You'll do nothing of the kind. First you'll come in and ask my pa properly for my hand, and then you'll join us for breakfast. Mother already counted you."

"Oh yeah? You mean you meant to make peace all along?"

"Of course. What kind of ninny do you take me for?"

♦♦♦♦♦♦♦

Abbie slipped her hand into the crook of Monte's arm as he drove the buggy to her pa's house. He lifted her down and rested his hand on the small of her back as they walked to the door. Pa met them there. "Come on in."

Abbie kissed his cheek, then stepped inside. Grant stood in the front room with Marcy beside him. He looked wickedly pleased with himself, and she hid her dismay. It wasn't fair. She'd come with such a good appetite.

Monte bowed over Marcy's hand. "What a delightful surprise."

What a smooth traitor he was. Marcy looked smug over his bowed head. Abbie smiled.

"Come on, everyone," Mama called. "Before the supper gets cold."

They gathered around the table, joined hands and prayed, then took their places. Pa passed Monte the platter of venison steaks. "It's nice to have you all together tonight."

Mama smiled. Grant's eyes twinkled. The hair on Abbie's neck rose. Something was afoot.

Mama turned to Monte. "You saw your sister safely off?"

"Yes. Though I was sorry for her to go."

Grant laid down his fork. "Well, Abbie, you had one sister-in-law leave, so I know you'll be pleased to hear you're getting a new one." He hooked his arm around Marcy's shoulders and grinned.

Abbie felt Monte squeeze her hand under the table. For once in her life she had absolutely no response come to mind.

Monte reached out his hand to Grant. "Congratulations, Grant. You've made a fine choice."

Abbie swallowed. "I'm ... very happy for you both." She couldn't manage more, but Monte made up for her lack.

"When is it to be?"

"The first of June. Marcy needs time to put together her trousseau. We're going to San Francisco for our honeymoon."

"How nice." Abbie forced her eyes to meet Marcy's. "I'm sure it will be lovely."

Grant's eyes softened behind their teasing glint. "It'll be good to get back, too, and settle into our own place. I've purchased the Craddock house in town."

Monte nodded. "Very good. That's a nice place."

Marcy sniffed. "It will be when I redecorate. Mrs. Craddock had the most appalling taste."

Abbie drew herself up. "Then for a wedding gift I'll give you red velvet drapes, brought all the way from Charleston."

Marcy turned in surprise.

"I'll show them to you when we have a chance." She felt, rather than saw Monte's amusement. Only a miracle would get her through the rest of the evening. She hardly heard a word that was spoken and moved automatically through the washing up while Monte visited with Pa and Grant, Marcy sitting like a porcelain doll beside him. She, of course, wouldn't lift a finger to help Mama.

At last Monte stood. "Thank you for a wonderful evening." He extended his hand to Grant. "Again, my congratulations." Bending low, he kissed Marcy's hand and she flushed.

If Abbie didn't get out she'd scream. Her family crowded the door behind them as Monte handed her into the buggy. Marcy leaned into Grant's chest and her dimples deepened. Abbie waved limply as Monte smacked the reins and started home. The creaking and bumping of the buggy hardly penetrated her daze.

Monte glanced at her. "Well ... that was news."

"News! Any simpleton could see it coming. Marcy was bound to have him no matter what."

Monte laughed full out. "My darling Abbie. Life will never be easy for you, will it? What was that you used to play ... the helpless maiden trapped in the jungle?"

"Wild animals I could face. Outlaws and Indians and blizzards
. . . but this, this is beyond me."

Monte hooked his arm around her shoulders. His eyes shone
with pride and amusement. "Abbie, I have come to know above
all else that *nothing* is beyond you."

Acknowledgments

Throughout this work there have been many who have stood by me, kept me focused, and more importantly, reminded me to "lighten up." Top on the list are my prayer partners and sisters in Christ, Marianne, Romona, Joey, and Margaret, for all their hours of listening, encouraging, and much laughter. Thank you, ladies.

As always I thank my family. Your faith and understanding bless me daily.

Thanks to my editor, Barb Lilland, who always has an ear ready, a gracious spirit, and a true sense of humor, and to the other hard workers at Bethany House Publishers.

And mostly, thanks to my Savior and Lord for whom it's all done anyway.